VERONICA
OR THE TWO NATIONS

DAVID CAUTE

VERONICA

OR
THE TWO
NATIONS

Arcade Publishing • New York
Little, Brown and Company

First U.S. Edition 1990

This is a work of fiction. Names, characters, places and incidents
are either the product of the author's imagination or used fictitiously.

Library of Congress Cataloging-in-Publication Data
Caute, David.
     Veronica, Or the two nations / David Caute. — 1st U.S. ed.
        p.   cm.
     ISBN 1-55970-101-3
     I. Title.   II. Title: Two nations
PR6053.A856V4   1990
823'.914 — dc20   90-81247

Published in the United States by Arcade Publishing, Inc., New
York, a Little, Brown company

10 9 8 7 6 5 4 3 2 1

BP

Printed in the United States of America

Author's Note

A number of initials and a few acronyms have wormed their devious way into this novel. Most of them reek of Britain then and now, and so they should. Some may be less familiar to the American reader, but to spell them out in the text would be to split the semantic envelope inside which the dominant narrative voice shelters. I mean the truculent shorthand employed by those living on the inside track.

A glossary of initials and acronyms can be found at the back of the book.

VERONICA
OR THE TWO NATIONS

ONE

In July 1939 I arrived home from boarding school to find that Veronica had come to live with us. I had not known of her existence but Mother explained – rather tightly, I thought – that this new person was a distant cousin – the distance was apparently both genealogical (at eleven my vocabulary was extensive) and geographical: with Veronica came several bottles of South African plum jam. I fell in love instantly. Half a century later, as I write this memoir, my love remains undiminished.

Veronica was usually four years older than me but only three between August and October. (I should have written 'than I', but our slipshod media are now pressing good grammar into the spitting image of pedantry. I notice that BBC newsreaders refer to the Government in which I serve as a plural entity – would that it were so.) About Veronica's lineage and changed circumstances little was said; she herself was shy about the subject and my mother a veritable guillotine on't – apparently Veronica's upbringing had been an 'unhappy' one and I was forbidden to inquire further. The pressing task, Mother confided, was to get the girl's colonial accent into a proper mould. About this, as about everything else, Veronica was marvellously responsive; she rapidly adopted the 'princess' accent of the RADA-trained actresses we heard in the cinema.

She was a film fan and ardent picturegoer who – am I telling tales, my darling? – confessed to me that she would have gone to the cinema more often but for Mother's remonstrances.

Mother's intense disapproval of Veronica was transparent from the moment of her arrival, although our new 'cousin' (Mother in a friendly mood) or 'guest' (less friendly) seemed to me a paragon of good behaviour and helpfulness. Particularly frowned on was my helpless habit of staring at the beautiful cousin or guest. 'Don't gape,' Mother would mutter in my ear. Veronica herself was held partly responsible for my habit. 'Don't encourage him, Veronica,' Mother would intervene when my engaging new friend allowed me the small boy's privilege of a delicious tangle and tussle against hopeless odds.

'All she's interested in is film magazines and Hollywood stars,' Mother said on one vexed occasion after she had found her little boy humiliatingly pinioned to the carpet and clearly very happy about it. 'Mind you,' (voice lowered), 'it's a small miracle that she's no worse than she is.'

I inquired.

'Her mother,' muttered mine, 'traipsing from one man to the next.'

Another time Mother said, 'There are things a boy can't understand.'

This formula was acceptable. Any deficiency common to all my sex was something to be proud of and somehow Elizabethan. It's women who bridle when told they are 'all the same'. What women and girls alone could understand were things like lengthening hems and monthly periods. And war, of course, affirms male dominance. Mr Chamberlain quavered on the radio and we all looked up at the sky, craning our necks, as never before – sirens, blackouts, gas masks, shelters, alarums and excursions. Our fate lay in the secure hands of Wing Commander (then Group Captain) Henry Parsons, my father.

October 1939 brought Veronica's sixteenth birthday. Not sure what to buy a girl of that age, I consulted Mother.

'Nothing expensive,' she said. 'She's been dreadfully spoilt.' Mother was busy at the ironing board with the wireless tuned in to (most likely) the Brains Trust. 'Why not buy her a book? It's time she read something better than women's magazines.'

At the age of seven I had been sent to a coeducational boarding school in Hampshire called Greendale. It was a 'progressive' (Mother said) school housed in a rambling Edwardian-Gothic mansion which I couldn't classify at the time but knew to be hideous. (Harold Rascoe was the first to come up with 'coed' but he isn't with us yet.) Mother was herself an Old Girl, and her sisters too, and now she was a Governor. The Headmaster was a balding creep and miser called Rowley (no first name). When the time came to read *Nicholas Nickleby* in the Lower Third, we at once recognized Rowley in Dickens's pedagogic tyrant, the terrible Yorkshireman Wackford Squeers, and henceforth a summons to Rowley's study was called 'a trip to Yorkshire'. Rowley installed sand bags and red fire buckets all round the school. We emptied them at every opportunity. That Greendale should burn down – and its rotten paintings, each of which now carried one, two or three stars for priority in case of fire – was our most ardent wish.

Our most intimate enemy was Matron, a peevish spinster and super thyroid who yelled us into submission and herself out of these pages. 'You can't be sick here!' The plumbing was grim; the cloakrooms were always awash and we were always to blame. As for the food, ugh. Rowley could say 'There's a war on' in six 'Allied' languages, including Latin and Greek, but the constant Sight Unseen was food. My letters home were not well received: 'Father and I are getting a bit tired of your complaints,' Mother wrote. Acute displeasure was signalled by the absence of a food parcel. This was a terrible blow because my only escape hatch from constant punishment by the dormitory bullies of Top Landing, Brophy and Charrington, was handing out slices of Mother's fruit cake.

Father would have preferred to send me to a more traditional public school for boys but his own had been a pretty minor one and Mother's 'progressive' views prevailed. No doubt they realized that no war would be won on any playing fields disgraced by my disabilities. Mother had read some foreign novels, Bernard Shaw and J. B. Priestley; Father knew how to erect a tent in a hurricane and how to inspire fear by drawing back the corners of his mouth. He never shouted and never beat me (I was too delicate, Mother explained), but I sensed there had been some lively arguments between them on this subject. I didn't see much of Father; I remember his uniform and cap badge (a blue heart and red crown tipped by outstretched wings) but I can no longer hear his voice. I am proud of him and he comes at the top of my CV.

With Father you were always welcome to ask questions of a practical sort (I knew quite a lot about Spitfires, Hurricanes and Messerschmitts), provided they were not Official Secrets, but more penetrating 'whys' were not encouraged. Actually . . . I *was* told certain things in confidence, despite the 'Don't Tell Aunty & Uncle or Cousin Jane and Certainly Not—' posters and the 'Careless Talk Costs Lives' ones. In 1935 a research team had discovered that a plane reflecting radio beams could cause a green spot to wiggle in a catho-ray tube twenty miles away. A chain of 350-feet high radar masts had been erected along the coast. Each radar sighting was reported to a filter officer at Fighter Command HQ at Bentley Priory. I am of course not at liberty to disclose who told me all this, but my informant did have a way of inspiring fear by drawing back the corners of his mouth.

Most things were not to be questioned. One went away to school and that was that. Britain was best as self-evidently as the sun was in the sky. (Actually, Mother was always ready to explain why the sun was hot, et cetera, at a distance of 93 million miles, because she had read Julian Huxley and listened to the Brains Trust.) National superiority was just a fact, in the bloodstream, like driving on the left of the road or not asking why LSD meant pounds shillings pence. We played a unique role in the world – but quite different from all the hysterical German screaming about 'Destiny!' and 'Lebensraum' – bad taste for starters and who needs to strut about like a goose, boasting? The German mixture of barbarism and genius (Mother stopped talking about 'the two Germanies' when the war started) was clearly something that had to be put, firmly but quietly, down. Nor did you need those huge, multi-syllable words to pull it off; when the word 'Weltanschauung' came our way in the Fourth we just laughed. Our fathers and elder brothers were shooting Weltanschauungs out of the sky by the dozen. The radio news gave our losses as well as our victories – that was our strength, to face up to the set-backs, whereas the Germans pretended they won every battle (which in fact they did, though more scared than we were, et cetera).

In fact, I never felt wholly part of 'we' or 'us'. At an early age I saw through the smug, myopic patriotism of my family and my school. I lacked, as Father periodically reminded me, the team spirit. I wasn't supposed to show fear. Whenever 'our' ack-ack started showering shrapnel on Hampstead and Mother was too exhausted to herd us down to the shelter, I took the opportunity to creep along the darkened corridor to Veronica's bed. She didn't mind being woken and let me curl up to her, even though she knew I'd exploit her hospitality. But later, in the cold, forbidding hour before dawn, V gently expelled me for fear of Mother's anger.

(Thus I called her, I alone – V for victory – though never in front of Mother.)

Coming as she did from South Africa – still a solid pink in our atlases – V was terribly short of friends her own age. Once, waiting in the cinema queue, she fell in with an older girl who was serving with an anti-aircraft crew and who came from the North of England, reputedly a savage region. V brought this Mabel straight home for cocoa and biscuits. I was in bed by that hour but Mabel told V and Mother how much swearing there was on the guns and how even the girls were soon saying f- and b- and b- my pants all the time. V thought this sounded pretty spirited and she liked Mabel a lot but Mother wouldn't have her back in the house. She had opened her home to two foreign refugees, a German and a Pole, but she wouldn't have a 'common' girl from the North, though Mabel was clearly homesick in her billet. V didn't tell me about this episode while Mother was alive.

Today I regard the Britain of 1940 with critical affection. My parents served their country loyally, he in blue, she in her green WVS uniform – yet the impression which remains is a blur of thick ankles, sensible shoes and displeased serge pleats.

Naturally they sent V to Greendale. She arrived there two weeks after the outbreak of war. Mother told us both to say that she was my cousin if anyone asked and to say nothing if anyone didn't. No one did. But I was prepared to disown her – what is childhood if not a chapter of shabby betrayals? V immediately sailed into the remote reaches inhabited by girls who were half-way women and therefore practised civility (of a somewhat hysterical order). V's arrival attracted lewd comments from spotty boys driven half mad by the fevers in their uninformed (I almost wrote 'uniformed') cocks. Long after Matron had turned out Top Landing lights and pressed her ear to the door, Brophy and Charrington would announce to their acolytes of the lower decks the names of the senior girls who were currently getting 'jiggered' – a word which, marinated in English imprecision, meant both the whole hog and something more plausible. V was soon top of the list; according to Charrington's 'reliable sources', Veronica King had already been jiggered by the entire male half of the Sixth minus the 'shagspots'. Smut blocked our drains and pipes; every thought was recycled into filth; the news that Veronica was brilliant at games was instantly 'And we know what games'. I choked with humiliation but dared not speak.

Jiggered: I didn't believe Charrington, of course, yet could not help observing from a discreet distance when V walked in the company of the broad-shouldered, broken-voiced louts of the Fifth and Sixth forms. My eyes were fangs and my heart ached. Her infectious laughter, and the truculent toss of her head, I understood only too well. She was *it* – and I just a skinny squirt who sang with the altos in the school choir.

V's flowing auburn hair got under Mother's skin. She itched to wield the big scissors. Hairpins, ribbons, buns, pony tails – they wrestled through a series of edicts and compromises. Only at bedtime was V allowed the full splendour of the hair she brushed with loving devotion. In certain respects V's wavy hair resembled my own: the dark hue of Oxford marmalade with golden lights. V said my hair was wasted on a boy and Mother immediately sent me to the barber for a scything on account (she said) of the air-raid shelter and hot-water rationing.

Mother had built the shelter soon after Chamberlain came back from Munich waving his piece of paper because she believed in foresight just as she believed that least said, soonest mended and a stitch in time saves nine and (of course) waste not, want not. If Mother was into proverbs for a penny, she was in for a pound. I remember the musty-mildew smell of damp brick and gas mask and Leo's rancid sweat mingling with the stifling odour of night. Our other refugee lodger, Albert, had temporarily been spirited away into detention, because he was a Socialist, a Jew and a German – though Mother wouldn't hear a word against him. I preferred Leo because he was a Polish officer and a gentleman, who explained to me how Poland had won every battle before losing the war – but he sweated rather seriously whenever the sirens went. Leo made it clear that only Hitler could have forced him under the same roof as Albert, who carried his fountain pens in his outer breast pocket like a shopkeeper. Leo was devoted to my father (who barely noticed his existence) and wished he was young enough to fly Hurricanes.

People were leaving London and Mother was tremendously involved in the evacuation of children. I wasn't one of them; my role was to 'set an example'. Her swishing serge skirt said, 'Daddy doesn't run away nor do we.' As for the grown-ups who fled the country or to the country, Mother despised them as 'shirkers' and called the hotels and country houses where they shirked 'funk holes'. Mother also reported, in disgust, that one London home out of every eight now stood empty.

'You'd think English people would have more pride,' she said – then suddenly told V that *she* could leave London if she chose. V looked astonished.

V was tremendously popular among the other girls at Greendale. They didn't seem to resent her instant success with the boys (which she affected to ignore). Her performances on the hockey pitch, in the gym and the swimming pool won her general acclaim – V modestly explained that in South Africa one is more or less involved in sport round the clock. (I had associated South Africa with food, raw materials and loyalty.) V possessed the social gift of appearing to be surprised and delighted by whatever was said to her. Her word was 'Gosh!' and it caught on among the girls like wildfire – though she rarely used it when alone with me. Soon all the grumblers and groaners were transformed into radiant goshers. There was one thick, big-boned ugly girl with a pathetically obvious (our shorthand for 'pathetic') crush on V, doggedly plodding in her wake, begging admission to her charmed circle, where the breathless password was 'Goshnicky!' Her name was Nancy Lunt. She had a large house in Surrey and a horse called Winston. Heaven for Nancy was 'Nicky' astride Winston at a gallop. V, of course, had done quite a lot of riding in South Africa.

But V's athletic prowess did her no good with Mother. Her first term report from Greendale was a disaster: leaves much to be desired, poor concentration, lack of this and that, atrocious spelling.

'Oh dear,' Mother murmured as her eyes fell from one boxed subject to the next. 'Well, we're going to have to try harder, aren't we?' V readily agreed that we were. Mother's politeness to V was sinister; if my own habitually excellent reports ever slipped in any regard, Mother came down on me with the slap in time which saves nine, but the rebuke was a token of kinship and love; her relentless politeness towards V meant, 'I am not your mother, you are only a cousin/guest here.' It also meant, 'Of course with an upbringing like yours . . .'

Later that evening I crept into V's room and found her close to tears. I sat on the bed and took her hand.

'Cheer up.'

'You can talk, you smug swot.' She rumpled what hair of mine Mother had allowed to remain a target for Hitler's bombs.

I said, 'You'll play hockey for England, get married, have babies, and who will care whether you can conjugate Latin verbs or spell "antidisestablishmentarianism".'

'Spell *what*?'

I grinned puckishly but she was thinking about what I'd said. V's destiny was clearly 'wife and mother' – after she'd sent all the young beaux crazy and danced the night away with a bloke who'd danced with a girl who'd danced with the Prince of Wales, though we didn't have one at the time. V's future was semi-detached within sight of the crenellations of Windsor Castle.

'You think females are nitwits?'

I affected to ponder this gravely. Life had become a series of manoeuvres (but somehow all one motion) to be alone with V. At Greendale, impossible; at home, Mother's censorious tread on the stair. Love is both a foreign body, the object of desire, and a force long dormant in oneself.

'How much pocket money do you get?' I asked.

'None of your business.'

'It's just that, for a negotiable fee, I would consider giving you extra tuition in – '

She caught my wrist and began to twist. 'Impudent squirt.'

'If you were to consider objective factors rationally . . . ow!'

My arm was behind my back and my face pressed into the bedspread.

'Say uncle.'

I held out in the hope that she would climb astride me but on this occasion I was denied that privileged private view of her remarkable legs – she too was listening for Mother.

Father's view of our school reports was rather different. Although he didn't say so, perhaps out of deference to Mother, you could tell that he regarded academic attainment as irrelevant for girls. The glowing accounts of V's sporting prowess, not least her leadership and team spirit, brought a rare smile to his stretched features and reluctant lips (or so I assume – I can't remember his face despite the surviving studio portrait). V was a future *victrix ludorum* (about the only Latin that Pater knew) and he obviously wished she were his own daughter rather than unmentionable's.

He led me to his study, a holy of holies which only the cleaning lady and Mother entered in his absence. It had a big antique desk with some locked drawers. Here he sometimes laboured on official papers in a slow, awkward hand. A lump would form in my throat as I strove to win his approval; I could recite by heart the sector stations of No. 11 Group, Fighter Command; forty years later they remain as familiar to me as amo amas amat. The red, white and blue circles of the RAF, with their outer rim of yellow, embodied everything that was 'us'; pure evil – *them* – was a black cross edged in white. I knew that the ME109 was the best German fighter and that its flight endurance was limited to one-and-a-half hours. (When the Tate Gallery bought Roy Lichtenstein's *Whaam!* I smiled and I was still smiling when She decided to reconquer the Falklands without including me in her 'War Cabinet'.) But you couldn't be sure with Father; on some occasions he was responsive to questioning but at other times he would clam up with references to Mister Knowall, Miss Leaky Mouth or Miss Teacup Whisper. In later years I recognized this capricious spirit when we discussed whom to prosecute and whom not to prosecute under Section 2 of the Official Secrets Act. (Such decisions are, of course, entirely the prerogative of the Attorney General.)

So Father led me to his study, my report in his hand, a family version of a 'trip to Yorkshire' or *Yorkshire at Both Ends* by Michael Parsons. I had always been fearful of authority and have never kicked a sign warning me to keep off the grass. While Brophy and Charrington would rub silver milk bottle tops on to pennies, brazenly passing them off as florins in the local shops (despite getting caught more often than not), I would worry that a torn postage stamp would anger the Royal Mail into non-delivery. I remember what Father said on that occasion but not his words. You couldn't win wars, he explained, without the 'boffins'. Brains were needed and first-class ground control, BUT the Battle of Britain was won when the fighter pilots were still boys in school: camping together, mucking in together, climbing together, he didn't say jerking off together. That, said Father, was where Character was formed. He looked at me. He had pilots under his command who wrote poetry; he'd seen young men come in with their kites on fire and half an hour later they were lost in some Russian novel. If they were mindless stevedores (the noun and adjective always went together) Jerry would be laughing. But the main thing was

Character. Which meant pulling your weight.

I was nodding in the desperate solemnity of genuine concurrence. I craved his approval. I asked him whether he'd like to see my most recent drawings of Spitfires, Hurricanes and Dorniers.

'Take your mother,' he said. 'The work she does.'

Would he consent to view my drawings? It wouldn't take a moment to fetch them.

'Take your sister,' he said.

Could he have said it? If ever there was an only child it was me. To this day I can't share anything. Mother once told me that having me had almost killed her – as if it were my fault – and the doctors had warned her never again. Then Father was saying that if I'd had a sister like Veronica I'd have someone to emulate but there was a colour in his skin I didn't recognise, a kind of suppressed candlepower, as if the warrior of the heavens had stalled in some obscure valley below sea level. It struck me that Mother never seemed particularly happy during Father's rare appearances at home, but a boy's mind knows how to cut out.

That night, curled in bed with the window open (Mother believed in fresh air), I nursed the heavy stretching limb which threatened to burst at the seams, and willed myself into a private (precious word) arcadia where there were no air-raids, no Rowleys, no Brophys, no Wing Commanders, no tent-skirts in green serge. This was a world of luminous messages conveyed by silent morse codes and invisible semaphores known to me alone; a sleepy meadow of long grass and buttercups where, by stealthy stalking, you might catch sight of a beautiful girl who was always drifting away, wrapped in her own dream. Then she would turn and laugh saucily: 'Catch me!' With pounding heart and clumsy legs I would stumble after this swift, nimble nymph.

The heaven of that meadow was its emptiness. During my childhood I had made a virtue out of the solitude imposed upon me. Not only had Mother chosen 'Never again!' but she had also deserted me for long periods when Father was serving our far-flung Empire and piloting Gordons and Furies (I could draw them) from bases in India or the Middle East. She was an officer's wife. I tracked my parents across the map; blindfold I could place a sharpened pencil on Ismailia, Amman, Basrah, Peshawar – names which remain as familiar as amamus amatis amant. (Of late a succession of sumptuous tele-films has offered me various second-hand imperial parents; I only wish David Lean's epigones conceded that childhood takes place in black and white.)

These cigarette-card explorations were pursued not only at Greendale but also with Aunt Phyllis, to whose house in Cornwall I had formerly been sent for the school holidays. Phyllis was Mother's elder sister – the younger one was called Amanda and lived in South Africa and had a beautiful daughter I'd never heard of – and an absolute brick. She loved her garden and collected butterflies. Each morning she seemed to be pulling herself out of some tragic loss into the day – I would now say into a Laura Knight painting. Everyone in the village respected her. A fisherman called Trelawny (she always used his surname) used to bring her mackerel fresh from his catch. He often came up the hill for a cup of tea. He took his boots off outside and scrubbed his large red hands but he still smelt of fish. I concluded that Phyllis liked the smell or the idea of it. She was always finding rare additions to my collections of Imperial postage stamps and cigarette cards depicting regimental regalia. I collected Churchman's cards, discarding the practical tips: how to mend a bicycle tyre, how to plant lettuce – and then, when the war came, how to make a garden dug-out, how to protect your windows, how to arrange sandbags, how to extinguish an incendiary bomb (this card showed a chain of rather smartly dressed women passing buckets but everyone knows that very little water survives after a bucket has been passed from hand to hand).

Aunt Phyllis was quite attached to her family tree and photograph album – clearly she had been badly hurt when both her parents, Grandpa and Grandma French, champions of what Phyllis called *la vie méditerranéenne* (something fuller, Greeker, more wholesome, I later surmised, then *méditerranée*), were drowned in a boating accident while holidaying in Greece. Both of my other grandparents, on Father's side, had died long ago and I had the impression that our family had exceptional difficulty in staying alive. Phyllis talked about Fate and Hydra, a Greek island, and the terrific risks that Father took. She taught me to swim and to map-read across country because she wanted Father to be proud of me and (perhaps) pleased with her. One could detect a faint flush in her cheek when she told me what a gay young man Father had been, and how he cut quite a dash, chancing his arm shooting crocodiles on the Nile, and generally sowing his wild oats. I'm sure Phyllis knew I wouldn't quite understand but she needed someone to talk to, and she loved me because I was Mother's, or so I assumed. I was never short of assumptions on any subject.

Phyllis couldn't resist hinting that she was sitting on some kind of family secret but there was no way I could get at it. I remember one photograph in her album, taken in Alexandria some time in the 1920s. It showed Father and another young man standing on a tennis court with Phyllis and her youngest sister, Amanda, all four dressed in sporting whites. There was an Egyptian in the background, also smiling at the camera, probably a groundsman. Phyllis explained that Mother wasn't in the picture (black and white of course) because she had taken it.

'Your mother was always the organizer. I was the dreamer, my head full of Siegfried Sassoon and Rupert Brooke, and Amanda, of course, was frightfully young and only interested in the Charleston.'

Aunt Amanda looked quite beautiful in the photograph. She had gone off to live in South Africa and Canada.

'So many husbands,' Phyllis confided with a wink, 'one is never quite sure of her current name.'

Amanda had even married a Jew. I asked Phyllis about Jews. She said, 'They have a tragic history,' as if that was not quite enough of an excuse for being whatever they were. I said I didn't think Mother ever corresponded with Aunt Amanda. We were sitting on a rock during a blustery day trip to Land's End and Phyllis refastened the ribbon which held her straw hat against the wind.

'Well, Michael, that's all ancient history.'

Aunt Phyllis loved books, particularly E. Nesbit, whose *The Railway Children* became my World's Best Book in the Aunt Phyllis era, not least because Father in the novel was inexplicably away from home and it turned out he'd been in prison, unfairly of course. What most fascinated me, however, was the impressive array of servants employed by the parents of these 'ordinary suburban children' who (said their author) lived in 'an ordinary redbrick-fronted villa with coloured glass in the front door'. I re-read several times the brief passage in which the parlour-maid was rebuked, and soon afterwards summarily dismissed, for speaking out of turn. There was also a cook and a 'between-maid'. When the hero Peter – with whom I identified closely, both of us ten – felt hungry for pigeon-pie, 'Mother asked the Cook to make a large pigeon-pie.'

I asked Aunt Phyllis about all this. She said that in 1905 'people like us' had lots of servants, who made life easier and more difficult. 'Of course,' she added, 'your own dear parents still employ native servants when they're living abroad.'

I absorbed these paradoxes into a slow, alkaline chemistry – my parents had failed me. At school I never admitted that we only had a charwoman who came in twice a week – indeed I invented servants whom I regularly dismissed for idleness and insolence. During a boring debate in the House one muggy afternoon I slipped out of the backbenches and into the back row (always) of the cinema showing *The Servant*, a teasing and laconic tale of a power struggle between a wealthy, complacent bachelor and his ambitious manservant. I sat through the film twice, plotting to dismiss my own man. Skipping a crucial division, I received my first warning from the Whips.

When Mother came back to England I missed my holidays with Phyllis. The news of her death shook me and I cried. It was she who had told me about death (perhaps we both felt that talking was a kind of insurance against it), and now life had caught up with the imagination. Mother went down to Cornwall for the funeral but wouldn't take me. Some years later V told me that Phyllis had been in love with a married fisherman who had four children. Apparently she had bumped herself off when he stopped coming to tea.

V had never been to Cornwall or met Trelawny; and Phyllis (it now struck me) had never mentioned Veronica's existence.

TWO

Incest in the ancient world [wrote John Ford in the *Spectator*, two weeks after Anglo-French forces invaded Egypt] was on the whole an aristocratic practice: a guarding of the genes and an avoidance of dynastic entanglements; a keeping-at-bay of predatory foreign princes and of ambitious domestic upstarts. As Freud noted, incest between a brother and sister was a privilege legally reserved to kings as representatives of the gods. Jupiter lay with his sister Juno and Caligula boasted that he'd gone two better by having all three of his. The Egyptians set the pace for incestuous marriage: Isis married Osiris, the first and greatest of Egyptian kings and renowned cultivator of wheat, barley and wine grapes. Nephthy married Ser (guess the boy). In ancient Persian religious writings one finds references to incestuous unions as 'pious' (the experts tell us). The pre-Columbian Peruvian Incas were required by religious law to contract sibling marriages. It was a unique privilege: 'Only the Inca is allowed to be married to his carnal sister.'

Those of us who take our family tree from the Judaeo-Christian texts will, of course, note that we are all descended from the union of a brother and a sister. The Book of Genesis does not call them that, but the only alternative interpretation of Adam's rib would be a coupling between two hermaphroditic components of a single being.

Despite Adam and Eve, sibling incest was clearly a violation of Jewish law. The prohibition is found in Leviticus 18 (verses 6–18): 'None of you shall approach to any that is near of kin to

15

him, to uncover their nakedness: I am the LORD... The nakedness of thy sister, the daughter of thy father, or daughter of thy mother, whether she be born at home, or born abroad, even [her] nakedness thou shalt not uncover.'

However, when the punishments are handed out in Leviticus, there is a clear discrimination. Adultery merits death, as do homosexuality and bestiality; but sibling incest, though 'a wicked thing', merely deserves ostracism ('and they shall be cut off in the sight of their people'). The offenders live 'to bear their iniquity'.

The most vivid depiction of the taboo – and the grim consequences of its violation – is found in the tragic story of Tamar as told in II Samuel.

Tamar, the daughter of David and sister of Absalom, was desired by her half-brother Amnon. 'And Amnon was so tormented that he made himself ill because of his sister Tamar; for she was a virgin and it seemed impossible to Amnon to do anything to her.' So he, on the advice of an astute friend, pretended to be ill and asked his father to send Tamar to him with cakes. This she did, whereupon he dismissed his attendants and commanded her, 'Come, lie with me, my sister.' Tamar refused, 'for such a thing is not done in Israel; do not do this wanton folly. As for me, where could I carry my shame?'

But Amnon would not listen, 'and being stronger than she, he forced her, and lay with her'.

Having had her, he immediately rejected Tamar, ordering her to 'arise and be gone'. Now Tamar clung to him. 'No, my brother; for this wrong in sending me away is greater than the other which you did to me.' But the ruthless Amnon commanded his servant: 'Put this woman out of my presence, and bolt the door after her.'

Subsequently the incensed Absalom had Amnon murdered, and David's household was sundered by tragic divisions. But those who interpret this story as an abiding indictment of sibling incest (concluded John Ford long ago) are mistaken or disingenuous: the offence was rape.

THREE

When V and I took the train from Waterloo back to
Greendale in September 1941 she was approaching her eighteenth birthday and sat with one remarkable leg hoisted on the
other, commanding the unqualified admiration of the servicemen travelling in our compartment. I could never tell
whether she welcomed this attention or not. She pretended not
to. It was always my fear that Brophy or Charrington would
spot us together on the train or alighting at Greendale station.

Life in their company (ninety-one days, I used to tick them
off in my diary from the first night) was vile and brutish but not
short. According to Christopher Charrington, what united the
human race was bum, bowel and balls. As for Roger Brophy,
our gain was Hitler's loss. Actually, he was painfully British in
a haphazard sort of way, baffled by his own ape-like strength
and maddened by the itching knuckles in his huge, dangling
paws. For years I had retained my position as his prime target –
a swot, a squirt and a fart.

Before I went back to school Mother would hustle me round
the usual clothing shops, where we would collect boring grey
shirts and socks, and baggy serge games shorts. I would
shudder at the prospect of freezing runs and disgusting milk.
Our trunks were despatched by van via Waterloo at least a week
in advance. It seemed as if one was no sooner unpacking than
packing again – whereas the impression at Greendale was
precisely the reverse. When you got there the reality was
invariably worse than the premonition – particularly Brophy's

vile taunts and pokes while one stood shivering in underpants at the line of cracked basins. The first night back on Top Landing I would lie rigid under the two regulation grey blankets with my eyes closed, waiting. My tormentors liked to let me stew.

On the first night no sleep was permitted until three or four in the morning. Total attention had to be devoted to Brophy's account of his sexual adventures and triumphs during the holidays. Anyone caught not listening was punished. Normally he had jiggered every tart in Mayfair before moving on to Soho and other paved pastures of delight. Proclaiming himself to be suffering from syphilis ('the syph'), he promised to rub all our towels against his suppurating groin. At some time in the small hours of the morning he and his chief-of-staff, Charrington, announced that the coming term's 'campaign' would (as on all previous occasions) be to invade the girls' dorms by night and jigger the lot. Allegiance to this crusade was not optional. ('There is no alternative. We have only one option,' She tells us in Cabinet.)

Charrington, a tall, languid boy – a 'youth' before his time – with a twisted sense of humour and a lock of shiny black hair permanently masking his left eye, produced detailed tactical plans based on expert reconnoitres and fanciful logistics. The main thing, he warned, was to prevent the enemy cutting the 'lines of supply'. This probably meant Matron. He also report-ed that the girls, relying on their own formidable intelligence system, had posted sentries chosen for their way with a hockey stick. It would be a bloody affair, many would perish, but in the end the Prize would fall to the Commander-in-Chief. Brophy would jigger Veronica King.

Horribly torn in my loyalties and fears, I finally reported all this to V, swearing her to secrecy. She laughed.

The school was housed in an Edwardian mansion of many pretensions. Dormitories and classrooms were scattered at random across an estate extending for half a mile. Each morning the chamber pots were brimming and a line of boys stood writhing outside the overflowing, blocked, stinking, unbearable loo. (I gag to recall it.) Even during the war underpants had to be changed twice a week. All our clothes had sewn-on name tags with our personal school number. My tags were plain black; Charrington's mother had chosen a kind of gothic script, in green. Washing and eating were both performed in vile conditions. The crockery was all chipped particularly the cups and I used to drink with my left hand to avoid where everyone else's mouth had been and still was. Lumps of fat and gristle browned in disgusting gravy lay on every plate until Matron swooped with news of her war. (All grown-ups seemed very proud of the war they'd given us.)

One winter Saturday Father descended on Greendale in a staff car, his cap now adorned with a Group Captain's laurel leaves, his cuffs ringed with broad, multiplying bands of rank. I admired the sleek bonnet of the RAF car, little guessing what would befall it. The occasion of Father's visit was a girls' hockey match against (if memory serves) Headington High. There was no escape – I must stand at his side on the touchline while he loudly applauded V's dazzling, twisting runs, dum-mies, feints, swerves and goals – smack! – her auburn hair tied in a bobbing pony tail with a black satin ribbon, her breasts heaving enchantingly beneath her Aertex shirt. 'Well played, Veronica! Come on Greendale!' Hooray hurrah. He was just about the only parent *sur le champ* (as Charrington put it) and the object of keen scrutiny – the RAF, *quelque chose* (Char-rington). Huddled at his side, I realised that my murky connection with V was now irreversibly exposed – he spends his holidays in the same house as the school tart! (Brophy) – and all the worse for having been concealed. A few yards up the touchline Charrington was observing us with his usual blend of insolence and calculation. It occurred to me for one deranged instant that I might now be reassessed as a hero's son and a person of some consequence.

Then Father laughed. At the heart of the Greendale defence V's disgusting devotee Nancy Lunt had planted her oak-tree legs and was blocking Headington's attacks by all means necessary. If it wasn't an illegal body check it was deliberately locked sticks or intimidatory 'lifting' – the visitors from Headington were clearly in a state of flushed shock – and the referee's whistle shrieked in constant remonstrance. Beetroot-red, Nancy heaved like a hippo and stood her ground. Father laughed.

'Is she a Lancaster or a Wellington?'

Veronica the Spitfire – unspoken but understood. She had scored twice. 'Make it a hat-trick, Veronica!' Father bellowed. Then he made me shout as well – the Battle of Britain had been won by pilots who, despite the poetry and Russian novels, had shouted for the school before and after their voices had broken.

Now the steaming hockey girls were walking from the field with V's stick uplifted in three cheers for Headington, hip hip . . . As Father moved to congratulate her, Charrington lifted the perennial lock of black hair from his left eye then let it slide back.

Nancy, doggedly trailing V, her broad features smouldering, was introduced to Father.

'Jolly good of you to come, Group Captain Parsons. You must be jolly proud of Nicky.'

I wondered about her choice of word.

'Well, you kept them out,' Father told Nancy.

V and the Lunt creature went off to entertain the visiting team to war rations while Father and I took tea with Rowley and his awful wife and dog. Squeers was wearing his habitual rotting tweeds and his most obsequious fixed smile. The house smelt of linoleum wax, boiled-to-death cabbage and concentration camp: in a word, Yorkshire.

'I gather Michael's work passes muster,' Father said.

'We have the *highest* expectations of him, Group Captain. Should I say it? – an Oxford scholarship.'

'Well, he gets his brains from his mother. I was always bottom of the class.'

Rowley chuckled, globs of phlegm on his tongue. 'So was Mr Churchill, they say.'

'I preferred getting out of doors and fending for myself.'

Father then turned the conversation to the hockey match and Veronica, casually dismissing me and promising to take us both out for some 'grub' on a future occasion. I scanned his stretched features for a flicker of affection – for a father, but no, that's an adult thought. Two years elapsed before V reluctantly disclosed (along with the Mother-and-Mabel episode and Aunt Phyllis's suicide) that Father had in fact taken her out for a meal in town that same evening. When V had suggested that I would want to come too, Father had murmured something about dinners for the deserving. I never saw him again.

More accurately, I saw him again that night. After the slops called supper, the court martial had convened with Brophy in the Chair and Charrington languidly presenting the case for the Prosecution to m'Lud. He had no difficulty in proving that all assaults on the girls' dorms had been repulsed, with considerable loss of life among the commandos, because of prior Intelligence received by the Enemy. In short, a Spy. And who else, if not the School Tart's clandestine cousin?

To my knowledge the commando raids had never been mounted, let alone repulsed, but the indictment contained an uncomfortable grain of truth. V had failed to keep my warning confidential, the senior girls had made merry over it, and the message had been passed to Brophy that if he wanted his smelly underpants hung from Great Tower (as a pretentious Edwardian pinnacle was called), then the fourteen-year-old King Kong had only to show his face in the wrong place at the wrong time. Thus derided, Brophy had marinated his wound.

Charrington asked the court for the cold bath, the 'rods', and castration. I sensed that Father's uniform had got under his skin. Hysterical with fear, I committed the cardinal sin of claiming that Father was due to arrive any minute to take me out. Prima facie, this had to be taken seriously – the court was adjourned. At midnight it was reconvened. I fell on my knees and cried. I was made to confess that at home I washed and ironed Veronica's underwear, tried to crawl into her bed during air-raids, lusted after in a disgusting manner, and generally wanked myself senseless in her honour. None of this was quite so comic as it sounds. I was then held in an ice-cold bath and lashed on the buttocks with a leather belt wielded by Brophy.

Having sobbed myself into a shallow sleep, I was discovered

flying at eighteen thousand feet over the French coast, altimeter falling, *comprends*?, and desperately striving to gain height, the sky a brilliant bowl of ice-blue, sun in my eyes. Father had taught me that the most dangerous area of the sky is in the direction of the sun. Having abandoned the close V-formation of three planes, Fighter Command had adopted the German *schwarm* of two *rotten* (pairs) flying at different altitudes, so that they all enjoyed a clear view of the dangerous, sunny arc of the sky. If caught by an unseen attacker (Father had explained), the instinct to turn and run must be resisted.

'It's like skidding your car on ice. You must turn the wheel into the skid. When attacked in the sky, always close in on your opponent, reducing his fire orbit. Then you turn in ever tightening circles to get on his tail until one or other spins out of control or stalls his engine through loss of speed.'

Now, at eighteen thousand feet over the French coast, I begged Father to remind me quickly, quickly, how the pilot aims all the guns spaced out along the wings. The answer was irritably delayed and delivered: 'How many times have I told you -- the guns are harmonised to converge on a target 250 yards away – that's only two seconds' flying time.' I knew that an Me109 was circling above me, out of sight but *there* (as V had been *there* in my perennial dream of the arcadian buttercup meadow), and I also knew that Father was the German pilot. His voice crackled through on the intercom, harsh, mocking, Teutonic: 'Get above and behind me. Above and behind, boy. Fire, then turn. Don't hang on my tail or admire your work.' I knew that I was inhabiting a dream but this split consciousness did not diminish my terror; I hung in the sky, upside down like a fruit bat, naked, paralysed, contemptible, waiting for the burst from Father's guns, synchronised at 250 yards, 168 rounds per second. Waiting.

Two weeks later I was summoned from a maths period to attend on Rowley. Mother was sitting there in her thick green WVS tweeds, idly fondling Squeers's somnambulent dog. She told me I must be very brave, which I immediately understood. Father was dead but would continue to pass judgment on my conduct from wherever he was. Mother's own distress was rigidly concealed, if she felt any. Rowley, who had been wheezing in something resembling commiseration, and had even extinguished his pipe out of respect for a widow, felt duty-bound to remind me that I was not the first Greendale boy to 'suffer bereavement'. I nodded respectfully: I knew the code – a death is a test for the living – but I felt the need of a friendly face and inquired after Veronica.

'I wanted you to be the first to know,' Mother said. 'He was your father.' She already had her tenses under control.

I was sent back to Top Landing to pack. The train was slow and cold and I shivered all the way. My chattering teeth so got to V's tender heart that she began to cry for me. She smelt delicious, like a flower. Mother didn't speak to her. Finally, I plucked up courage to ask how Father had died, though I felt quite guilty about it.

'I am not at liberty to tell you, Michael. Not yet. Naturally it's something you can be proud of.'

The funeral service was C of E, naturally, though I'd never seen either of my parents inside a church except for social reasons. The three of us sat in the front pew beleaguered by the conspicuous absence of a wider family (most of the guests behind us wore RAF blue or WVS green) and I began once again to shiver uncontrollably. V took my hand. When Father arrived feet first with an RAF honour guard, she began to weep and I had a premonition that the Parsons family would henceforward live without status or money or authority.

I studied the coffin. What sort of shape was he in? Shot to pieces? Horribly disfigured? Unrecognisable? Mouth drawn back in a fearsome rictus? Whatever the truth, 'they' (the force invoked by Mother) had every right to conceal it. I am not impressed by the fashionable hullabaloo about 'freedom of information'. Knowledge is property; it is owned; only an administration which knows more than the general public is capable of governing them. The 'progressive' intellectuals forget that civilization and sanity are safeguarded by ignorance – imagine our lives if we knew in advance the date and manner of our death! Or of our loved ones' demise! Science is now hounding expectant mothers into tormenting dilemmas

23

unknown during the millennia when the pregnant woman hadn't a clue whether she was destined to give birth to a sheep or a goat. As soon as a woman has mental access to her own womb she commits infanticide.

As for the canting Socialists, they conceal their own corpses with the pious excuse that the 'Tory press' cannot be trusted with the truth. If I could have picked the lock of Father's pseudo-antique desk drawers I would have done so, but he had every right to padlock the evidence. As for Mother's systematic deception, good luck to her! Access to the files of those who pass judgment on us – *another* 'human right', we are told – merely discourages honest appraisal or creates festering resentments.

Charrington displayed an unexpected solicitude: 'Sorry about your Pop, Parsons.'

'It's OK.'

'You may have wondered about my own pater?'

I hadn't but it was prudent to display a civil interest.

'This is strictly between ourselves,' he warned.

It transpired that Charrington Senior, a High Court Judge with every prospect of making 'LCJ', had committed suicide with a carving knife ('quite a mess') after being discovered 'between the sheets with three tarts'.

Charrington Junior's one visible eye monitored my reactions with luminous intensity.

'Good Lord,' I said but without too much emphasis.

'Don't be wet, Parsons. The old lecher left me quite a pile. Want an Egyptian dried fig?' He lifted the lid of his well-stocked tuck box. My mouth was crammed with this delicacy when my host sharpened his tone:

'God, Parsons, you didn't actually *like* your old man, did you? He looked the most awful bore to me. My view is that if Jerry can wipe out an entire generation, life can only improve.'

I mumbled that my father had been all right.

'What about the lovely Veronica?'

I trembled.

'Something fishy there,' Charrington drawled. 'If you ask me, which you obviously don't, but I'm *telling* you anyway, your old man had hot pants for her. Probably jiggered himself to death.'

I turned and walked away, choking with shame: the code was to punch his nose, despite the taste of Egyptian fig on my tongue, but I was afraid. My eyes closed in anticipation of any blow and stayed closed. A couple of weeks later Charrington's mother turned up in a flashy outfit and much accompanied by a tall, willowy gentleman who bore an unnerving resemblance to Charrington. I tried not to stare but couldn't help myself. After their departure I foolishly inquired who the gentleman was.

'What?' Charrington gave me his blankest stare. '*What?*'

'It's just that you told me . . .'

'Told you *what*, squirt?'

He stood over me like a romanesque belltower. Brophy could twist my arm till I called myself a hermaphrodite incapable of riding a donkey side-saddle, but Charrington's smooth, marble features and empty voice projected the terror of the snake.

Somewhere at the other end of the school, out of earshot, V crossed her legs with a faint swish of tenderness.

V arrived home for the school holidays in a depressed and defensive mood. In her anxiety to gain Mother's approval she slaved at the chores, the shopping, the ironing, the darning, the evening meal, the Dig for Victory patch. It was painful to observe.

'Greendale's horribly expensive for you, Aunt Margaret,' she said to Mother at supper. 'I really ought to leave and get a job. I mean I'm a complete dunce and I've no right to be running around playing hockey when there's a war on.'

'You're barely eighteen, Veronica. I must see you educated if I can.'

Mother sent me up to my room. Hanging on the stairs like a bat, I could interpret their muffled voices, the contralto and the soprano, through the closed sitting room door. I heard a choke of protest, almost of remonstrance, from V – something about having visited the graveyard and seen the inscription on my father's – Uncle Henry's – tombstone. Mother said, 'It has to be

25

like that.' Then V said she was fed up with pretending and it would be better if she went away. Mother demurred, then asked:

'Is Michael behaving himself when I'm out of the house?'

'Behaving?'

'I'm quite sure you know what I mean, Veronica. Your effect on him is far from healthy, I'm sorry to say. The way he looks at you.'

'It's quite harmless, honestly.'

'Mm. Does he mix with girls of his own age at Greendale?'

'At that age it's a matter of honour not to.'

The following morning, with Mother gone at crack of dawn, her attaché case bulging with projects for sending East End orphans (urchins) to Greendale during the school holidays, I asked V what was the matter about Father's gravestone. She was standing at the kitchen sink and I was making a big show of drying up. She looked horrified.

'Mike, you were listening!'

I asked her whose side she was on – no reply. I said I thought she was my friend. She rumpled my hair. I pressed her about the tombstone inscription. She declined to be pressed.

'Why does Mum treat you like that?'

'Oh . . . because I don't really belong here.'

'You belong to me.'

'Belong to you, brat!'

'What I mean is, in my opinion, you belong here.'

'She thinks I'm a bad influence on you.'

I examined V out of the corner of my eye. 'What do you think about that?' Her proximity, and the subject under discussion, almost caused me to stutter.

V said: 'Too many questions, sir. Go and dig the garden.'

I loathed Mother's vegetable garden but I was V's devoted and obedient slave. I put on my wellies and went out into the clammy morning under the usual grey sky to dig for victory. Mother was a great one for under-cooked vegetables and never met another woman in the course of her work without conveying the divine message of that great sage, the Radio Doctor. 'After all, we aren't cruel to animals, so why should we be cruel

26

to vegetables? Why cook them to pulp?' asked the homely charlatan – and mighty was my amusement, twenty-seven years later, when a Labour Prime Minister appointed the Doc as Chairman of the BBC to dish the liberal establishment on a diet of raw carrots.

My gardening fork was sullenly prodding sodden clods of Mother's earth – there must be easier ways to bring Hitler to his knees. My periods of recuperation lengthened; resting my foot on the fork I made a study of the barrage balloons, calculating which of them was most likely to drag its cables through our tile roof. Presently V came out of the kitchen door in her wellies, chided me for my idleness, took the fork, and began to dig while I settled back to observe the thrust of her thighs and the enchanting motion of her breasts. With Mother gone for the day, there was no poll tax on looking.

As V said, I'd been making heavy weather of it. Within ten minutes she had covered more ground than I in half an hour.

'Jolly good show,' I said, with the standard ironic emphasis of the Lower Fourth; V responded with a delicious scowl. (Greeks and Trojans had fought for ten years to possess one such scowl.) Abruptly she was a girl again, one of us, and not the anxious, careworn young adult cleaving to matriarchal rectitude.

'Of course you're quite a weed.' She alone in the world could say this yet engender more pleasure than pain.

'We'll shake on that,' I announced, holding out my hand. This was a boy's game but V knew all the games and was four inches taller than me (we regularly measured ourselves against the kitchen door jamb at my excited insistence, using tiny marks that Mother wouldn't notice) so she straightened her back and removed the gardening glove from her right hand.

'You'll be sorry.' She kept her amber-green eyes firmly on mine as our hands tightened their grip and a part of me launched its familiar subversion below the belt. I felt a cord of steel emerging in her smoothly rounded arm; her lips parted in rehearsal for a smile; I winced, bent, and felt the wet soil greeting my knees. V laughed in the truculent *victrix* manner approved for the squashing of boys, then tactfully resumed her digging, no doubt aware of my difficulty in standing up. Such moments of happiness are not forgotten.

When V went off to Surrey to spend four days with Nancy Lunt, Mother insisted on taking me into the WVS and setting me to 'work' on the Urchins Conspiracy (as I privately termed her beloved London Boys' Programme – I'm not sure about the apostrophe, it probably depended on the whim of the old typewriter Mother used, a Woodstock like Alger Hiss). My task was to devise a timetable which would provide the plebeian brats with fresh air, enlightenment and exercise in equal measure. 'We must always think of those less fortunate than ourselves, Michael.' Her life was a beavering war against malnutrition, scabies, festering sores, impetigo (a contagious, pustular disease of the skin), chronic bed-wetting, broken families and the roaming anarchy of the gangs whose playground and battlefield was the rubble of the East End. I was regularly informed that nine-tenths of Stepney households had no bath – it never occurred to Mother that it might be their own fault. If Goering left a wall standing, Mother immediately posted a Ministry of Food poster on it. The locals tore them down and used them for loo paper.

Green tweed suit, beetroot jumper, schoolgirl felt hat: during the height of the Blitz Mrs Parsons led her flock down into the tube stations to spend the night on platforms and even on motionless escalators. Sensible shoes, thick ankles, blankets, hot soup, buns, tea, and a brisk sort of comfort. Who could have guessed that our paying guest recently released from internment, the German Jew superboffin Albert, would rather have held Mother in his arms than Marlene Dietrich? And did.

Mother admired not only Albert's intellect but also his 'moral posture'. Mine was poor. I was the one who filled the other person's glass first but less full than my own.

On the third day of V's absence in Surrey with Nancy and Winston, Mother surrendered to my sulking war of attrition and left me to my own devices. I penetrated Father's sanctum and gave the locked desk drawers several unavailing tugs. (The handles might have come away in my hand but didn't.) I browsed in search of a clue to his death but found none. After

28

that I took a fifteen-minute walk to the cemetery and examined the gravestone, wondering what had upset V. 'Group Captain Henry Parsons DFC, 1898–1941. Beloved Husband of Margaret and Father of Michael. He died for his Country.'

Home again, I closed V's bedroom door softly in case Leo was on the alert, then examined the photograph of her mother – a handsome woman with a rather vacant, Happy Valley smile (metaphor not available at the time). I kissed the glass: V's mum had not only given V to the world but had the decency to be seven thousand miles away. When I observe the unisex kids of the 1980s (I recently addressed the sixth form of a famous London girls' school – four out of five were wearing baggy denim trousers out of choice, whereas the young women serving in the forces, factories or Land Army of the forties longed to climb out of their utility uniforms and into something soft and feminine) it's difficult to recall how rigidly everything was differentiated in those days. Boys were supposed to lace their shoes straight across, girls diagonally; boys' coats were buttoned left over right, girls' coats right over left. The only surviving gender gap I know of is the bicycle crossbar.

With awe and tenderness I began to explore V's cupboards and drawers, pressing fragrant blouses and underwear to my cheek, enchanted by the sweet aroma, the divine aura, which belonged to everything she wore or touched. With tremulous care I unfurled her precious nylon stockings (virtually unobtainable unless you knew a Yank or could afford to spend two pounds in the black market), laid out a suspender belt, and experimentally fastened the clips to the stockings. After pondering these holy mysteries for a while, and having climbed out of trousers, shirt and vest, I stood before V's long mirror attired in stockings, suspenders and bust bodice (more common at the time than brassière), astonished by the faintly familiar hermaphroditic figure confronting me with sacramental gravity.

V's bra had a short bodice below the cups. I fondled the cups. I remember one day when alone in the street gazing into a shop window full of corsets, petticoats and suspenders, all displayed on wires with the naïve artistry of pre-designer civilization.

Stuck to the glass was a notice: 'A.R.P. Outfits.' I studied the prices, wondering what V spent on this vital side of womanly life. A bust bodice cost 4/6, most items were something like 6/11 or 9/11 (the '11' was the moral equivalent of today's '99'), the most expensive being a petticoat at one guinea.

V's stockings were too long for me and I had to roll up the tops to get the tight stretch I adored on V's beautiful legs.

Fastening the hook and eye of the bust bodice behind my back was no joke and I marvelled that women could begin their day promptly despite so intricate an operation. The bodice hung loose on my skinny chest. Increasingly careless of future detection, I stuffed my socks into the cups, then sat on V's bed, rubbed my cheek against her pillow, and took myself in hand – though not in Mother's sense of the term. The silence in the empty house was magical. I am a solitary creature, never bored by my own company. Only by a tireless effort of will have I forced myself through the noisy conviviality and relentless humbug of a life in politics. A moment after my climax a transvestite of no fixed identity stretched across the bed hugging V's beloved stuffed elephant – Rupert Bear meets Babar. Even in wartime innocence is not rationed.

How many of my Cabinet colleagues have been through a version of this experience I don't know. The *sondages* have probably been suppressed by the Cabinet Secretary, who is also Head of the Civil Service, the post that Charrington insists I was cut out for. My guess is seventy per cent excluding the females and the one or two born north of the border. As for the Shadow Cabinet, absolutely nil – devoid of imagination and sensibility, how can they aspire to govern a country?

I was asleep. Father had walked through V's door, carrying his flying helmet and wearing the insignia of the Luftwaffe. 'Take your mother,' he said, 'take your sister.' But in death my tight-lipped father had even less imaginative stamina than in life; soon he was supplanted by V herself, fresh from subduing Nancy Lunt's horse Winston, her riding crop magnificently raised. Not until EH blew his third general election out of four did I feel it safe to risk *Belle de Jour* at the Curzon in Mayfair. As luck would have it, a *Times* writer was sitting directly behind me but he knew the code and soon after that I flew to Paris to see Genet's *Le Balcon*.

My prudence eroded, I removed her stockings while half-asleep and started a ladder with the rough nail of my big toe. Such remorse: poor V. I found ten shillings from Mother's petty cash box and put them on V's dressing table. On second thoughts I put them back. Education means converting first impulses into second thoughts. V's door closed silently behind me. How large and silent our house was; if only V and I could live here alone. I rather resented our foreign lodgers, although Albert was always at his hush-hush lab and Leo generally kept to his room, nursing Polish wounds of honour in a fug of stale tobacco. Mother even talked of bringing in more refugees after hearing J. B. Priestley rolling his vowels on the wireless. The Yorkshire Pudding told the nation about a large house and garden in his neighbourhood which stood empty while its selfish owner sat out the war in America. Could that be right – *was* it right – with so many working men and refugees in need of billets and allotments?

I gave Mother my view: Priestley should mind his own business. She sighed in dismay. Mother called her social conscience patriotism but to my ear it sounded more than half-way to Socialism, though God knows she must have voted Liberal. I'm sure Albert put ideas in her head, she was much too soft on him, he was always presenting her with books, Penguin Specials and the yellow-and-magenta covers of the Left Book Club run by the Jewish Communists. It was Alfred who put Mother on to G. B. Shaw, the opinionated Irishman who ate only vegetables and therefore couldn't die.

In later years I learned about the Holocaust. I am a strong Zionist. I visited Israel several times, once as a junior minister in the Foreign Office. When interviewed in Jerusalem or New York, my position is that the Jews have finally rescued their unique cultural heritage from the poison of Marxism and the sludge of social democracy.

When Soviet Russia entered the war (through no fault of its own), Mother decided that her Plan for sending urchins to Greendale during the school holidays was a close kinsman to

31

Stalin's Five Year Plans. She regarded Uncle Joe as a Practical Man who Got Things Done and read Bernard Shaw, didn't overcook his vegetables, and probably listened to the Radio Doc. My own taste was for the cut and thrust of the Brains Trust. No Idea or Plan survived their scrutiny. I regularly tried out the riddles posed by Joad and Company on poor V: 'Why can you tickle other people but not yourself?' (Practical demonstration thrown in, followed by slaps and – bonus – twisted arm.) I hadn't heard of logical positivism but I was a natural. Treason excited me too, the do-it-yourself satanism of Lord Haw Haw's 'Geer-many calling'; that sneering voice could knock a Group Captain with a stretched smile out of the sky. Among the dreary Socialists who confronted us after the war, only Aneurin Bevan could match Haw Haw's sneering contempt; the Welsh demagogue's exhilarating diatribes sharpened my appetite for politics.

V returned from Surrey, Nancy and Winston. Once again Mother sent me to my room after supper. Something obsessive was haunting this calm, practical woman. I hung from the stairs like a bat.

'Veronica, I feel it my duty to tell you that Michael has been in your room while you were away. Of course a boy of his age doesn't fully understand what is happening to him. It's different for boys . . . much more explosive than for us.'

'Well, I don't mind,' V said, with what sounded like aggressive complacency. 'Mike has been a good friend to me.'

'Really, Veronica! I wish I knew whether you're completely naïve or not. There's clear evidence that he's been among your clothes. I won't go into the details.'

'But into my drawers you do go?'

I held my breath – never before had I heard V goaded to sarcasm. But Mother's response was curiously subdued.

'I don't blame you, Veronica . . . No one is responsible for her own upbringing.'

'It isn't my fault if you've never forgiven my mother!' cried V.

Whatever Mother's response to this, it was lost in V's tears. I had only once before heard her weep, when Father died, but our muffled moans in the face of fate are not the choking sobs precipitated by man's cruelty to man (I decline to pander to fashionable gender usage).

Mother's retaliation, when it came, was severely practical. She had just received a letter from Rowley lamenting that he had now lost his last male games teacher to the army. He therefore offered Veronica a temporary post as games mistress, with a room of her own in the Staff Annexe.

'And of course you'll stay at Greendale during the holidays to help with my London boys,' Mother added. 'I'm sure you'll be quite wonderful with them, Veronica.'

I crept to my room, stricken.

FOUR

[John Ford reviewed a revival of Ibsen's *Ghosts* at the Lyric Theatre – the *Spectator*, January 1959.]

A great fuss and furore was originally raised against this play. It would be tempting to conclude, by standard liberal logic, that it must be a good play, but it's paltry stuff. The whingeing artist Osvald and the maidservant Regine are ignorant of their true relationship. A marriage between them looks imminent by Act III, but as soon as Osvald's mother intervenes to reveal that the young pair have a father in common, the brave nonconformist Osvald collapses into meek silence. As for Regine, she simply takes off while her 'lover' gazes myopically out of the window in a Nordic trance. 'Has she gone?' he murmurs.

Ibsen, by pretension a radical nonconformist, he of the great white mane and the fierce eye as captured by Munch, retreats into an entirely conventional posture. His spokeswoman, Mrs Alving, who is flirting with faint forms of liberation, is even made to agree with the hypocritical, moralizing Pastor Manders: 'I wouldn't allow it for anything in the world.' Allow what? She means the sexual union of Osvald and his half-sister Regine.

We learn from Mrs Alving that 'there are dozens of married couples out here in the country who are related in the same way', yet the loathsome Manders is allowed Ibsen's last word on that: 'But in nine cases out of ten the [sibling] relationship is unsuspected – or, at worst, unconfirmed.'

So that's it! The main sin lies in the mind: ignorance excuses,

34

knowledge condemns. Indeed a long literary tradition points to a single conclusion: that if brothers and sisters could embrace one another in total ignorance of their relationship – it would be quite all right. The truth known to rare and ardent spirits is quite the reverse; the love derives its fullest joy and purpose from knowledge of the prohibition.

FIVE

V was assigned a dingy, damp bedsitter in the Staff Annexe, heated by a feebly spluttering gas fire. In winter she often wore her overcoat indoors. She didn't complain, of course, she was cut straight out of any Ministry of Propaganda film – those well-bred gels in spotless uniforms with tinkling-teacup accents who told everyone to cheer up and get on with it. I adored them all but I am lapsing into hindsight.

V was now not only my acknowledged cousin but also – imagine – our Games Mistress. The horrific promotion involved every known species of identity crisis, plus a few others. The appointment of a young woman to govern the male domain of sport (coeducation had brought the sexes not a step closer to coexistence) was interpreted as an insult by boys insanely proud of their breaking voices and patches of pubic hair. They were not going to take the insult lying down. The war, declared Charrington, was simply an alibi for adult bungling. Miss King, Brophy announced, while flicking a wet towel into my raw privates, was going to get it.

We stood shivering in shorts and singlets as V called the roll before the first confrontation, a cross-country run. Our new Games Mistress wore no more layers than we did because that was what leadership was about; no more, that is, except for the bust bodice whose white outline was mysteriously visible and invisible through her equally white Aertex shirt; but our pride dictated that the graceful limbs and seductive curves on which thirty pairs of eyes were fastened be instantly derided. Brophy set the tone with a ten-ton sardonic 'Yes . . . *miss*' when his name was called; Charrington's reply was theatrically delayed while he pulled the hair from his eye, and the frosty air was electric with sniggers as my surname came calmly out of V's slender throat.

V paused. 'By the way,' she said. 'Michael is my cousin. Does anyone have anything interesting to say about that? Nothing? Good.'

Yet what united her and me against them was offset by what separated us from her and me from everyone – the secrets of the night when I squirmed and thrashed in the sagging valley of my mattress, producing milkish pools which both fascinated and appalled me. Like a cat sniffing its own vomit, I was baffled by my helpless emissions.

The healthy, upright, clear-eyed young woman facing us on the sharp tide of morning, could she know or guess? She had been informed by Mother that I had been among her clothes but what do girls really know?

V's first motion of authority was rapidly followed by another: 'I want some effort out of you boys this morning. We're going to run three miles and –'

'Three miles!'

'Three miles, Charrington, and that means everybody. Stokeley Wood, the Yew Tree Inn, the old ford and back by Smythe's fields.' (Spoken as if she had been born among 'em.) 'No slacking and any rotter I catch cutting the course does an extra run before breakfast tomorrow.'

The pack set off along rutted paths of frozen mud, and soon the reluctant runners were stretched out in the familiar file, myself among the flat-footed rearguard straggling under the pain of stomach cramp ('stitches') and collapsed lungs sand-papered by the raw air. Brophy himself was torn between conflicting impulses: to demonstrate his powers of rebellion by leading bandit packs away from the appointed course; or to show Miss King what male running was about. In the event Brophy stormed to the front like a crazy carthorse stallion stuffed with (more hindsight) steroids.

Gliding effortlessly beside her wards, her ribboned pony tail

37

flowing, V moved up and down the line of runners, accelerating and slowing, offering encouragement, tending the crippled, gently chastising slackers. The planned rebellions and breakaways failed to materialize. Her sheer good nature and self-confidence commanded respect. After a couple of miles, with Smythe's fields in view, V quickened her pace, passing one boy after another until – out of my sight, but it was later much reported – she drew level with Brophy himself. Charrington (whose loyalty to Brophy was loosening as our lives moved on from absolute monarchy to Whiggish closet intrigue) later likened the spectacle to a race between a steam engine short of coal and an electric train. The barrel chest, apeish arms and rampant cock, which had for years been the dormitory's unofficial coat of arms, were in trouble. Not that our Games Mistress was 'racing' her young charges – merely keeping pace, exhorting greater effort, and giving Brophy something to chase over the last, torturing quarter mile. Standing at the changing room door, her breast barely heaving, her long (remarkable) legs ready for many miles more, she welcomed each of us home with a snappy word of encouragement. 'Jolly well run, Brophy . . . well tried, Mason, good effort, Faulkner . . .'

And for me, at the tail, a wink. Perfect tact.

Brophy, whose eyes were rolling with humiliation, took his defeat with the good grace of a steer smelling the slaughter house. He was undone (if life were so simple). Furiously he flicked a wet towel at my carroty groin.

Later, when the mown grass smelled of summer and Rowley ordered us to risk our health in the scummy outdoor swimming pool, it was the same story. V was mistress of every aquatic art and motion. While Brophy thrashed his knotted shoulders and oakish (oafish and oaken) legs in a frenzied froth of misapplied effort, jerking his head up for air, V glided tantalizing inches ahead of him, effortlessly graceful, her disciplined motions as regular as a metronome's. While Brophy practically destroyed the walls of the pool with his whale-like turn, V, by contrast, flipped through a sleek underwater somersault, gaining, gaining, and all those who watched the boy champion climb out of

38

the pool with maddened, rolling eyes, felt their fingerhold on manhood slipping away.

I hated water even more than fresh air.

V was the true amateur. The sports pages of the newspapers – admittedly pretty thin in those years – did not interest her. She could not have named a single Olympic champion or a single member of the England women's hockey team. She never really 'trained' for anything. She might talk tactics before a school match, but the main message was 'come on now, let's try harder, more effort, girls, we've really got to show them'.

She didn't defeat the fifteen-year-old boys in order to humiliate them. She did it to command respect and maintain control against the odds – odds which she very well understood. If the same boys found her distressingly attractive that was their problem. There was a time and place for everything and a boy was simply someone who didn't know it. In general girls at Greendale referred to boys as 'undesirable elements'. (Don't look now but we're being followed by two undesirable elements.)

But I am neglecting Haw Haw and Jerry. Seven weeks after the dreadful quarrel between Mother and V, on the eve of our return to Greendale, a Heinkel dropped a bomb straight into Mother's Dig for Victory cabbage patch, shattering all the rear windows and instantly killing the lady standing at the kitchen sink in the thick green uniform of the Women's Voluntary Services. Mother was alone in the house at the time. When the loving Albert arrived home from his super-secret lab, they had already taken the pieces away.

I was summoned to Rowley's study during the second course of the usual disgusting lunch: a morsel of leathery horse flesh, turnip reduced to yellow sludge, and a watery tapioca pudding generally known as fish eyes. Little did I know, as I took the trip to Yorkshire amidst the usual jeers and innuendoes from Brophy and Charrington, that I had received my last home-made fruit cake, my last bottle of homemade jam.

V, who had been waiting for me outside Rowley's house,

drew me into the front hallway and folded her arms round me very tight. She was fighting tears, fighting for words, taking on herself to break the news before Rowley staged his usual disgusting performance in his rotting tweeds, tamping his pipe, belching understanding, self-admiring pauses and a great display of callous Tact. Mrs R appeared with a mug of sweet tea which was apparently 'just the thing' for such moments. But death with a human face soon yielded to the Stalinism (hindsight) of Wackford Squeers – it was very far from clear (to him) who my legal guardian would now be, but in the meantime he was sure that the Governors would wish to do their best for me in honour of my mother's long devotion to the school, oh yes, oh certainly.

'As for the school holidays, Michael, that's something we'll have to solve.'

'Michael will stay with me,' V said firmly.

'It's something we'll have to solve,' Rowley repeated emphatically. 'Now . . . mm . . . more immediately . . . Mrs Rowley will accompany you to London to, er . . .'

But V insisted she could manage with the help of our lodgers. Her tender gaze kept returning to me: 'Mike, dear, I think you should stay here.'

I had once overheard Mother describing bodies so blown apart that they could not be reconstructed; wrong hands hastily sewn on to wrong arms; wrong heads stuffed into wrong coffins. I told V I was coming with her; she didn't argue; she had taken a WVS first-aid course and knew the symptoms of shock.

Albert had identified Mother at the mortuary. Trembling with grief and resentment, I insisted that he describe the condition of her body (V was trying to distract me by offering to take me out to buy a new bicycle – a bicycle! – as if I were a child!) and when Albert stalled I threatened to go to the mortuary myself, as I had every right to do as next-of-kin. Every time I gingerly picked my way through piles of rubble into the shattered kitchen and recognized some familiar object or utensil belonging to Mother, I began to sob hysterically while the three adults tenderly comforted me.

'You are a brave fellow,' Leo insisted as I dug deeper into a despicable performance which would have confirmed Father's worst fears about my character.

'Your poor, dear mother,' Albert kept sighing. His round boffin glasses had misted over but he was the soul of competence, assuring V that he would contact Mother's usual building contractor – six windows needed to be replaced, half the roof had been blown away, and there was a strong smell of leaking gas. Later that day the family solicitor, Mr Underwood, arrived carrying copies of two wills: Father had left everything to Mother and Mother had left everything to me so that was fine. But Mr Underwood (whose existence was a novelty to me) seemed deeply troubled.

'There is the question of, er, guardianship,' he told us. 'Michael's only surviving, er, adult relative is your mother, Veronica.'

V and I exchanged agnostic glances. V had confided to me that her mother hardly ever wrote to her from South Africa – so how could Aunt Amanda possibly serve as my guardian?

Mr Underwood, who had been alive during the Boer War if not the Hundred Years War, cleared his throat and mumbled about a 'serious conflict'. Let us not waste words on Underwood: in a vocabulary which was archaic, anachronistic, atavistic and arcane, he managed to convey that Father's will (or Will) had appointed Veronica's mother to be my legal guardian in the event of Mother's death – BUT, hm, mm . . . Mr Underwood found another frog in his throat while V and I sat before him in our best suits, our knees pressed together in perfect humility and attentiveness.

'However . . . after your brave father's death, er, your dear mother made it clear to me that she opposed this, er, arrangement. Er, quite fiercely. She therefore made a will of her own, appointing, er, me or my surviving Partners as your, er, sole legal guardian.'

'Which will prevails, sir?'

The old fool looked a bit surprised by my directness. 'Er . . . in theory your, er, mother as your, er, surviving parent . . .'

'Fine,' I said.

'I am nevertheless painfully conscious, Michael, of your, er, father's wishes . . . hm . . . That is to say, if Veronica's, er, mother wished to apply in an English court . . .'

Stymied by his own dilemma and by the wondrous ambivalences of Law, Mr Underwood then produced a key, unlocked the drawers of Father's desk, and removed the contents. Observing this act of rape, I coldly pondered the Greendale School Motto, 'Self knowledge and the fullest possible development of personality.'

Or, alternatively:

I said, 'What about my father's papers?' and gestured towards the locked drawers of the antique desk (I had the naïve belief that whatever they contained belonged to me). I felt V's hand on mine. Kneeling, she pulled the drawers open, one by one, most tenderly: Mother had destroyed everything. The next day V and I returned to Greendale, our hands clasped throughout the journey. I had a feeling that there was something she wanted to tell me but I didn't press her.

Charrington solicitously took me aside.

'I'm awfully sorry, Parsons. Look – you do know about the Fund, I suppose?' Silence being the acceptably dignified token of ignorance, I waited while Charrington lowered himself into a stage whisper:

'Between ourselves and *entre nous*, and I wouldn't pass this on to anyone but your good self, some old Jew who'd robbed the poor for fifty years sent his brats here, then left the School a filthy pile.'

We were walking along Front Terrace (as a ragged stretch of worn gravel was dignified). Charrington carefully pulled the lock of hair from his left eye then cupped his hand under my elbow:

'In strictest confidence, the Jew's Fund is earmarked for destitute orphans but Squeers has stashed the money under his floorboards – to spend on his syph. You do know about VD, Parsons? My Pop has it badly. In the end it rots the brain cells and drives you into the bin. The symptoms are quite observable in both Squeers and his dog, who regularly sleeps between man and wife and sometimes gets mistaken for the latter, *comprends*?

Your only course, quite honestly, is to confront him without delay.'

There was a school dance. V taught me some steps and I trembled at her touch, our licensed closeness, but I refused to go to the dance. 'Mike,' she said, 'I bet a lot of girls are longing for you to ask them.' I didn't believe her, nor did she. I wasn't going to spend a nauseating evening sipping lemonade while V was swept around in the arms of great spotty louts. Nowadays, I notice, young people dance with anybody or no one or their own shadow – a very sensible evasion of the potential pain of rejection.

A constant problem was V's acolyte Nancy Lunt, now Head Girl (on account of her universal unpopularity, we supposed) and therefore free to haunt V's room at will. Whenever I put my head round the door I was met by Lunt's hideous Lesbian scowl – she was probably a hyperthyroid, what with her popping eyes and general excitability. She insisted on marching off to the dance with V on her arm and her petticoat showing at the back.

I wandered the grounds on that summer evening, brooding vastly and plotting spasmodically. When it was all over the doors of Great Hall (so called) were flung open, emitting a blaze of light in contravention of the air-raid regulations. I positioned myself in the shadows of an elm tree (any old tree, I don't know) until V emerged with Lunt still on her arm.

I heard V say, 'We ought to check the junior dorms, Nance.'

'Oh gosh, Nicky, those squirts, not yet.' (Normally 'Gestapo' Lunt couldn't have enough of the police raids, charging into Top Landing looking for delinquents to report to Rowley. Charrington reckoned she hankered after corporal punishment and capital punishment as well.)

Nancy was leading V towards the woods. Presently her heavy arm, a match for Brophy's any day, fastened itself round V's waist, and she began cooing and giggling. As the Bard says, 'On such a night as this . . .' I followed discreetly, worried that I might step on a dry twig and give myself away. Lunt was soon spilling out her filthy infatuation in little whimpers, her big hippo body quivering in its hideous taffeta ball gown. It was a kiss she wanted and V was turning her beautiful face from side to side in gentle but firm refusal.

'Oh Nicky, you're so cruel! I love you so much!'

'Ssh.'

'And you hate me!'

'Ssh! Of course I don't, Nance – it's just that I don't kiss girls.'

My heart was hammering: who *did* she kiss? I was still wrestling with this when the Lunt creature buried her face in V's neck – not exactly *mens sana in corpore sano* – followed by the slurping sounds you heard in hall when the pink, rubbery discs known as Luncheon Meat were served with beetroot, absolutely disgusting, then V broke free and ran back towards the school as fast as her high heels would allow – to have removed her shoes would have put her precious stockings at risk. She passed within touching distance of my tree. Lunt was now whimpering like some cow elephant which had mislaid its baby. My heart threatened to leap from its cage as she slowly tramped past, sniffling – fortunately sniffling is incompatible with sniffing.

Of course I kept all this to myself and, besides, I'm too honest a writer to believe a word I write, even under severe provocation from the women's committee of the GLC and Islington Borough Council – item: wrestling mats for Lesbians.

Squeers summoned me to Yorkshire and told me, through clouds of pipe smoke, that he was disturbed by recent reports of my work. Potential Oxbridge scholars could not afford any backsliding, right? I nodded and waited. Reminding me that he was customarily addressed as 'sir', Rowley concertinaed his several chins in recognition of my recent bereavements.

'In such cases introverted melancholia is not uncommon.' And that in turn led to certain bad habits (like double negatives?). He named one of them: 'whacking off'.

'In the bad old days they used to threaten us with blindness –

44

just as nannies once warned naughty children that Boney would get them. You won't go blind, Michael, but you will continue to sit through your lessons with your eyes half closed if you persist in whacking yourself senseless.'

I was choking with fury but he wasn't through yet. Matron's report on the state of my sheets followed: 'deplorable'.

'It destroys concentration, Michael, and drives the mind into morbid fantasy.'

I had nothing to say (though not for the aforementioned reasons). Squeers came at me again:

'Let me prompt you, hm. You are floating off into sleep and you imagine a particular person in your, hm, arms. She might be real or imaginary; a film actress or a girl at this school; or a nude lady from a magazine.' He paused in italics. 'Who is it?'

I came up with Cleopatra, Queen of Egypt.

'Ah.' His pig eyes twinkled in triumph – a boy who whacks off for Cleopatra must be scholarship material.

'Don't let her destroy your declensions and conjugations, Michael.' Yellow, broken teeth leered at me between lips of rotted rubber. 'You have balls, Michael, I have balls, and Hector here has balls.' (He motioned to the filthy, shaggy, drooling hound which lay, permanently asleep, at his feet.) 'We have to learn to handle them, don't we, hm? Basically, that means hands off. Their time will come.'

Descending the staircase through the familiar concentration camp stench of cabbage and lino wax and burnt Yorkshire pudding, my mind and I slipped their handcuffs. If only my feeble, hesitant father had been man enough to override Mother's 'progressive' pretensions and insist on sending me to a real public school – a place where 'sir' meant something. In any event my rebellion would be Napoleonic not Jacobin.

At the start of the school holidays Greendale emptied like a bucket of slops and I moved into a damp hole in the Staff Annexe which Rowley grandiloquently called a bedroom. When V protested on my behalf she was reminded that there was a war on. Since it was she who volunteered for fire duty practically every night of every week, that wasn't news to her. Another reminder was a notice pinned inside the front door: 'Staff are Responsible for their Own Blackout. Also for any Fine Incurred in Connection with the Same. Carelessness in Such Matters is Unpatriotic.'

V and I were together, and alone, at last. Our tiny kitchen boasted a wall-mounted gas heater for hot water (ha ha), an electric cooker, an iron plugged into the light socket, a cracked sink and wooden draining board from which cockroaches emerged to do their daily PT, and a clothes rack suspended by rope and pulley from the ceiling. We also shared a Hoover Model 375 whose dust bag announced:

> IT BEATS
> AS IT SWEEPS
> AS IT CLEANS.

The main threat to our domestic happiness was a ferocious spinster called Miss Murdoch who lived next door and normally had her ear to the wall or the keyhole. The old bitch smelt of moth balls and was perpetually snooping and interfering and asking V to turn her radio down. But at least she wasn't Mother and couldn't make V cry.

V made stupendous efforts to learn new recipes and to perform small miracles out of four weekly ounces of bacon or ham, eight of sugar, cheese and fats, I forget the rest. I've never been much interested in the social history of the war, which is nowadays called 'the people's war' in progressive television documentaries. However, who can forget the awful Radio Doc urging us to eat liver and kidneys, damning sugar as a menace, and drivelling on about 'my old friend the dandelion leaf'. Darling V took all this tremendously seriously and I was free to love her and whistle while she worked.

After supper V would usually knit while listening to the radio and waiting for Miss Murdoch's thumps on the wall. It was a Philco 'People's Set' 444 in plastic. Mother had told me she bought it at the time of the Coronation for six guineas. My habit was to read while listening to the radio and looking at V. 'Mike, you're looking,' she would rebuke me. I protested my innocence in voices borrowed from the wireless – Tommy Handley as head of the Ministry of Aggravation, Colonel Chinstrap ('I don't mind if I do') and other beloved characters who kept a nation laughing under the searchlights and bombers. Millions of homes were listening. I've never cared for the millions, but the radio warmed and eased the difficult spaces between a boy of fifteen and a girl four years older. Handley's innuendoes brought blushes to her cheeks:

HANDLEY (*to his secretary*): I have power to seize anything on sight.

SECRETARY: Oh, Mr Handpump – and me sitting so close to you.

I was torn between the restless impulses of a mischievous boy with sticky hands and the gravitas of a young gentleman. I displayed constant, gallant appreciation of V's clothes and regularly advised her on the styles and colours that suited her. V used the word quite a lot: 'Does it suit me?' or, studying knitting patterns, 'Would it suit me, Mike?' I brushed my hair down like Hitler's to provoke her into rumpling it up; she still said it was 'wasted on a boy'. Occasionally I was able to lure her into a small physical tussle but my excitement and tumescence disturbed her and she was continually dousing flames by pulling free of me with a gentle reprimand or woman's habitual alibi, 'Can't you see I'm busy?' But she did let me brush her long auburn hair; as a reward I was allowed to kiss her mouth but only for a split second and with closed lips.

I had not been enthralled by the spectacle of the East End urchins roaming their own devastated habitat on the few occasions when Mother had succeeded in dragging me down to Stepney, Limehouse or Shoreditch. I liked them even less when they invaded Greendale – Mother's brainchild scheme. They spilled out of their coach in fighting heaps, yelling, yelling, yelling, kicking gravel in each other's faces, overturning sand buckets, snot dangling from their noses. They more or less relieved themselves where they stood and shovelled their food into their grimy faces with their knives. They were totally hostile to any environment not their own; their only possible response to the unknown was to attack it.

V was wonderful. She took them on hikes, played football until her shins were bruised, taught them how to put up a tent and light a fire out of damp wood; she expended their energies in the gym and she scolded them if they failed to wash or clean their teeth and smacked them if she caught them smoking. She ignored their ritually obscene language, the litany of filth which gushed mechanically from their mouths, the interminable 'Fuck offs' and 'Fuck yous'. 'It's not their fault,' she said. They adored her. She was 'Miss'.

These urchins were all aged between eight and eleven, anything older being, in Mother's opinion, impossible to handle. But even the youngest of them knew that Miss was a lush dame. When she stripped down for PT or cross-country runs (they loathed the soggy, empty, pitiless countryside even more than we did – we at least owned it), the chorus of 'approval' was so deafening and so persistent that V was forced to wear slacks and sweaters. 'Cor! Corr! 'Ey, Bert, take a look a' those tits!' For my part I could tolerate neither their lusts nor their delinquency nor their vandalism.

Their lives were ruled by gangs and gang leaders. Observing their social habits was a form of anthropology. King Pin of the Mob was a ten-year-old bruiser, large for his age, called Bert Frame. He carried the flushed-barrel profile of a master butcher in miniature. (According to Mother, these kids had never eaten so well as during the war.) Bert was clearly on to blackmarket rations. His word was law and normally lawless. He traded in shrapnel, bits of German fighters he'd shot down with his bare hands, clothing coupons either stolen or forged, Woodbines and Capstans, dirty pictures, and mighty blows with hoof and paw. He had a way of looking at me which was the incarnation of insolence: a slow, savage, mocking stare. I tried to avoid the urchins but they were soon brashly transgressing the frontiers they had been set, roaming everywhere in warring packs, honking like geese and screeching like seagulls. (Forty years later one hears the same honking from their sons.) You had to shake out each shoe in case you found one of them curled up inside.

48

V insisted on inviting them to tea in the staff Annexe. I protested vehemently but she was stubborn. They arrived in twos and immediately began to search for objects to filch. I would have required them to empty out their pockets on departure – though often enough the stolen goods fell straight through the holes in their short trousers – but V wouldn't allow it.

Recently I watched a television programme about an exchange visit between some sixth formers from a public school and a comprehensive school. It wasn't a great success. Neither group felt at home or at ease. The cultural revolution of the sixties was mainly a media event. Mangled vowels and northern stresses (suck-cess for success), previously confined to gardening programmes, stand-up comedians or radio serials, suddenly surfaced among newsreaders, political reporters and cultural pundits. The Americans imported the Liverpool sound to Shea Stadium, David Hockney dragged his vowels up and down the coast of California, and the children of the professional classes deliberately blunted their accents; but the class structure survived until our own Government was elected to place it on a sounder – because more rational – footing: initiative, energy, enterprise.

'Two nations,' wrote Disraeli, 'between whom there is no intercourse and no sympathy; who are as ignorant of each other's habits, thoughts and feelings, as if they were dwellers in different zones, or inhabitants of different planets.'

V admired my brain and gallantly strove to improve her own. ('Mike, I'm such a dunce.') The arrival of the London urchins seemed like the moment to induct her into a novel which had caught my imagination and which I've never ceased to reinterpret, Benjamin Disraeli's *Sybil. Or the Two Nations.* In fact Mother had given it to me but I didn't open it until after her death.

Disraeli's England was a revelation, both painful and exhilarating. Not many decades ago the ancestors of our urchins had practised infanticide as extensively as the denizens of the Ganges. Unwanted children were regularly starved, poisoned or sent out 'to play' – to be run over. Death alone kept them down.

The Labour politicians who had been received into our wartime National Government by Mr Churchill may have been decent individuals but behind them (I warned V) lay a pent-up force of envy and destruction biding its time. For V's benefit I read aloud Disraeli's descriptions of the vast concourse of rough and desperate persons assembled on Mowbray Moors round the rocks called the Druid's altar – flaming torches, the hot breath of anarchy, rank conspiracy. I conducted V through the secret trade union rites of initiation in the warehouse, guarded by sentries wearing dark cloaks and black masks; here the industrious worker John Briars was denounced for accepting piece-work and earning forty shillings a week – whereas the idle rabble would stick to day work and twenty shillings. A resolution was passed to expel any member who took pride in the quantity or quality of his work. The initiate was made to swear to obey the committee slavishly in all its directives, such as 'the chastisement of Nobs'. I wasn't sure what a Nob was but it sounded like M. Parsons when Bert Frame's evil eye lay upon him.

Mob-rule prevailed (I told V): Hell-cats burning down the tommy shops in a licentious passion of rage, all trammels of civilization discarded. Never mind Messrs Attlee, Greenwood, Bevin and Morrison; look for the shadowy Jacobins and Bolsheviks at their elbows, men of brutal and grimy countenance, grasping hammer and sickle, commanding that all labour shall cease until the Queen (or our King) submits to their demagogic demands. 'I was always against washing,' declares Disraeli's Tribune of the People, 'it takes the marrow out of a man.' Did that cap not fit Bert Frame and his cohorts perfectly?

V, knitting patiently during this exposition, commented that it pretty well fitted Roger Brophy as well. 'Remove Matron and which of you would clean your teeth?'

I explained to V that the delinquencies of boys of our social class were transient acts of theatre; our Destiny was to wash and we would, at the appropriate time, do so.

V replied that our soldiers and airmen kept themselves every bit as clean as their officers. I demurred, begging to inform her that in Communist Russia baths were forbidden and proper washing restricted to once a month on pain of Siberia.

'Are you sure, Mike?'

'Yes.'

'The Russians are putting up a jolly good show, aren't they?'

'It has never been said of barbarians that they can't fight.'

V usually let me have the last word. For her the meaning of *Sybil* lay not in the broad realm of masculine understanding but in the finer (narrower) tuning of feminine sympathy. Sybil's religious compassion for the poor and her love of the good (if simple-minded) nobleman Egremont was spiritual food enough for V. The message for her was the One Nation of Crown and Cottage – the poor were our responsibility, not (as I argued) their own. The poor had been shamefully exploited by Egremont's elder brother, Lord Marney, and it was no surprise to V that they rioted; yet they were decent folk at heart and Sybil had personally chided the local men she knew into shame and restraint at the height of the insurrection.

V's devotion to Egremont, shared with Sybil, irritated me. If she set out to find a good-natured but idiotic old Etonian Knight of the Round Table, I would be left alone. I reminded V that Egremont had passed most of his life crossing from Brooks's to Boodle's and from Boodle's to Brooks's. She frowned and shook her lovely hair and said no, that was surely some other, minor character in the novel. I insisted though I knew she was right.

V and I could now go to the cinema whenever we felt like it. The cinema queues stretched right round the building, the usual redbrick thirties edifice with a few narrow windows (cinemas don't need windows) and the obligatory rounded part at the entrance. The architects of the thirties were obsessed by streamlining but buildings neither move at speed nor move at all. I hadn't thought this out but I was vaguely conscious of inheriting a world full of clumsy mistakes.

V was a fan. She fell in love with most of the stars though not really. There was Leslie Howard as the man who designed the

Spitfire; David Niven played his ace test pilot. V was always susceptible to scenes of emotional understatement, as if she was still learning to be properly English:

SHE: Do you think you'll be away long?

HE: This one won't be over quickly.

SHE: I suppose it's no use asking *you* to take care.

HE: Does it matter to you so much?

SHE: I rather think it does.

In those days directors still showed respect for the script and employed real writers. Comradeship, grit, self-sacrifice, the muted claims of love – V could never have enough of it. During the holidays, when Greendale's pupils had abandoned the place to London orphans and V was 'Miss' rather than 'Miss King', she would let me hold her hand in the cinema.

There was one snag. The town of Greendale was situated only five miles from an airfield taken over by the 8th American Air Force. As a result we suffered our share of air-raids and stray bombs, but the serious factor was the human one – a German occupation could not have been much worse apart from the token Heil Hitler-ing which no one took seriously anyway, except a few Jews determined to make trouble for themselves. Our friendly American conquerors gave us candy and took our girls. They told us that everything in England was 'small': houses, shops, rations, cars, people. We were cordially invited to regard ourselves as Lilliputians, as quaint miniatures of the real thing which, in its hugeness, existed somewhere known only to them. They brought with them every item that any human being could need except Mom, the home town, and women. Gallant and glamorous and broad-shouldered in their olive-green uniforms cut out of the finest cloth, these homesick allies loaded with money haunted the streets and cinema queues, chasing skirt. Hey, why don't we have ourselves a good time?

Over-paid, over-sexed, over here.

To shuffle forward, with the queue, in V's company was like politely fending off bandits while clutching the Crown Jewels. They came at her with the monotony of rain; they clustered like flies on glue-backed paper; they were never short of something to say or propose; they offered me chewing gum and called me sonny.

I became a reluctant expert on B17s and B24s, the Flying Fortresses and Liberators which were flying high-altitude daylight 'missions' (it sounded almost religious) over Europe. It was odd – probably impossible – to imagine these candy-dispensers at thirty thousand feet, blasted by flak. Their morale was still bullish; despite their two per cent 'downs', they lived on their own high and it was we, the earthworm civilians, who felt like casualties.

Their approach to sex seemed utterly innocent and guileless even to a boy who hadn't had any – you couldn't imagine them saying anything dirty. We, who never got it, knew it was a disgusting, shameful business – any civilized person understood as much.

As soon as the Americans had marked a local girl like V as 'class' (as distinct from 'on the make', 'easy' or 'tramp') then we were quickly into 'history'. History had class: 'You have a lot of history here.' Enter Westminster Abbey, the Tower, and a pile of stone called Buckingham Palace, where 'your Royal Family' waited every night to be bombed like everyone else. (I am a republican by sentiment, a monarchist by observation of my countrymen. I would rather execute Charles I than pray with Cromwell, the Greatest Englishman Who Ever Lived.)

Open and extrovert (I prefer 'extravert') our Americans paraded their lives and biographies with naked innocence. Whatever they felt they said; in our view words should conceal or disguise feeling. The world was a marketplace, everything up for grabs, including self. Some of them approached V under covering fire by talking to me – 'You her brother, son?' – of eight-man aircrews and the mysteries of altitude. 'You like Hershey bars, son?' Quivering with hostility as I was, I absorbed information like blotting paper and could have written a small (if incorrect) thesis on why pilots, bombardiers and navigators were commissioned officers, whereas your wireless operator, flight engineer and gunner were not. These Americans talked of rank because they knew it was in our bloodstream – it was like a rope thrown from ship to shore – but off-duty it seemed to count for little and the tail gunner with his sights on V never stepped back out of deference for the pilot. Their occasional token salutes would have disgraced the Marx Brothers. On the few occasions I had walked down the street with my uniformed father, RAF men and soldiers had straightened their backs and swivelled their heads to left and right.

V was never rude to her American suitors – never rude to anyone. Nothing and no man disconcerted her. Occasionally I observed a flicker of genuine interest in her eyes; I monitored her with intense concentration, trying to glean the geography of her desires and emotions. I noticed that V immediately put up defences if a man was too obviously handsome. When the pressure became too blatant ('I'll be waiting for you right here on Tuesday', or 'Silk stockings? – no problem') V quietly produced her exit line:

'You'll have to excuse us. Goodbye.'

She was capable of saying 'goodbye' to a man who would be standing next to us in the cinema queue for a further half-hour. If necessary the goodbye could be really fierce. No cowboy attempted to ride it. It had class and history. Less pressing but tedious suitors would be shown off the field with 'We wish you luck' or 'Your mother must worry whether you'll ever come home'.

Obviously V despised the flirtatious behaviour of other young women. She would never dream of painting her legs, still less of drawing a seam up her calves with a brown make-up pencil. She called all that 'sad'; it wounded her patriotism.

Inside the warm cinema popcorn and Hershey bars crackled from every direction. Once the main film began V would let me hold her hand. If the film was very good my hand was allowed to rest against her thigh. My hand did exceptionally well during *Waterloo Bridge*, when Vivien Leigh had to conceal her tragic secret from handsome Robert Taylor. Love, tragedy, shame, suicide, all in a London fog – V almost wept.

We cried our way through *Mrs Miniver* with Walter Pidgeon and the lovely Greer Garson (for whom my heart later heaved in *Random Harvest*), about a family pleasure boat crossing the Channel to the beaches of Dunkirk. The people of England came to the cinema twice a week to forget themselves in Atlantic storms, North African deserts and Olde England (mainly filmed round Henley though I didn't know it at the time). Our semi-detached civilization suddenly discovered its soul in depth-charged submarines and Constable's 'The Haywain'.

When the film was brighter stuff V and I bantered our way home on the last bus, each accusing the other of falling in love with the hero or heroine. V was particularly vulnerable to teasing about her namesake Veronica Lake, a thick mane of whose luxuriant hair fell provocatively across one cheek in *I Wanted Wings*, starring the dishy Ray Milland and William Holden. (I caught V experimenting with this style, but it was impractical for a games mistress who wanted to see what was going on.) A single swing of Lake's sequinned box-shoulder said it all: 'C'mon get me, fella, if you can.' V didn't know – never knew – that Lake was born Constance Ockelman and that she was held to be causing accidents among women workers in munitions factories; at the request of the US Government, Paramount patriotically changed her hair style when she played a nurse in *So Proudly We Hail*. V never knew that Lake was discovered twenty years later working in a Manhattan cocktail lounge, having twice been headlined for drink convictions; never knew that when she died in 1973 she'd been married five times.

SIX

This may be the moment [John Ford wrote in the *Spectator* shortly after the Profumo scandal broke], to review a new paperback edition of Herman Melville's *Pierre or the Ambiguities*. The old joke about the Herman Melville Prize for the most meaningful literary silence seems inescapable – would that Melville himself had won it by not writing this awful novel.

His hero Pierre longs for a sister: 'He who is sisterless is a bachelor before his time. For much that goes to make up the deliciousness of a wife, already lies in the sister.' (One can scarcely imagine greater nonsense. It is the mother, not the sister, whose role overlaps with that of wife in ways too familiar to modern psychoanalysis to require recapitulation here. No 'Oedipus' ever killed his own father or brother because he fell in love with his sister.)

As in many tales of sibling incest, the hero of *Pierre* starts out unaware that his father had an illegitimate child. Pierre does not discover the existence of his half-sister Isabel until his twentieth year, by which time he is engaged to nice Lucy.

Impoverished and unloved all her life, Isabel moves into the neighbourhood and cannot resist writing to Pierre, revealing both her identity and her love for him. Our hero, having already set eyes on this young woman at a sewing circle and found her beautiful, is immediately thrown into melodramatic turmoil. Pierre breaks off his engagement to Lucy (causing his mother to expel him and die of a broken heart), then carries

Isabel off to New York, presenting her as his wife (no doubt a nobler deception than the one Abraham resorted to in Egypt, where the great Jewish patriarch presented his own wife, Sarah, as his sister in order to save his whatever is the kosher equivalent of bacon at the hands of the ever-lustful Pharoah). At this juncture Melville's windy, discursive, high-flown novel loses its nerve. Isabel is Pierre's 'wife' in what sense? Melville decorously shrinks from an explicit answer and often refers to their adjoining 'chambers', though we are left in no doubt that their mutual love has a strong sexual dimension.

Melville's saccharine sentiments lead him into a dense and suffocating impasse.

We notice that Pierre (like Ibsen's equally insipid Torvath) worships the memory of his dead father before discovering that this noble figure had been guilty of dissolute lechery. Since the beloved half-sister is the product of that disillusioning lapse from honour, Pierre is catapulted into chivalrous concern for his dear, betrayed mother and his cast-aside, illegitimate sister. To the rescue, our gallant young knight, cock in the air but securely padlocked to the codpiece of romance.

Pierre, a Proteus of Christian chivalry who addresses the victims of his affections as 'thee', clearly believes himself motivated by nothing baser than compassion and guilt; yet he is soon driven deep into duplicity. Although his fiancée Lucy and his sister Isabel meet in New York, Pierre keeps each in ignorance about his relationship to the other and both young women are conveniently too meek or stupid to expose his game, despite the unhappiness and jealousy he causes them. One might applaud Pierre's Machiavellian defence of his passion but for the fact that Melville's bleeding-hearted hero continues to regard himself as the victim of an Unkind Providence. Finally, in a scene which effectively suspends the suspension of dis- belief, Isabel and Lucy join Pierre in the prison cell (to which he's been committed after killing his bad cousin Glen, suitor to Isabel) as a prelude to a triple suicide.

Very well. Scholars insist that Melville was engaged in complicated parodies of mid-nineteenth-century romance, with echoes of Bunyan and Milton. But Bunyan was an honest

Puritan fanatic and Milton had the guts to blame Adam and Eve for succumbing to lust off the apple tree of incest:

> Carnal desire inflaming, he on Eve
> Began to cast lascivious eyes, she him
> As wantonly repaid: in lust they burn.

Alpha for Milton. John Ford's Giovanni and Annabella also 'burned'. Melville's sibling couple are too wet to burn.

SEVEN

We lived through the school holidays, V and I, in extraordinary isolation. Greendale emptied, we stayed behind. We possessed a damaged house in London but no home because no family; or friends. If I was shipwrecked, she was my raft. My sixteenth birthday came, V couldn't afford much of a present, and she cried that morning for me and my predicament. I took her beautiful and bewitching face between my hands and kissed her on the mouth. 'You,' I said, 'are the only present I need.' It was too prettily said, perhaps, but deeply felt.

It was a late summer evening in '43 and the urchins had been herded back to their dormitories and dens. The dimming sky was still splashed in extravagant bands of fire and the surface of the swimming pool was smooth and sluggish, a darkening jade. V's white costume slid into the water almost soundlessly. Sixteen on the day, I followed clumsily, feet first, limb by reticent limb, into the shallow end, then bravely began to dog-paddle in pursuit of the sleek white phantom. She vanished. I flapped around, spluttering; hands caught my feet, pulling me down. Water in the nose is a marvellous antidote to Milton's burning. She glided away to the deep end, leaving me to administer my own recovery. But she, *victrix ludorum*, was in a playful mood (my birthday, after all) and came at me again, hauling my legs into shallower water, then allowing me to clasp my arms round her waist until my shame pressed into her thigh and she broke away into a few rapid strokes, shy, troubled, prudent, Rose-of-England. (And I, a clever sapling with

59

unspoken claims, stick-thin and never quite to be trusted.)

I shivered and splashed clumsily towards her. She swam round me in slow circles, wary yet seductive. Bravely I called her coward and she said 'Oh?' and was gone. A flash of white under the water and I was swept off my feet, pinned against the side of the pool. 'Beg?' she asked. Fired up, I gave it all I had and was quickly forced to submit. 'Beg,' she insisted. She allowed my wet-dry lips to touch her mouth; I pulled her hand to my cock, which had come up and out of my trunks like a hungry periscope, and whispered 'Please'. She was rigid with hesitation. I said 'Please' again (perhaps repeatedly) and she dropped her gaze, leaning forward and resting her wet forehead on mine. Her hand was agonisingly slow, reluctant, amateurish even – as if a boy's parts were news from nowhere – but then she caught the accelerating rhythm of my breathing and her hand quickened, firmed, suddenly admitted its knowledge. I discharged then clung to her.

She made us a nightcap of cocoa, mostly water but a little milk, like the preceding half-hour. I chatted sensibly of other things to lift her spirits and varnish the event in normality, but when we sat down with our steaming mugs she shook her head in something like despondency:

'Gosh, Mike, how can I know what's right for you?'

'You're right for me.'

'That's too glib an answer. I'm serious.'

I told her she was the most beautiful creature I'd ever seen – including Vivien Leigh and Veronica Lake. A faint smile came up; V was a romantic at heart and vulnerable to chivalry even from a toy man. But a maternal frown quickly closed down the smile.

'Mike, do you miss Dad and Mum terribly?'

'Sometimes . . . I'm no longer sure who I am. I have a name, that's all. I suppose I'm "an orphan".'

She took my hand. 'I wish I could bring them back to you.'

'I don't think Mum treated you very well.'

V was silent. Then she said: 'Mike, darling, I don't think, I honestly don't, that I can go on pretending. There's something I've really got to tell you.'

Pure Ealing Studios, but that's the way it was. Whenever the chance arises of viewing those old films again, the ones that V and I saw together, I go – I lied my way out of a ministerial meeting in Brussels to sit through *Waterloo Bridge* right underneath it, at the National Film Theatre, rigged out in a false moustache, mirror shades, a knitted balaclava and that bittersweet flavour which attaches to any memory of V.

V clasped my hand tight and told me she was my sister. 'Not just half but three-quarters.' She'd obviously given much thought to this quantification and I suppose I'd always known. (I ask myself this question more frequently than any other.)

For an unmeasurable moment I suspected she was playing a bent card to fend off my fires once and for all. And so she was. But she could not have feigned the luminous tenderness with which she said, 'So you've got me for a sister in everything but name. Rotten luck for you. No more hanky-panky, right?'

The Parsons family, then, was rooted in a lie like rhubarb in a compost heap. Our shame lay less in the truth than in the lie itself – we felt, both of us, trapped by two dead parents, one of whom had belonged to us both. I was more clear-headed about it than V. Who would believe us? Rowley? V's birth certificate told a different story; birth certificates do not lie. V's treasured collection of letters from Father, written in that unmistakably awkward, laboured, sloping hand, letters extending back to the age when she had learned to read, more than confirmed her claim, but she felt, and I felt, that these letters were too private to show to anyone.

'Don't tell anyone,' I said. I had no wish to inherit my father's sins. 'Do you promise?'

V looked quite stunned. 'If that's what you want.'

This is what V told me:

In 1923 the three sisters Phyllis, Margaret and Amanda French had been living in Alexandria, where their father was serving as an army doctor. Phyllis, the eldest, was a dreamy, rather spiritual person; Margaret, the least handsome, was bookish and busy with good works; Amanda, only eighteen, was gay, frivolous, the toast of the town.

To Alex came two young air force officers who were close friends: Henry Parsons and John King. Henry courted Phyllis in a rather diffident fashion and his proposal was slow to come. John King pursued Amanda fervently but she was not to be tied down, not yet. Margaret, meanwhile, passed messages and acted as go-between.

Then Henry and John's squadron was posted to India. In a flurry of last-minute courting John once again knelt before Amanda and she, to everyone's surprise, not only accepted but insisted on a rapid marriage before his departure. Her sisters suspected that she was pregnant and they were right. The baby, when it came, arrived six months after Amanda's marriage and was christened Veronica. A photograph of mother-and-child was sent to India, along with messages of congratulation to Flight Lieutenant King. Amanda planned to sail for India as soon as the baby was old enough.

John King turned out to be rather less sporting about it than anticipated. In a letter to Margaret he expressed his distress: he had never (he swore on his honour) lain with Amanda before their wedding night. 'She never gave me the chance, actually.'

Margaret felt she had to show the letter to Amanda, who shrugged: 'The baby is Henry's, so what?'

As if to confirm his grievance, John King soon afterwards got himself killed in a flying accident. A letter from Henry Parsons broke the news. 'Beastly luck.'

Some months after the French family returned to England, Henry Parsons was posted home from India (V was hazy about the dates). Margaret decided to talk to him privately, to tell him that he ought to marry Amanda. But it was a difficult mission because Phyllis was still in love with Henry and had maintained a dedicated correspondence with him, living in hope. Margaret and Phyllis had always been close – but Margaret was also in love with Henry and secretly hoped that he would marry neither of her sisters.

V smiled sadly. 'By this time just about everything was a secret from someone or everyone.'

Henry agreed he should marry Amanda and become father to his own daughter, but Amanda herself spiked the plan. She had loved him once but now she wasn't having him whether she loved him or not. Her pride was furiously engaged – even when she'd got him into bed in Alex she'd been unable to extract a proposal, though she told him she was carrying his child. He hadn't fancied marriage. 'Have John,' he'd advised.

As soon as Amanda said no, Henry fell in love with her. He also adored his child, Veronica. Faced with his belated passion, Amanda married a South African stockbroker she didn't love, and took Veronica off to live in Johannesburg.

The Union Castle liner had barely rounded the corner into the Bay of Biscay than Henry proposed to Phyllis. Phyllis said no, then yes, then fled to Cornwall to pursue poetry and pottery. Scarcely had her train rounded the corner into Dorset than Henry proposed to Margaret.

'And the world,' V said in her Hollywood, March of Time, voice, 'got Michael Parsons!'

But Henry's heart now belonged, obsessively, to Amanda and little Veronica. His letters flew down the Atlantic to Cape Town like palpitating pigeons. At the age of five V wrote her first letter to her father (whom she had met but couldn't remember).

'We had to write to him at his London bank so your Mum shouldn't find out.'

Amanda presently divorced the stockbroker (after he'd been 'wiped out' when the Great Depression hit Table Mountain and the Rand) and married a Canadian businessman who hadn't been wiped out. After a spell in Vancouver – V had vivid memories of sailing off the Pacific coast but it was too cold to bathe – Amanda left for South Africa again and married a Jewish wine exporter. (It was at this point in time that Aunt Phyllis started forgetting Amanda's married name; here, at least, I could contribute one small verse to the many chapters provided by my big sister, for these had been the years when my mother followed my father from one foreign posting to another, leaving me to spend the school holidays with Aunt Phyllis in Cornwall.)

According to my mother, Aunt Amanda had never returned to England. But V explained that this wasn't true. Shortly before V came to live with us in Hampstead, Amanda brought her on a Union Castle liner from Cape Town to Southampton. By this time Wing Commmander Parsons was back in Britain, training fighter pilots. V recalled the intense excitement of the journey – her first visit to the 'Home Country' since she was old enough to remember, and her first prospect of meeting her father. They stayed in a London hotel – Amanda had plenty of money from the Jew – and visited the sights. But they didn't visit Auntie Margaret.

They went down to Brighton to stay in the Grand Hotel. A man was waiting for them at the station, dressed in civilian clothes, and she hurled herself into the arms of this stranger 'with a feeling I've never had before or since – love, I suppose'. Her parents shared a hotel bedroom and she felt sure they would get married after her father had divorced Auntie Margaret and her mother had disposed of the wine merchant. To this end, Amanda had engaged a private detective who could attest on Margaret's behalf that her husband had committed adultery in the Grand Hotel. (My mother, of course, had no idea that Amanda was in England.)

Divorces took time, however. Father insisted that V had reached the age when she needed a sound English education; she must not return to South Africa. At first Amanda protested vehemently; despite her several marriages she had only one child.

'How do you imagine Margaret will feel about it when you ask her for a divorce?'

Father told her to stop fussing and V, who was allowed to listen to these exchanges, suddenly and secretly divined that it was herself Father wanted, not her mother.

'Did your mother share this premonition?' I asked.

V didn't know the word. Amanda had surrendered and returned alone to South Africa.

'Every time you and I got the train to Greendale from Waterloo, I used to remember waving goodbye to my mum – but I couldn't tell you.'

'Did you mind being separated from your mother?'

'Oh, Mike . . . Dad had come to mean so much to me. Mum was a lot of fun, I mean totally the opposite of yours, but there were always rows, storms, accusations, divorces. We were always packing our cases and moving on. I just wanted to belong somewhere properly. And England, it's the home country, isn't it?'

I gazed at my beloved V, long and slow, no one to say no.

'Can I kiss you?'

She let me.

I had been brooding about this secret family saga (Parsons and French) that V had unfolded, sifting, testing, weighing. Eventually I asked V whether she hadn't felt a bit low in deceiving me about everything.

She touched my cheek. 'Darling, they both insisted, Dad and your mum.'

I wore an unforgiving expression.

'OK,' she admitted, 'at first I felt quite happy misleading you. I was part of an adult conspiracy and you were only a child. It didn't matter since we'd never met before. But after I went to Greendale I realized that if Dad married Mum it would mean the break-up of your home. I began to feel really bad.'

'Did he ask Mother for a divorce?'

'No. Either he got cold feet about his position in the world or he never really intended to. Maybe it was me he wanted – your mum certainly came to that conclusion.'

'Oh?'

'Oh yes. But are you old enough to know this?'

I grabbed her – I recognised a deliberate provocation and a license for a roughhouse – and we fought on the bed, I (as usual) much over-excited and liable to kick over a table, she constantly muffling her giggles and hushing me with the spectre of Miss Nosey Parker Murdoch. Anyway, I got on top, vibrating with anticipation as V's skirt rode up her kicking thighs, and was wondering what to do next when V abruptly killed it by lying dead still and speaking in a grown-up manner.

'My mum suddenly got very angry. She wrote to your mum from South Africa and dumped the Brighton weekend and the private detective and all that in her lap. Oh Lòr'! Can you imagine?'

V arched her eyebrows as high as they could go.

My erection was refusing to subside.

'Up to that mo' your mum had merely resented me but from that mo' on she really hated me. I mean she took it all out on me – things you never heard about. So naturally I wrote to remind my own mum that I was living as a guest under your mother's roof and that what she'd done was completely unforgivable.' V dabbed at her eyes. 'I haven't heard from her since.'

I took her hand, aghast for her yet pleased that she, too, had no one else. 'Oh poor V,' I said.

'I also told Dad that he'd bloody well better stay married to your mum or I'd vanish for ever. But she, of course, thought I was scheming to separate them. How could I possibly explain?'

'What did Dad say?'

'Not much. He got more drunk more often, that's all. Actually – it runs in the family.'

She produced a small bottle of gin and poured herself some, downing it neat. I watched in amazement.

'Dad – drunk?'

'Yes, Mike. When he was drunk he used to try and fondle me in an unfatherly way. Remember when he came down to watch the hockey match? That evening he took me out to dinner. When I insisted that you should come too, he said something about "dinners for the deserving" and took me to a place where there was dancing. He . . . never mind. He said I looked just like my mother when she was a young woman living in Alex. Do you understand?'

'No.'

'You should do,' she said rather aggressively, reaching for the gin again. 'You're certainly a chip off the old block when it comes to feelies.'

'I never saw him drunk.' It still rankled.

'How did he really die?' she asked gently, taking my hand. 'On a test flight for a new, highly hush-hush night fighter?'

I waited, paralysed.

'Well, darling, it's in for a penny, in for a pound tonight, so

66

I'd better tell you that our father, yours and mine, got plastered at a senior officers' dinner at RAF Northolt and drove his staff car into a tree on the way home.'

She ran a hand through my hair as if to quell my rising hysteria. Probably it was the worst moment of my life. Not – I've analysed it again and again – because of these revelations about Father; not because I really believed he'd done things to V or killed himself while drunk; but because at that moment it seemed clear to me that the person I had been left with, whom I'd loved most, adored and trusted – was a vixen, a vicious liar, a fantasist, an unscrupulous imposter and a tart to top it all.

'I suppose you enjoy spinning yarns at my expense? Because there's no one left to contradict you, you feel you can say anything you like. Mother was right about you. With an upbringing like yours, you never stood a chance.'

'Have a drop of gin,' V said, wild-eyed with despair and terror. She more or less forced some down my throat. I spluttered then felt better and hurled myself on her. She didn't resist but she didn't help either and in the end I was sobbing helplessly in her arms while she milked me into my hanky.

EIGHT

In the field of prose fiction [John Ford wrote in the *Spectator* while students fought riot police in the Latin Quarter of Paris] no depiction of incestuous love between brother and sister compares in beauty and audacity with Thomas Mann's *The Holy Sinner* (1951) – though this title bears no correspondence to the original German, *Der Erwahlte* ('The Elected One'). With exquisite artistry Mann forges the pains and penalties of sibling passion into an immaculate conception.

We are in the age of Christian chivalry and the incest taboo is absolute. The offenders are the son and daughter of Duke Grimald of Flanders, Wiligis and Sibylla. Twins of great beauty, their double-birth had caused the death of their mother in childbed. Proud and vain, they pay court to one another from an early age, taking erotic delight in their separate sexes, magnetized by their biological identity, flattered by the social gulf that separates them from their father's subjects. They alone are good enough for one another.

They tease and flirt. 'We envy you,' said she, 'your differences, admire them, and are covered with shame, because we are broader in the hips instead of in the shoulders . . . even so my legs are high and slim, leaving nothing to wish in this respect.'

Wiligis expresses the aristocratic élitism of sibling incest. 'I have had eyes alone for you who are my female counterpart on earth. The others are foreign, not equal in birth like you, who were born with me.'

The old Duke clearly entertains barely sublimated designs on

68

his daughter, for he woos and fondles her under fatherly phrases, and turns away every foreign suitor for her hand. The night of his death his son Wiligis dances on the paternal grave by making love to his sister.

When Wiligis climbs into bed beside Sibylla, she feigns innocence – 'What means, my brother, this wrestling?' – but she is not innocent. 'Only you must not aim to part my knees one from the other . . .'

Now the faithful hound Hanegiff howls his own ceaseless protest at their bedside; exasperated, driven by unstoppable love and lust, Wiligis cuts the dog's throat. Sibylla's protests grow weaker: 'Oh, away and away! O angel boy!'

The monk-chronicler of this story comments: ' . . . out of all bounds they loved and that is why I cannot quite rid me of well-wishing for them, God help me!' Their love continues, moon by moon, and neither seeks a spouse, despite their father's dying command. They parade their affection, hand in hand, as a ducal pair, and soon there is whispering at court. Wiligis discovers that a loving brother – albeit a prince – cannot defend either his own honour or his sister's when he is discreetly taunted; to do so would amount to a confession.

In time Sibylla becomes pregnant and their panic matches that of John Ford's lovers Giovanni and Annabella. In Mann's novel, like Ford's play, it is noticeable that the sister's pregnancy immediately tosses the loving brother back from possessing man to frightened boy. But, whereas Giovanni and Annabella, mere bourgeois of Parma, rush headlong into her marriage, Mann's royal sinners take refuge in the protection of a great, wise and loyal knight who owes them absolute allegiance.

Avoid pregnancy, then? Unfortunately, such prudence must suggest a degree of calculation incompatible with the romantic imagination which, alone, can offer redemption and even charm an old monk into a semantic wink. Youthful incest must wear the badge of passion and innocent abandonment.

Wiligis now confesses that he had been engaged in a covert contest with his father over Sibylla: 'in jealousy [he] often drove me from your side – that drove me to your bed.' But now he fears exposure and shame. The Baron Eisengrein manufactures a solution; Wiligis will mortify the flesh by departing on a crusade, thus giving the baron a pretext for taking Sibylla under his liege protection, as acting Duchess, during Wiligis's absence.

Sibylla's baby is born in secret; it is in every way a perfect child but Eisengrein decides that 'honour and politics' dictate that it should be put in a tub, warmly wrapped, and sent out to sea, to discover God's will. Wiligis, meanwhile, has died during his journey to the East, apparently of a broken heart – his love for his sister had become a debilitating addiction.

The years pass. Sibylla, faithful to her dead brother, will marry no one else despite the pressure from suitors and advisers. Then comes the 'wooing war' between Burgundy and Flanders – a rejected royal suitor embarks on a long and destructive campaign against Flanders in support of his claim to the Duchess Sibylla's hand. But now a gallant young knight appears on the scene, a stranger called Grigorss, and almost single-handedly wins the war for Flanders. Sibylla promotes him to be her seneschal and then, rather fancying the much younger man, and much moved by entreaties to marry for the good of the Duchy, joins herself to Grigorss in wedlock after praying to the Holy Virgin for guidance.

The young husband Grigorss is, of course, Sibylla's own son, rescued as a babe by holy fishermen in the Channel. To Sibylla and Grigorss a daughter is born. The child is:
– the granddaughter of twins;
– the daughter of her own grandmother;
– the granddaughter of her own mother;
– the daughter of her own brother.

Yet no one seemed to notice, even though – as the chronicler slyly puts it – 'she had her head on the wrong way.'

NINE

At the top of the sleeve, the men of the US 8th Air Force sported a large badge decorated with a white star and – in the case of air crews – with two golden wings. They, the flyers, were the élite. We knew it, but they told us in any case.

V had already read *Gone With the Wind* in long, absorbed sessions. We queued for an hour to get in to the film, steadily propositioned by the 8th Air Force – 'Goodbye,' said V more than once – then settled in to our seats, amidst the crackling popcorn and candy bars, to fall in love with Scarlett O'Hara and Rhett Butler. V had already confided to me that Vivien Leigh belonged to Laurence Olivier (whose *Henry V* had set me dreaming – there was a joke of the time: Olivier, Old Vic, Vic Olivier).

We came out of the Ritz pulverized by three or possibly four hours of epic passion and civil war. It was indeed true that things were big over there. I'm not sure why people spend money on celluloid wars when they have a real one – no doubt the semiotic-structuralist film journals patronized by the progressive lumpen-intelligentsia are loaded with explanations. The last bus had gone and we began the three-mile walk home hand in hand. Presently V began to hum 'The White Cliffs of Dover', a favourite with the Ritz organist, then carried on to 'Shine on Victory Moon'. It was a lovely night, a friendly country road, the school was on holiday and I entertained renewed thoughts of brotherly love.

From behind us came the distant hum of a vehicle. Presently

narrowed headlights pierced the darkness and a jeep drew up beside us. The driver saluted respectfully.

'Good evening, ma'am, can I give you people a ride home?'

V never accepted lifts from Americans but my stride had been slackening and I had begun to complain of sore feet.

'We're going to Greendale School,' she said reluctantly.

'Just show me the way.'

Lieutenant Harold Rascoe had entered our lives.

I can recall every detail. V got in the front (the passenger seat was on the right side), I in the back – but there is no back to a Jeep, just a painful metal ridge and a spare wheel. The driver insisted on introducing himself and shaking hands – a firm, warm clasp. Politeness seemed to dictate that we yield our own names, though it felt like an intrusion if not an imposition. We then 'gunned' away. Harold Rascoe told V that he still hadn't 'gotten' used to driving on the 'wrong' side of the road but – he went on – an English country road was a whole lot nicer place to be than at forty thousand feet over Germany.

'Oh yes,' said V politely.

The driver then told us about his surname. First he spelled it, then explained that the 'a' was pronounced 'o'. We then passed through 'Moscoh' and 'Moscow', 'tomahtoe' and 'tomaytoe' – and up to the locked gates of Greendale School.

V thanked him but – couldn't we predict it? – the American seemed reluctant to accept her firm goodbye. Were we, he inquired, related? – even by night he discerned certain physical similarities. This was the first time any stranger had put such a question and the effect of it was to give the American a forged *laissez passer* into our lives.

'We are cousins,' V said, 'since you ask.'

The lieutenant ignored the sting in the tail and suggested that we meet again the following day, a Sunday.

'Oh no, we couldn't possibly,' V said.

As evidence of his good intentions he extracted a handsome wallet in tooled leather and presented V with his personal card.

'Harvard men never take no for an answer. Expect me shortly after noon.'

I waited for V to send the bounder packing with a resounding, Ealing Studios 'Goodbye!', but she merely said 'Goodnight' while unlocking the smaller, pedestrian's gate. A cheerful salutation came from behind us and then the jeep roared away.

Walking across the gravel yard to the Staff Annexe, I vented my feelings, keeping my voice down on account of Ma Murdoch.

'Why behave like a common tart?'

V gasped at the insult. 'Mike!'

'If you think I'm coming with you tomorrow – '

'Did anyone invite you, twerp?'

And so a happy evening dissolved into acrimony at the sudden appearance of a third party.

By the time I got up on that Sunday morning V had gone to minister to the London urchins. I settled down with a book in her room and didn't move until she returned. She threw me a hesitant glance, half a smile, as if to discover whether we were still quarrelling, then took down her prettiest frock from the tiny utility cupboard which passed for a wardrobe.

'Please don't look,' she said.

Normally she let me watch. I sometimes believed that my constant desire had set her imagination smouldering at the outer rim.

I listened instead. In an age of undergarments, of hooks and eyes and suspender clips, listening was like a form of understatement; V's body, however, outran the imagination. Presently she began rummaging through the small Japanese box in which she kept lipstick, powder and mascara. These shameless preparations finally brought my fury out of its cage.

'You're not really going out with that Yank?'

'He seemed quite nice.'

'Nice! You're certainly doing yourself up!'

'Anyway, he probably won't show up. Americans aren't gentlemen.'

'Ha ha.'

'There may be some good grub up his sleeve, Mike.'

This was a thought. Despite the Ministry of Food, Lord

73

Woolton – I little imagined that I'd one day be introduced to the great man – and the Radio Doc, a good meal stood on my horizon of possibilities close to the act of jigger.

How Harold Rascoe located our quarters I don't know but the Jeep came skidding across the yard to the Staff Annexe a few minutes before noon and cheekily bleeped on its horn. V opened the window, gave a small wave, took her handbag and white gloves (a pretty pillbox hat was perched on her carefully done-up hair) and blew me a kiss.

'Bye then.'

There was a sardonic note in this since I had already slithered into my best suit and cleaned my shoes – hardly gestures of hair-shirt defiance. Sensing that she needed my company on this occasion, I played my favourite game of attrition, hands deep in my sulking pockets. At this juncture a third party intervened to spring the lock on our quarrel; behind V's shoulder Miss Murdoch was hovering in the corridor.

'Is that American man in the car for you, Veronica?'

'Yes, Miss Murdoch.'

'Kindly tell him not to sound his horn like that.'

'I will, Miss Murdoch.'

'You were very late home last night.'

'I'm terribly sorry if I disturbed you. Actually, I wouldn't call it "home".'

'The pictures again, I suppose? It can't be good for Michael, at his age. And probably not suitable either.'

When V passed on the rebuke to Harold Rascoe he looked mortified. 'Put it down to natural stupidity and a beautiful day.' His admiring gaze spoke of another source of beauty and I had to admit, as he warmly clasped my hand, that in daylight he looked quite presentable himself.

We gunned out of the yard with a roar calculated to send Miss Murdoch bananas, a fruit I could barely remember. Clearly the man was a fool. I relaxed a bit.

'Well,' said he loudly (in a wind of his own making, which forced V to hold on to her little pillbox hat), 'first things first. I happen to know a place, an inn, where a man can eat and believe it. They don't seem to know there's a war on.'

He showed his teeth in a Rhett Butler smile. Harold, I soon realized, would never be short of something to say. As we sped through the soft green countryside he announced that he was living with a problem; the name of the problem was Betsy Lou. Here he paused for V's reaction. There was none. Bad luck.

Betsy Lou, it transpired, was a B17 bomber, a 'hard luck' ship which preferred the ground to the air. 'You take her up and immediately she goes bad on you. Back you come, test every part, she seems perfect, up you go again, tuck into formation, cross the coastline – and she doesn't like it. She begins shaking a wing to show her feelings. You turn her around.'

V was assessing the man. I leaned forward from my uncomfortable but sporting perch in the back:

'Maybe your Flying Fortress has no stomach for Goering's yellow noses.'

His head swivelled. 'You certainly have the vocabulary, Mike.'

V shot me a glance which I understood: she didn't want our father mentioned. I said, 'My father was an officer in Fighter Command.'

'Was? – I'm sorry.'

Harold knew the country round Greendale better than we did. My parents had never possessed a car; they spent what little money they had on school fees and the house. (Invite our prospering working class to divert a fraction of what it spends on cars, video-cassettes and drink to the education of its children, and its tribunes cry out in horror. Yet the involvement of our population in education – and hence the standard of education on offer – would leap forward if parents contributed towards its cost by direct payments. You own a house, you look after it – you may even learn how houses are designed and built. But give houses, health care and education away free and everything is treated with sulky indifference, the petulant carping against 'them' which is the hallmark of under-development.)

'Gas', as he called it, made Harold Rascoe lord and master of churches and inns unknown to us; indeed our miniature landscapes, layer upon layer of history, now resembled film sets

75

erected for wealthy invaders. The man even had the impertinence to tell us what we were seeing: Tudor, Jacobean,
classical, Georgian, a storm of information until we drew into
an 'olde' coach house straight out of a film set at the back of
which lay a charming lake where swans obligingly paraded their
haughty necks.

'Oh how lovely,' V said with a slight swing of her skirt.

'It's your country, Veronica,' the American said.

'Full of history,' I said.

He laughed, flashing his perfect teeth and leading us to a
reserved table on the verandah, overlooking the swans. Tall and
broad-shouldered, he had the lazy, assured motions of an
athlete.

'When does the ballet begin?' I asked.

He laughed again. 'As a matter of fact, Mike, I majored in
history at Harvard. Are any of you people averse to some real
claret?'

The proprietor was hovering at Harold's elbow, keeper of the
seals of his client's other weekends. The menu was disclosed
and discussed in a purred whisper on a 'most favoured' basis;
the treasures under the counter must not be divulged to
irregular guests at neighbouring tables. The tables had been
placed at discreet intervals, each one an island with its own
specified price. Harold ordered fresh Scotch salmon and a
saddle of beef 'all round'. When the waitress uncorked the
bottle she poured a small amount into his glass; he sniffed,
sipped, looked thoughtful, nodded. I had never seen this done.
At home wine appeared only on adult birthdays, frothed from
the neck of the bottle, was made in England, and was always
said by Mother to be 'very good value'.

V shyly lifted the American's cap from beneath his chair and
examined its badge, a shield with an eagle clutching a sheaf of
wheat and a sheaf of arrows, all crowned by a rosette.

'Tell me about your father, Mike,' Harold said.

'He was a Group Captain. He came down over the Channel
while test-flying a new hush hush night fighter.'

'He must have been a fine man, a brave man, Mike.'

I nodded modestly and sipped some wine. It tasted ugh.

Harold seemed to think it was very fine. He kept sniffing it and murmuring about its 'bouquet'. He told us that he'd spent time in France before the war – he knew the Paris picture galleries and the 'nightspots' in Montmartre – then he drew the conversation round to football and Harvard. Evidently he had played the one for the other.

'Our kind of football.' Broad grin, teeth.

'Isn't it more like rugby?' V asked.

'In Rugby the ball can't be passed forward,' I interceded.

'You a sporting man, Michael?'

Harold's shoulders were rippling under his jacket of fine olive-green cloth; if the proprietor had produced an oblong football from under the counter our host would no doubt have thrown it right over the lake.

'No. Veronica was *victrix ludorum*. That means –'

'I know some Latin,' Harold said. He turned to V. 'What do you play, Veronica?'

'I quite like hockey. And swimming. And tennis.' She smiled shyly. 'I can get by in the gym.'

I said: 'She could easily play hockey for England – if she knew they had a team.'

She looked at me in mock reproach. The American was reading us both, the cousins who looked closer than cousins. When would he inquire about V's parents? I asked him whether he knew that all the swans in England belonged to the King.

'I didn't know that, Mike. So if we eat one for lunch we get sent to the Tower?'

He was obviously pleased with this comment but V told me afterwards that she was quite shocked at the suggestion that one might eat a swan. A goose yes, but not a swan. (Not until many years later did I learn from the Lord Privy Seal that a certain number of swans had been culled for the pot under a special royal dispensation.) Indeed the whole blackmarket smell of this lakeside heaven disturbed V. I suppose we were all going through a kind of socialist ethic – the moral horizons of the officer class had been narrowed to ration-card egalitarianism. Even Dig for Victory allotment plots were divided into the standard dimensions of postage stamps. None of us could understand why Americans believed they could both win a war and have a good time. No wonder this fellow's kite, the Betsy Lou, was permanently grounded!! And how many others?? Did any of them ever reach Germany!?

Harold may have read the direction of my thoughts because he now informed us that he never went aboard his 'ship' without his medallion. He showed V his medallion.

'For good luck?' she asked.

He nodded gravely in recognition of her acute perception.

'Right. Luck is half the game. But every man's number comes up when it must.' Then he groaned theatrically in my direction. 'Mike, I'm sorry, that was unforgivably crass. I just wasn't thinking.'

Assuming himself to be forgiven instantly, Harold conducted us, hour by hour, through his 'pre-mission routine', listening to the RAF Lancasters going out, waiting for their return, 'feet on the floor' at two-thirty a.m., leaving his most precious possessions under his pillow, briefing at three, stand-by at four-thirty.

V said: 'The salmon was lovely.'

'Have some more. It can be arranged.'

'Oh no, no, please.'

The saddle of beef arrived under a silver lid and it wasn't a swan. With it came the pre-flight briefing:

'The Intelligence Officer reveals the target. Could be docks, factories, submarine pens, anything Jerry wouldn't want to say goodbye to. It all looks very clear on the reconnaissance photographs; when you get over there it's different.'

I suppose I ate my roast beef and horseradish sauce as if my life depended on it, an unbelievable treat. V ate like a lady. The American's monologue was now locked into automatic pilot:

'It's worth eating a healthy breakfast, Veronica. It may be your last. Anyway, it's going to be goddam cold up there and an empty stomach is no help at all.'

I thought: these lines are supposed to be spoken by the woman waving goodbye, not by the hero himself. Then Harold started dressing himself: woollen underclothes, the hot suit which plugged into the 'ship's' heat outlet, fleece-lined boots and gloves also wired up, finally the Mae West, inflatable life

preserver and parachute. I was on to a second helping of beef –
V winked encouragement, overcoming her scruples on my
behalf – before we heard the final zip.

(I said: 'My father never talked about it. He just did it. He
was a real man.' The American wiped his mouth with a napkin,
laid a wad of money on the tablecloth, and walked away
without a word. 'Well done,' V said, 'he's quite awful.')

Soon we were into strawberries and cream and boarding the
Betsy Lou along with Harold and his 'contingency packet' of
foreign money, maps and concentrated foods. The pilot lit the
four engines, one by one, the ground crew pulled the chocks
from under the wheels and V quite suddenly burped. She went
red. Harold was too much the gentleman or the monomaniac to
notice; *Loo*tenant Rascoe was bounding down the runway.

'You're the pilot?' V asked.

He smiled ruefully. 'To every pretty girl and brave young
boy the pilot is *it*.'

'Oh no, I just –'

'I'm a bombardier, Veronica. I carry a beautiful piece of
equipment called a Norden bombsight. So secret that it's
removed from the ship between missions.' Harold paused
before delivering the *coup de théâtre*. 'When I carry it to the
plane I'm wearing a loaded pistol.'

By this time my mind was as content as my stomach;
certainly V would never consent to 'date' this vulgarian again.
Even though the Betsy Lou slept on the ground day and night,
week after week, Harold was now conducting us aloft in his
plexiglass bubblenose; V covered her glass with her hand to
refuse more claret just as we crossed the Dutch coast and met
the first flak.

'Problems begin when the Me's rise to meet you – oh boy! do
I hate the sight of those yellow noses! The golden rule is to stick
in tight formation. Stray from the pack and they'll pick you
off.'

Loaded with food, fuzzed by wine and warmed by sunshine,
I half closed my eyes and fixed them on a pair of courting
swans. Harold was turning the knobs of his Norden, moni-
toring the crossed hairline, giving adjustments to the pilot,

correcting for speed, drift and wind. I refused coffee in honour of the extraordinary lingering aroma of strawberries.

'It's not as easy as it sounds, Mike, you really buck and bounce up there.'

Startled, I opened my eyes.

'Mike,' V said reproachfully.

'Probably he hasn't had a real meal in years,' Harold said.

I knew then that he was reconciled to a state of war between us. When he released his bombs over Germany it was 'maybe in a cluster, maybe in a line' and then they were turning for home with the Me's on their tail and buddies going down in flames, small puffs of white as they jump and . . .

' . . . you think Oh my God, it could be us, it could be us.'

V looked a bit embarrassed. 'We're very glad to have America with us in the war,' she said, playing with her napkin.

If the Yank wasn't already head over heels for her, that did it. Leaning towards her earnestly, he took advantage of the Grand Alliance to touch her hand.

'Believe me, Veronica – Mike – I wanted the United States of America in this war right from the day Hitler went into Poland. But we have some very strong isolationist sentiment at home. It wasn't easy for Mr Roosevelt at all.'

V said she very much liked Mr Roosevelt.

Harold nodded gravely. 'I guess that's a very great man, our President. And your Mr Churchill – great men for great times. In my view Charles de Gaulle could be cut of the same cloth.'

V didn't know too much about Charles de Gaulle and I yawned. Harold's tender gaze was fixed on my sister.

'Do you know the most beautiful sight in the world, Veronica?'

Through heavy eyelids I observed the colour creep into her face. The American grinned: 'It's the coast of England rising out of the sea at the end of a mission. Hot food, a warm bed, country sounds, a bird in a tree, a harvester at work, a dog barking, friendly people. That's where we're lucky. A soldier in the field doesn't get that.'

The afternoon drifted on through more of the same bilge. Presently Harold drew from his tooled wallet more crisp pound notes than I'd seen in my life. They all looked brand new as if manufactured in the USA.

'It's really awfully kind of you,' V murmured.

'On the contrary – kind of you and Mike to lend your delightful company to a stranger. But come now, I haven't heard about you people. Are you teaching school at Greendale, Veronica?'

We strolled round the lake, V saying she felt awfully guilty about her work when she ought to be in a munitions factory like Mr Bevin said or on the land or in the services. She'd never said any of this to me and I didn't care for it – neither for her sense of guilt nor for the impulses which moved her to confide in this unappetising stranger from the U.S. of A.

TEN

Sartre reports that as a child he had no sister and accordingly invented one [wrote John Ford in the *Spectator*, reviewing a new production of *Altona* a week before Britain's first woman Prime Minister took office]. Much moved by a novel, *Les Transatlantiques*, about a young American boy and his sister, Jean-Paul Sartre had fallen in love with the girl, Biddy, and dreamed of writing a short story about two lost and quietly incestuous children.

The fantasy persisted. Echoes of it can be found in the relationship of Orestes and Electra in *The Flies*, of Boris and Ivich in *Roads to Freedom*, of Frantz and Leni in *Altona*. But only the last couple go through with it.

Sartre tells us that what attracted him to sibling incest was not so much the temptation to love as the prohibition against making love. Wavering at the door of genuine perception, Sartre impedes his own entrance by setting up temptation and prohibition as antitheses. In reality the two are the positive and negative poles of a live wire. He then digs himself a shallow funkhole; 'I liked incest, with its mixture of fire and ice, enjoyment and frustration, so long as it remained platonic.'

How, then, do we explain the goings-on in his play *Altona*, which emerges as the most honest affirmation of sibling lust in modern literature? No bogus dichotomies between temptation and prohibition impede Leni as she addresses her brother Frantz:

'I need you, the heir to our name, the only one whose

caresses stir me without humiliating me. I don't amount to anything, but I was born a Gerlach, which means I am mad with pride – and I cannot make love to anyone but a Gerlach. Incest is my law and my fire. [*Laughing.*] In a word, it's my way of strengthening the family ties.'

(This last line is weak and redundant. The point is already made.) The grand bourgeoisie is experiencing in vulgarized form the same erotic bonds of blood, inheritance and power which bewitched the young sibling twins in Thomas Mann's novel, *The Holy Sinner*. Frantz says:

'Oh, little sister! You are there and I clasp you. Kind sleeps with kind – as it does a thousand million times every night upon this earth.'

Leni reflects:

'He desires me, but he doesn't love me. He dies of shame, and he sleeps with me in the dark . . . So? I win. I wanted to have him and I have him.'

Sartre is doubly to be congratulated on observing that in sibling incest one partner (Leni) is invariably the mover, while the other is fascinated into compliance – a point missed by John Ford and Thomas Mann, whose lovers display equal ardour (even if the brother makes the initial running out of courtly convention). Yet Sartre tosses us a huge escape clause: Frantz and Leni are the children of a Nazi industrialist, they are living in limbo, incapable of coming to terms with the post-war world, and Frantz is close to crazy with his imaginary crabs. Incest, then, emerges as merely a landmark in Sartre's famous geography of evasion – *mauvaise foi* – the escape from responsibility and free will. In short, we are invited to digest the incestuous bond between Frantz and Leni as the pathology of a defeated and demented ruling class. What a pity. Or, as Leni herself screams at one point, 'Coward!'

That Sartre's celebrated brain and equally renowned existential battlefield can yield such blatant contradictions and evasions need surprise no one familiar with his recent runs down the slalom slopes of global politics. Let us say that no modern writer has contradicted himself so brilliantly so often and leave it at that.

Three years ago I discovered that the bugger had been writing under the pseudonym John Ford for twenty-five years. Shaming to admit as a professional journalist, but I hadn't cottoned on to the real identity of this 'Ford' – a respected Tory MP with his libido on full display – until the *Spectator* went through one of its very latest terrific teacup storms (change of proprietor, change of editor, marching orders, squeals of fury, daggers thrust into corpses). I used to think I was in a hard trade putting my foot in the door of queer vicars or lifting photos from the sitting rooms of train disaster victims, but compared to the Jacobite *liter-arti-parti* we hacks on the *Globe* and the *Mirror* are Twiggies.

I gathered from my *Spectator* squealer – several glasses of something expensive went down him before he consented to swallow my lunch at the White Tower – that the identity of John Ford had been an 'open secret' to the *** [can't spell foreign words but it begins with 'cog'] for years.

'Of course he's always been something of a puzzle: unmarried, by reputation celibate, yet certainly not gay; and that obsession with incest, absolutely nonstop – but the very successful can afford to be, don't you think?'

'Afford to be what?' I dared to ask.

'Oh – puzzles.'

Room 20 of the Prince of Wales Hotel, Llanfairfechan, offers a lovely view of the Menai Straits and Puffin Island. I imagine that hasn't changed since August 6, 1945. New management, of course, and new décor, juke boxes, fruit machines, television, credit cards. I had telephoned in advance with a special request for Room 20, giving my name as Maxwell just for the sound of it.

'Room 20 is a double room, sir.'

'Yes, I know.'

'Very good, sir. How will you be paying?'

'In cash.' (Just to put Visa, Access and Diners clean out of business.)

Signing the register, I flipped back the pages to August 6 of the previous year, explaining to the receptionist that I'd oh something or other, lies lies, and there he was, 'John Ford' – Jesus! Every year in the same double room on the same date under the same pseudonym for forty years! Mad! A word of thanks here to the unfair competition of the Japanese manufacturers of miniature cameras, excellent for photographing entries in Welsh hotel registers under conditions of stress (to invoke the buzz word of the hour).

In Room 20 I felt the bed. Well, that was a new mattress. It was an odd feeling, climbing into this bed, their bed – I'd never forgotten those legs of hers on the cross-country runs and in the gym. I'll get you, you bastard! I'll bring you down.

Lovely view, though, and time for a walk along the sands before a gossip in the bar and dinner, imagine them walking together, Mr and Mrs Michael Parsons, unmoved by the bomb on Hiroshima, bumping their sibling hip bones in joy, unaware that their curtain was about to come down.

No reason why I shouldn't return to the hotel a day or two before the coming August 6, 'Mr Maxwell' plus photographer, to record the annual visitation of John Ford. Then I could publish and little Michael would be damned.

ELEVEN

I had laid the book on her pillow. It was second-hand, faded, dull-looking.

'What is this, kind sir?'

'It's a present for m'lady.'

'*Four Jacobean Plays*? Is it for my improvement?'

'For your pleasure. Please open the book at the marker.'

She absorbed the title of the designated play in silence. I could sense her faint recoil.

'Should you be reading such things, Mike?'

I sat beside her on the bed. 'The play is about love, the love of Giovanni and Annabella, both attractive young people, well respected and admired.' I paused thoughtfully, my gaze on V's crossed legs. 'But their love is their undoing.'

'Like Romeo and Juliet, you mean? Do they come from quarrelling families – or is one of them already married?'

'Not from quarrelling families. From the same family.'

V was wrestling with this.

'Giovanni,' I went on, 'goes to his confessor, the Friar, who tells him: "Leave her, and take thy choice, 'tis much less sin."'

'Why leave her? Why less sin?' asked V.

'You must read the play and find out. Listen:

> I have too long suppressed the hidden flames
> That have almost consumed me; I have spent
> Many a silent night in sighs and groans,
> Run over all my thoughts, despised my fate,
> Reasoned against the reasons of my love.

V said: 'Did you find it in Mowbury's? I only wish we had more money to buy you books.'

'As Doctor Faustus said, "O, would that I had never seen Wittenberg, never read a book."'

'Wittenberg?'

'Never mind,' I said impatiently, 'just read this. Aloud.' I thrust a Jacobean passage into her lap. V's eyelashes dropped shyly over the page and Annabella's revealed passion. She read but not aloud.

> I blush to tell thee – but I'll tell thee now –
> For every sigh that thou has spent for me
> I have sighed ten; for every tear shed twenty.

'Isn't that beautiful?'

'Yes, it is,' she murmured.

'Won't you say the lines to me?'

'You know I'm rotten at acting.'

'Must you be acting? May I kiss you?'

Term had resumed when Harold reappeared. It was a Saturday afternoon and V was out on the games field with the juniors. I was browsing through her underwear drawer when I heard the distinctive crunch of tyres on gravel. The horn half-sounded, then checked itself. The American came up loaded with Hershey bars, Life Savers, tins of Tang, Prem and Spam, and six pairs of nylon stockings. He pumped my hand as if we were old friends.

'It's certainly a small room,' he said.

'Small country. Small people.'

He laughed. '"With a lot of history."' He examined the photograph of Father on the mantelpiece, a formal studio portrait, artificially lit and posed. I knew that what most saddened V was the lack of any photograph showing her parents together.

'This is Veronica's father?' Harold looked puzzled.

'Yes.'

'He was also in the RAF – like yours?'

'Yes.'

'I didn't know that. Quite a flying family.' Harold glanced at his watch and inquired after Veronica.

'Was she expecting you?' I asked.

'Not exactly. Telephones certainly make the world an easier place.'

Idly – and clearly ill at ease with idleness, not least in company – he picked up the volume of Jacobean plays I'd given V, opened it at the marker (V had made no progress) and studied the title page. Whatever passed into this man's mind invariably came straight out of his mouth:

''*Tis Pity Shees a Whore* by John Ford, first performed by the Queenes Maiesties Servants at the Phoenix in Drury Lane in 1633.' He thought about this. 'That wouldn't be Queen Elizabeth, then?'

'She wasn't exactly a Jacobean.'

'Who then?'

'Henrietta Maria, Queen of Charles I. You probably know the Van Dyck paintings.'

He nodded. 'In that case more Carolingian than Jacobean? You're reading this, Mike?'

'Yes. As a matter of fact, "Carolingian", more commonly "Carlovingian", can only refer to Charlemagne.'

'I stand corrected.' He smiled easily, flipping the pages in search of what he called 'the story line' (he may have said 'scenario'). His eyebrows then obligingly rose:

> Shall then, for that I am her brother born,
> My joys be ever banished from her bed?

Harold read it aloud twice to 'get it straight'. Satisfied as to its meaning, he said: 'I guess the answer was yes.'

'Many are the aphrodisiacs in the garden of intellect,' I told him.

He appraised me. 'I hadn't suspected that you would be into this kind of stuff.'

'You mean literature?'

'Not exactly.'

He then suggested a walk round the school. 'You can show

me "the places of terror and the places of joy" – Cicero.' The prospect of parading this gleaming Yank before three hundred attentive kids held no joy at all; but kind fate intervened in the shape of V herself, marvellously clad in singlet and shorts. The sight of the bombardier threw her into confusion and her blush deepened when Harold asked whether she had received his letter – not a word about it had she expended on me. The American's vulgar pile of gifts – a god called More – merely increased her discomfort:

'Oh no, I couldn't possibly.'

'I hope the nylons are the right size,' he said, studying her long and beautiful legs with brazen admiration. V nervously lit a cigarette – she had recently taken up the habit – then carried her clothes to the bathroom to change. From the window I could see a group of kids examining the Jeep parked in the gravel yard below.

Fortunately what passed for lunch in Rowley's Yorkshire had drawn them away by the time we emerged to take another ride to another feast, this time at the Crown Hotel in Greendale. On the way into town Harold informed us that he'd flown four missions over Germany since our last meeting: Bremen twice, Karlsruhe, Dortmund.

'Big fires, bright enough to turn night into day.'

Again a table had been reserved as if V's availability had been taken for granted, but Harold pre-empted any offence by assuring her that 'good luck requires good management'. Lifting his hand in lazy salute to a pair of American airmen seated at a table across the room, he ordered the food, then turned the conversation to *Gone With the Wind*.

'It was wonderful,' V said. 'I'd love to see it again.'

Harold looked charmingly reproachful. 'Veronica, believe me, that film is a whitewash.' He sniffed the wine, nodded to the waitress, lit a cigar and stretched his immaculately creased legs. 'All those Southern slave-owners, the Confederates, are decent gentlemen in the film, enlightened patricians, right? And their cheerful black slaves, happily devoted to master and mistress – oh *sure*. I mean do either of you know what slavery was really like? The degradation and cruelty of the human

89

beings bought and sold like cattle, the men chained in the fields. How many black kids knew who their father was?'

V was visibly swept away by this sudden display of principled compassion, though with regard to the issues she was in a fog thicker than the one shrouding *Waterloo Bridge*. (Even I had difficulty in tacking a century on to the American Civil War, though the rifles and uniforms had looked quite modern.)

'Listen,' Harold persisted intensely, as if we had just thrown up a host of clever objections, 'I'm not going to whitewash the Yankees and if you look into Abe Lincoln's record he's not the spotless idealist of the history books. The carpetbaggers swarmed down South and that wasn't a pretty business. But I just know too much about the power of the Klan in the South today – and not only in the South, Veronica! – to find it easy to forgive Hollywood for peddling trash like that.'

V, picking at her food, bravely admitted that she'd always thought all Americans were Yankees. And could he please explain what the 'clan' was?

'You've never heard of the Ku Klux Klan?' He looked to each of us in turn with insufferable forbearance.

I said I knew that George III had lost America but nothing much after that until Clark Gable and the Marx Brothers.

'You mean George III kind of "lost" America the way Columbus found it?' he asked.

'The Vikings found it,' I said.

'You have to forgive my ignorance,' V said. But I didn't agree about forgiving and let the bastard have it between his bomb-sight eyes.

'In our schools,' I announced, 'the study of history is linked to the development of civilization – art, architecture, literature, music. For these things one doesn't have to travel much beyond Europe, as I'm sure you agree.'

V gasped and put down her knife and fork. I had noticed that Harold used his own knife in an odd manner, cutting slices then laying it to rest at the rim of his plate as if it might get exhausted. I assumed this represented a late bid for gentility on the part of a population entirely composed of immigrants.

Harold was assessing me. 'I think I get it,' he said.

90

V stayed silent out of loyalty. But to whom? Harold soon switched on the charm again – apparently Harvard Law School had made him the man he was. I rose to fight again while eating steadily through his food.

'I thought you studied history.'

'Correct, Mike. The Law School is strictly postgraduate.'

V was suitably impressed. 'You've got two degrees?'

(And she had two legs with a prized space in between.)

I sat on my own uncertainties. Although 'destined' for Oxford from an early age, I had very little notion of how a university worked. We were not trained to conceive our own questions; our elders laid down the tramlines of legitimate inquiry. Anyway, anyway . . . Harold, having done all that, had moved to the West Coast of America and taken a job with a 'major studio' as a 'contract lawyer'.

'Gosh! you work in Hollywood?' V was helplessly awed.

Harold then told us how much all the different MGM stars got paid.

'Is MGM the one with the roaring lion?' V asked.

'Sure – but he doesn't get paid.'

He flashed his Rhett Butlers and she laughed obligingly – she kept laughing every time she thought about the lion not getting paid, totally sickening. Finally his arm encircled her shoulder to protect her against his own wit and magnetic charm. He then told her (he'd stopped pretending about me) that most of the famous film stars were really Jews from eastern Europe who had adopted English-style names. He cited chapter and verse while V listened wide-eyed.

I asked him if he was anti-Semitic (on the principle of try anything once). This spiked the fun. Harold looked very solemn as if he were practising a miracle of self-control despite severe provocation.

'Mike, we're all Americans or none of us are.'

'Is,' I corrected him.

'Is.' Harold gave it to me like a Hershey bar – (now fuck off, sonny.)

V hastily asked him whether he actually met the film stars in the course of his work as a . . . a . . .

'Contract lawyer. Meet them, Veronica? You trip over them. Garbo, de Havilland, Davis, Welles, Grable.' He smiled ruefully. 'Until Uncle Sam called my number.'

'You didn't volunteer?' I asked. 'I thought you wanted America in the war from the day Hitler invaded Poland?'

V said, 'Mike.'

'No,' Harold reassured her, 'your young cousin has a good memory and should be allowed to exercise it. I guess I wanted America in the war more than I wanted Harold Rascoe in it. I grew up spoiled – too much money and too many parents. My dad has married three times and each time I got a pay-off – I had my first La Salle Straight 8 at the age of sixteen. We had a party on Long Island and I wrote it off. My dad got me another.'

'You're used to getting what you want,' I suggested.

'I doubt it, Mike. What you really want is what you can't buy.' The words were redirected at V. He lit a cigar and gestured to the waitress for more coffee.

A lump called Lunt waylaid me as she was pinning notices (*diktats*) to the notice board in Big Quad (so-called) while I was humbly creeping from A to B. 'Parsons!' she bellowed. 'Come here!' The cow then invited me to tea. Tea with the Head Girl! Would there be lemon curd tarts?

When I foolishly mentioned the invitation to Charrington he pulled the hair out of his eye and drawled, 'She'll jigger you as the price of a currant bun.'

A jar of home-made Surrey strawberry jam lay on the table and the kettle was hissing as I knocked timidly on the dot of the appointed time. 'Come in!' Lunt bellowed belligerently, followed by, 'Oh it's you.' Commanding me to sit down and help myself to 'scoff', Nancy announced that there was no point in 'beating about the bush'. Since my mouth was deeply engaged with hot crumpet and jam, I didn't inquire which bush.

'People are talking,' she said darkly, 'about Nicky.'

'Hm?'

Lunt's statuesque bust heaved and she grabbed a crumpet for herself. 'It's that American. He's after Nicky.'

'I didn't imagine he was after me.'

'Don't be clever, twerp. This is serious. I mean the man's a bounder, a complete cad, but Nicky simply won't hear a word against him.'

I buttered another crumpet. 'Takes two to tango,' I murmured.

'If that Yank walks off with your sister where will you be?'

My jaw slackened its masticatory motions. 'My sister?'

Lunt looked guilty, sullen, aggressive all in one. 'Nicky told me.'

I shrugged. 'It's her story.' (Prodigious powers of rapid recovery have carried me to where I am.)

'You don't mean Nicky made it up!'

'These are family matters.' I was looking around for the cake. Couldn't see any. There had to be cake.

'Well, I'll tell you a family matter, young man. I saw that American's Jeep outside the Annexe after midnight. I was checking the fire hydrants, actually . . . I mean, Nicky's completely innocent – what if that bloke gets her into trouble? And that's not the worst of it. Old Murdoch reported Nicky to Rowley. He summoned her to Yorkshire and gave her a terrible wigging, an ultimatum in fact. Damn it, Michael, we've got to do something!'

'Is there any cake?'

It didn't do to tell the Head Girl that *Nancy to the Rescue* looked a mile further from reality than *Harold Strikes a Home Run* (baseball having recently been added to his list of sporting enthusiasms). Neither E. Nesbit nor Arthur Ransome would help in this fix; nor Buchan nor Biggles. In reality no such precise thoughts survived the vast eruption of jealousy I experienced at this report of V's treason. Thanking Lunt rather curtly for the cakeless tea, I went straight to the Staff Annexe for a showdown. V's 'Hullo, Mike' didn't sound right and the anxiety in her beautiful eyes was all too evident.

I said: 'That was pretty rotten, getting yourself summoned by Rowley, and spending the night with that cowboy, and telling Nancy Lunt that I'm your brother. How many pairs of nylons has your "virtue" cost this Yank?'

My own tears followed V's. Her grief horribly confirmed everything that Nancy had told me and tears also generate themselves – observe any child who, having grazed a knee, continues to cry because he's crying. Pretty soon V and I were together on the divan sofa, her damp face against mine and my hand pressing the no longer inviolate flesh above her stocking. Oh the sweet, tender fragrance of her! Such was her sisterly concern and womanly contrition that she submitted to my hot embraces even when they extended to her breasts. Realizing that I had to be quenched, she serviced me with a hand considerably bolder and less amateurish than its swimming pool prototype on my birthday.

You think badly of her now, reader? Or you don't?

'Mike darling,' she said, 'whatever happens I'm not going to leave you. I promise, yes, cross my heart. I've explained everything to Harold and he completely understands. Anyway, he could be posted anywhere any time, Italy, the Pacific, it wouldn't be right for us to get married until the war's over. Harold thinks the world of you, Mike, he really does.'

So. So *they* were now talking about me, whereas previously she and I had been talking about *him*.

V had a lot to say.

'I'm sorry if you didn't want me to tell Nancy about – '

' – You promised not to tell anyone! Remember?'

'Did I, darling? I felt I had to tell Harold, it's been so wonderful to find someone I can talk to because he's so kind and understanding about everything. Mike, please don't be angry. I know it's wrong to . . . to do it before one's married but Harold flies over Germany night after night and – '

' – Does he?'

'Yes he does and one day he won't . . . [tears] . . . he may not . . . I mean he's the only man I've ever loved and there may never be another if he's . . . [tears].'

'Killed?' I suggested.

She looked at me sharply. 'Don't you want me to be happy, Mike?'

* * *

With half-term approaching, Harold wrote to V announcing that he'd been granted short leave and would be taking us both up to London for 'a good time'.

'You go,' I sulked. 'I don't want to spoil your fun.'

V wrote back to Harold arranging to meet him at the Crown Hotel in town – she had taken to heart Rowley's warning about Harold's visits to the school. (But for how long?) On the Saturday morning we caught the early bus each carrying a small cardboard suitcase. V had advised me to take toothbrush and pyjamas 'just in case' but she made it sound like 'just in case we break down on the way home' and I was both too trusting and too excited about the anticipated spending spree to give further thought to toothbrushes or spare socks. V was wearing her prettiest frock and looked ravishing.

Harold and his jeep were waiting for us outside the Crown Hotel. Standing with him, hands in pockets, brash, chewing gum, were the two American servicemen he had greeted in the hotel restaurant when he took us out for lunch. Though friendly, there was no disguising their envy of Harold's good fortune; bored and short of girls, they would no doubt spend the day kicking their heels on street corners, rattling the idle money in their pockets.

'Keep an eye on your sister, son,' one of them said to me as Harold loaded us into the jeep. His wink was as heavy as the drop of a portcullis.

We were on the road and out of town before Harold commented: 'Mike, I know you feel complicated about the "sister" business but I happen to believe it's in everyone's interests to normalize this thing and that means being completely open about it.'

He then asked V whether she had told Rowley. Shyly she shook her head. Harold said she should.

(I leaned forward from the back 'seat' and reminded him that Veronica was already in hot water with Rowley on his behalf.

('We're quarrelling already, Mike?'

(I said that if he thought up a better answer I would be interested to receive it. And would he kindly drive with both hands on the wheel rather than with one on Veronica's knee?

And was a legal speed limit unknown to the civilization of the Far West? And who the hell did he imagine he was anyway?)

And some more. But neither Harold nor V seemed to hear me. He sped past a slow-moving column of bren-gun carriers – V sighed in admiring reproach – with his left hand on her knee. I noticed that she smiled even when his jokes fell flat and kept giving him her 'oh you naughty boy' look. His cultural pretensions ran neck and neck with puerile banalities. The 'people of London', he told us, had given American servicemen a 'wonderful time' during the weekend of July the Fourth. Bands had played 'The Star-Spangled Banner' and 'Home, Sweet Home' in Hyde Park. On the other hand the Rascoes were descended from Huguenot stock – the Rasqueaus of La Rochelle, hence the French 'a'. He reminded us that 'your Duke of Buckingham' had laid siege to La Rochelle – this was followed by a thumbnail sketch of the French Wars of Religion and a description of some vivid paintings depicting the Duc de Guise's Catholic League on the rampage. Harold had personally viewed these paintings during a pre-war trip to Paris, a city he described as 'something else'.

After the war he would take us to Paris. After the war I would visit Mr and Mrs Rascoe in America.

I almost forgot: on his way out to the boat at Cherbourg he had 'stopped by' at Bayeux to inspect the famous tapestry. It was 'pure propaganda', of course, like *Gone With the Wind*. His namesake, King of England, had 'gotten' a raw deal at the hands of the Norman Ministry of Propaganda, who depicted Duke William – 'the Mussolini of his time' – riding into battle carrying a bishop's mitre. Harold (the bombardier, not the king) had visited the battlefield at Hastings to 'check out the storyline'.

We were approaching the south-western suburbs of London, Kingston and Richmond. Leaning forward from my hideously uncomfortable and demeaning perch in the rear, I inquired earnestly whether the modern town of Hastings was built on the old battlefield of 1066.

'Part of it,' he said, but I noticed a fraction of hesitation. He then told us about the World Series and the World Fair.

It seemed that 'the World' was installed across the Atlantic.

By mid-morning we were crossing Hammersmith Bridge and were soon among the familiar, reviving advertisements pasted to the red double-decker buses: Maclean's tooth paste, Black and White whisky, Oxo cubes. An aching homesickness possessed me; for the first time since Mother's death I wanted to put back the clock and be warned that it was time for bed by a solid woman with thick ankles and a voice which never admitted uncertainty. I suggested to V in a dramatically confidential whisper that maybe we should go up to Hampstead to see Albert and Leo, but she tossed her curls like a tart and said it would ruin the day.

Harold parked the jeep near Oxford Circus and we plunged into a succession of department stores: Selfridge's, John Lewis, Liberty's. V paraded across carpeted floors in one costume after another, swivelling and pirouetting before mirrors while our benefactor sat back and imperially chewed his cigar. He dealt out money as if he were playing Monopoly. As for clothing coupons, he had clearly printed his own. (Since June 1941, the ration had been sixty-six coupons per person per year. A man's new coat absorbed twelve coupons.)

'Veronica could be a top model,' he confided to me, man to man. 'When she arrives in Hollywood, Grable had better watch out.'

Then it was my turn: suits, shirts, shoes. V took even greater pleasure in my gifts than in her own – she no longer uttered small cries of protest. Frequently she squeezed my hand before tucking her arm through Harold's. Not a few of the austerity-worn natives stared at our profusion of carrier bags with obvious resentment but V had shed her inhibitions, her innate sense of fair's fair, and abandoned herself to good fortune. Harold took us to the Lyons Corner House at Marble Arch for a blow-out feast, ordering me a Knickerbocker Glory packed with tinned fruit as exotic as the distant forests and plantations where, according to my illustrated encyclopaedias, they grew.

Harold's contented smile was as stable as a log fire.

'I know what you people have been through.'

'We don't fly bombers over Germany,' V reproached him.

'You know something? I'd find it a lot easier to hate the Germans but for their music. When I see those cities burning, Veronica, I can hear Beethoven and Brahms coming up from the ashes. Does that surprise you? Maybe we should take in a concert tonight at the Albert Hall?'

V said, 'Oh yes,' but without enthusiasm.

'Frankly, Mike, when this war's over people of your generation are going to ask some awkward questions. I mean why wasn't Hitler stopped dead in his tracks in thirty-six, eh? Why were the Western democracies so scared of Joe Stalin that they handed Czechoslovakia to the Nazis on a plate?'

I didn't know about this – not even Mother had discussed it. As for V, the choice of an evening was the lady's. She finally chose Noël Coward in preference to Sir Malcolm Sargent and Bernard Shaw; we, the intellectuals, gracefully concurred. Harold paid 10/6 for front-row stalls, bought a large box of chocolates, placed V between us, and held her hand throughout the performance (of which I remember nothing at all). She didn't offer me the other hand. I got as many chocolates as I could eat.

During the interval Harold gave me more of his man-to-man routine, soliciting my opinion about the relative merits of the Normandie, the Embassy, Quaglino's, the Paradise, the Café de Paris. I proudly informed him that the last had received a direct hit from a bomb and I'd never heard of the rest. I wasn't shy of professing ignorance to a man who thought the Battle of Hastings had taken place at Hastings and who even claimed to have visited the site. (I had of course never been inside a night club, although Brophy and Charrington claimed to have jiggered their way through most of them.)

Harold drove us past Rainbow Corner, a converted Lyons restaurant at the corner of Shaftesbury Avenue and Windmill Street, which was now the biggest GI club. Apparently Hollywood stars appeared at Rainbow Corner. 'It's also', he added, 'a place where people shack up.' He talked big and fast about Glenn Miller, Fats Waller, Duke Ellington, New Orleans and Greenwich Village, as if he knew every one of these famous performers and places intimately. 'Progressive jazz' was

Harold's thing, Charlie Parker, Dizzy Gillespie, Miles Davis, Thelonious Monk, all of whom were 'real bitches' – this phrase rather threw V at first.

In the event Harold drove us to a place in Soho called Jack's. As he threaded a passage through the narrow, blacked-out streets, he kept snapping his fingers together and saying 'Bop', very cool, as if it was the password to the inner life.

'Of course,' he mused, 'they're all smoking hay.'

He meant the musicians but at first I assumed he was referring to the tarts for sight of whom I was eagerly scanning the pavements and about whose pox condition we had often heard from Brophy – he claimed the best test was to tug their hair. If it all came out in his hand he wore a rubber. Years later I visited a large, municipal brothel in Hamburg, hoping not to meet fellow members of the Shadow Cabinet in the courtyard where whores from all over Europe paraded. One of them reminded me, from a distance, of V until, catching my interest, she sidled towards me, paused for inspection, then swung irritably away as she read my revulsion.

Jack's was bursting with Americans. Harold was clearly on intimate terms with the proprietor, a big, smarmy spiv with Brylcreemed hair and 'blackmarket' engraved in his crooked smile. Why hadn't he been conscripted? Although every table was apparently taken one was found for Lieutenant Rascoe. As on our first outing with Harold, there was the official menu written on a card and the other menu whispered in his ear: oysters and thick, juicy steaks. V went off to the powder room to do her nose and hair.

Harold threw me his disgusting wink: 'Feel guilty afterwards, Mike.'

V was already tipsy on champagne when Harold began to unfold to us his miserably spoilt childhood in Great Neck on Long Island Sound – the imported Rolls-Royces, the six servants, the huge parties, and the throng of guests who invariably arrived uninvited. Yes, Harold had a sister but no brothers – one day most of it would come to him. V asked about his sister.

'Daisy? She's pretty cute, pretty spoilt also, and always

waiting for someone big and decisive to pick her up and solve her life.'

V blushed. 'I know how she feels.'

Harold took her hand. 'But you have found that guy and Daisy hasn't.'

'I'd like to meet Daisy.'

'You will, soon enough.'

Jack's seemed very noisy to me but Harold explained that here one heard Fats Waller music and Glenn Miller music, horns, trombones, saxophones, smooth and clever like Harold. He also disparaged pre-war British nightclub music as 'dreary, sugary, Henry Hall stuff, like wallpaper'. V looked rather hurt, although she didn't contradict him. We all knew that the lowest-paid GI earned five times as much as a British private. Worth repeating – over-paid, over-sexed, over here. After a few more drinks V became rather drunk and emotional about something that I personally could live with – she said a lot of married women whose husbands were abroad took off their wedding ring in the evening and went dancing. This upset her a great deal – 'When a man is fighting for his country.' God knows what she was trying to say – perhaps she divined that by the end of the war our handsome Allies would have sired seventy thousand bastards.

Assuring V that Jack's jazz was 'simply the best in town but I'm not talking about New York or New Orleans', Harold led her on to the crowded dance floor, commandingly gathered her in his arms, cheek to cheek, thigh to thigh, his great paw, gleaming with the rings he left under his pillow before a mission, encircling her slender waist. She was the prettiest girl on the floor by far. How many others had Harold brought here? Brylcreem Blackmarket would know.

Sitting alone at the table, the youngest male in the place, I felt conspicuous and pathetic. ('God, you're pathetic, Parsons': see C. Charrington, *Collected Speeches*.) Now the band had hotted up into a furious jitterbug (was this the epistemological source of 'jiggering'?) and the Americans were leading their girls into a furious display of athleticism – V did it as if she'd done it all her life, her legs shamelessly flying up either side of Harold. I felt the full force of my sister's betrayal; she had concealed so much of herself from me while pretending to be my friend.

We ate our steaks, V replenished her vivid red lipstick, as precious as gold (I see now that she belonged to a generation which felt bound to inspect and service its face every half-hour) and then Harold remarked, with his usual wink at me, that you could always tell a girl with a boyfriend in the Parachute Regiment (he probably said Airborne). She asked why, on cue:

'Because she rustles as she dances.'

They danced again. I could see them whispering together and knew that I was the subject (object) of their concern. I saw Harold catch the greasy proprietor's marble eye and beckon to him – a quick, manly exchange. A few moments later a painted creature emerged out of the crowd, smiled at me, and sat herself at our table in an explosion of cheap scent.

'I'm Belinda,' she said. 'Lonely?'

I felt my cheeks burning. This was it! A real tart!

'Want to dance, dear?'

I said I wasn't much good at it.

'You'll get the 'ang soon enough.'

And then I was on the floor, no longer a spectator, only inches from a real woman's low-cut gown, getting the 'ang. Soon I forgot my clumsy feet and surrendered to the extraordinary sensuality oozing out of this creature – I quite forgot about tugging at her hair – whose hips swayed shamelessly against my groin. Once or twice I caught a glimpse of V with Harold, her expression slightly anxious, his blatantly self-congratulatory. My erection came quite suddenly and couldn't be checked; Belinda pretended not to notice – presumably it was part of the job.

I was wrong. She drew very close, her pert, Cockney mouth to my ear: 'Feels like someone wants to do it. Just say the word, darlin' – 'e'll pay.' Adding, with native warmth, 'Money don't mean nothin' to them, do it?'

I cleared my clogged throat. 'Where?' I whispered.

'Upstairs, dear. Oh it's very comfy and clean.'

My eye caught V's across the floor. She smiled and blew me a kiss. A kiss of encouragement? Blind rage possessed me. They had conspired, she and he, to destroy my claim on V, my claim to protect her interests, to guard her virtue, to love her as grown men love women. Had V betrayed my feeling for her, our sacred secret, to Harold?

'No,' I murmured.

'Well, yer' only a kid,' the tart said consolingly. 'Try and count sheep, duck, or yer'll never be able t'walk back t'yer table.'

It was well after midnight when we left Jack's. I had vaguely assumed that we would head back to Greendale but Harold roared down Oxford Street to the Cumberland Hotel – evidently V had packed our little cardboard suitcases with callous premeditation. Harold strode ahead of us through the grandiose and rather vulgar hotel foyer to the reception desk while V and I lingered in the background, she trying to be friendly, I sullen. The place stank of hoarding, blackmarketeering, bulky profiteers, glittering women in marzipan make-up, kept women, Jews.

Harold strode back, a cigar between his teeth, holding two keys attached to embossed metal tags. Perhaps he was a Jew after all.

'Room 215 – that's you, Mike. It's even got a shower – if you're interested.' Another wink.

We took the lift to the second floor, V and I clutching our precious gift parcels, in silence. Stepping out into the thickly carpeted corridor, Harold laid a hand on my shoulder.

'Well, Mike, it's been quite a day and wonderful to have you with us. If you're up early and feel hungry, just go down and order anything you want. Tell the waitress to put it on my check – that's room 218. OK?'

V said, 'Goodnight, Mike, sleep well.' She gave me a quick peck on the cheek and I walked to my room, not looking back (though I did). I didn't use my toothbrush. Climbing between crisply laundered sheets which seemed wasted on me I tried to extract my imagination from 218. Presently my cock fastened on Belinda and I wanted, with all my being, to call her back, to abandon myself to her skills, to be inducted at last into full manhood. I could imagine her frisky little body shamelessly writing under me – if only she would walk through the door into this big, sleek chamber of curves and convenience, this private place set apart from leering jazz musicians and the knowing winks of amused adults. So clean, quiet and private here.

I got up, dressed, pocketed my key, closed the door very quietly (each calculation as clear as my passion), and took the stairs down to the lobby, determined to find myself a Belinda on the street! I glanced furtively towards the reception desk, convinced that the adults behind it would forbid me to step out of the hotel – I was a minor, did I have permission, the usual. Sure enough, I had taken half a dozen steps towards the revolving doors when I heard a woman's voice ring out, 'Sir!' – and knew it was my number. I slouched back to the reception desk with lowered gaze – like a trip to Yorkshire.

'Your key, sir, if you're leaving the hotel.'

I told her I had no intention of leaving the hotel.

Back in my laundered bed, I went, angrily protesting, to the Friar:

GIOVANNI: Marriage? Why, that's to damn her. That's to prove her greedy of variety of lust.

Defeated, I felt my soapy fingers slipping from my beloved Annabella:

GIOVANNI: You must be married, mistress.
ANNABELLA: Yes? To whom?
GIOVANNI: Someone must have you.
ANNABELLA: You must.
GIOVANNI: Nay, some other.

But V had never said, 'You must.' There was no 'variety of lust' in V. As for Giovanni, my paragon was grown up – a graduate! – assured, handsome, yet even he had had to bury his pride, stifle his passion, before the idiotic suitor Soranzo:

SORANZO: Here's to your sister's happiness and mine.
GIOVANNI: I cannot drink.
ANNABELLA: Pray do not urge him if he be not willing.

And my sister's prescription for me? – new shoes, a Knickerbocker Glory, champagne, oysters, tarts. I curled up in the
crisply starched sheets like a hedgehog and not long afterwards
Harold's oysters came up on the oyster-coloured carpet of the
Cumberland Hotel.

Next day Harold took us rowing on the Serpentine. Barrage
balloons floated overhead like gaseous elephants. Harold rowed
most of the time, strong, lazy strokes, then offered me the oars.
I made a hash of it; we floundered about in jerky, erratic circles.
V took the blades, let her skirt slide up her thighs, and we sped
through the water, each thrust of her body a celebration.

TWELVE

I was tipped off about the Prince of Wales Hotel, Llanfairfe-chan, by Bobby Dukes. Bobby is the reason why English football clubs are banned from the Continent. An ungainly hulk in his late twenties or early thirties (so much flesh obscures the proper contours of age), he carries a beer belly as prominent as his permanent air of restless resentment against 'them'. Purpose-built for the Saturday special train and the Sunday National Front rampage through Brixton (or Stuttgart, even better), he can bellow 'Here we go here we go here we go' or 'one nil one nil', and he's capable of occupying the front steps of some sleepy Gothic Rathaus and bellowing simultaneously 'Hitler Got It Right!' and 'Who Won the Bloody War!' but he wouldn't know the words of 'Land of Hope and Glory' or 'There'll Always Be an England'. A month after he was sacked as ministerial car pool chauffeur I got to him with some tenners and a couple of tout's tickets for the semi-final of the Cup. Normally Bobby Dukes joined the Nazi legions haunting the terraces at Stamford Bridge (Millwall when Chelsea were away north of the Humber), but, as he candidly explained, nowadays there were too many police informers and too many dawn arrests. 'It's no longer safe to carry a dangerous weapon.'

We sat in the stand at White Hart Lane and smoked our way through one hour thirty minutes plus injury time of negative football, mass hysteria, and boredom. Just after the interval Bobby started shouting 'one nil' and looking about for some-one to contradict him, but these weren't the terraces and you couldn't even decently piss into a beer bottle or on to the punters below. Bobby Dukes had been personal chauffeur to the Rt Hon Michael Parsons until he'd been involved, once too often, in a drunken driving accident.

Bobby doesn't read the *Globe* – too left-wing – but he'd picked up a copy in the local betting shop (even though he'd promised his wife to stop) and had seen one of my circumspect stories on his former boss, so here he was at White Hart Lane, on the look-out for my cheque book and recalling a trip up the M6 to North Wales, where the Home Secretary was scheduled to address the assembled chiefs of police.

'On the way up he asks me why I support the National Front. I said to him, "Sir, don't get me wrong, but if you was true to your principles you'd do the same."'

'What did he say to that?'

'Nothin'. Then I says, "In my opinion, sir, the only aristocrat in Britain today is an unemployed black homosexual." He says why. I says, "They're the real racists, aren't they, the West Indians. I mean they get away with murder, I mean that." So Mr Parsons says, "Keep your eyes on the road, Bobby." I says, "I am, sir, I'm fully capable of driving and talking at the same time like that American president who could walk and chew gum." Mr Parsons never laughs, he's a cold fish that one. Clever though. So I told him: "Where I live, in Ealing, they're spending ratepayers' money, my money, on homosexual clubs and gay videos for schoolkids. And don't imagine I let my wife and kids near the White City Estate. I mean when I came out of the Air Force I had no work at all, I was eating crusts, I was making a pint last three hours, so what did I do? In this life you don't lie down. I got up off my arse and I got myself a job as a driver."'

A foul just outside the penalty area. Bobby insists it's a penalty. He doesn't know or really care but he needs the aggro. Then the other team won't take their wall back the full ten yards or is it metres now and Bobby hurls himself into a tunnel of noise at the small, sunny end of which are GT sports cars, shares in British Telecom, a profit on the sale of his previous one-bedroom flat in Acton, and kicking the other fellow's fingers off the ladder. Bobby despises unions, hates blacks, and believes everything he reads about social security spongers.

'What about working-class solidarity, Bobby?'

He gives me a glance. 'Frankly, Mr Frame, I don't go for any of that. I mean, people talk about "sticking together against the bosses" – but by my way of thinking it's one against one and one against all in this life. I told Mr Parsons as much.'

'He agreed?'

'He said he understood my way of thinking.'

'That's all?'

'Not a talkative man – to the likes of me.'

Bobby says – keeps saying – how he hates his father (a mechanic NCO in the RAF) for neglecting his education, for moving him from school to school, for leaving him with only one 'O' level. 'In Religious Studies, if you can believe it. That's not a lot of use, is it? – unless you want to become a vicar.'

Married twice, Bobby has a small son.

'I'm going to back him up to the hilt, all the way that's certain – unless he turns out bad, you know. I mean I reckon I can make it to Australia or South Africa if I can put some money by. I mean I reckon they'll hold out against the blacks down there. They have to, don't they? Rest of Africa, it's gone, I mean the blacks are too easily led, don't get me wrong, we are too, but a bloke was telling me that to get into Zimbabwe they strip-search you if you're white.'

'What did Mr Parsons have to say to all that?'

'Why should he listen to my opinion? I mean I'm just dirt to him, aren't I?'

Back in fifty-nine, when I was a cub reporter on the *Mirror*, the paper had blasted 'I'm all right, Jack', a close cousin of 'You've never had it so good', but the materialism of the Macmillan era was a harmless playground romp compared to the savage, survival-of-the-fittest social Darwinism of Bobby Duke's eighties. Everything – the whole postwar social settlement – is being sold off and dismantled. Money alone rules. Profit is the yardstick of every human transaction.

We were streaming from White Hart Lane now, with forty thousand others, one nil and Bobby itching for his brawl.

'So what's the story, Bobby?'

'Well, like I said, I drove Mr Parsons up to North Wales, right? So we peel off the M6 near Chester and I glance at my mirror and the man's asleep. Ten minutes later, maybe twelve, I don't want to tell you anything false, a voice in the back seat says "Veronica" – quite clear, almost as if he was awake, but he wasn't. Five miles on, and he says it again: "Veronica."'

Bobby and I pushed on, with the crowds, passing the corner shops which couldn't resist the flood of custom but would lose half their stock by the end of the afternoon.

'That's all?'

Bobby Dukes looked a bit abashed at my lack of interest and barged against a couple of coloured boys who hadn't been to the match because it's too dangerous despite the increasing number of coloured club players. They said something in sharp cockney accents that sounded like a blackface echo of my youth and I pulled Bobby back to his former Master's Voice.

'After the speech to the police chiefs in Llandudno, he sends his hangers-on back to London, all those Parliamentary Secretaries and Deputy Under-Secretaries, and he tries to shake off his personal detective too but that lad wasn't having it, he said, "It's my job, sir, and maybe your life." So then Mr Parsons tells me to drive down the coast road to a place called Llanfairfechan, entirely the wrong direction of course but you don't argue. He'd ordered lunch in a private room at the Prince of Wales Hotel – his minder stood guard outside the door and sent me to the local. After that Mr Parsons decided to stay the night. Odd, really.'

'Remember the date?' (But I knew the answer almost before I had asked the question.)

'August the sixth.'

We had reached the tube station by now and Bobby had begun to use his elbows in the mêlée surging for the stairs.

'Did you ever drive him to his home in Wiltshire?' I asked.

'Coombe Bissett? He goes there most weekends.'

'A big house for one man?'

'Yeah.'

'Ever been inside?'

'Yeah. Well, not really, I mean I've used the toilet and had a cuppa in the servants' quarters . . . His housekeeper reckons it used to be a hotel.'

'Or a nursing home?'

'Could be. She says he keeps one bedroom permanently locked but then there was this roof leak and the builders went in there and she found two cupboards full of women's clothes, old-fashioned ones, you know, dresses, underwear, nylons, shoes, perfume, jewellery, you name it, and a big glass jar stuffed with human hair.'

'Colour?'

Either he didn't hear me, or he didn't want to. Bobby Dukes was barging through the dense mass of waiting passengers and football fans to the front of the platform, shoving, kicking, revelling in the ugly glances and curses he attracted, longing for a riot. He knew he was losing me and my cheque book but this was Saturday afternoon and his natural greed had surrendered to an almost religious sense of ceremony.

Call him a working-class Tory but I knew in my nicotined soul that Bobby was in the 'family' – mine, not little Michael's.

THIRTEEN

Harold was posted to Rackheath air base in Norfolk. V took it bravely.

During a single week of October 1943 the US 8th Air Force lost 148 bombers while attacking targets at Gydnia and Schweinfurt. V listened to the familiar BBC voices which contrived to blend objectivity with regret: 'This is the news and Stuart Hibberd/Alvar Liddell/Frank Phillips reading it' (just in case Haw Haw managed to worm his way into Broadcasting House).

I was now honoured by regular letters from Harold, man to man. 'Sadly, a down-rate of seven per cent per mission is where we're at,' he informed me, 'but this is between you and me.' Apparently the .5 cannon carried by the B17s could not cope with the new breed of German night fighter. His sentiments were nothing but generous: 'One day, God willing, I shall be proud to have Mike Parsons as my brother-in-law. But Hitler may have other plans.'

I hoped so.

The living, meanwhile, could take comfort in the beauty of the East Anglian countryside. Harold the scribe treated us to generous quotations from Ketton Cremer's book, *A Norfolk Gallery*:

'From any point of vantage, the gentle landscape of farmland and woodland rolls away, mile after mile, to the dim horizon or the sea. Slowly and subtly the colours [Harold loyally transcribed the English spelling] change with the seasons and crops; corn and roots, stubble and ploughland . . .'

Harold appended a comic account of the US 8th Air Force's attempts to cultivate vegetables alien to the English climate, including green corn, peppers and 'master beefsteak tomatoes'. Apparently the 'down-rate' on these was close to one hundred per cent.

On a cold weekend in December, V set out for Rackheath, a long journey involving many train connections and obvious emotional risks – this was the first time in their relationship that she had done the travelling. I saw her off at Greendale station. She looked a peach in the puff-shouldered suit and imitation fur coat that Harold had bought her in London and she smiled bravely as she mounted the two-carriage puffer which would take her to Reading. As it snorted away V leaned from the window, blowing me kisses, until swallowed up by the tunnel. I suddenly remembered the distant summers in Cornwall, Aunt Phyllis putting on her adventurous voice to read to me from E. Nesbit's *The Railway Children*.

I walked back into town and fell to browsing among the dusty shelves of Mowbury's second-hand book shop, my favourite haunt and normally quite empty, since books are the most unpopular commodity in the history of the world. It was in Mowbury's that I had discovered Ford's *'Tis Pity . . .*, Ibsen's *Ghosts*, and Thomas Mann's *The Holy Sinner*. I now found a novel called *Pierre* by a certain Herman Melville. It looked boring and windy but a promising addition to my highly specialized private collection, so I paid sixpence for it and took myself to feast on fish and chips in the local British Restaurant. Money had begun to trickle through from our family solicitor, Mr Underwood, although he stubbornly kept most of our miserable inheritance tied up in Defence Bonds, Savings Certificates and other patriotic pieces of paper. His letters solemnly assured me (V, of course, was disinherited) that a fifteen-shilling Savings Certificate would be worth all of seventeen and six in five years' time. And didn't the hairy Squander Bug grimace from every hoarding, satanically urging us to extravagance?

I found a table, tucked into the grub, and propped open *Pierre* with a salt cellar. But almost immediately a couple of

American airmen took the table adjoining mine and began to chat me up. I pretended not to recognize them but they were unmistakably the pair we had twice met in Harold's company, inside and outside the Crown Hotel. Despite their olive-green uniforms they made a striking contrast. One had knife-sharp features, a prominent, hawkish nose, hair plastered straight back with a parting down the middle (which I associated with double-breasted suits and England cricketers on cigarette cards) and a hard-boiled accent which drilled holes in my ear. In later years I could have identified it as Bronx or Brooklyn. His companion was a slow, dreamy, amiable Farm Boy type with rosy, flattened features and a permanent bemused smile beneath his mop of curly hair – as if he was listening to Country and Western music on invisible headphones.

Brooklyn made the running: 'Aren't you the fella with the pretty sister?' My eyes flickered away from his sardonic grin to my book. 'Veronica – isn't that her name?' he persisted.

I nodded, my mouth crammed with soggy chips.

'She's certainly a lovely lady. Wasn't she dating our lucky pal Harold Rascoe?'

I noticed that he pronounced 'Rascoe' with a rasping 'a'. Did I know that Harold had been posted to Rackheath? I nodded. And was my sister still dating him? I shrugged agnostically, a mere boy.

Brooklyn placed a Hershey bar beside my plate. 'I bet Harold hands out plenty of those – plenty of everything else, too – nylons? panty hose?'

Farm Boy gurgled his amusement but his expression was benign. Had it been two of our own hair-shirted servicemen moving in on a boy with a posh accent, they would have begun to lift the chips from my plate. Americans took nothing less than one's woman.

'Sow howah's things with your prurty sistah?' Farm Boy inquired.

'She's fine,' I said.

'Engaged to ol' Harold, urs she?'

'I don't think so.'

'No rocks on her finger yet?' (This was Brooklyn. The

question of an engagement ring hadn't occurred to me.) 'Harold, Huguenot, Harvard, Hollywood,' he rasped. 'Boy, does he love those aitches.'

The Battle of Hastings surfaced in my mind but I maintained a blank, uncomprehending innocence.

'What's your name, son?'

'Michael.'

'Fifteen at a guess?'

'Just sixteen.' (The 'just' seemed feeble.)

'So what's your candid opinion of our Harold, eh?'

('No worse than the rest of you.') I shrugged again.

'Brave guy, eh? A real flyer,' Brooklyn persisted, and then they both fell to heavy chortling. 'Should we tell him, Joe?' Brooklyn asked Farm Boy.

'Aint ah tole you, Frank, ah says good lurk to ol' Harold if he whanta shoot a lahn and cohn ahnotha li'le English gurl.'

'Hey, Mike, did Harold tellya his Dad's loaded?' Brooklyn asked.

'Loaded?'

'Jesus.' Brooklyn impatiently rubbed his fingers together for the benefit of the deaf and the dumb.

'Well – yes,' I admitted.

'Big mansion on Long Island Sound full of oak panelling taken from old English castles?'

'Something like that, I think.' I was interested now.

'Tha's a sho cohn,' said Farm Boy wisely.

Brooklyn flashed me his stiletto smile. 'Harold's pop is a teamster from Lansing, Michigan, son. He spent the entire Depression outa work.'

'A teamster?'

'Jesus. Drives trucks.'

Farm Boy came in: 'Ol' Harol' tell yews he wahs in school at Harvard? Played furtball for Harvard, did huh? No wehys huh duhd. Murchigan Stayt wahs as neah t'Ivurh League as Harol' evah gurt.'

'Listen, son,' said Brooklyn, 'Harold aint content connin' the local chicks – I'm not sayin' he don't have the style to call himself the Niagara Falls – but the goddam louse gotta crack his ass about it to the boys over a coupla beers. Don't kid yourself.'

Farm Boy produced a packet of Camels and they both lit up. I had abandoned the attempt to finish the cold, congealing mess on my plate.

'Harold tellya about those visits to Paris before the war, Mike?' Brooklyn asked, screwing his eyes against the smoke. 'Take it from me – all crap. Bullshit. Hitler gave that boy his first trip out of the United States.'

'He give yuh the ol' Hollywood routine?' Farm Boy asked.

'Harold has never been nearer Hollywood than Lansing, Michigan,' Brooklyn said. 'He peddles life insurance, door to door. Not a dime to his name till Uncle Sam came for him. That's why his pretty English "fiancées" never get their rocks. You can lift cans of meat and candy bars out of the PX stores but not diamonds – not yet anyway.'

They both laughed. I mentally recalled the expense Harold had lavished on our outings. Brooklyn seemed to read my thoughts.

'OK, Harold spends big. He borrows big, too – how much does he owe you, Joe?'

'Coupla hundred bercks.'

'Then you're lucky.'

I said: 'Obviously you don't like him.'

'Who says that?' protested Brooklyn, opening the palms of his hands in a gesture of innocence, a token of fair dealing. 'Harold's a lota fun.'

'But he gets the girls?' I said.

This didn't go down too well. Farm Boy's complacent pink features betrayed a hint of turbulence.

'Ah jahs dohn rate a man who's cohnin gurls ha's flahin missions ovah Gahmny when ha's sittin on hahs ahss in th' PX stores. Nahthin pahrsnl min'.'

'But he's a bombardier,' I protested.

Oddly, I found myself prey to conflicting emotions: elation at Harold's exposure – and chagrin that I (leave out V) could have been taken for a ride despite my reservoirs of ill-will. I didn't want V sleeping with Harold, but still less did I want her abandoning herself to the son of an unemployed truck driver.

114

'OK, the guy's a qualified bombardier,' Brooklyn said. 'He was commissioned on the seventy-second day of training in Colorado in the regular manner. But that aint nothin'. You arrive over here and you've never flown a real mission – a real yellow-nose Me9 coming at you aint no photograph.'

'Yeah,' Farm Boy sighed wearily, as if his concurrence was reluctantly given, 'when ol' Harol' flah hahs fahst mission for rahl ha jahs abaht drahpd hahs bahms everywhahs 'tween hah and Hahland.'

'Second time out it happened again,' Brooklyn said. 'His crew was real mad, no kiddin'. In your Air Force they'd have taken the man's wings but we have this big crazy thing called compassion, we have psychos on big salaries, we have morale boosters, so they gave Harold a run of nervous reaction tests.' He lit a new Camel, adding: 'For crying out loud.'

'Fuhnk tests, bah. Harol' fluhnkd th' laht.'

'He still has his wings,' I objected.

Brooklyn nodded and sighed. 'I guess Harold Rascoe has a silver tongue. Maybe he promised to introduce the medic to a sweet little Rose of England, eh? So someone puts him in charge of the PX stores. To get his courage up.'

They both split their sides. Under the stress of this hilarity Farm Boy's vowels more or less disintegrated.

'Th' onlah thungh ol' Harol' evah gurhts uhrp's ahs –'

Both collapsed in helpless laughter. They cried.

'That's a helluva thing to tell this boy,' Brooklyn eventually rebuked his friend. 'Hey, son, don't look so sore.'

I asked him whether Harold's real job at Rackheath was managing the PX stores.

Brooklyn stubbed out his third cigarette. 'They may have appointed him Supreme Allied Commander for all I know.'

Rising from their table, they emptied their pockets of Hershey bars and gum, and wished me luck.

How tranquil our little country stations were in those days. It was still the great age of the train; friendly branch lines to almost every hamlet; a buxom female porter waddling cheerily behind her trolley, birds twittering from the telephone lines, signals which went up, middle and down on wires, locomotives sleepily shunting into sidings looking for somewhere to doze.

V's train was late. I paced up and down the platform flapping my arms and blowing vapour in the frosty air. Someone had discarded an old copy of the *News of the World* on a platform bench. A vicar and his wife, exposed as brother and sister, had been sentenced to the front page.

My mind probed the tunnel, emerging fastened to E. Nesbit's *The Railway Children* and the fact that the world record speed for a steam locomotive was 126 m.p.h. set in 1938 between Grantham and Peterborough by a Pacific class engine called Mallard. I was romantically devoted to the railway children, those honourable, courageous, loyal, innocent siblings. Alone and ten with Aunt Phyllis in Cornwall, I had loved gallant Roberta (Bobbie) passionately – out of that love V herself was born. Miss Hilary Levinson, who at this time taught me English and Latin, and for whom I felt something akin to respect – she, a club-footed widow called herself 'miss' with stimulating stubbornness – advanced a theory about E. Nesbit which, generalized, smelt of the leather-and-wood-polish of an Oxford scholarship.

'Nesbit,' said Levinson – Brophy and Charrington called her a witch – 'Nesbit offers us a portrait of perfect, and therefore impossible virtue, thus inviting us, her readers, to imagine how people really are. We invest both reality and dream in the text she provides; we torture her lines into our own, singular arabesques.'

That was Levinson's style all right!

'Bollocks,' exclaimed Brophy loudly, with a belch worthy of the village drunkard.

Levinson also said that the brother and sisters in *The Railway Children* were sexually 'type-cast', despite their father saying (for the record) 'Girls are just as clever as boys' and asking his younger daughter, 'How would you like to be an engine driver?' Levinson, who spoke mysteriously of 'covert messages' and 'reinforcement', once showed me a photograph of a woman she called Rosa Luxemburg, whose life and death excited her most passionately. Endlessly eloquent about the destinies of male and female in life and literature, Levinson spoke of 'ontology' and 'teleology' and watched me, alone of my class, ravenous with ambition, sink my hound's teeth into these juicy foreign rabbits.

Gazing at the unsmiling tunnel mouth from which V's train would emerge, I thought of Miss Levinson's famous complaint:

'When the children hear a train coming in the tunnel why is it *inevitably* Peter, the boy, who shouts "Come on! Quick! Manhole!" and hurries his sisters to safety?'

'Well . . .'

'And then,' she went on unstoppably, 'the doctor lectures young Peter: "And we are much harder and hardier than they are . . . And their hearts are soft too . . ." And why does Peter do Latin "because he's a boy"?'

I smiled diffidently – my way with this Jewess.

It was Miss L's burden that she could never convert me to socialism. 'It's impossible', she once told me during a very slow, club-footed tête-à-tête round the school buildings, 'to be intelligent and reactionary. How can you not be a *philosophe*, Michael, a son of Voltaire and the *Aufklärung*?'

'Miss Levinson,' I said, 'for we who are not Jews, it's different. We recognize quality and quantity as incompatible. What is good is by definition scarce. What the majority wants is by definition wrong. Tory democracy is not democracy at all – it's the rule of the meritocracy endorsed by the mediocracy.'

Levinson pointed out that the first of these terms had not yet been coined (indeed I was the pioneer) and the second probably would never be. Dear Miss L, so admirably keen to create a gender-blind world (unlike the womb-wallowing 'sisters' of today's 'Movement' – ugh – swallowed up by the radioactive slit between their legs). She never spoke of my cousin Veronica – the recoil was almost physical between Golders Green and Table Mountain.

Waiting for V's train, the signals looked like the railway children's signals. Not much had altered in forty years. Levinson had proposed the tunnel as a metaphor – sniggers from Brophy and Charrington – for vision. Today her phrase means narrow-minded but Miss L understood that the visionary is never wide-angled or broad-minded. 'I'm a fanatic,' she once whispered to me, almost clutching my hand – even in this progressive, coeducational school, members of staff must *not* touch the children – 'are you a fanatic, Michael?' Something spurted: if only I could have put Levinson's mind and mouth inside V's face and body.

Once or twice I'd made V read aloud the passage where Peter's sisters tie him to the settle with rope – 'let's play at bone-setting' – then leave him to rot as a punishment. When Aunt Phyllis first read this passage to me during a visit to St Austell, I had a kind of Stone Age erection; my mind kept delaying Bobbie's departure until, succumbing to temptation, she pulled up her skirts and sat astride her fettered, squirming brother, inflicting on him unnameable tortures. My insistence that V should play this role was finally satisfied. Carried higher up fever's pinnacle than Bobbie could ever have portered me, she tickled the soles of my desperate feet until I begged release not from my fetters but from my unbearable pleasure.

'Close your eyes and think of Hitler,' was V's customary exit line under such importunate pressure.

Finally the signal flipped up and a few minutes later there was a distant chugging, an inconstant sound which came and went as if the incoming train kept changing its mind, until it suddenly grew emphatic as the gallant engine burst out of the tunnel. The train squealed to a halt, steam hissing from its pistons.

V looked radiant in the same puff-shouldered suit and imitation fur coat. She offered me her cheek as I took her case and led the way to the bus stop with my longest strides.

'How did it go?'

'Oh it was wonderful. Harold sends you greetings and hopes to be with us on New Year's Eve.'

'Was he flying missions during your visit?'

'No, thank heavens. Actually' – a tremor in her voice – 'their plane was so badly damaged crossing the Dutch coast that it's been grounded.'

'Surely there's no shortage of planes?'

'Harold says they've been assigned to training the new boys. It's called orientation.'

No use pointing out the contradiction between these two versions to a woman, still less one who insisted on believing she was in love. When we were comfortably seated in the bus I asked whether she'd met any of Harold's colleagues at Rackheath.

'Actually, I wasn't allowed inside the base. Harold says the security's much tighter now than it used to be. He found me a room in a sweet little hotel about ten miles away.'

'Ten miles seems a long way. Isn't it odd he didn't introduce you to any of his friends?'

She gave me a look. 'Darling, our time together is rather precious.'

'We've never met anyone who knows him, have we?'

'Of course we have!'

'Who?'

She was silent. I had hurt and offended her. Why must I immediately rub the glow off her happiness? If women were by nature alien to systematic logic, creatures of instinct and intuition, why not let her be true to herself?

'Well,' I pressed, '*have* we?'

'No,' she whispered.

'Has Harold proposed to you yet?'

'Well . . . we both feel . . . No, not formally . . . I mean, there's no hurry, is there?'

I took her hand. 'As long as you're happy.'

She squeezed.

We spent Christmas at Greendale. I had wanted to take V to London to visit Albert and Leo but she had her hands full with the urchin hordes. The Rowleys invited us to Christmas lunch along with Miss Murdoch and a dozen of V's barbarians who shouted non-stop, grabbed food, spilled gravy (Mrs Rowley's brown water was worth spilling), quarrelled over slices of greasy goose, fought over crackers and paper hats, snatched nuts, overturned glasses, and constantly blamed each other. 'Please, Miss, Bert's kicking me!' 'I'm not! Liar!'

Bert Frame was a great kicker. Any allegation levelled against him was invariably well-founded. Only Brophy could have tamed him but Brophy and Charrington were feasting with their wealthy families far away. (Nothing humiliated me more than my permanent, impoverished captivity at Greendale.) At eleven years of age Bert Frame had a pale, drained face that oozed resentment and impertinence. He was never without a grievance. Nothing was good enough for him. 'Miss, Jack's got more meat than I 'ave!' Whenever I caught his eye I received a hideous scowl: 'Stuck-up snob!' Presented with a slice of Mrs Rowley's disgusting Christmas pudding (packed with carrots and turnips, I surmised), the boy hacked at it furiously in search of a sixpence. Finding none among the brown rubble on his plate, he burst into howls of protest. The sixpence turned up in my slice.

'Would you like it?' I asked him (earning a fond glance from V).

The boy looked at me, then at the sixpence. He was torn. Pride and greed vied for mastery in his bullet head. Immediately the other urchins stretched out their grubby hands, 'I'll 'ave it I'll 'ave it! No you already got one you bugger!' Competition from his fellow proletarians resolved Bert Frame's doubts. Without a word he extended his hand.

'What do you say to Michael, Bert?' Mrs Rowley chided him. He looked at her.

'The word is "thank you",' she said.

Bert looked at me as if to discover whether I too was demanding his capitulation to common decency. I gave him a condescending wink, part youthful complicity, part commiseration that he was what he was. What came back at me was a length of brown-stained tongue.

Not long afterwards V emitted a cheerful shriek and slapped her thigh. It emerged that one of the boys crawling under the table had tried to run his hand up her skirt. When the offender was dragged up by his short hair, he (no prizes who) pointed a protesting finger at me: 'Well 'ee does it!'

This requires an explanation – at the time I alone knew what it was.

The roof of the Staff Annexe was in such disrepair that old Squeers had finally consented to allow scaffolding to be erected at the rear of the building. Workmen appeared rarely – there was a war on, et cetera – but the urchins soon grew bold and swarmed up and down like monkeys. Grubby faces were forever leering into the tiny bedroom I occupied during the holidays but the main tactical objective, of course, was to get a good look at 'Miss' in her knickers or, even better, 'starkers'. V now had to dress and undress with her blackout curtains drawn.

Her indignation did no good. This was what most disturbed her; not so much the peeping Tom aspect as the steady erosion of their respect for her authority. I reminded her of *Sybil*, adding that when tame lion cubs reach a certain age their bestial nature asserts itself and they must be put in the wild. But V only redoubled her efforts to bring civilization to the deprived offspring of Shoreditch, Stepney and Limehouse.

The Staff Annexe was unbearably cold. The roof was a sieve, fuel was rationed and hot water as rare as Rowley could make it. The pipes froze then burst. V never complained. Her solution to numbed limbs was exercise. Although they hated countryside, mud, ploughed fields, woods and biting winds, V regularly shepherded the urchins across two or three miles of frozen earth at a brisk gallop. She allowed gloves and jerseys but insisted on shorts – from which protruded bruised knees, scars and matchstick legs blue with cold. Their teeth literally chattered but she had their circulations going by the end of the run.

Occasionally I showed good will by turning out with her and acting as sheepdog. Grown tall now, and with new strength, I was more than able to keep pace with the urchins and 'bite' the ones who tried to cut for home or get 'lost' in the woods. Bert Frame was the only one I couldn't handle but V's solution for him was the same as it had been for Brophy: challenge him to prove himself the fastest and the leader of the pack. But, whereas V had run in ahead of the hulking adolescent Brophy at the finish, she always took care to let Bert Frame, reputed to be in his twelfth year, 'win'. It was of course a class distinction; Brophy had been reared to try harder if beaten; Bert, the leader of all the street arab gangs, would simply have burned down the school. Brophy knew he had a stake in the nation; Bert was his own nation.

One day shortly before Christmas V and I had come in from such a run, longing for a hot bath but resigned to disappointment. A steady trickle of warm water ran from the rusting tap into the stained, yellowing tub in the freezing bathroom; it was only a few inches deep before the tap began to run cold.

'You have it,' V said.

I insisted that she must have it.

'For heaven's sake, Mike, it'll turn to ice while we're bickering.'

I tugged the curtains together, locked the door, pulled off my shorts and climbed in the bath. 'Come on,' I said, 'there's a war on.' V hesitated, then tossed her garments in Hitler's face. She trusted me not to look.

We sat in the tub back-to-back, noisily passing a bar of Pears soap one to the other and humming 'The White Cliffs of Dover' with chattering teeth. I was the one facing the window. The curtains were drawn but there was a gap. I heard a scuffling sound on the scaffolding and immediately saw a young face glued to the frosted glass. I scowled fiercely but the urchin's eyes were boldly varnished in triumph. I climbed out of the bath and pulled the curtains together – more scuffling and sniggering on the scaffolding.

Whether V actually saw the face at the window I doubt. In any event she said nothing but swiftly wrapped herself in a towel and got out of the tub. I rubbed her back vigorously, then descended to her lovely buttocks, drawing a muted squeal of protest. There was a sharp rap at the bathroom door.

'Veronica? Veronica! Is that you in there?'

V and I exchanged glances.

'Yes, it's me,' V called.

'I'm sure I heard voices.'

'I was just singing, Miss Murdoch.'

But the old bitch wasn't letting go. 'Is someone in there with you, Veronica?'

'Don't worry, Miss Murdoch, we just discovered a few inches of hot water.'

'I'm standing here until you both come out.'

V fastened her dressing gown, unlocked the door and bravely stepped out into the corridor.

'So what's the trouble with you this time, Miss Murdoch, more complaints, spying again?'

'You will not adopt that tone with me, Veronica. Frankly, I'm surprised at you. What would Michael's poor mother think?'

'What are you trying to say to me, Miss Murdoch?'

'Well, I –'

'What is going through your mind? Come on, Miss Murdoch, we want to hear what we've been doing in the bathroom.'

'That, Veronica, is something you will have to explain to Mr Rowley.'

The old hag beat a dignified retreat down the corridor. V came back into the bathroom and offered me a brave smile. But that was more than I could offer two days later when, amidst the debris of Christmas dinner, Bert Frame was hauled from under the table, his roaming paw red with crime and his finger pointing at me: 'Well, 'ee does it!'

Shortly after Christmas a number of unpleasant developments occurred in rapid succession. Harold appeared on New Year's Eve to take V to a ball; they stayed away all night and returned on New Year's Day with a magnum of champagne. V was wearing a diamond engagement ring; the rock itself was large enough to fill the Big Hole at Kimberley. Harold explained the difference between a bottle and a magnum, then said:

'Mike, share my happiness. Your sister has consented to become Mrs Harold Rascoe.'

V kissed me on both cheeks rather anxiously.

Gallantly I gave the toast. Poor, darling V – no *Tatler* or *Country Life* engagement photographs by Cecil Beaton or Norman Parkinson for her. No one to throw a great party in her honour, or give her away, or wish her well: no family, no friends, apart from a boy twisted by desire and jealousy. So Harold shot the cork against the ceiling (a squeal of rage from Miss Murdoch next door – V refused to invite her because she'd ratted to Rowley) and I lifted my glass in salutation: 'To Veronica and Harold. May you both enjoy all the happiness you deserve.'

Little hope of the Luftwaffe or the German flak providing a reprieve if the man's 'combat missions' were confined to the PX stores at Rackheath.

Harold and I stretched ourselves in chairs on that New Year's Day of 1944 while V rustled up a lunch out of Harold's imported luxuries. Brimming with self-esteem and very much in his man-to-man mood, Harold confided that he had 'almost' joined the International Brigade in Spain while a student at Harvard.

'I wish I'd gone, Mike. It's on my conscience.'

'But surely not on the Red side?'

'It was the democratic side, Mike.'

'What – raping nuns and so on?'

'Aw, come on, that was just fascist propaganda. Scare stuff. Who killed Lorca, eh?'

I didn't know who Lorca was but informed Harold that mob rule remained – now as always – the greatest possible danger to civilization. Harold said that 'mob rule', as I called it, was invariably an indictment of the ruling class, a by-product of social breakdown.

'In short, Mike, it's the symptom not the disease.'

'An odd view for the heir to a fortune to hold.'

Harold betrayed no unease. 'I'm not sure I want the privileges I've inherited, but I'm quite sure I didn't earn them. You know something, Mike? My father once said to me: "Whenever you feel like criticizing anyone, just remember that all the people in this world haven't had the advantages that you have had."'

I found these words so interesting that I took pencil and notebook and begged Harold to repeat them. He looked faintly disconcerted: 'Hell,' he said, 'they hardly rate a dictionary of quotations.' But I was persistent and he humoured me; I noticed that each word came out precisely as before, without variation – despite the obvious clumsiness of 'all the people in this world haven't', which would be better rendered by 'not everyone in this world has'.

I informed Harold that I had managed, by dint of perseverant browsing in Mowbury's, to acquire some of the modern American authors he had recommended: Dreiser, Sinclair Lewis and Dos Passos – but not Hemingway or James T. Farrell. Harold's eyes radiated enthusiasm and delight; he most earnestly solicited my opinion of each of the aforementioned writers while simultaneously reaching into his pocket and presenting me with a pound note to cover the cost of these acquisitions. Presently – I was in no hurry – I came to F. Scott Fitzgerald.

'Gosh,' said V, 'you have been busy, Mike. I wondered why I hardly ever see you.'

Harold and V were exchanging proud glances as if they were my parents or something when I began reading out of my notebook the memorable words attributed by Harold to his father. 'Maybe,' I added, 'your father had been reading *The Great Gatsby*' – some edge in my tone stilled V at her gas stove. 'Word for word,' I went on, 'your father's advice is that given by Fitzgerald's Gatsby. Of course Gatsby also occupied a mansion on Long Island Sound, which may account for the coincidence. He too suffered uninvited guests at his lavish parties – just like your father.'

Harold smiled appreciatively. 'Great reading, Mike! – and malice may not be a fault in a critic. As a matter of fact, Fitzgerald frequently visited with us [with? *with*?] and I daresay he borrowed from life as novelists do.'

'You knew Scott Fitzgerald?' V asked him in awe.

'Sure. In my view Scott and Zelda have always wanted to live inside a movie. Cut to Antibes. Dissolve to the Ritz in Paris.' Harold smiled, showing two rows of perfect white teeth.

I wasn't done. 'Did your father serve with the Artillery in the Great War, winning countless medals before moving on to Oxford? Did he say "Old Sport" at every opportunity and love a girl called Daisy? Perhaps he named your sister after her?'

125

'My father isn't in the past tense yet. When you visit with us after the war, Mike, I hope you'll have the opportunity to ask him these questions yourself.'

'Is Daisy the name of a woman in the novel?' V asked me a bit uneasily.

'Yes,' I said with my ultra-nasty smile. 'She is a creature of fiction – like Harold's father, his father's house and his father's son Harold.'

Accusations had been building up behind my grinding teeth like angry rats scuffling to burst from their cage, and now the lock had sprung loose. The vast indictment levelled against Harold by his colleagues Brooklyn and Farm Boy, rehearsed in my mind over and over again, every detail, was sounding, booming among the champagne bubbles. Drawing on my last ounce of wisdom, I walked prudently out of the room.

'Sorry,' I murmured.

When the new term started Nancy Lunt returned wearing the hard hat of a member of staff and took up residence in the Annexe. She was never out of V's room. About one thing only were Lunt and I in agreement – V's engagement to 'that Yank' was a disaster. But Nancy was too thick to sign a treaty with the young 'squirt' who, she darkly hinted, was unnaturally devoted to his sister.

During the second week of January I received a summons to Yorkshire. Rowley's belching pipe had generated the usual pea-soup fog in his study.

'Just a chat, Michael. Sit down.'

Miss Murdoch had reported the bathroom incident. On top of that the Head had received an anonymous note scrawled on a filthy piece of lined paper with jagged edges, apparently torn out of an exercise book. He showed it to me:

Mister Roly that snob mikel Parson has it with miss King in the barth. She jurked him of I seen it. A witnis.

Every word had been underlined. I told Rowley that the author of the note was a London boy called Bert Frame, who regularly climbed the scaffolding outside the Annexe and made obscene propositions to Veronica.

Rowley nodded. 'I have talked the matter through with Veronica. She insists that you and she are brother and sister.'

'Yes, sir.'

'You yourself are now convinced of that?'

'Yes, sir.'

'Even though your father and your mother registered Veronica as your cousin?'

'Yes.'

'May I ask whether this revelation has altered your feelings towards Veronica?'

'Feelings, sir?'

He nodded in the no-further-explanation-required manner cultivated by detectives. It didn't do to be too neat or clever about this so I made a show of fumbling about. 'Well . . . she's my best friend . . . obviously . . . my only surviving relation . . . I mean she's the kindest person I know.'

'Anything else?'

'No, sir.'

Rowley then opened one of his desk drawers – the permanently hibernating hound asleep at his feet stirred and drooled – and produced a number of books and exercise books. I recognized them at once as my own and broke into a cold sweat.

'I have deemed it my duty, Michael, to examine the contents of your dormitory box.'

I might have pointed out to the old bastard that he had always promised – a declaration of progressive principle, no less – that dormitory boxes were private; a 'sanctuary', he called them, a 'nursery' in which 'the mysteries of individuality' could 'flower' without 'fear of hoe or roller'. Oh yes! A boy or girl's dormitory box was also a 'refuge' for that 'exquisite exile of the spirit' indispensable to the 'full development of the creative personality'.

Why protest? Hypocrisy and betrayal were the rules of adult life; power alone defined morality. The sweat clinging to my neck and the palms of my hands might have promoted the very rush of juvenile indignation that Squeers was waiting for. I said nothing.

'Mowbury's must regard you as a valued customer,' Rowley mused. 'Here we have an anthropology textbook with one passage heavily pencilled in the margin. Allow me to read it to you:

Among the Wutamba tribe in the Gold Coast one may observe siblings of the opposite sex playing together without any obvious inhibition or sense of shame. Brothers and sisters frequently dance in the naked state, twisting and writhing as if engaged in a mixture of play and combat. During such displays male erections are often in evidence. In certain villages siblings with maturing bodies engage in forms of love-play with encouragement from the local musicians, whose gourds and tom-toms whip the dancers to a mounting frenzy. When questioned, the elders of the villages adopt a relaxed attitude to the possible consequences, including coitus.

Rowley closed the book and asked me why this passage had been marked.

I said: 'I suppose the attitude of the village elders might be construed as a West African version of progressive education.'

His yellowing teeth broke through the blubber of his mouth.

'Very good. An Oxford scholarship is still in prospect. The stamp of the true scholar is also that of the true lawyer: skill in disputation.'

He then opened my precious volume of Jacobean plays (which I had withdrawn from V's room when Nancy Lunt began to poke about).

'Easy to see from the thumb prints which of these plays has enjoyed your closest attention, Michael. And we find certain passages marked in the margin, others heavily underscored. Act 2, scene 1: Giovanni describes his feelings after possessing his own sister:

I envy not the mightiest man alive
But hold myself in being king of thee
More great than if I were king of all the world.

128

I may have nodded. He leaned across the desk towards me, as far as his stomach would allow.

'Have *you* ever had occasion to feel such elation?'

'No, sir. These levels of experience are found only in literature. The play is the purest fantasy – an allegory about repression, I assume.'

'Excellent! Oxford reaches out for Greendale's brightest. But – may one ask – do such fantasies appeal to you?'

'Very much, sir. Murder, too. If you care to examine my school text of *Macbeth* you may find some of Lady Macbeth's murderous incitements also marked in the margin.'

Rowley grinned: 'But you're not plotting a murder, is that it?'

'Precisely, sir.'

'Are you familiar with the attitude of Bazarov and his friend Arkady? – the brightest young minds have a mission to raze every convention which does not prove, on scientific inspection, "useful". Or perhaps you haven't read Turgenev?'

I had but said I hadn't. The old bloater needed to score. His next thrust took me by surprise.

'If I may quote another passage from Ford's play which you have underlined with the most vigorous strokes of your pencil:

> Busy opinion is an idle fool,
> That, as a school-rod keeps a child in awe,
> Frights the inexperienced temper of the mind.

How am I to interpret that, Michael?'

I said: 'You have always taught us at Greendale to question the conventional wisdom.'

'To question it, yes. One should not blindly repeat the Ten Commandments as dogma – but that is not a license to disobey them.'

(More 'progressive' humbug but I nodded respectfully.) 'I agree, sir. My interest is in the Platonic Idea as it manifests itself in Art.'

He jammed his pipe back between his teeth. 'Now here are your diaries and notebooks. I find several entries which relate to incest. For example, you record that between 1660 and 1908 intercourse between brother and sister was not a criminal offence in England. The only inhibition was under canon law . . . mm . . . until the . . . can't read your writing.'

'The Prohibition of Incest Act of 1908.'

'Very interesting – but where is the Platonic Idea, or the Art, in that? Sounds like social history to me.'

'Yes, sir,' I said dutifully.

'And you were discovered sharing a bath with your . . . with Veronica. She explained to me that you were both frozen and that hot water is scarce in the Annexe. Mm . . .' Rowley picked up the greasy anonymous note and let it drop on his desk. 'The lower classes may be deficient in spelling but not necessarily in veracity. Mm . . . Michael, I'd like you to talk to a doctor, a trained psychiatrist.'

I reddened with humiliation. The insult! As if I were some kind of emotional invalid! A child to be 'cured' of his own disease!

'I see no need, sir.'

'I do.'

'This doctor, does he – '

'She. Better that you see a woman.'

'Does she understand sexual politics?'

Rowley gaped. He had never heard the phrase, nor had I. My precious books and notebooks went back into his drawer. A few days later I was summoned to an interview at Greendale General Hospital.

I knew nothing of other contemporary journeys, of cattle trucks and gas chambers, and it wouldn't have distracted me from my own burning grievance if I had known. What infuriated me was Squeer's refusal to return my precious books. *My* books! Obviously I suspected V's involvement in this treachery, she whom I loved with a consuming passion.

FOURTEEN

You could tell at once that she was lonely, or forsaken, as elderly people are, and in need of company. At first glance Kate Bracewell was the sort of dear old thing who keeps you waiting in shops and post offices while she spins out her transaction, relating her little difficulties in minute detail, weaving webs of delay. But Kate still worked part-time as a consultant paediatrician in a London teaching hospital and after weighing my metal she opened a briefcase whose locks snapped back click click!

'Bloody amazing,' she said, waving my documents. 'I'll keep these if I may.'

I'd better explain (after all, my chapters aren't literature). It was another doc, a geezer called Yardley, who'd tipped me in Bracewell's direction. He'd also passed on to her the John Ford file in the *Spectator* – hence the amazing and waving. So here she was, in my office at Globe House, ten floors up and on equal terms with the dome of St Paul's.

'Are you sure *he* wrote these articles, Mr . . .'

'Frame. Bert. Yes, quite sure, Doctor.'

'Call me Kate,' she insisted. '*He* never would.' She rolled her eyes, quite a party trick, I noticed.

'Sorry?'

'When he was a boy undergoing treatment. During the war. He never called me anything – too standoffish.'

I lit a cigarette with a token gesture of hesitation, she being a doc and all, but she snatched one from the pack and lent across to my throwaway lighter, showing a pair of boobs in good nick for seventy, which she must have been.

'He was your patient at Greendale General Hospital, Kate?'

'Yes, dear – but doctor-patient relationships are confidential.' She winked and I saw some eyelashes not entirely her own. Being a pro with the standard soul of saddle leather, I knew when to put the boot into an upper-middle-class rump.

'So why are you here, Kate?'

She pulled a pile of stuff from her snappy briefcase, old volumes and school notebooks. 'The birth of John Ford,' she said. Saliva ran out of the corners of my several mouths. 'He wanted it all back after the war . . . but I "mislaid" it. Even in 1943 he struck me as a dangerous character – and *very* political. At the age of sixteen he'd coined the phrase "sexual politics" – bloody amazing.'

My shorthand hand raced down my reporter's notebook.

'All you have to do', she went on bossily, 'is to reprint his schoolboy notes alongside the John Ford articles – and it's curtains for the Tories.' She burst into a rough smoker's cough, a real hack, at the prospect. 'Anything to bring those buggers down.'

'Why?' I was playing the prole's dead bat.

'They want to wreck the entire NHS, haven't you noticed, Mr Frame?'

'How did you get hold of these books and notebooks, Kate?'

'Rowley confiscated them.'

'Did he!'

'Rowley was –'

'The Headmaster. I know. I was a London orphan at Greendale. A worm on the scaffolding. So Parsons was in big trouble with the Head? Tell me, Kate, do these notebooks contain any reference to Veronica King?'

'Not directly. But indirectly the books and notebooks are exclusively about his fierce passion for her. She was . . . his sister, you know . . .'

'His cousin, surely?' I played the innocent.

Bracewell's smile was full of secret knowledge. 'Half-sister, actually – and far from blameless. A compulsive seductress beneath a disingenuous innocence.'

Suddenly Doc Bracewell looked guilty; I could tell that it was an ancient guilt, like rust.

Do I hate this Government? It's more like a dull ache. I still pay my dues to the party and the union. Keeping faith. Saturdays, I was with the print workers on the Wapping picket line. One or two Saturdays. I wanted the miners to win, too, though they were cruelly led. I keep faith after my fashion. After three defeats you begin to ask, 'Are we mad?' Like the last Christians or something. Canvassing is cruel, the old women peering at you through the curtains, waiting to be mugged; the guilty looks on the council estates, 'We haven't made up our mind,' which means no. The widow who tells you that Mr Jones died last year and she won't be going out to vote any more, too dangerous. The working class terrified of itself.

Wasting evenings canvassing the neither here nor there lodgings in main streets where bells are unnamed or don't work and no one will come down anyway though they sometimes stick a head out of the window. The ten valuable Patels in the corner shop but no way of getting at them after closing hours, just a rich smell of Tandoori. Even the Asian shopkeepers are crossing the floor, tightening the knots of their ties, talking of rates and taxes.

The white building worker whose only thought is to deport 'them'. If you're patient and a bit lucky, he may still vote Labour because 'I always have'.

It's funny, almost: you can stand outside a tube station during the evening rush hour with a wad of leaflets and you can predict each person's reaction as they walk towards you. Anything half tidy, half clean, it's 'No!' (The made-up little girls in black executive suits with a slit up the skirt who giggle nastily, 'We're bored with politics.') Anything scruffy and falling apart, it's 'Right on, mate'. Same with the houses. A neat garden, a freshly painted front door, and you're out of luck. In my Mum's day every working woman washed her doorstep and swept her bit of pavement every day. Today? – you have to be joking. The nation resembles an overturned litter bin. No pride in anything. That's one thing She's right about.

Don't bother with the posh streets. They bark only seconds before they bite. 'I thought my vote was *my* business!' (The bitch wouldn't say that if your rosette was blue.) Husband comes to door in cardigan and fulminates against 'that bunch of Reds in the Town Hall'. Their crime, please? Well, the Marxist rabble raised his rates because they wanted to put central heating in council flats, build new houses, accommodate the homeless, fund the support services and the libraries, assist tenants being booted out by rapacious landlords, do something for the blacks, rescue teenage mothers from despair. Disgusting. They even squandered money on bringing black rock groups to the public parks on Sunday afternoons. Trouble is, the black afternoon begins about nine in the evening – we do have cultural problems.

The *Globe* is supposed to support Labour but you might wonder. We never fail to refer to Labour Council leaders as 'Town Hall chiefs' just as we never fail to 'expose' 'top brass' spilling out ratepayers' money on a portrait of Winnie Mandela to be painted by a black woman. 'Blatantly racist . . . storm of protest.' BARMY! is our kindest word of abuse. (BLIMEY! is out of fashion; even East Enders have to move up-market.)

Oh, we're still the good people, but helpless somehow against the little Michaels with their wealth and stealth. I covered the annual Levellers Day do at Burford. With the approval of a sympathetic vicar the WEA have attached a plaque to the church wall, commemorating the three rebel soldiers who were shot right there by Cromwell's troops. A prayer, a wreath or two, and then sing 'The Red Flag' if you know the words. All very quaint, bearded lecturers from my old college, Ruskin, nice anorak people who listen to Radio 3 or don't eat meat, gentle Tawneyites full of concern, and an upper class dame from Maidenhead peddling her forthcoming Shelley celebration. ('Sign language for the deaf available.') Reclaim the great heritage! It's not my heritage.

To find the afternoon seminars you're invited to walk for a mile and get lost. Empty streets – it's Cup Final afternoon.

That's the measure of our great Movement – staging its festivals of remembrance on Cup Final Saturday. How do I drive seventy miles home to my video without somehow being forced to know the result of the match? I'd warned the surviving remnants of my family: 'Only tell me the final score and I'll kill you.' A butch girl who probably thinks Liverpool's a city jumps up belligerently and wants to know whether the meeting on 'Black Women and the Peace Movement' is to be for women only. It's a struggle not to call the stupid bitch 'darling'. Didn't I survive the Blitz so that she could have abortions-on-demand?

Little Michael and his legions have us by the short hairs. Three election victories on the trot. The tarts on *Marxism Today* call it 'cultural hegemony'. Take the latest Parsons onslaught:

Addressing the Young Conservative Conference, I asked: 'If we kept the money and spent it ourselves, rather than having it recycled through a slow and bureaucratic apparatus, might we get a better bargain?'

One thing is certain: the 'progressive' middle class intellectuals have suffered the total collapse of their Keynesian religion. But the disastrous results of their 'Commonwealth' remain our crippling inheritance.

In 1910 public expenditure absorbed 13 per cent of the Gross National Product; by 1963, 43 per cent; by 1975, 60 per cent. Where will it end? At 101 per cent?

The Treasury, traditionally the guardian of the national purse, has been dragged down into the orthodoxy of high public expenditure. The Treasury should be on tap, not on top. We must turn a deaf ear to bright young officials who are forever identifying 'new needs' and discovering fresh areas of deprivation which can only be solved – so they claim – by fresh injections of public money.

There will be outcries, of course, protests – we will be accused of vandalism and worse.

Pluralism, competition, market forces – these are the watchwords for the future. The nation will survive only if its fittest elements prosper.

I have no doubt we will also meet with opposition within our own party. In the sixties we embraced the 'hand-out' solution – give the unions whatever they demand, wring our hands helplessly as the budget deficit and the trade deficit mounts, plead for a national incomes policy. There are elements within our party who talk of 'one nation', an organic community rooted in the benevolent paternalism of the old squirearchy. They should remind themselves that an archaic Britain of heraldic shields suits very nicely Americans, Japanese and Germans who are not afraid of the dynamic tensions of a pluralist society. They prosper at our expense.

In 1835 Disraeli produced his treatise, *Vindication of the English Constitution*, written under the influence of Edmund Burke and the romantic poet Coleridge. Disraeli attacked the utilitarian belief that the interests of all can be achieved by allowing each individual or family to pursue its own interests. He also disparaged the 1832 Reform Act which for the first time admitted middle-class urban dissenters to the Lower House. Disraeli was wrong on all counts.

Impossible to avoid mixed feelings about the young Dizzy. The dandy squandering his father's money by cutting a dash at the races and in salons of influence does not appeal to me. The shopkeepers from the chapels called Sion, Bethel and Bethesda no doubt lacked breeding and refinement but they represented a genuine interest. I would have been with Robert Peel at that time or the Manchester Liberals – Bentham even.

Rationality must always prevail. When Disraeli became leader of the Tory Party and Prime Minister, he did not forget his disgust at the appalling social conditions prevailing in the new manufacturing industries – he imposed Factory Acts, sanitation rules, inspectors – but he did abandon his archaic, romantic vision of the Commons as representing a single, ancient estate of the realm, the knights of the equestrian order, Coleridge's 'franklins'.

In 1867 he further enlarged the franchise and simultaneously promoted the Tory Party as champion of a property-owning democracy. Unlike Salisbury he perceived that conservatism and democracy are natural allies (given intelligent leadership) against the bastard-feudal barons of Organized Labour.

The great enemy since the French Revolution has been the Leviathan of Collectivism. This new creature, which wears many heads (TUC, CGT, AFL-CIO) and speaks many tongues, is monstrous in its clamorous claims for power and privilege – the Rule of raw Envy. Its perennial weapon, now as in 1789, is the Mob (which we daintily term the flying picket). The recent roughhouse scenes at the gates of our mines were invariably the same scenes depicted by Disraeli on Mowbray Moor. The miners' message was identical to that of the picketing print workers at Wapping on the Isle of Dogs: 'Dare to work and we'll break your head.' Pandering Welfare only inflames the disease; I am sometimes reminded of Disraeli's comment that 'scanty food and hard labour are in their way, if not exactly moralists, a tolerably good police'.

'Sometimes' reminded, little Michael? Oh, you have to be posh to be 'sometimes'. I'll getcha.

FIFTEEN

The doctor's name was Bracewell. She wore a twin-set and flared skirt and clearly thought she was the cream into which any tom cat would dip his whiskers. Having offered me a cup of tea and a sandwich biscuit layered with the usual ugh, she explained that sex was on the whole a good thing and nothing to be ashamed of. Did I agree?

I shrugged.

'Adolescence can be an extremely frustrating time,' she went on. 'We are physically mature but society denies us emotional fulfilment and genital release.' Did I agree?

I played with my newly arrived Adam's apple.

'Have you ever fallen in love with any of the Greendale girls, Michael?'

'Love is girls' stuff,' I told her.

'Do you find any girls of your own age physically attractive? No need to be shy with me. And please call me Kate.'

'Difficult to say.' (If it was an offence to call her 'doctor', she could do without any form of address. She had fine breasts which she took care to display to advantage. I assumed she was another paid-up member of the 'progressive' conspiracy, a quack.)

'Maturity, for example? Do physical and emotional maturity attract you in a woman?'

I shrugged. There was a noticeable tightening round her mouth. I knew with all my being that when women said 'woman' it meant something different to when I said it: they turned both desire and normality inside out.

'Dr Rowley tells me you're an exceptionally intelligent boy, Michael, a potential Oxbridge scholar with a flair for self-expression. I can't believe you're as inarticulate as you make out.'

I said, 'Are you a Freudian or a Jungian?'

She made a note in her book, then asked me whether I had been greatly disturbed by the loss of my parents.

'I miss them, naturally. Particularly my mother.'

She made a note in her book.

'And your father?'

'I didn't see much of him. When I was younger he was normally posted abroad. Then the war started . . .'

'Perhaps your father was rather an elusive man in more ways than one? He withheld love – or distributed it sparingly – like a reward for good conduct? Perhaps he wanted you to be more courageous, more "manly" – in a conventional way, I mean.'

I was shaken to hear these familiar truths, for the first time, from the mind and mouth of another. This woman was laying a dangerous claim to be human.

I said: 'Possibly.'

She made a note in her book. 'Did that quality in him leave a wound? Resentment even?'

'Hard to say.'

'Do you feel that your father loved Veronica more than you?'

'Probably.'

'But of course you had no idea at the time that she was his daughter?'

I nodded.

'Has that knowledge changed things?'

'I can't understand why my parents should have lied about it.'

'I suppose Veronica could be mistaken – is that a possibility?'

'You mean Veronica could be lying,' I said. 'Psychiatrists shouldn't use euphemisms.'

Dr Bracewell's mouth tightened again. She took refuge in her notebook.

'So your revenge may be directed against your parents? They betrayed you twice, didn't they – the second time by getting killed.'

'Revenge?'

'Yes, Michael. Isn't incest a form of revenge – a cry of protest? Even as a thought, an idea. Obviously Dr Rowley has shown me your private collection of books.'

I was silent.

'Are you interested in power, Michael?'

'Power? No.'

'Dr Rowley told me that you used the phrase "sexual politics" to him. He was very struck by it. So am I – a quite brilliant coupling of normally dissociated ideas.'

I said I had no recollection of using any such phrase – and what did it mean? She didn't answer directly but pointed out that parents exercise power over our lives – in death as well as in life.

'Believe me, Michael, we all of us conduct an inner dialogue with our parents from the cradle to the grave. When love fails, that dialogue may turn into a war – a war in which there is only one active party.'

I nodded respectfully.

'Tell me, honestly, did your feelings for Veronica precede or follow the revelation that she's your half-sister?'

'I've always liked her, if that's what you mean. She's been a true friend to me, you know.'

She wrote in her book.

'But you're also in love with her – as a woman. Isn't that correct?'

Fearing that V had let cats out of bags, I said: 'She, too, has been rather short of love, you know.'

Bracewell made a note and smiled sympathetically. 'Is that why she let you share a bath with her?'

'Good lord – that! Didn't she tell you about our hot water supply?'

'Oh yes, I do understand that. And what about her American fiancé, Harold?'

I shrugged.

'Do you feel jealous of his attraction for your sister?'

'Why should I?'

At this juncture Dr Bracewell re-crossed her legs with a sexy swish. There was a ring on her finger. I wondered whether she maintained a steady line of questioning while being jiggered.

'Michael, you are here for your own sake, not for mine. I cannot help you if you will not help yourself by telling the truth. We don't have as much time as I would like.'

'May I ask a question?'

'You don't require permission to ask, Michael.'

'Does everything in that notebook of yours go straight back to Mr Rowley?'

Bracewell re-crossed her legs again. 'Well – '

'How can a doctor claim a patient's confidence without a pledge of confidentiality?'

Her little mind raced. I was pleased by my own performance and couldn't resist on more jab:

'Let's call you a gendarme with a pleasant bedside manner, Doctor.'

She wrote hectically in her book but I could see she was playing for time, trying to put the pieces of herself together inside the sexy twin-set. And why did she varnish her nails pink – what kind of a doctor was that?

At that moment a pert, starchy nurse poked her head through the door and mentioned that the next patient was waiting. Bracewell sighed with relief and regret.

'Let's talk again,' she said, fishing for a suitable smile.

Potential Oxbridge scholars were rare as parrots at Greendale and did wonders for the school's phoney prospectus. Rowley wasn't looking for a pretext to expel me – just shuffling responsibility to Doc Bracewell (the approved 'progressive' tactic). As for V, she had made herself indispensable to Squeers; she alone was capable of maintaining law and order among the boys on the games field; she alone could restrain the London urchins from burning down the school during the holidays – though for how long?

As for Quack Bracewell, the ridiculous woman reported that I was a reasonably 'adjusted' boy suffering from a single, destructive fixation brought on by a succession of rejections, traumas, desertions. (Intellectual foundations of the Welfare State. Lumpen intelligentsia. Morbid philanthropy.) Therefore the fixation must be removed. V must go.

Bracewell called us both in, V and me, and told us point blank.

V was frightfully upset. She protested passionately: What would become of me during the school holidays? Who would cook my meals and mend my clothes? Who would keep me company? (I had thought Bracewell attractive but seeing them together I recognized that they stood in different leagues of beauty.) I knew V was reliving her more painful exchanges with Mother through this nail-varnished doctor.

Bracewell provided no solutions. She assumed, vaguely, that Mrs Rowley would take me in as a lodger during the holidays. V then announced that if she was forced to leave Greendale she would find work in London and I would spend the holidays with her at home. Bracewell's mouth tightened; she asked me to wait outside.

Ten minutes later V emerged looking shattered. All the way home she refused to tell me what Bracewell had said to her.

The twin-set doctor moved fast. Two days later V received a visit from a lady carrying an attaché case. OHMS. She came from the Labour Exchange – we were living under our own form of National Socialism – and spoke of the nation's urgent need of 'mobile woman labour'. The OHMS woman flipped through her folders. Now that Miss Nancy Lunt had joined the staff there was a clear case of duplication, of two women doing one job. The District Manpower Board took a dim view. A fit young gel, unmarried, should do her bit in the aircraft or munitions industries: welders, fitters, railways, farms – women could do it. Not to mention the ATS, the WRENS or the WAAFS. 'A Group Captain's daughter might long since have enlisted in the WAAFS,' she added primly.

This remark gave us our clue to the source of the assault; Rowley wanted to retain V's services; Bracewell was the only other person in a position to disclose that Miss King was the daughter of the late Group Captain Parsons. Departing, OHMS urged V to volunteer before she was conscripted. 'That way you'll have more choice.'

Had we overlooked Nancy herself as the informer? She, too, knew that V and I shared the same father. Could she be revenging herself for V's engagement? Perhaps Lunt had decided to clear the decks, dispose of V, and ooze her way further up Squeers's stinking armpit? On balance I doubted it; the hippo was still miserably besotted, a moaning bag of crush, and quite capable of following V all the way to a munitions factory or a squalid farm in Suffolk. Anyway, Nancy was a good sport and wouldn't rat.

V was terribly downcast by the OHMS woman's visit. I now renewed my demand that she divulge what Bracewell had said to her after pointing me to the door. Tormented, V ran her fingers through her flowing hair. I sat beside her on the divan sofa and took her hand.

'Speak.'

'She was quite horrid, Mike. She said that I was entirely responsible for your . . . your . . .'

'State of mind?'

'Yes. She said I'd compensated for an emotionally . . . rotten . . .'

' – an emotionally deprived childhood?'

'Yes.'

'Unstable?'

'Yes . . . by . . . by, well, by turning myself into a . . . certain kind of woman.'

'What kind?'

'She said I'd led you on. Played with you. She said she'd heard that the London boys made . . . very suggestive remarks about me . . . that the younger boys at Greendale also talked about me . . . that I'd flaunted my "affair" with Harold in front of the school. She said it was inexcusable to share a bath with you, that I . . .'

V began to cry. I suppose she now knew what I'd always known, from the cradle: women are incapable of innocence.

* * *

Dear Mike [wrote Harold],

Thank you for your letter. I think I understand why you wrote it. Anyway, I'm resolved to give you the benefit of the doubt.

Your main concern is that I am a stranger, a foreigner too, with only my own claim to be the man I say I am. You insist that you have reason to doubt my credentials and my good faith (a diamond engagement ring notwithstanding). You ask for a letter from a 'reputable referee', preferably my commanding officer, refuting serious allegations allegedly made against me by two unnamed 'colleagues' in the US 8th Air Force. I can only regret that you could not, or did not, cite your sources.

As Veronica's brother you claim to be fulfilling the protective duties of a deceased father. Let's leave aside whether a boy of sixteen can adequately discharge such duties (which, after all, are a function of experience and maturity). I'll give you the benefit of the doubt on that one, too.

Everything I have told you about my background and biography is accurate. Yes, my dad is rich, I grew up on Long Island Sound, I went to Harvard, studying history, then law: yes, I visited Europe before the present war. Equally: no, my father was not an unemployed truck driver (the word is 'teamster', by the way, not 'teamer'), I did not grow up in Lansing, Michigan, and I did not attend Michigan State University.

Yes, I do work in Hollywood for MGM as a contract lawyer. My claim to have met many of the stars is neither 'fraudulent' nor 'a motion in a long chain of mendacities' – I have to admire your flair for language, in case you were wondering.

On and on we go. Have I really been flying missions over Germany? Yes I have. I ought to know! – but that, of course, is no answer to a budding star of the English Bar like yourself. Did I fail my 'funk tests'? No, sir. Am I, all the while, the covert manager of the PX stores? No, they have guys specially trained for that. The tops of their heads are flat, to balance things on. Why, you ask, did Veronica not meet a single one of my flying colleagues when she visited with me here at Rackheath? If that was what she wanted (there was no hint of it) I am greatly at fault. I guess I was jealous of my short time alone

144

with the woman I ardently and admiringly love. Jealousy is an emotion you may understand.

You say that 'all' American servicemen carry photos of their families in their wallets and display them at the first opportunity. Maybe they do – I happen to be myself first and an American second. My sense of who I am doesn't require snapshots.

Clearly you have been engaged in some detective work of your own. Why did I claim to have visited the site of the Battle of Hastings *at Hastings*? OK, it was a slip of the tongue. You have also pounced on convergences between my claimed upbringing and passages from *The Great Gatsby*. Evidently my explanations did not satisfy you. As the French say, *tant pis*.

We come to what the lawyer in me might call 'circumstantial evidence' (leaving behind the hearsay and innuendo). You insist that my professed political beliefs are simply 'incompatible' with the privileged family background I claim. You cite in particular my views on *Gone With the Wind* and the Spanish Civil War, which you characterize as 'outright socialism'. That's news to me. Maybe the patterns of politics in England and the United States are rather different. We in America have recently lived through something called the New Deal, not just a list of legislative achievements but a profound upheaval in our attitude toward public life and public values. The progressive wing of the Democratic Party is, believe it or not, full of Ivy League graduates from what we call WASP backgrounds. It may be that in England social class determines political allegiances (though you may have overlooked Labour leaders like Stafford Cripps, Clement Attlee and also the Fabian intellectuals). I suspect that England still awaits its New Deal: when it comes, Mike, you may think again.

I hope this disposes to your satisfaction of the 'phantasmagoric' Harold Rascoe. I now turn, even more painfully, to the 'real' Harold whose conduct you find unworthy of a suitor for Veronica's hand in marriage.

You accuse me of a 'vulgar display' of wealth. (Yes. I'm familiar with the common English quip: 'Over-paid, over-sexed, over here'.) I guess it's a fault in our culture: to give is a token of affection. A man who loves a girl must manifest his devotion by acts of material endowment – I guess the man is by tradition the bread-winner and he demonstrates his credentials, his potential, his capacities, by putting his hand in his pocket. Primitive, certainly, but are things so different over here? Of course I understand the resentments felt by English people – Yanks moving in to buy up their girls. I wouldn't quarrel with your stricture 'imperialism', though you may not care for the word when you think of India, Africa and other parts of the globe shaded red.

Meals, gifts, shopping expeditions, our trip to London – all these figure in your indictment, your catalog of crimes. I emerge from your pages as a cynical blackmarketeer peddling counterfeit money and forged clothing coupons. Should I remark that you didn't exactly toss the clothes I bought you in the Thames? – or are the relatively poor defenseless against the relatively affluent? Listen, Mike, I'm sorry, truly sorry, about the trip to London. Veronica and I were guilty of a bad error of judgment. We thought you were enjoying yourself but you were hating every minute of it – as you say, your own home town, a scene of bereavement, was crassly transformed into a 'pleasure palace'. And that night in the Cumberland Hotel, I wince at your words.

Finally, I enclose three documents as a mark of my respect for you and my honorable intentions toward Veronica. The first is my complete service record, including the number of missions flown, signed by my commanding officer. The second is a recent letter from my father welcoming my engagement to Veronica (you will see that he also alludes to my work and prospects at MGM). The third is a family photograph taken in our Long Island garden. My dad needs no identification; the lady at his side is my second step-mother; the girl on his knee is my sister Daisy; the man with his arms round her shoulder (and mine) is F. Scott Fitzgerald.

You wrote your letter in 'strict confidence' and asked me to reply in the same vein. You explained that you were anxious to avoid 'unnecessary pain' to Veronica – I gather that you have very nobly never voiced your doubts and discontents to her. A skeptic might conclude that though your discontents are real enough your doubts exist on a plane of consciousness (well known to psychiatrists) half-way between conviction and invention. But let that pass. I shall not mention our correspondence to Veronica unless you do.

Please write me when you can. I would like to hear that we can be friends. I almost said 'again', but that was my delusion, wasn't it?

Sincerely . . .

V took the bus into Greendale to visit the Labour Exchange. She was kept waiting for two hours in a bleak hallway with a brown linoleum floor, a vast array of public notices and exhortations pinned to the wall, and no chairs. Her intention was to appeal to 'the Director' but in the end all she got was the same OHMS attaché case woman who was determined to cook her goose.

V protested that her work with the London Boys' Programme was sponsored by the WVS (she mentioned my mother) and therefore 'war work' for women according to the National Service Act. V had been doing her homework.

But OHMS had Dr Bracewell in her ear. Veronica was a bad woman. Nancy Lunt could perfectly well cope with the London boys.

'Wasteful duplication. I regret that you have ignored my advice to volunteer, Miss King. Things can be easier that way.'

As V was leaving, OHMS mentioned tersely that she had lost her fiancé at El Alamein. She seemed to feel it was V's fault.

V showed me a letter she had received from Harold. This was something she never did and I took it from her with a trembling hand – the bastard must have ratted. But there was no reference to our correspondence, merely cordial greetings to me.

Harold's letter was mainly devoted to a harrowing description of a catastrophic USAAF day-time raid on Berlin involving 730 bombers and 796 escort fighters, mainly Mustang P51s. Only one hundred of the fighters had reached the target. The Gefechtsverbände had swarmed up over Berlin into the Ameri-

147

can bomber boxes, wreaking havoc and bringing down 69 Fortresses and Liberators. 'Darling, I didn't really expect to see you again.'

'Tell me what you think, Mike?' V asked shyly.

Sensing that she was suffering from unbearable anxiety, I merely murmured my sympathy and slipped a consoling arm round her waist. Her own comment, when eventually it came – and it obviously forced its way out through several barriers – took me utterly by surprise.

'So unlike Father. All those exact numbers. Dad would have said, "We're not having it all our own way" – and finish. He didn't shove military secrets in the post, did he?'

It was the first word of criticism she'd ever levelled against Harold. I remarked that Americans have statistics the way the French have wine. 'Drunk on them.'

She was lost in thought. 'Mike.'

I waited.

'If Harold would marry me ... immediately ... they couldn't conscript me.'

'Oh. I thought –'

'Thought what?'

'Well ... his letter. You –'

'I was just being silly. It's because I'm so afraid for him.'

'Marriage means babies. You'd have to resign your job here.'

'I know perfectly well how not to have a baby. I'm going to write to Harold.'

The end of term was only two days away – and no doubt the end of everything. Rowley's appeals to the Manpower Board on V's behalf had proved unavailing. With every post we expected the conscription notice.

The School Yard was piled with trunks and tuckboxes to be collected by the trucks of the Great Western Railway. The air was shrill with excited voices. Charrington took, as was latterly his custom, my hand. 'Michael, why don't you drop by during the hols. Some good fishing in prospect.' But the invitation was no sooner uttered than it was forgotten.

Then silence. All gone. Greendale empty. Forty-eight hours until the urchins arrived.

V and Nancy went down to the gym to inspect the gear. Lunt was in a terrible state of sniffling gloom and foreboding. I thought of taking a look in her room, a pretty squalid horsebox of a place packed with photos and drawings of her beloved Winston. After a while I found what I wanted.

I then went to V's room and searched through her Japanese cosmetics box. I knew the geography pretty well and I was in luck – a fat pack of Harold's rubbers made in the USA.

Half an hour later V came into view, crossing the gravel yard. I had a fairly shrewd idea of what must have been happening in the gym and it was ten-to-one that V would insist on leaving Lunt to mop up the tears. How beautifully she walked. Such elegance, such assurance – such style. My naked body vibrated with excitement then sank back on to the divan sofa, quivering beneath its risen masthead.

V stared at me.

I said, 'I've been good, haven't I?'

She nodded gently and took a further step towards me.

I said, 'Just once. Before they take you away. Just once – I beg you, just once. I've loved you, haven't I?'

She was within reach now but I didn't touch her. My clenched hand opened and slid the rubber on. V's eyes widened further and her lips parted. 'It won't take a minute,' I whispered. 'You're the only person I've ever loved.'

Her eyes filled with tears. She lifted (I'm sure she did) her skirt with the graceful motion of women about to bend the knee in courtesy and curtsy. Historians may dispute V's exact motion, or its portent, at the moment Nancy Lunt barged in, as usual, without knocking. There are no Cabinet Papers on this and no Thirty Year Rule, but Lunt's long howl (like a vixen caught in a trap – 'Oh, Nicky!') and my sister's most private garment in my hand were evidence enough.

V managed to bundle Nancy out of her room and lock the door before Miss Murdoch emerged, fuming, into the corridor.

SIXTEEN

Dr Simon Yardley still carried traces of a Brum accent like fur on his tongue. An Audi or two sat outside his Harley Street clinic and he had the resigned, faintly amused, air of a man with an expensive wife borrowed from the shelf above his own. Yardley wasn't shy of publicity either; a leading light in the British Medical Association, and a Senior Consultant Pathologist, he'd recently spread himself across television and radio to slag the 'criminal decimation and dismemberment' of the NHS by a Government which he called 'the most retrogressive since the War'.

Quite a character but he let me smoke in his consulting room – I can't think, let alone take shorthand, unless I smoke. I smoke while eating and I smoke in the shower.

'So you knew Parsons during the war?'

I nodded. 'I even kissed his sister on VE Day. She was a peach.'

Yardley was flapping casually through the John Ford file I'd sent him. 'Interesting that Parsons should insist on a point regarded as unproven by most of Byron's biographers – that he had sex with his half-sister Augusta.'

'Just as Jupiter lay with his sister Juno, by Jove,' I added in my version of Greendale Avenue.

'Interesting,' said Yardley (again), 'that Ford, otherwise employed as our Home Secretary, should congratulate Caligula on having slept with all three of his sisters.' He snorted incredulously and slapped the papers in his hand: 'She can't know that Parsons wrote all this!'

'She won't be pleased.'

He gave me an ugly Midlands stare. 'Why haven't you published the fact?'

'No point in throwing a single stone at a bloke in armour.'

'Hm. Interesting[!] that Sir James Frazer assumed that the legal prohibition on incest indicated a natural instinct in favour of it. Freud pursued the same line in *Moses and Monotheism*.'

I nodded respectfully and mentioned a former patient of his, Miss Veronica King, whom he'd treated in a Wiltshire nursing home, and also a certain Dr Albert Harting, now resident in the German Democratic Republic.

'We're off the record,' Yardley said, or warned.

'Agreed.'

'In the end, but only when cornered, Parsons did admit to me that he'd had her. But he always insisted they were cousins. Couldn't break the bugger on that. Harting told me they had the same father. According to his version, Veronica had always known this, but Parsons himself had been misled by both his parents.'

I may have looked worried because Yardley hastened to reassure me: 'Veronica told the little bugger the truth after his mother was killed. In the nursing home she always referred to him as "my brother". She'd lost part of her mind, of course, but not all of it. She was transparently honest – so was Harting.'

'You said that Parsons admitted the affair when "cornered"?'

'Yes. He changed his story when he discovered that I knew about her overdose and the police report. They'd shared a bedroom, you see, in the Prince of Wales Hotel, Llanfairfechan. You didn't know that? Glad to be of some help to the Fourth Estate.'

'Why?'

'Why what?'

'I was born in a slum. My readers play Bingo and smash up football terraces and spread litter through city centres.'

'But you're not our national problem, though you might like to be.' He said it as if I'd just failed the Mercia Examination Board Matriculation. 'The rot lies in the new class,' he went on. 'Not the socialist model, as explained by Orwell, Burnham and

Djilas. The rot lies somewhere between sitting room and drawing room, between leasehold and freehold: if Britannia had paid her military caste better . . .'

'So what's the diagnosis, Doctor?'

'For incest, chum? I'm fucked if I know. What I do know is that he destroyed, yes wilfully destroyed, a very nice young woman. Have you met Bracewell?'

'Who's he?'

'She. She might be the eyewitness you're looking for.'

He scribbled 'Dr Kate Bracewell' and the name of a London teaching hospital on the back of a prescription form. For an awful moment I thought he was writing out a bill. He must have read my thoughts again for he offered me a real Brum grin at the consulting room door: 'No charge today.'

As Dr Yardley had commented, with the air of a don reaching for the port, 'This wouldn't be the first private scandal to rock the present ship of state.'

True enough!

I was still working at the *Mirror* when last instructed to put my infamous boot in a famous door.

'You disgust me,' the lady had snarled, 'I wouldn't discuss anything with you.'

Such venom! I'd merely asked if she was pregnant by a Cabinet Minister! 'You disgust me.' And why?

At that moment she was still hoping that her lover would divorce his wife and marry her.

But when he didn't there was no limit to the publicity she sought (in the unpopular press, of course) to bring him down.

You can't win!

Take a wedding photo, put it on the front page, who objects? Catch the same couple three years later leaving the divorce court and you're 'the gutter press'.

Later we made an offer for an exclusive photo of mother and child.

Heavens! What a disgusting proposition! 'Sell ourselves? – never!'

Well, never is a long time in the life of a jilted mistress.

Next morning you discover that the competition has won a five thousand pound contract to take the same photo. Naturally we retaliate with a story accusing her of exploiting her baby.

'Her pleas for privacy will no longer gain her popular support now that she has made her child public property.' So who can look God in the eye at the end of the day?

Tory Central Office launched a whispering campaign ... she'd got herself pregnant on purpose because the affair was petering out ... she'd blackmailed him into proposing under duress – and more.

Talk about dirty tricks.

But I had to agree. I mean if she'd really loved the sod she'd have had an abortion. You can bet it was no accident.

Women use their bodies that way. It gives young working-class girls without education or prospects a minimum social status, a claim to attention. An educated woman in her thirties may play the same game.

Mind you, her Ministerial lover boy is as slimy as a bar of wet soap. Taste of honey and lemon. In the middle of his catfish mouth there appears to be another mouth which does the speaking. He gives a huge interview to a Tory Sunday newspaper editor, in the course of which his own voice is conveniently ventriloquized into that of 'friends' and 'colleagues' – straight deception. Whatever the purpose – purposes, old boy, are libellous – the effect was to damage the reputation of the woman and spread misinformation about their past relationship. I didn't say disinformation.

Oh boy: if only she'd run as an Independent Conservative in the bastard's own constituency, taken him on at the hustings, 'Are you the father of my child and did you promise to marry me?' – oh boy what a story that.

Not a single camera crew would have surfaced in any of the other 649 constituencies throughout the campaign. I do not claim – none of the various Bert Frames has ever claimed – to be anybody's peach melba.

* * *

What do they know about me? Better: what is there to know? (You tell me.) Already they're using the lobby system against me. 'Senior sources', 'senior Tory MPs' and 'sources close to the Cabinet' are letting it be known that I am paying off an old, very personal score. It appears that little Michael's generous mother, WVS, had aroused my rancid resentment by bringing too many second-hand clothes and toys to our Limehouse home. Then I'd been pitifully homesick (in the manner of slum children) when sent away from home under Mrs Parsons's WVS holiday scheme for orphans – so more family resentment. All that charity scorned!

Labour MPs come up to me in the corridors genuinely puzzled:

'What's it really about, Bert? For God's sake, lad, think of Palmerston Asquith Lloyd George and the six divorced members of the present Cabinet. Think of the minister whose grown-up daughter finished herself off on heroin and booze at Oxford. Half the Cabinet has children on crack or heroin, Bert – all that new money chasing a good time. How can you possibly choose a target who's not only a bachelor, but an austere recluse and palpably not queer?'

I light up. 'He screwed his own sister. Screwed and ruined her.'

A dismissive smile. 'Oh, didn't we all?'

I take out my notebook. 'Can I quote you on that?'

The look I get says: Can't we base our politics on something better than squalid muckraking? But what they mean is: You may fall off your penny farthing.

The conversation drifts windward of speculation: Her mistake last time was to keep the targeted minister in his job – would She repeat the error with little Michael?

Who could forget Parsons's comment on his colleague's downfall: 'A deeply shattering event . . . I am deeply sad to see him go'?

The question put to Parsons on the Nine O'Clock News was: Had the PM been wrong to refuse the culprit's offer of resignation at the outset?

'The PM', little Michael had most sweetly rejoined, 'is a

deeply loyal person to people She believes in and to causes She believes in. I think She did the right thing.'

One could imagine the Michael Parsons interview on prime-time television: a sleeve on his heart rather than his heart on his sleeve.

Q: When did you first tell the Prime Minister the truth?

A: I am not prepared to discuss that.

Q: Did you tell her before or after the *Globe* made its accusations?

A: I am not prepared to discuss that.

Q: Did you offer at any time to resign?

A: I am not prepared to discuss that.

Q: Now, Mr Parsons, you claim you have been libelled in the *Globe* and other newspapers.

A: Yes.

Q: Well . . . you've been accused of sibling incest . . . which is something you wish to legalize . . . so . . .

A: Yes, but it isn't yet legal and anyone who has committed it, er . . . acted illegally. Obviously.

Q: Isn't that splitting hairs?

A: No court of law would say so. Besides, you must understand that to legalize a practice is not to legitimate it. A man may be materially damaged if accused of homosexuality, though it's lawful – he might very well lose his wife. There is no law against returning to work each afternoon incapacitated by alcohol – but, if I accused you of making a habit of it, you'd probably sue me.

He has style, I'll grant, the plain style of the elaborate mind. At least little Michael will never be heard talking of 'the downside' and 'the upside'; of 'bullish' and 'bearish'; of 'the bottom line' and 'negative growth'. He once wrote in the *Spectator*: 'Politicians turn life into clichés. The proper mission of literature is to turn clichés into life.'

SEVENTEEN

Rowley insisted on driving us to Greendale station in his Ford 10. Our trunks would follow later, courtesy of Great Western. Stung to the quick, summarily expelled, given no opportunity to defend herself, branded in shame, V carried her suitcase and her stigma out of the Staff Annexe at the very moment the coach disgorged its awful load of East End urchins. They spotted her at once – and me – raucously demanding explanations and offering coarse insinuations. Poor darling V, her excuses ('Just a day or two, I'll be back soon enough!') sounded hesitant and hollow. Nancy Lunt watched her departing darling from her window, bloated with grief, riven by V's freezing scorn, her protests of innocence dismissed more scathingly than Rowley had put aside V's own explanations.

His interview with me had been brief. 'You know Latin and you know the meaning of *in flagrante delicto*. Yes or no, Michael? and no clever speeches.'

I said no. He stated the accusation bluntly but refused to divulge his source. It could only be Murdoch or Lunt (I insisted). His pig eyes narrowed in forensic triumph. Why? What had either of them seen to make me so sure? Nothing, I replied, but Miss Murdoch had resented Veronica's beauty for years and Miss Lunt was so jealous of her engagement to Lieutenant Rascoe that she was capable of anything. Besides (I confided) I had asked Lunt to volunteer for war work in Veronica's place; her resentment was beyond reason. Squeers listened, sucking his pipe through the gaps in his yellow teeth, then called in V herself and announced that the scandal had reached such a point that he could no longer 'hold it down'. He had not only Dr Bracewell breathing down his neck but also the Labour Exchange and certain members of staff; he had been accused of moral weakness, of myopia and of opportunism – soon the Governors would intervene. He offered us both a 'clean sheet', excellent references, no stigma at all: but Go! 'Go home, go to London, you'll find war work there of your own choosing – this school can no longer accommodate you.'

Rowley hastily scribbled a list of recommended 'academic' schools in north London. V wouldn't touch it. Her revulsion was almost physical. I took it.

'You'll get your scholarship to Merton or Magdalen,' he assured me, wheezing.

I wanted my confiscated books back. 'Out of my hands,' said Rowley, showing me his swollen empty paws. 'It's entirely up to Dr Bracewell.'

(That's state medicine for you – that vast Leviathan of paternalist do-gooders. No private practitioner would assume such arrogant prerogatives. He knows who pays his fees. Very well: one day they would be made to squeal.)

We left Greendale like convicts, hustled out of the back gate. Thank God it was the holidays, with only the East End urchins to constitute a Greek chorus of furies celebrating nemesis – all those knowing, leering pairs of eyes, those monkeys of the scaffolding.

V refused to speak a word to Rowley as we waited on the station platform. She even rejected his parting handshake. Once we were alone together in the crowded train she really let her hair down. I'd never seen her in such a rage. Apparently Rowley had shown her the anonymous note he'd received, written in capital letters – another note, another accusation! Only one person (V and I agreed) could have written it – V had immediately recognised Nancy's notepaper and distinctive, thick-nibbed pen.

I glanced cautiously at our fellow-passengers.

'Can you remember what it said?' I whispered.

'Every bloody word. DEAR HEADMASTER, VERONICA KING

AND MICHAEL PARSONS OFTEN COMMIT INCEST. I HAVE JUST SEEN SUCH AN ACT IN HER ROOM, SHE DIDN'T EVEN BOTHER TO LOCK THE DOOR. I AM APPALLED AND DISGUSTED. YOU MUST TAKE IMMEDIATE ACTION OR I'LL WRITE TO THE GOVERNORS. [SIGNED] A FRIEND OF DECENCY AND GREENDALE SCHOOL.'

V had committed three of four trivial errors of memory but naturally I didn't point them out.

As for Rowley, for whom V's contempt was limitless, he had refused to bring Nancy to his study for a confrontation – some justice! Back in the Annexe a distraught, weeping Nancy had protested her complete ignorance and innocence – 'Nicky, Nicky, I would never do a thing like that, I'm not a rotter!'– and it now enraged V that she had let Nancy know what it was all about (even though Nancy, of course, had been the culprit). I very gently pointed out the illogicality of this to V but the shock and humiliation had pitched her into the wildest irra-tionality: she was 'sure' that bloody Dr Bracewell was some-how behind it; she was 'sure' Miss Murdoch had been spying on Bracewell's behalf. She was 'sure' that Rowley's arm had been twisted by that Labour Exchange woman.

'I told Nancy that she's a disgusting Lesbian and a rotter and she'd better never cross my path again. When I think what I've had to endure from that sow.'

Poor V – shaken to the core, her foundations in landslip, head spinning all the way to Waterloo. But fear not, Father, your daughter has Character. I took her hand.

'It was my fault, really.'

'No it wasn't.' She was dug in on this – I was beyond blame, it was a point of honour – her brother. The sight of the war-ravaged London suburbs did nothing to divert her. I knew that Harold was hugely on her mind but she didn't mention him.

'Don't worry, darling,' she murmured, 'I won't let you down. We'll get you into a *real* school this time.'

To save money we took buses from Waterloo to Hampstead. Depositing our cases under the stairs, we sat on the top deck so that V could smoke. Suddenly she gripped my hand with painful intensity: 'Marry me, Mike?' Her beautiful face was possessed by the most ghastly luminosity: a fever. 'Well why not, why not? We have our birth certificates . . .'

I touched her cheek. 'Accepted.'

'You'll want to marry someone clever,' she said. 'Not a dunce.'

The bus was threading up Regent Street. My attention was torn between the Bruegelian scenes below, the voyeuristic pleasures of the top deck of a bus, and the intense, burning introspection of the gorgeous person at my side.

Her mood alternated abruptly between grief and truculent defiance. 'I could sue Rowley. For defamation. Ruin him. We could have pots of money out of that bloody school, you and me. We'd buy you hundreds of books . . . and a typewriter! Wouldn't you like a Remington? And shoes – such huge man's feet you've grown.'

Islington. What a long journey. I became conscious of hunger.

'When you go to Oxford you'll need money,' she said wisely. 'You must entertain, throw grand parties on the lawns, join all the clubs, pay for your round, go to all the London theatres – cut a dash! Oh yes, darling, you must.' She turned to gaze out of the window but her mind's eye remained inner-directed. 'Harold was going to pay, he promised, but of course that's all over.'

'Over?'

She laughed bitterly. 'Don't worry. *She'll* inform him.' A pause. '*They* will.' A pause. 'Anyway, I can't . . .' She couldn't finish.

The bus was climbing Haverstock Hill.

'We're English people, you and I. This is our country. No one is going to push us around. We don't just marry anybody.'

She produced a small, half-empty bottle of Gordon's gin from her bag.

'Have a drop, darling. Go on, be a sport.'

'Not here,' I whispered. 'It's forbidden.'

Without a glance to left or right she drank from the bottle then handed it to me. 'Dare you. Show me you're a man. Can't marry you unless you're a man.'

159

I scanned our fellow passengers, put the neck of the bottle in my mouth and tilted my head back too hastily. I gagged and shuddered – it tasted like petrol. V's eyes opened very wide and her finger went to her lips: 'Our secret.'

We had to walk the last quarter-mile, I carrying both our large suitcases, V tottering, the gin bottle almost empty. When we got there it didn't look like our house at all; it had shrunk; peeled; it was begging permission to collapse. The shame it displayed at our arrival mirrored the chagrin I felt at its long neglect.

'Your mum,' V hiccupped.

'What?'

'Your mum, watching us . . . fr'm th'w'dow.'

I walked to the back of the house. The gravel path had long since vanished, overgrown with weeds. Limp, dirty grass stood shin-high. The bomb crater remained exactly as I had last seen it eighteen months earlier, plumb in the middle of Dig For Victory, except that it was now filled with brown water, floating timbers, bits of roof. V held on to my arm as we entered the sitting room, smiled insanely at the chaos, the piles of boxes, the camp beds, then closed her eyes and lifted up her chin, as if asking to be tested for 'butter' with one of the meadow buttercups of my boyhood dreams. I swept the débris from a sofa on to the floor and laid V down upon it.

'Home,' she murmured. 'Dear, darling, Mike.'

The condition of the house can be described but not conveyed. Albert and Leo had not expected us; having evaporated into phantom landlords charging a nominal rent (which was rarely paid), we had abandoned every claim to their respect and consideration. Nevertheless, my immediate reaction was one of outrage, of betrayal. Such filth and dilapidation was an insult to decency, to trust, to hospitality. The house had degenerated into a refugee camp, an animal warren. Albert had not yet returned from work when we arrived; as for Leo, he wrung his hands in a charade of helplessness as the storm clouds gathered in my face. How he had aged! His once spruce moustache, meticulously trimmed whenever my father came home, now resembled a leek withered by drought. Wringing his knotted hands, filthily dressed, the Polish officer and gentleman muttered incoherent apologies as I climbed the stairs amidst rat-like scurryings, foreign whispers of alarm, gaunt, tramp-like figures darting into the shadows (not a light bulb worked). Ghetto eyes stared out of dark corners, glazed with defiance, as I inspected each room in turn – mine, Mother's, V's – opening doors, kicking aside piles of cardboard boxes and kitbags, my hands clasped behind my back like an adjutant. Reaching the top floor I found the roof still open to the sky, nothing repaired, walls and floor saturated. Our home had been stolen from us by the detritus of occupied Europe – wretched histories, baroque tales of bereavement, pathetic pleas, a great moaning of babylonic tongues. Each refugee branded by his own cursed fate.

Pathetically they produced their soiled bits of paper, their 'documents', 'licenses', 'permits', 'references'. I didn't bother to read them. I too had lost two parents to this war. An officer knows when to listen and when not to listen.

By the time Albert returned home my temper was sharpened by acute hunger. Betraying no surprise at our arrival – V was still sheltering in sleep – his bright eyes twinkling in warm welcome behind his round boffin glasses, the German warmly embraced me.

'But why did you not write? We would have prepared a dinner party!'

I wasn't having it.

'This is no good, Albert. It won't do. It won't do at all.'

'Michael, if we had known you were coming . . .'

Leo renewed his own protestations to Albert: 'I always tell you it's a wrong thing, this. No gentleman – '

But clearly Leo had never been of any account to Albert.

'Too many guests?' Albert asked me. 'Ja, ja, too many . . . but . . .'

'But what?'

'It's difficult, Michael. So many people without homes . . .'

'I not responsible,' Leo mumbled, his moustache drooping.

161

'I thought a Polish officer is always responsible,' I snapped.

Albert laid a calming hand on my arm. 'Michael, it is me you must reproach. I believed your good mother would have wanted us to shelter these poor people.'

'This house is mine now.'

'Ja, ja, but you were not here. I am a social democrat, understand. We who have suffered unkindness must not ourselves be unkind.'

He was an appealing figure, this Jew; still young (though rapidly balding), unmarried, uprooted, very polite and always confident of his own values, his own judgment. He alone of the ten 'lodgers' I had paraded on the landing earned his living and wore a decent suit. Mother had admired him intensely – his most casual utterance was gold-plated with wisdom. I knew that either Albert would rule this house or I would; the disadvantage of my years allowed for no compromise.

'Veronica and I have returned to live here. This is our family home not a doss house or refugee camp. It's a private house, understood? Private. All these people here are unauthorized squatters. They must leave.'

'Leave?' Albert shrugged. 'Where shall they go?'

'That's not my affair.'

'This not Michael's affair,' Leo echoed me dutifully.

'The fate of Hitler's victims is everyone's affair,' Albert said. 'Your dear mother –'

'Kindly allow me to speak for my own mother.'

'But it is not her voice I hear –'

'I will not have my home collectivized! Understood? *Verstanden*? This is not the headquarters of the Popular Front. Or of the International Brigade. Good God, two of your guests have stuck a portrait of Stalin on the wall.'

'And of Churchill,' Albert said. Even now there was not a hint of repentance in him. My rage expanded.

'I thought you were supposed to supervise the repair of the roof. Look at the place – shambles, dereliction, pools of water, woodrot, filth, stink.'

'There was no money,' Albert said. 'The builders went away. Your solicitor could not release the money.'

I was discomforted, even abashed, but dared not show it.

'Tell these people they're guilty of trespass. Order them to leave immediately. Otherwise I shall call the police.'

There was a wail from our audience of vagrants: police they understood. Their heavy breathing and moaning was rank with the acquired inertia of the parasite. We were fighting a war on behalf of these wretched people but they invariably mistook kindness for weakness. Having collapsed into hopeless lethargy they had lost the will and capacity to help themselves. Creatures of charity, abject scroungers and scavengers, they blamed their fate on the world and the war. (But among every group of prisoners there are some – a few – with the will to escape. The others prefer a certain dinner to an uncertain liberty.)

The over-reaching state is the enemy. Free men determine their rights and obligations by contract. But here was mob anarchy. Legitimate authority must assert itself – not the Nazi kind, nor the Stalinist variety, and not the nanny-state of whingeing social democracy either.

A room was hastily cleared for Veronica. All our cultures converged on that small point of consensus: the lady must have her privacy. Albert was clearly disturbed by her comatose condition and wanted to know if anything had happened – and why we had returned so suddenly from Greendale, but he didn't get far with me. I snuffed out a suggestion that we call a doctor.

'All she needs is sleep and a house she can call her own.'

The following morning Albert stayed home from his hush-hush laboratory where (Mother used to tell me) the war would be won or lost. So far it had been neither. Our astute physicist at once went to work on V, appealing to her good nature, urging her to use her influence over me on behalf of the destitute refugees. One by one they came to 'the lady' to petition her with tales of persecution and flight, of tragedy and death.

'How awful,' she said, and 'you poor man' and 'I'm so sorry for you'. But she remained loyal to me and my judgment. 'It's Mike's house. He's the master now.' There was a silky, supine almost erotic quality in that 'master' which reminded me of her

163

tone on the bus from Waterloo Station. Besieged on all sides, Albert began to grow angry; he even suggested that at the age of sixteen I had no authority to decide anything. V turned on him very fast:

'And you think you have authority – here? Would you like to leave as well?'

It was V's tone which did the trick. In truth I was quite apprehensive about going to the police, imagining a stream of bureaucrats and OHMS do-gooders invading our home, listing the number of rooms, preaching J. B. Priestley, issuing lodging permits to every applicant, conscripting V on the spot, and asking what school I attended. There was always Mr Underwood, of course, but he would no doubt be receiving a letter from Rowley . . .

Within two days we had reduced Albert's contingent of squatters from eight to four. When Albert was at work I had found it possible to shout the weaker spirits out of the house, but four (two of them Germans – the bloody Germans – and all of them hard-core Bolsheviks) refused to budge. They offered to confine themselves to one room on the top floor, to help with the spring cleaning, to repair the roof free of charge – anything except leave. They talked a great deal about 'the anti-Fascist struggle' which, I gathered, was something bigger and better than a mere war against Germany, Italy and Japan.

Each evening, when Albert returned from work, the remnants of the Party cell gathered round him. There were tense discussions, mainly in German, a rebel commune on the top floor. Albert would then approach V and me, as commissar negotiator, my 'good mother' forever on his tongue.

'It surprises me,' I told him, 'that a former German national engaged in highly classified war research should keep such company. Do they pass the secrets straight to Stalin?'

In retrospect I have to be grateful for this cold war of attrition. Every altercation drew V closer to me, strengthened her loyalty, and brought me to manhood in her eyes. I dealt with one last-ditch defender, an Austrian 'poet' who claimed to be a friend of someone called Brecht, by tossing his kit bag and grimy mattress into the garden; the 'poet' snarled 'Hitler!' at me but took himself off, limping. Apparently he had a septic foot.

Albert's three remaining friends departed the following day.

EIGHTEEN

The biting medical rabbit called Yardley had been pulled from the nuclear hat of a Red physicist called Professor Albert Harting who lived, for inconvenience, in Leipzig.

A senior colleague on the *Mirror* with good contacts inside the Secret Service set me on to a retired MI5 officer who'd once been famous (not to me) for catching Reds in and under beds. Rusk by name. He seemed convinced that the country had been 'sold' the moment he retired. This being so, Rusk was happy to sell it over again, for a consideration.

I knew more about selling houses than selling countries but apparently this embittered geezer had something good on Michael Parsons. His English was such that I wasn't always sure what he was saying. Rusk insisted that his contract with MI5 had been 'arrogated without prescience'. As a result Rusk also had a right to be 'aggravated' and was therefore talking to me off the record and 'strictly presumptively'. There was to be no 'flaunting of the rules'. Was that clear?

Crystal clear. Indeed I'd adduced precisely that.

'Otherwise you'll be gambling with my patience,' Rusk warned.

This reactionary gumshoe seemed as keen to stop little Michael in his prime ministerial tracks as I was. Apparently – did I believe Rusk? – Parsons had many years ago shopped a German-born physicist called Dr Albert Harting. 'I'm not insinuating that,' Rusk explained helpfully. Little Michael had taken no initiative and even when approached he'd sought refuge in repeated professions of affection for his victim.

'The little fart took me in,' Rusk said. 'He really indulged himself. Chairman of the Oxford Conservative Association, but "loyal" to an old family friend who'd been his lodger during the war, he ran me round the block in a downright deviant manner. When he finally dropped the dirt on Harting into my lap I presumed I'd uncorked him but later I had reason to recapitulate.'

I gathered that no firm corroborating evidence had come from other sources – Harting's fellow scientists 'gave him the dry clean', reported Rusk – but it was the Klaus Fuchs era, the political dogs were barking, and Harting got booted back to East Germany (though brought up in Hamburg).

'Parsons had it in for that German and I've never discovered why.'

I said: 'Perhaps Harting knew too much about something else,' but this drew not a flicker and Rusk gave me the slow withering stare he reserved for morons. Was Harting aware, I asked, that Parsons had shopped him?

'I'd be interested to ascertain,' Rusk said, pocketing my colleague's cheque. 'Any such conjecture would be problematical, to say the least.' He limped out into Ludgate Circus in his bent trilby and Aquascutum mac, ready for anything.

What does an East German press visa have in common with spaghetti? No prizes: it doesn't grow on trees.

Here was my biggest break in years but the break resided hundreds of miles away behind Iron Curtains, Berlin Walls and – for all I knew – iron bars as well. Or dead. I thought of applying for a general visa – 'Patterns of Socialist Development in the German Democratic Republic' – and then hunting down Harting on the side, but you don't mess with the men who built the Wall, particularly if you work for a paper trading in one-line paragraphs. I applied for a research grant from my old college, Ruskin, but gathered that my professional life during the past twenty years had disappointed them. I paid a call at 23 Belgrave Square, where I knew the press attaché of the Federal Republic, posed some less-than-clumsy questions, then took the short walk to number 34, where the Democratic Republic flies a different flag. My story was the Cold War, Western Imperialism, Spy Mania; I was anxious to discover 'changing perspectives' thirty years on. Obviously scientists who had worked in Britain would be of particular interest to our readers – I mentioned Harting, Fuchs and one or two others. The DDR official kept nodding and scarcely looked at me, in both respects the opposite of what I had expected from my devoted hours with Le Carré. I didn't get a visa. Every time I telephoned my case was 'pending in Pankow'. Ten months later some considerable Comrade must have fallen out of the Politburo or the Volkspolizei because I got a call saying Dr Harting would see me. Just Harting – no other name was mentioned. It was chilling – they read your real intentions by nodding and not looking at you.

Dr Harting was living in a garden suburb of Leipzig in one of those large comfortable houses our scientists can't afford. Quite elderly but still very alert, the Comrade Professor, as he now was, spoke better English than I did, which reminded me of an old Limehouse joke about the Messerschmitt pilot who was shot down in Bethnal Green, couldn't understand a word his captors said, and politely inquired whether he was in England. There was coffee, cakes, a beautiful piano and a Frau Harting who spoke with the kind of American accent you learn at the Diabolical Language Training Institute in Moscow. When I'd got through the Cold War stuff I said:

'Dr Harting, you must be amused to have been a friend of our future Prime Minister.'

Harting looked at his wife as if for guidance. She went off to telephone Pankow or Moscow but of course I was light-years behind them. They were just being polite. I knew the proletariat but not the dictatorship of the same.

'Parsons,' I rambled on, 'is of course an ultra-right hawk in military terms. He's dead against any interim disarmament deals. We in the Labour Party regard him as extremely dangerous.'

Dr Harting looked grave, distressed, peace-loving. 'Michael was always very reactionary. Ja ja. But he was still a boy and extremely intelligent – I hoped he'd grow out of it.'

I asked whether Harting had still been in touch with Parsons at the time of his expulsion from Britain. The answer was no, but something was being held back. It seemed time to tell Harting that little Michael was largely responsible for his expulsion.

'Yes,' Harting said. 'I guessed.'

I was about to say 'Now's the time to pay him back' (the journey from London to Leipzig had been littered with bureaucratic obstructions, despite the visa, and there were no ashtrays visible in the polished Harting drawing room) but checked myself in time. Harting didn't seem like a vengeful person, merely the sort to invent a bomb designed to wipe out a whole city.

I said, 'Progressive forces in Britain would be grateful for any further information you can give us. We are all working for peace now.'

My host smiled indulgently, as if I'd just lit a birthday cake of candles for him to blow out. 'You know what they say, Mr Frame. In the Socialist countries everything matters and nothing is permitted. In the capitalist countries everything is permitted and nothing matters.'

But peace was the word I'd used and the Comrade Professor began to fill my notebook, punctuated by many sorrowful disclaimers of malice and affectionate references to little Michael's late mother, 'a very dear friend of mine, a fine woman'. I guessed this had been, broadly, little Michael's tactic with Inspector Rusk when shopping his friend Albert three and a half decades earlier. Harting conducted me through the history of the Parsons family from the time that Mrs Parsons took him in (perhaps in more senses than one? or is a Limehouse boy condemned to see the dirty side of everything?). I also learned that Group Captain Henry Parsons had not died 'in the service of his country' during the test flight of a new fighter, but had driven a staff car into a tree after a party at RAF Northolt.

'Does Michael Parsons know that?'

'His mother never told him. There were other things she didn't tell him. But he always found out – we in the DDR

169

regard him as one of the most astute figures in the present British ruling class.'

Albert Harting wept a little as he described the death of Mrs Parsons. Later, after a long absence at Greendale, Veronica King and Michael Parsons had suddenly returned home without warning or explanation. There followed the cruel expulsion of the other 'guests', all of them Harting's friends and comrades.

'Gestapo.'

'Pardon?' My pencil hovered.

He shrugged. 'Michael behaved like the Gestapo, English model.'

Even I found this a bit much but I'd had my rear end searched by too many Volkspolizei on the way to Leipzig to start asking which fucking nation began the fucking war anyway. I therefore tactfully inquired about the relationship between little Michael and Veronica King.

'That was not a political question,' he said quickly. The subject was clearly odious to him. As every hack knows, when the subject gets odious the subject gets real.

'With respect, Professor, I don't see it like that. Even a Marxist must surely agree there is such a thing as personal politics.'

He thought about this, sighed, shook his head in puzzlement. 'No, no, your categories are false.'

But his wife, who was now back from her chat with Honeker or Brezhnev or Lenin, contradicted him. 'Mr Frame is right. Speak, Albert.'

Dr H. groaned at the heavy emotional duty exacted by Customs and Excise of World Peace (had his reticence been a con?).

'They moved, the two of them, ja, into the big bed in the master bedroom. I was shocked. Shocked.'

'Albert was shocked,' added Frau Harting.

'Veronica had always known,' Harting said. 'At first I assumed that young Michael remained innocent but . . . In the end I felt compelled to explain to him – but he already knew. Already, ja?'

'Knew what?'

'Michael's mother should have told him,' Frau Harting said. 'That boy bitterly resented having been deceived by his parents, isn't that so, Albert? [Harting nodding.] It was a kind of revenge on Michael's part. I've never met him but I know him better than Albert does. Men are poor psychologists.'

The word 'revenge' lodged in my ear – was this my own driving force as I uncovered an infamy far more vile than my dirty little imagination had guiltily (and disbelievingly) concocted forty years back? Veronica King's betrayal stung as sharply as if it had occurred yesterday. We were all betrayed, we slum kids who'd surrendered our precious cynicism to adore and trust that one immaculate, beautiful paragon of English womanhood, English friendliness, and English decency. By the time I dutifully asked the Hartings how they explained Veronica King's behaviour I had passed beyond hope of an explanation.

Harting looked genuinely stricken. 'Nicht verstanden,' he said. His head bobbed on his neck like a punished punchbag.

'Guilt,' explained Mrs Harting, decisively flashing a striking Indian bracelet. 'The girl felt intense guilt on Michael's behalf, understand? She felt responsible for his predicament. But none of this will be clear until we know what happened during those two years at Greendale School. That is the key to the lock. There was some great sadness in her life, Albert.'

'Did you ever meet the American?' I asked Harting. 'The airman.'

The guarded glances exchanged between the Professor and the Frau Professor were not feigned, I'd put my life on it. In the silence that followed the whole Soviet-bloc intelligence system lost its job.

'Leo did once mention something of interest,' Harting told me cautiously. 'One day in 1944, when Veronica was in St Bartholomew's Hospital –'

'Why was she in hospital?' I cut in.

'You don't know that? Her injuries? Really, you should do your homework, Mr Frame . . .'

But Frau Harting rebuked her husband. The British ruling

class, she reminded him, was devious, machiavellian and secretive. Chastened, Harting reported how an American officer had come to the house, engaged in a long conversation with Michael – 'including some shouting by the American, ja?' – and had departed after being sick on the floor, twice.

'Only Leo was at home. Michael made Leo swear never to tell anyone.'

My notebook was filling.

'Not even Veronica?'

Frau Harting smiled at my naïvety: 'Particularly Veronica.'

I said, 'According to rumour she became engaged to an American bombardier.'

Frau Harting's expression registered acute satisfaction.

'According to Dr Yardley,' said Harting, 'Veronica tried to kill herself when she learned of this American's death.'

'Ach no,' Frau Harting said.

'Yes, Bettina, the doctor told me.'

'Ach no. That Dr Yardley never discovered the whole truth.'

'And you are wiser, dearest, you who have never set foot in England?'

She addressed herself to me: 'It is not news of death which kills our spirit, Mr Frame, but news of betrayal – or shame.'

I asked Harting to tell me more about his knowledge of brother and sister after the war.

'I was in America for some months – New Mexico. When I returned Michael had sold the house. My possessions had been deposited in a warehouse. I wrote to Michael but he didn't reply. I went to see him in Oxford. He was not friendly. He refused to speak of Veronica. He wouldn't even tell me where she was. But I found her.'

'How?'

Abbreviated, this is what Harting told me:

Shortly before his death, Leo had written to Harting. They had never been good friends – ach, politics, the Polish question – but now Leo was lonely and afraid. He told Harting that in August 1945 a letter had arrived for Veronica from the US Air Force in the Far East. He had put it in a clean envelope and sent it on to the Welsh hotel where Veronica and Michael were spending a week's holiday. Leo had never seen Veronica again but after some months, when Michael was living in Oxford, a doctor called Yardley had visited the house in Hampstead to collect certain of Veronica's possessions. Or so he said as he began to sift rapidly, methodically, through books and papers as if looking for evidence of something. Apparently he departed disappointed.

Leo would dearly have liked to visit Veronica but he was too ill to thread his way through the obscurities of the English countryside. He wrote to her but received no answer. By the time he wrote to Albert Harting he had forgotten the address of the nursing home but he remembered it was in 'Willshire'.

'Within a month Leo was dead,' Harting said. 'Michael sold the house.'

'But you managed to trace his sister?' I asked Harting.

'I did. Dr Yardley asked me many questions. He detested Michael. That doctor could smell incest but he couldn't prove it. Poor Veronica. She used to sit cross-legged on her bed, holding my hand. Sometimes she would cry. She could no longer make much sense of things. A year later I was deported from Britain.'

'This warmonger Parsons must be put down like a dog,' Frau Harting said. But the death sentence was pronounced in an oddly dispassionate way – the Communists notoriously preferred to do business with Tories, Republicans and Christian Democrats than with reformist Socialists claiming the workers' allegiance.

Presently the comrade maid announced that dinner was served.

Over dinner I absorbed the scenario (no doubt little Michael would find the foreign word, *ambiance* or whatever): the heavy shelves of books, the piano, the metal music stands, the woodcuts and lithographs on the wall, the reproduction Picasso dove of peace, the standard photo portrait of Comrade Honeker. The small red medal pinned to Harting's lapel. Whose side was I on: theirs or little Michael's? Who had killed my Dad at Dunkirk, who had bombed us into the underground? The answer wasn't difficult: Limehouse need no longer fear Leipzig. Neither they nor their ruthless Soviet masters would ever attack us again: little Michael and his Sugar Plum Fairy Queen were It, plus the cold smart tarts who lacquered culture on greed in the pages of the *Spectator*. I experienced a horrible little tenderness towards our looney Left borough councils and the pathetic vegetarian softies in anoraks who gathered every year at Burford parish church to wail over three Leveller soldiers shot three hundred years ago. I'd witnessed real thuggery among Scargill's flying pickets and during the printers' Saturday night vigils at Wapping, but so fucking what? Take away a man's livelihood and you won't get the Ten Commandments. You can choose your friends but you take your allies where you find them. Mister Churchill had taught us that lesson.

After dinner a handsome tray of liqueurs came out and Frau Harting attempted to explain little Michael to me in the light of Herr Doktors Marx and Freud. After fifteen minutes of it, mainly above my head, I concluded that for geezers of my background it was always too late, despite Corporal Braine, the WEA and Ruskin College. Little Michael would be perfectly at ease with Frau Harting's brilliant lecture and he'd murdered his own sister, like the infatuated brother in the old play, but with a shabbier kind of cold steel. In my humble opinion.

'You either hate the guts of the ruling class, Frau Harting, or you don't.'

She rebuked me in the kindest manner. 'We must not forget the objectively progressive role played by ruling circles during the Great Patriotic War.'

'Sorry – the what?'

'The Second World War,' Harting hastily corrected her.

Just one problem nagged at my sense of triumph during the journey home: Harting was attributable but how can you plausibly quote an expelled German Communist, a citizen of the DDR, against a British Tory minister? The voice in my ear was not only Charrington's ('Disinformation, my dear fellow') but also my editor's ('Red Spy's Revenge'). Rusk believed Harting had been innocent of espionage (though no Red was wholly innocent of anything) but he'd never say so on the record. When it came down to a figure as powerful as the Rt Hon Michael Parsons, every witness was either dead or off the record.

Unless he stumbled.

NINETEEN

Albert didn't speak to us for some days after the last of his Party cell had been expelled but we were happy and V celebrated by cleaning out the master bedroom and laying Mother's good green Irish linen (to my surprise our anti-Fascist refugees didn't seem to have stolen anything) across the big bed – a fine thing, with an antique headboard – once occupied by my parents.

'This is your room, Mike,' V said.

'No, yours.'

She moved from one side of the bed to the other and lit a cigarette (I have never known anyone with such innate grace of movement), then poured herself a little gin, drank, grimaced, and drank some more. I watched, enchanted; here, in our own purged home, there were no school bells, no Nancy Lunts, no arriving urchins, no headmasters, doctors, pharisees. No parents either – and the dead have no opinions. They turn in their graves like Father Christmas comes down the chimney.

V sat on the bed and said: 'When you were twelve, during the first air-raids, you wanted to climb into this bed but your mum wouldn't let you. Remember?'

'But you let me.'

Tossing her lighted cigarette out of the window, she laid her arms on my shoulders, her green-amber eyes level with my mouth.

'I might let you again.'

I kissed her eyes and presented myself at Brutus Hill

Grammar School for enrolment in the History Sixth. Rowley had written me a generous letter of reference, regretting that I had been compelled to leave Greendale by 'family circumstances'. Brilliant pupil, excellent prospects, both parents lost to the war.

I wouldn't classify Greendale as a proper public school but Brutus Hill was a clear step down the social scale. At Greendale everyone spoke with the same accent except the children of rich refugees; at Brutus Hill most of them spoke a London version of the King's English and couldn't have read the News on the BBC, but there was no idleness, no affectation, no Charringtons and no pretence that anything counted more in life than doing better than the next boy. No Rowley crap about 'mixed ability' or 'non-competitive values'. At Brutus Hill the boys wore uniforms, even in the Sixth; they kept rows of pens in the breast pockets of their crested blazers; they competed (and cribbed) furiously. I learned to respect the ambition and dedication of these sons of trade and toil.

At home I had my own study, a good desk and bookshelves on which I could have spread out my precious private collection had Dr Kate Bracewell ever returned it to me. It didn't matter now: literature is a poor substitute for the real thing. V, meanwhile, secured her position under the National Service Act by volunteering as an auxiliary in the Fire Service. Given the new danger of 'flying bombs', this filled me with alarm and I begged her to find a post in the WVS (which could be dangerous enough).

'No, that's one outfit I'm steering clear of. The WVS are responsible for the London Boys' Programme at Greendale. God knows what Rowley has told them. I don't want a lot of your mum's old hen chums snooping and spying here.'

Unanswerable. But did it have to be the Fire Service?

'Time I did my bit,' she said. Oh, she grew more and more beautiful, my sister. How could it have occurred to me that she wanted to die?

Some workmen came to fill the bomb crater in the garden and repair the roof. By night the Doodlebugs swarmed in. The first V-1 arrived in June, the first V-2 in September. The RAF got some, ack-ack knocked out others, but at least half of the V-1s made it. V was often out on duty at night and I would stand at a darkened window (though the rockets were blind and pilotless) watching the fiery tails of these pitiless creatures which piddled along, growling and spluttering, until the engine cut out. Then you held your breath as the thing fell with a ghastly roar. With the V-1s you at least had a chance to dive for cover but the V-2s came so fast that the impact preceded the sound of arrival, which resembled the rumble of a train entering a tunnel. V, who came and went in a zip-up boiler suit with wide trousers and a tin helmet, told me that the first V-2 explosions were attributed to gas mains, but as they proliferated there were jokes about flying gas mains. Once again we lived with the warble and wail of sirens.

I thought of V in the thick of falling masonry and flying glass. I had brought her to this danger; I alone was responsible. And I knew enough of the Greek playwrights to understand. She would come home at any hour, exhausted, filthy, yet manifestly exhilarated by the infernoes she had survived. It was with a horror akin to elation that she told me how she'd held the hand of a young woman on a stretcher who was in such a state of shock that she couldn't remember her own name.

The British working man, meanwhile, displayed his patriotism by going on strike. The number of working days lost to strikes during 1944 was 3.5 million, the highest figure for ten years. The coal industry was far the worst, then as now. The general view in the Brutus Hill sixth form was that every striker should be imprisoned or conscripted. I shared this sentiment but insisted on rational calculation, pointing out that coal miners could hardly be replaced by landgirls – or us – and the miners knew it. Such insights added to my reputation for political acumen; no one suspected ambition.

One night V came in after toiling for hours in a terrace of houses which had collapsed like a pack of cards after being hit by a rocket. In the house which received the direct hit the wife and children had taken refuge in the Anderson shelter at the back but died from the blast. The remaining houses had to be searched. The collapsed floors were jacked up by the civil defence workers and it was then V's role – young and agile – to squeeze through dangerous narrow apertures in the rubble and search for survivors. She found a middle-aged woman lying on a sofa, covered by fallen timbers, yet miraculously unhurt. In the next house V's torch discovered a young woman huddled over her baby; both were dead but the baby was still warm.

'She must have instinctively shielded the child from the blast but then her own body suffocated it.'

Often V arrived home in the middle of the night having walked alone for miles. She rarely came straight upstairs, she needed her gin. The official quota for spirits was one bottle per person every two months, but there were known to be considerable stocks in bond and many cases disappeared in transit. V's smile did the rest and she was rarely short of gin. Her side of the bed was the one nearer the door. You couldn't predict her mood; she might fall asleep immediately (it was a privilege to hear her breathing deepen), or lie rigid, or whisper my name. Her physical passivity in my arms felt like a decision against her nature – one sensed a powerful spring refusing to release its full energies because bespoken elsewhere. No climax on her part and none feigned, just a happy sigh for me.

In fact I'd prefer an utterly frigid woman to one who derived more pleasure from me than I from her. V wasn't frigid but the greater pleasure was always mine. I enjoyed the teasing due to a younger brother – and the granting of what did not properly belong to him. I beat against her like a bird against the hot glass of a lighthouse – but I could count on her to open the window before I broke my wings.

She always preferred darkness. In summer she would draw the blackout curtains. The seeing eye is a greater source of guilt and shame than the sensuous finger. The pressing of flesh is primal, an infant-like state of innocence, and the eyes close as a token of helpless surrender. But open the blinds, admit the day, and there can be no excuses.

> My sister's beauty being rarely fair
> Is rarely virtuous; . . .

Sated as my senses were, I began to want more – to expel the ghost of Harold from our bed. I had almost used up his rubbers but couldn't use up the man.

What Albert and Leo made of the master bedroom didn't bother us. V's unconcern was part and parcel of the almost anarchic defiance which had possessed her since our summary expulsion from Greendale. She not only drank and smoked but swore as freely as any fireman. Yet she remained herself; her extraordinary dignity, her capacity to excite devoted loyalty, the devastating flick of her skirt when the devil licked her ear. Even Leo shed twenty years when V smiled at him. In January 1945 everything froze, there was skating in the parks, V flashed across the ice with me in hopeless pursuit, and Leo fell into a new confusion of hope and despair as the Red Army finally launched its great offensive across the Vistula. When Warsaw had risen against the Germans the previous August, the Russians had not stirred and Leo had wrung his hands in anguish; now, as his country passed from Germany to Russia, his elation was shadowed by foreboding.

During December 367 people were killed and 847 injured by flying bombs. January was worse.

When I got home from school a trembling Leo broke the news. I sat paralysed while the old Polish gent tugged at his ridiculous moustache and walked in small circles of commiseration. It was Albert, returning late from his max. sec. lab., who took charge and drove me to the hospital by taxi. I didn't have the nerve to go alone.

They had operated and she was 'critical' – splinters and flying glass had been removed from her head but there might be more, lodged deeper. We weren't allowed to see her. A nurse explained that she was under morphine and on a drip. I asked whether her face had been injured. The nurse gave me a look and inquired whether I was her brother. No, I said, cousin. 'It could have been worse,' she said. Albert paid for the taxi home.

'Ach,' he sighed and briefly gripped my arm. No longer the self-assured young man who had driven Albert's comrades from the house, I now appealed to him for counsel and prognosis: 'Will she be all right, what do you think?'

He sighed again: 'Let's hope.' Then added: 'You are very close to her, eh?'

Out of my palpitating panic I clutched at the hem of a longer garment: 'When I graduate we will be married.'

'No,' he said. In the darkened taxi I could make out the firm set of his smooth features. 'No, Michael, you cannot marry Veronica.'

'You think I'm too young?'

'Ja ja,' he said but then he sighed and shook his head.

Intensely curious, my regular caution subverted by the shock of V's injuries, I pressed him for an explanation. 'Just an infatuation – is that it?'

'Michael, I should explain to you that –' He broke off and pretended to clean his glasses. 'Some other time, my young friend. This is enough for one night.'

Two letters arrived for V. One was from Nancy Lunt. I recognized the handwriting and applied steam to the envelope. Pleading her innocence and parading her broken heart, Nancy blamed everything on Miss Murdoch. 'Oh Nicky, I'm so utterly horrified that you should believe I'd ever do anything to hurt you. Please, please write to me.'

With two touches of glue I re-sealed the envelope.

The second letter was stamped '8th USAAF' and postmarked Rackheath. I re-lit the gas under the kettle.

> My darling Veronica,
> Life without word from you is scarcely bearable. I think about you day and night. Friday we came back from Hamburg on three engines. Normally your love would power the shaking ship home, pulling me through the sky, but all I felt was desolation and a diminished will to survive. The one letter I've received from you extinguished the great light of my life. You assure me that it's nothing I have done, only something you have done. What can this mean? What am I to believe? Why did you leave Greendale?

My bewildered mind travels in two directions. In a moment of loneliness you were unfaithful. Your sense of honor took over. You say you would return my engagement ring if you could entrust so valuable an object to the Royal Mail. Why return it? There is nothing to forgive. Many women wouldn't say a word. Please do not allow your shining honesty to kill our happiness.

Or you have fallen in love with someone else? But that simply does not figure. You would surely tell me, wouldn't you?

A third possibility simply won't go away. Not long ago Mike wrote me a letter. It was 'in confidence' and I replied in the same spirit, providing him with some facts and assurances about myself. My letter went unacknowledged. The nature of Mike's letter was such that I cannot bury the suspicion that he has indicted me in a court which allows no defense.

In an earlier letter you told me that Mike had been 'unwell' and had been to see a hospital doctor. You didn't elaborate and I've heard no more about it. I simply ask: has this got something to do with it?

Veronica my darling, you are so good and beautiful, there is no woman on earth your equal. You are the sun and the stars to me. If you love another, may he be worthy of you. Please write me. I can take the truth whatever it is. What I can't take is not knowing and not understanding.

Your sad and bewildered fiancé,
Harold Rascoe.

V hadn't mentioned that she had written to Harold, indeed his name had not passed her lips since we left Greendale, but I could divine her fears. Whoever had denounced her to Rowley, falsely claiming to have witnessed V *in flagrante delicto*, was indubitably inspired by a hatred so malign that it would inevitably extend its work of destruction to Harold as well. V may well have wrestled with draft after draft of tortuous explanation, to discover that she could clear her own name only by compromising mine. It was beyond her nature to do that; neither could she bring herself brazenly to lie her way to safety. Too late: the trial had caused the crime.

Not difficult to imagine the curse lying upon her shredded letters to Harold, the same curse that had branded Annabella when the Friar discovered her relationship with Giovanni:

> Ay, you are wretched, miserably wretched,
> Almost condemned alive.

The Friar had offered her a special hell:

> There stands those wretched things
> Who have dreamed out whole years in lawless sheets
> And secret incests, cursing one another.
> Then you will wish each kiss your brother gave
> Had been a dagger's point.

V underwent a second operation to extract metal splinters buried in her skull. Her head was wrapped in iodine-stained bandages but her face had suffered only minor scars and the nurses instructed me to be cheerful. (Apparently my long face was an offence, as if I were undervaluing their efforts.) V was in pain but she never complained. She did once ask whether Harold had written. I said no.

Harold wrote again.

> My darling Veronica,
> No reply to my last letter. I cannot believe that you, of all people, could be so callous and cruel. No, I cannot. Something's wrong. You're in trouble and refuse to shout for help, I'm sure of it. I have to get to the bottom of this, it's driving me mad, and the only way is to come and see you. I must talk to you.
> I've been granted a 48-hour pass next weekend. Expect me on Saturday. If this nightmare is dispelled and all the misunderstandings cleared up and our love restored, then we will have the Sunday together as a feast of happiness.
> Darling, I want you to know that I have been posted to XXI Bomber Command, 20th Air Force (General Nathan F. Twining). I leave for the Pacific in three weeks' time. In the circumstances I would like us to be married before I go. Or is this a case of the beggar asking for the crown?

I do beg one thing – that you be at home next Saturday, even if it is destined to be our last meeting. I love you with my whole heart and soul, my wonderful Veronica.

Your devoted, adoring

Harold Rascoe.

I had been expecting this but it nevertheless threw me into turmoil. If Harold got to V's bedside that would be that. A wedding in hospital, straight out of Ealing Studios, why not? It requires only the intervention of Fate in the guise of disaster to heal a lovers' quarrel – I had seen a Hollywood film in which a couple on the verge of divorce were reunited by a San Francisco earthquake which buried their children under a building. (The children were OK.) Marriage was the inevitable sacrament for a young woman who had escaped death by a hair's breadth of brain tissue. There would be Instant Baby before Harold's departure (which was probably a con anyway) and after that it wouldn't matter whether the Japanese fighters had more luck than the Luftwaffe. I could feel Harold's manly hand pumping mine on departure: 'Take care of her for me, Mike.' (Heavenly strings wailing behind the clouds.)

During the following week I went to Brutus Hill every day but my concentration kept lapsing. The eyes that studied Cassius's Tiber-side tirade against Caesar – 'and this man is now become a god!' – were glassy with introspection. No doubt there were three main causes of the English Civil War (always three causes) but ten or none would have suited my mood just as well. My head crawled with feverish schemes.

One minor blessing: Albert worked on Saturdays. After all, Mother, he's just about to win the war. I told Leo that I was expecting a 'confidential' visitor and would be glad not to be disturbed; which meant 'stay in your room'. Leo 'understood' at once (among gentlemen) and almost saluted. Of course I prayed that Harold would not come but there he was, larger (as they say) than life, resplendent in olive-green, his cap crowned with an eagle and many gifts under his arm. Whatever his own misgivings, he bravely concealed them, smiling broadly and thrusting out his hand as I opened the front door, feigning mute astonishment.

'Good Lord!'

'Weren't you expecting me, Mike?'

'Well – no. How are you?'

His handsome features clouded: all the bad weather and Megs of his own fears raced in to dull his rustproof smile. As I led him into the sitting room, he glanced around warily, feeling the silence of the large, shabby house, then planted his feet wide, as if claiming territory, and jangled the coins in his trouser pockets.

'Well, Mike, you've shot up.'

'Won't you sit down?'

'You weren't expecting me?' he repeated.

'No. But you're very welcome, of course.'

'Veronica must have gotten my letters?'

'She didn't say anything.'

'Well where is she?'

'She's out on fire duty.'

'*Fire* duty!' (I nodded.) 'But that's helluva dangerous work!' (For a moment he sounded like the teamster's son from Lansing, Michigan.) 'I mean it's crazy with all those V-1s coming down.' Still declining to sit down, he jangled his coins. 'You didn't give Veronica any of that stuff I got from you?'

'No.' I shuddered. 'You must accept my apologies, Harold. My ear was poisoned by two of your 8th Air Force friends in Greendale.'

'And you say she didn't mention I was coming to town today?'

'No.'

'Does the postal service operate in this neck of the woods?'

'I think so, yes.'

He sighed and sank into a chair. 'She must have had my letters!' He kicked his heel on the carpet. 'Will she be back soon?'

'One never knows. She went out only an hour ago, Sometimes she's gone for twenty-four hours. Depends on the "weather".'

'I've been posted to the Pacific,' he said.

'Really?'

'The big bomber war is now in the Pacific, Mike. That's the 20th USAAF, General Nathan F. Twining. A great commander, believe me. He's the best and deserves the best. We now have the long-range B29s, the Supers, hitting Japan from the Pacific islands. I'll be joining XXI Bomber Command on the Marianas. Do you know where they are?' I shook my head. 'Got an atlas?'

One had to admire the man's spirit. All this was for V's ear and his heart must have been in his boots. A sweet odour of hair oil and after-shave emanated from my companion as we bent over the atlas, his neatly trimmed finger nails indicating Okinawa, 350 miles south of Japan and still under enemy occupation, then Iwo Jima, also in Japanese hands.

'That's the fighter screen we have to get through on the way in to Tokyo and Osaka. It's tough. Then they hit you again on the way home. Anyway, that's where they want Captain Harold Rascoe.'

He grinned and tapped his shoulder where a grey square was now sewn to the epaulette, with a single stripe of white running smartly through it. I congratulated him.

'So now you believe I really fly airplanes?'

We closed the atlas. Harold sank back in his chair, morose.

'So what the hell has *happened*, Mike? Why did you and Veronica take off from Greendale like this?' (he snapped his fingers). 'And then Veronica writes me just one letter saying she wants to break it all off – no explanation at all. What am I supposed to believe?'

He lit a cigar, a large one. I found him an ashtray.

I said: 'It's up to Veronica to tell you.'

'Oh sure. You're just an innocent young kid, eh? It wasn't you who wrote me that ten-page indictment? Maybe she never received my letters, maybe you got there first?'

A creaking of floorboards upstairs – was Leo getting restless or curious? A visitor was a rare event and Leo's life an empty one.

'If you don't mind,' I said, 'I think we might keep our voices down.'

'OK, point taken. I mean . . . listen, Mike, if she has another guy she only has to tell me, right? I can take it.'

I nodded.

'Does she still wear my ring?'

'I . . . I'm afraid not.'

'So there *is* another guy?'

'I'll make some coffee.'

'I've brought a little Scotch whisky, Mike. Would it bother you if I opened it?'

I said: 'Keep some for Veronica.'

He checked his motion towards the pile of presents and carrier bags. 'She drinks?'

'Like a fish. She also smokes Lucky Strikes in case you've got any.' I went into the kitchen to make coffee and find a tumbler, Harold following. 'Sorry no ice.'

I pointed out the spot where the bomb had fallen.

'My mother was standing right here.'

Harold softened a bit. 'Terrible, terrible.' He carried the tumbler into the sitting room, poured himself a thick one, then returned with more than a hint of the old Rascoe swagger.

'Want to see the house?' I asked.

The house wasn't what he'd come to see but time was on his hands and he said why not. I explained about the lodgers, then showed him my study. 'Quite a den,' Harold commented. 'So where are you in school now?' This having been explained, I conducted him to the master bedroom. 'You'll have to forgive the mess,' I said, and indeed the bed was unmade, with several of V's garments (carefully) strewn across it, a nightdress, stockings, a pair of knickers. Harold stood on the threshhold, awed by the footprints of his beloved; he inhaled as if to soak in her scent, her expended breath, the lingering aroma of her love. But even without his Norden a bombardier's eyes look twice and there on the bed, on a chair, on a chest of drawers – Jesus! – was a used shirt, a pair of grey trousers, a bar of shaving soap, a pair of size ten shoes.

'I don't get it,' he said.

I nodded. 'Sorry. It was the only way I could tell you.'

I made for the stairs but the grip on my arm was firm.

'Just spill the beans, Mike.'

I gave this the silence it deserved. Harold could live with the Luftwaffe but not with silence. His grip slackened and we went downstairs. He poured himself another thick one.

'So what's it all about?'

I said: 'They punish the messenger – by tradition. On this occasion the messenger is also part of the message.'

'Aha.' (Warily.)

'Do you know the work of John Ford?'

'The movie director?'

'The Jacobean playwright.'

'No, but I still insist I went to Harvard. Could we come to the point?'

'Veronica and I were expelled from Greendale.'

Harold refilled his glass, thicker this time.

'*Both* of you?'

'Yes, both. For the same offence. You can find it in one of Ford's plays.'

'What offence?' Harold asked quietly.

'That of kith and kin.'

'Don't be smart with me!' Harold bellowed. Again I heard Leo shuffling about upstairs. 'Jesus wept! This country! Oh, you're a cute kid Mike. A few years older and you'd have won this war single-handed. Maybe we need a Goebbels over here. What is this – the Old World's revenge on the New? We have candy bars and Cadillacs but you have culture and decadence? We have a John Ford but you have a better John Ford?'

His gaze was now glassy and unfocused. A cigar butt lay dead in the ashtray beside the smouldering end of a Lucky Strike. The whisky bottle had a hole in it. Harold kicked petulantly at the pile of elegantly wrapped gifts on the floor.

'Are you kidding? Veronica and *you*?'

'The worst offence, of course, is to be found out.'

'Shit. Fuck you, sonny boy. I could break your neck. I might too.'

The door inched open. Leo's moustache followed by Leo. He

studied the scene, picked out the American officer's epaulettes, then observed the American officer vomit on the carpet. Leo looked puzzled: officer – gentleman – vomit – bounder: war.

'Everything all right, Michael? I hear some commotions.'

'My guest is just leaving, Leo.'

Harold took in Leo, read him, then straightened himself.

'I'll clean that up,' he said. He took a couple of steps towards the door and was sick again. 'On second thoughts, sonny, it's all yours.'

The sirens were wailing as Harold walked unsteadily across the overgrown lawn to the garden gate, grimly clutching his presents. A Doodlebug passed overhead, spluttering, then cut out, but Harold didn't look up or check his stride.

Before Albert came home I had a word with Leo.

'This is in confidence, Leo. Between gentlemen, yes?' My Polish friend stiffened and brought his heels together in acceptance of my authority. 'That man – ' I said.

'The American?'

'Yes, yes, the American. He's a cad.'

'Of course, I see that. No officer in Poland – '

'He made Veronica very unhappy. Took advantage of her.'

'I see that. In the old days – '

'Never mention his visit to anyone. Not to Albert – '

'Albert! Of course not!'

'Not to Veronica either. For her sake. Never. On your word of honour.'

He bowed. When I offered him the remains of Harold's whisky, his eyes glowed with gratitude. I went back downstairs and renewed my struggle with the two stained patches on the carpet. Mother had once said that salt is the thing for wine stains but she'd proffered no advice on the right condiment for USAAF vomit.

TWENTY

The window of Sir Christopher Charrington's chambers in the Temple may provide a view of the boundary line between the Cities of London and Westminster but I didn't look. I had long since forgotten who I was or why so many versions of myself were available. The illustrious QC had agreed to an interview after surprisingly little delay, the formula agreed being 'unattributable background material for a profile of a potential Prime Minister'. Pointing me to a chair and apologizing, very graciously I thought, for nothing in particular, Sir Christopher poured the sherry and explained his dilemma:

'Close friends may be the best sources, Mr Frame, but the best sources may cease to be close friends.'

Charrington knew who he was. So did little Michael.

I asked him whether he'd consulted Parsons himself before agreeing to see me. This was a blunder on my part and bad weather came up on the distinguished barrister's serene countenance. (They say he earns too much to accept a position on the bench.)

'I'm not his spokesman or press officer,' said Sir Christopher. 'But we are close friends since Oxford days and Michael is godfather to my eldest son, Jeremy.' Charrington picked up a copy of the *Spectator* from his desk and asked his secretary to photocopy an article for me.

'Shall we begin at Oxford, then, immediately after the war?'

I said fine.

'As soon as Michael was elected Secretary (later Chairman) of the University Conservative Association, his articles gained acceptance in *The Times* and the *Daily Telegraph*. He also began to write occasional pieces for *Tory Challenge* and established useful contacts in the Young Conservative department at Central Office. When the Party Chairman, Lord ('Uncle Fred') Woolton, appealed for a million new members, we launched a brilliant recruiting drive and got them within three months. Michael's contribution earned him a special commendation from Uncle Fred. If my memory serves, Michael also attended weekend courses at Swinton College, near Ripon in Yorkshire.'

'What kind of a Tory was he – at that time?'

'Well . . . my own hero was Anthony Eden. I was mainly interested in maintaining our position in the world, you see. The social question didn't much preoccupy me. With Michael it was always paramount. He was looking for a Peel or a Disraeli. What he found never quite suited him: R.A. Butler.'

Charrington passed rather rapidly over Parsons's National Service. Having himself served with a posh infantry regiment in Malaya, maybe he felt little Michael had slithered out of his gentlemanly obligations. Anyway, we shot through those two years in a couple of sentences.

'I was in Korea,' I said.

'*Were* you? After his military service Michael joined the *Financial Times*, where he soon gained a reputation as an extremely able political and economic analyst. Discussions among the young staff of graduates took place in the downstairs canteen. Logical positivism was in vogue; propositions were not "meaningful" unless they could theoretically be disproved. The central question for my generation was the relative decline of the British economy. Leading politicians were entertained at lively dinner parties and cross-examined on strategies for achieving economic growth without chronic inflation. Few passed the test.'

(I noticed that Charrington spoke of his generation as if I were not part of it. By 'generation' he apparently meant one per cent of it – the genocidal generation.)

'My view is that Michael was influential in moving his young colleagues from a neo-Keynesian to a neo-classical position – I say "neo" because he insisted on the desirability of floating exchange rates and the deregulation of currency movements. This may be the orthodoxy today but at that time, I assure you, Michael was regarded as something of an extremist – though not in manner, of course. Michael has never displayed the impatience and even contempt a clever man must feel for those who resist his arguments but cannot refute them. That, by the way, is one reason why he has so few enemies in the Party?'

'Where are his friends – other than yourself?'

Charrington thought about this. 'He may not need friends. However well one knows him – and I may flatter myself in this regard – there is always a fine barrier of muslin, a kind of filter.'

'To be blunt, sir, he's secretive?' The 'sir' escaped like a mistake in an ammunition depot, leaving a mess behind. But Charrington shrugged off the question and continued with his admiring account of the rise and rise of Michael Parsons. Was it possible he didn't know his friend's squalid secret?

'In 1953 he was accepted on Central Office's list of approved parliamentary candidates, along with seven hundred others hunting for a constituency, preferably a safe one. Michael didn't have much money at that time but money wasn't really a problem since the Conservative Constituency Associations now paid a candidate's full election expenses and his agent's fee.

'He began to appear before constituency selection commit-tees; normally there are a hundred candidates for each nomina-tion of whom about a dozen will be selected for interview, though the number varies. One talks for twenty or thirty minutes, then fields a few questions, most of them asked by the Chairman.

'Michael was still frightfully young, of course, by the stand-ards of the time, in his mid-twenties I suppose – and a bachelor. This may have been something of a drawback: as you probably know, when the shortlisted candidates come before the con-stituency's executive council, the candidates' wives are expected to prove their sociability and "vicar's wife" spirit. Michael himself sensed a muted message: when you're old enough to marry, my boy, you may be old enough to become an MP.'

'But he showed no sign of marrying,' I interjected. 'No girl friends?'

'He wasn't queer, if that's what you have in mind. Rather shy, perhaps. I never doubted he would bag a constituency if he persevered. His *curriculum vitae* was excellent. Father: Wing Commander decorated for gallantry, died for his country. Mother: well remembered for her services to the WVS. Michael himself, Chairman of the Oxford Young Conservatives, an officer of the Oxford Union, a first-class honours degree, excellent references from the head of his college, his tutors and from his CO in the army. His employers at the *Financial Times* gallantly affirmed that "we wish him luck in his application but would be sorry to lose his services". 'Charrington chuckled to himself. 'I remember him once quoting some Jacobean lines:

> How did the university applaud
> Thy government, behaviour, learning, speech,
> Sweetness and all that could make up a man!'

'I take it "government" means self-control?' I asked.

'Yes, yes, decency generally. "Let men say, we be of good government." Henry IV, Part I.'

I asked when Parsons had quoted his Jacobean lines and where they came from.

'Long, long ago. I believe the lines are John Ford's but time plays havoc, mm.'

'You've said nothing about his school.'

'What?'

'Your list of references . . . nothing from Greendale?'

'Ah yes, I forgot. The Headmaster of Brutus Hill Grammar School . . . mm.'

In Charrington's view Michael Parsons's initial rejections by Conservative constituency associations were due, apart from the age factor, to a basic error of tactics on the part of the candidate.

'When invited to appear before the selection committees, Michael at first made the mistake of addressing them as if they were the downstairs canteen of the *Financial Times*. He talked about policy (if not about logical positivism), but these local worthies weren't interested; they were more concerned with "loyalty" to the Party leadership on some hot issue of the day. Are you loyal, dependable, solid? Will you let us down? Are you sincere, hard-working and decently ambitious? Are you too clever by half; a cold fish; are you charming but a waffler; are you tough but not ruthless? He was once asked, somewhere north of the Pennines: "You're not an intellectual, Mr Parsons?" He had long since prepared his reply: "As Stanley Baldwin said, 'an ugly name for an ugly thing'." (Actually Baldwin had been referring to the word "intelligentsia", but Michael was confident that local Tory worthies would neither know nor care.) In a sense he's not naturally cut out for politics. He derives no pleasure from pumping hands or slapping backs.'

'He's naturally cut out for what?'

'Ah. He would be the natural head of the civil service. He's really happier behind the scenes.'

'But?'

'But there are . . . shall we say . . . "urgencies" in Michael which demand a more direct kind of power. Difficult to describe. Almost as if he had scores to settle . . . Anyway, he got his Parliamentary constituency at, I believe, the fourth or fifth attempt. Bagged a Home Counties seat with a fairly safe Tory majority – recently made gilt-edged by convenient boundary changes. As you know, Michael was elected to Parliament in 1959, at the age of thirty-one.'

Charrington shrugged apologetically as if to say: Of course you know all this. Was he as innocent of my intentions as he seemed? Did his radar not pick up my bloodshot Limehouse eye?

'In 1962 Harold Macmillan sacked seven of his Cabinet in a night of the long knives following by-election reversals; as a leading Liberal put it, "Greater love hath no man than this, that he lay down his friends for his life." In the subsequent reshuffle Michael got his first junior post – an astonishingly rapid promotion. In private, I remember, he expressed his growing disenchantment not only with Macmillan himself but also with Rab Butler and the whole consensus doctrine known as "Butskellism". He was convinced – I wasn't – that the new National Economic Development Council and National

Incomes Commission would fail in their objective – to buy off the trade unions. The unions could not be bought off, only broken. Michael was, as usual, right.'

'Right?'

'He understood before most of us that, if you smash Socialist institutions and conventions, you leave the Labour Party naked.' Charrington lowered his gaze politely as if my privates were showing through trousers half a century old.

Charrington then recalled how, in 1963, the Conservative Party grandees staged their usual coup d'état from above, putting Lord Home in the saddle. Michael Parsons, having lost faith in Rab Butler, left the Government with Iain Macleod, who became editor of the *Spectator* –

' – to which Parsons himself has been a consistent contributor.'

'Yes.'

'Under his own name?'

The Queen's Counsel stared at me evenly. (Had I snarled?)

'Why yes. At least I'm not aware of any pseudonym.'

Charrington then described how, following Labour's victory in 1964, Parsons had backed Edward Heath in the consequent Tory leadership contest.

'Heath reminded him somewhat of his hero Sir Robert Peel – remote, brisk, cold, modern-minded, efficient. Michael liked to quote Daniel O'Connell's description of Peel: "His smile was like the silver on the lid of a coffin." But whose coffin? I sensed at the time that Michael recognized in Ted Heath a kindred spirit; both bachelors, similar social backgrounds, both "Peelites" – and "so much buttoned-up loneliness, then sudden bursts of temper, like fits of coughing".'

'These were Mr Parsons's words about Mr Heath?'

'I wouldn't want to be quoted on that. I think he was also applying them to himself – though his own temper is a pretty even one, in my experience. His angers lie below the surface.'

In January 1970 Parsons had taken part in the Selsdon Park meeting of the Shadow Cabinet, a publicity exercise to promote Tory policies on tax cuts, competition, more selectivity in welfare benefits, and law and order.

'We won the election that summer but the anticipated Cabinet job didn't materialize – he was quite upset and asked me what he'd done wrong. His compensation was a leading role in the Think Tank preparing the Industrial Relations bill.'

'A major fiasco.'

'If you say so.' (Charrington's sardonic glance reminded me that I was here to ask questions not to pass judgments.) 'Later Ted gave him a junior post in the Foreign Office. It was after our two defeats in 1974 that the deep split in the Party became visible. Michael was on the platform at Preston when Keith Joseph delivered the first of his eloquent speeches reversing the post-war consensus. Michael shared Sir Keith's view of inflation as a self-inflicted wound caused by expanding aggregate demand through deficit financing. Nothing would come right until Governments got the money supply right.

'I admit I urged him to be cautious. He said: "You lose your teeth if you don't use them." He also said something else which I found revealing – not least because we were at school together. Michael told me that when he was a boy the smoke from the camp fire always seemed to blow in his direction – regardless of where he positioned himself. He came to the conclusion that this wouldn't matter provided he was the one making the fire.'

I wrote this in my notebook.

'Unattributable,' murmured Charrington, stretching his long, cross-country runner's legs beneath their pin-stripe trousers.

As Charrington recalled, by 1975 Heath had lost three elections out of the last four.

'The Tory Party doesn't believe in failure. Michael deserted Ted and embraced – for want of a better word – Margaret.'

'A real marriage of minds, I hear. When you consider how many heads have rolled since seventy-nine, anyone who has lasted the course must be part of the course.'

Charrington was again unhappy with my intervention. 'If you say so, Mr Frame. Mm.'

I coaxed him back to history.

'To begin with She operated through the Cabinet committee system, with the Cabinet office taking the minutes, but these formal committees were soon downgraded, yielding to small, informal ad hoc groups dominated by Her close confidantes. Those not on the inside track, including some ministers, increasingly felt they didn't know what was going on. Morale was not improved when some of them learned, on the bush telegraph, that they were "wet". Michael said it was the French Revolution in reverse.'

'He doesn't always keep his trap shut, then?'

'Discreet indiscretion. His wit is a natural faculty but he knows where and when to deploy it – at the clubs, private gatherings, that sort of thing. I remember a remark of his to the Reform Group: the old adage, *Qui trop embrasse, mal étreint* ("grab all, lose all"), had, he said, finally been reversed. As French is decreasingly understood at court, such quips go unpunished. So was his remark after a Cabinet session, "We are all *arrivistes* now."'

'You'll have to translate.'

There must have been a raw wall of plebeian hostility in my throat, for Sir Christopher immediately discovered that my sherry glass was empty. Suddenly he became effusive, as if my good opinion was precious to him.

'To be perfectly frank, Mr, er, Frame, Michael has never been at ease with Her implacable zeal, Her beehive voice and honeypot hair (or the other way round, if you like), Her Home Economics, Her Victorian mythology. "Queen Victoria today defended Thatcherite values," is one of Michael's jokes. He admires Her thirst for conflict, Her Iron Lady resolution, but is less keen on Her bossy "forefinger" school of oratory, Her relentless "best clothes" look. As Michael once said, "At least Golda Meir looked like a witch."'

I laughed appreciatively and remarked that the Prime Minister seemed incapable of tolerating a normal journalistic question. Why was I going over the top to embrace this Tory shit?

'Quite incapable,' said Charrington, as if me and he were now the best friends in the world. 'She invariably tells the victim that he really ought to know better. Michael says that when the Director General of the BBC was invited to lunch he flinched every time She reached for Her handbag.'

I said: 'One day some exasperated hack is going to blow his career by inviting Her to interview Herself.'

I'd lost my way. Was this the Chelsea Flower Show or what?

'Oh, She wouldn't notice,' exclaimed the barrister merrily. 'She cuts in on everybody, including Her own ministers when She summons a dozen of 'em to appear with Her on a platform to launch a brave new initiative. As Michael remarked after one such disaster, "At least Indira Gandhi only silenced her opponents."'

And how, I asked, would Sir Christopher assess his friend's political prospects? (Seething at my own tongue-in-arsehole. His 'friend' had done his own sister, right?)

'So many contingent factors. But I've noticed of late that Michael has attracted both breeds of speculators, gossips and gamblers alike. A milky way of little stars and starlets girdles the brightening planet. He is suddenly "in the running" – though never seen to run. A possible successor though not an heir apparent.'

'I suppose he feels some gratitude?'

'To Herself, you mean? Michael regards gratitude as a dangerous sentiment. He once told me how he was about to climb the short flight of steps from St James's Square to the London Library when he realized that the man ahead of him was courteously holding the door open until he arrived. Michael naturally bounded up the steps, slipped, and tore something in his leg. He later remarked that his own misguided gratitude cost the other man far more lost time than if he'd walked up the steps in the normal way.'

'How would you place Parsons – the wet end of the drys or the dry end of the wets?' (Choking on my own gentility, playing posh with this piece of asparagus.)

Charrington laughed out of polite deference to my wit.

'In senior common rooms it's well known that Michael has privately opposed some of the cuts but it's also understood that for departmental reasons his hands are tied. Open rebellion would serve no purpose. In the meantime he prudently steers clear of Black Book seminars at Peterhouse or invitations to write for the *Salisbury Review*. Safer to stick close to Her own favoured think tanks; it's always a pleasant promenade from Westminster down Birdcage Walk to the Centre for Policy Studies in Wilfred Street or past the Abbey and New Scotland Yard to the Adam Smith Institute in Abbey Orchard Street.'

'I wouldn't know,' I said, sour as a cider apple, then asked whether Parsons was distrusted by the radical extremists. Charrington re-crossed his long legs.

'Of course there are some sharp exchanges. Even Michael is regarded as wet by bright-eyed doctrinaires, pure disciples of Hayek or Friedman, who want to go the whole hog according to the pitiless logic of monetarist marketeering. Some of them never read anything more human than computer print-outs. Their culture is pure daisy wheel and dot-matrix. When Michael explains that the greatness of Disraeli is mirrored in Dickens's *Hard Times*, their eyes are like frosted glass. When Michael explains that you can't properly understand *1984* without also reading *The Road to Wigan Pier*, they write him off.'

Gently Charrington cleared his throat of heresy.

'I wouldn't want to be misunderstood, Mr Frame. All sections of the Tory Party share the same basic goal: not to allow the other side to regain the intellectual initiative they squandered in the reckless street rioting and university occupations of sixty-eight. Never again to allow trade union barons to hold the country to ransom. To create a society where livelihoods are earned – not dished out like spaghetti from a vast public pot which never cools.'

Swallowing this poison neat, I asked Charrington whether Michael Parsons was capable of galvanizing the Tory rank-and-file. His speeches to Party Conference were well received (I suggested) but scarcely provoked adulation. A two-minute ovation was just about his ceiling.

Charrington sighed a bit.

'You're absolutely right. What they still adore about the lady is Her wild stuff, the rhetorical blasts at the 'anti-racist mathematics' supposedly fostered by the Inner London Education Authority; at the kids' books tenderly depicting Dad in bed with another man. When She goes witch-hunting the wild ones pardon Her trespasses. If the Argies have learned their lesson and the Spaniards are too sensible to invade Gibraltar, She has to make do by bashing gays. Michael could never do that. I happen to know that buggery has always distressed him but two of his most prized possessions are a Hockney swimming pool and a first edition of J.R. Ackerley's *My Dog Tulip.*'

Kicking myself livid for sipping sherry and playing the game instead of sticking my boot in, I took myself to the roughest pub I knew, tattoos and bare torsos, to look for a fight and read the new 'Parsons's Pleasure' which Charrington had had photocopied from the *Spectator* to assist my education. The byline was simply 'Godfather'.

I am godfather to a friend's son, who I shall call Nicholas. He got a fair degree from Oxford but since then has holed up in the Socialist Republic of Brent doing bugger all. His father's anxious – and increasingly waspish – voice being unacceptable to Nicholas, I offered to have a go:

'Dear Nicholas,

'I do realize that you feel an understandable reluctance to be shoved into a tidy slot. If you had chosen an inspirational vocation in preference to the conventional ladders of advancement, then your father and I would, of course, have wished you luck. But your life seems to have reduced itself to a series of temporary expedients and to bumming rather unscrupulously off Social Security. If this sounds like the familiar voice of the bourgeois world, then beware of the painful moment when your friends and kindred spirits slip out of their counter-culture into regular employment. As someone who is very fond of you, I'd hate to see you a stranded spectator to this inevitable grape harvest.

'I am not urging you to cross any picket lines of the soul. But beware the "down with everything" nihilism so fashionable among educated young people today. They curse the world as if they weren't part of it; their duties are as few as their grievances are various. Sooner or later you'll find all ritual rejectionism rather dull and lifeless. It's a convenient alibi for not getting up in the morning. You have great intellectual gifts but for some time you have cultivated a flat, curtailed style of speech which suggests that you distrust man's capacity to express himself with fluency and wit. I fear that your vision of integrity is the old Roundhead one – smash the icons! This is reinforced by a recent youth culture extending back to the late James Dean and the Beats: an honest young man never completes a sentence. It's as if the daffodil, granted only a few weeks of life on this earth, decided that its bright petals were too vulgar to display. Believe me, disengagement is a kind of slow suicide.

'Obviously you have caused your father considerable anxiety. Is this deliberate? When I was a boy during the war it was always an open question whether one would ever see one's father again – "Father won't be coming home," my mother told me one day. But your generation is alienated both by *our* remembered war and by your own peace. Too much security equals boredom – and the bored soon become boring.

'"Does life have any meaning?" I once heard you ask. I'm not a religious man myself and I recognize no force, or principle, or rationality, beyond man himself. So what is man? He is partly a creature whose nature and needs are pre-determined by biology (like other animals); but he also belongs to a uniquely endowed species with a remarkable capacity for creative endeavour. "Oh yes," I can hear you say, "he is capable of destroying life on this planet either by nuclear war or by massive pollution." You're right. But you won't stop him doing so unless you crawl out of bed. (Did you ever read Kafka's *Metamorphosis* by the way?)

'What Kipling called the "Great Game" (he meant international espionage and intrigue) is really Life itself. We know this as children, instinctively, but then as young adults we wrap ourselves in the dull colours of weary moralism and we forget. We forget how to play and how to pretend. We imply, with a yawn, that nothing is worth doing unless the world is perfect. Would anything be worth doing if the world were, indeed, perfect? I imagine that in Utopia few curtains are drawn apart until mid-afternoon.

'You once spoke of journalism as a possible career. Beware! What Churchill said about the Germans might equally apply to the popular press: always at one's throat or at one's feet. I dare say each of us in politics has his own particular splinter under the nail. I knew my one as a boy; he would dig in his nose, inspect the result, then swallow it. When his ignorant mind was confused his eyes would lapse into indifference, as if taking no print of what they saw. Nowadays he never misses my press conferences; the years have given his features the leathery impassiveness of a cigar-store Indian – a face as friendly as the main door of a prison.

'Please forgive these inadequate and unsolicited thoughts. They are inspired by affection and concern. Need I add, yet again, and always more apologetically, that if you ever want a job in this world I can find you one?

With fondest regards,

Your devoted godfather.'

TWENTY-ONE

V's recovery was painfully slow. She suffered high temperatures, terrible headaches, sleepless nights and bouts of delirium. The hospital doctor prescribed phenobarbitone. The sight of her own scarred face had such a devastating effect on her morale that I removed every mirror in the house, including the small one she kept in her handbag.

But youth and a strong constitution gradually restored her. The iodine-soaked bandages came off, her shaven head began to flower, her face healed, she lay in bed listening to the Philco radio and painting her nails, I returned the mirrors. Leo would sit with her, reminiscing for hours about battles won and wars lost in Ruritania. Whenever Poland won a battle he kissed her hand. Whether he was ever tempted to break his oath of silence about Harold's visit I don't know – I once overheard him telling V that the type of Pole who emigrated to America was 'riff raff' and 'good riddance'.

Several times V asked me – always with an apologetic smile – whether there had been any letters from Harold while she was in hospital.

'I just thought you might have forgotten about them.'

'I'm sorry – nothing.'

She took my hand, eyes lowered. 'Mike, I want to see him.'

'Then write and tell him.'

'I've tried to. But every time I try to explain I –'

'Don't explain. Just say "I want to see you. Please come soon. Veronica."'

She looked radiant then downcast. 'You don't want me ever to see Harold again.'

'Whatever will make you happy.'

She wrote the letter according to my suggested formula and asked me to post it. I had a further suggestion.

'Why don't I send a telegram as well?'

'Oh darling Mike – would you?'

I chose a post office where I was not known. Harold was presumably no longer in England, but I guessed the 8th Air Force would send it on to him, they were awfully keen on care and compassion. The message read:

'Should have told you truth stop marriage impossible for reason Mike gave you stop good luck and goodbye stop Veronica.'

No reply ever came and V never inquired (such self-control). But one could read the vast, mounting grief in her beautiful eyes.

The other war didn't much divert me from my pursuit of an Oxford scholarship. Zhukov, Montgomery, Eisenhower – they had one duty: to finish Hitler before I was conscripted. Increasingly irritated by the Allied doctrine of Unconditional Surrender – more pandering to the Russians – I kept a lazy eye on the war in the Pacific. The Philippines fell in October, Okinawa not until April 1945. Heavy casualties were reported and many planes lost. I took V to the cinema when I could spare the time from my studies (she was resolved to wear a headscarf until her auburn hair was fully restored to its former glory).

So restless at night was my poor sister that I had temporarily moved into a spare room. One evening Albert came into the kitchen to cook his usual frugal meal and found me at the stove.

'Veronica is a wonderful girl,' he said. 'So brave. So strong.'

'Yes, she is.'

'I am glad, Michael, that you now have your own room.'

V's recovery was never complete. She remained dependent on phenobarbitone. It was a losing battle to keep her from mixing the barbiturate with gin. As soon as she was strong enough to go out and buy her own she became quite cunning in hiding the bottles. The results (as a hospital consultant had warned me) were appalling: screaming depression and wild accusations.

By the time the Allied armies were closing on Berlin, V was spending several hours a day making herself up. She would parade about the house in the clothes Harold had bought her, or sweep into 'dinner' wearing the white ball gown he'd given her for a New Year's Eve fling. I say 'dinner' because V's devotion to cooking and housework was now rather spasmodic – 'Tell the maid to do it,' had become one of her favourite retorts. But you could never tell, her moods were variable; she even began digging a new vegetable bed round the rubble-filled crater.

On a warm spring morning I found her pottering with bulbs and lettuce seedlings in the garden. She seemed cheerful and almost sober.

'Hullo,' she said, 'why aren't you at school?'

'Don't like school, miss. Hate school, miss. Please let me awf, miss.' I then handed her the letter.

Her face lit up. 'Oh gosh!' she cried, 'oh wonderful wonderful, oh my clever brilliant darling!' She rushed into the house to tell the news to Leo, who waved down, rather wearily, from his window on the top floor; then she came running out and embraced me again. 'A celebration! We must go on the town!' Stepping back from me, she lent seductively on one leg. 'Do Oxford gentlemen take their sisters boating on the river? Or is that reserved for clever ladies?'

'They take their beautiful cousins on the river. And to commem. balls.'

She smiled. 'Their cousins. Agreed. Shake on it.' She extended her hand. When I took it lightly she began to squeeze. It was a fraction of a second before I realized that she was deliberately carrying us both back five years, to this same garden, when my frail frame had laboured on Mother's wet clods of earth under the barrage balloons and then V had come out in her Aertex shirt to show me how it should be done and I had challenged her to a 'shake on it' and been squashed. My trousers had swollen then as I felt the cord of steel in her arm

205

and burned under the triumph in her eyes. It was rather chastening for the new Oxford scholar to experience the same sensation below decks but at least I was master now and could confine myself to a chivalrous grip of her hand until she grew tired and – yes, she did remember – sank gracefully to her knees before me.

'Oh kind sir, you may be a scholar but you are no gentleman.'

I drew her up and kissed her sweet mouth. (Was Leo watching?) It was our first such kiss since she had come out of hospital.

'A scholar must be rewarded,' I murmured.

'A scholar must wait,' she whispered. 'Does he love me?'

'Yes.'

'As much as ever?'

'Yes.'

'As a sister?'

'Yes.'

'As a mistress?'

'Yes.'

'As a wife?'

'Yes.'

She looked at the bomb crater. 'Can't grow veggies there. It wouldn't drain. Shall we take Albert and Leo to Jack's?'

'Jack's!'

'Why not?'

I was about to say: Because Jack's means Harold and it isn't Harold who has won the scholarship; because Jack's is part of the most humiliating day I can remember; because last time we went to Jack's you and Harold tried to set me up with a cheap tart – but I knew this had to be V's celebration, V's return to the world from the edge of death.

'Will we get a table?' I wondered.

'I'll ring them. I always get what I want. That's why you'll have to marry me.'

We took a taxi. V wore her white ball grown. Albert, full of nuclear euphoria (hindsight again), sported his best suit and was in the highest spirits. Only Leo, whose health was failing (we had discovered he was suffering from angina), had to make an effort to keep pace, but he was very gallant about it and wore his most rakish silk cravat. V had trimmed his hair, moustache and sideburns before we set out. Winking hugely at Albert and Leo in the taxi, she said she hoped I'd brought my scholarship letter with me because we wouldn't have to pay the bill.

'I pay,' Albert said.

'No you do not,' V said. 'It's my do for Mike.'

'It's on me,' Leo said, displaying his clubman's English.

Jack's was as crowded as ever and no different – I shuddered. She had brought us here in search of the man she loved. Every inch of floor was jammed with servicemen and their girls, the jazz was loud, audible conversation a struggle unless you shouted, nearly everyone was shouting. V told the waitress to produce the proprietor. 'He'll remember me.' After a while the identical greased-down blackmarketeer stood at our table.

'You remember me, don't you – and Lieutenant Rascoe?'

'We have so many guests, madam.'

'And you had all sorts of lovely things under the counter.'

'Everything's on the menu, madam.'

'Not for my fiancé, it wasn't. We've got plenty of money, you know. Even English people can have money.'

I had been keeping an eye on Leo throughout this exchange, but he was too far under the weather to pick up signals.

V ordered champagne. 'For my brilliant cousin.' She turned to Leo. 'Isn't he a handsome young man?'

Leo smiled faintly. 'He thinks so.'

'Will you dance with me, Leo?'

She swept him on to the floor, waited for him to lead, then subsided into what looked like a slow foxtrot although every-one else was jitterbugging or jiving (or jiggering).

'This must be a proud day for you, Michael,' Albert said. 'If only your poor, dear mother were here to enjoy it. And your father,' he added hastily, 'your brave father.'

V led a weary but happy Leo back to the table and gaily sipped more champagne.

'My fiancé brought me here,' she announced. 'A very

handsome man. He spoilt me dreadfully but I could never have enough of it.'

'Don't upset yourself,' I murmured in V's ear.

'Do I look upset?' she shouted. 'I'm having fun, aren't I?' She turned to Albert. 'You're a wise man, Albert. We can't have everything we want in life, can we? You and Leo have suffered far more than we have, far more.' And she gaily toasted this in more champagne – V drinking too much again, eyes sparkling, eyes wild, eyes roving for Harold. The food was a long time coming and I asked her to dance.

'Oh, I was *wondering* when the distinguished young scholar would ask me.'

V danced rather lazily, eyes roaming, a faint smile on her lips, occasionally glancing at me as if to confirm I was still there. Then her mood changed abruptly.

'How's Vivien Leigh?'

'I haven't been good to her.'

'Chasing other women?'

'One in particular.'

'Oh. Oh.' She drew closer. 'And pray tell me her name.'

'Her name is V.'

'That's an odd name. Is that how you've thought of me all these years? And what about that creature you insisted on dancing with here, Belinda wasn't it? Oh I haven't forgotten your little erection, was she more to your taste that this V you speak of?' She arched her back, lightly brushing her body against mine. 'I got you up this morning in the garden, didn't I? Shall I do it again, mm?'

'No.'

'No? Who shall I sleep with tonight, then? Albert? Leo?'

I whispered my passion in her ear.

'Well?' Her lips brushed mine.

'Please be kind,' I begged.

The vehemence of her reaction astonished me – an almost diabolical, Hyde-like change of chemistry.

'Kind! Ha! Haven't you got everything you want? Do you deserve kindness? Aren't you a complete bastard?'

Presently she subsided into semi good-humour but she was

drinking steadily, relentlessly, and it was the devil of a job getting her out of the place. In the end Albert paid the bill and we all lent a shoulder in carrying her out into Soho. I found a taxi in Piccadilly and managed to guide it back to the pavement outside Jack's where two refugee gentlemen were supporting a giggling young woman whose attractive physique and loud remarks turned every passing head. I took the jump seat while V sat wedged between Albert and Leo. She soon lifted her foot, placed it on my knee, and drew her long white skirt up her thigh above the knee.

'Goo'l'gs, Leo?'

'The best,' the old Pole agreed, but gallantly not looking.

'Alb't, wha'y'th'nk, eh?'

Albert took her hand. 'Dear Veronica.'

'Y're d'v'lish hands'me man, Alb't.'

'Ja?'

'Tell ... V'ron'ca ... y'r ... h'sh h'sh secr'ts.' Albert laughed in the Schleswig Holstein manner. V's mood altered. 'N'ver too late f'ra man. I'm on th'shelf, y'see. W'shedup. W'sh I wer'a man.'

'None of us would have guessed,' I said.

Her attention now focused on me. There was quite a long silence – V thinking – but her eyes were intensely mobile with mischief. Then she tugged at Albert's sleeve.

'Know s'm'th'ng, Alb't? Me an'Mike ... Mike an'I ... go'n't'g't marr ... marr ... marr'd.'

Albert's expression reminded me of an odd coincidence; on both occasions it had been in a taxi that he had received this news of our impending 'marriage', once from me, now from V – once when she lay close to death in hospital, and now when she was restored to health and beauty with her ball gown displaying her legs.

'You ... you ... g'vem'away.'

Albert didn't understand. He looked at me.

'She says she wants you to give her away at her wedding – like a father,' I explained.

Albert patted her arm. 'Ja ja.'

'I'm going to marry Mike,' V said quite clearly, with Ealing

Studios precision. She was drunk all right, but less plastered than she'd pretended. 'Wedding next month. Isn't that right, scholar and gentleman?'

I took her hand. 'Yes.'

'No.' Albert said, and once again there was an unsuspected iron shadow across his smooth features. V and I had finally forced him to take the proposition seriously.

'Wh'no'?' V demanded petulantly, drunk again, by convenience.

Perhaps he thought I was too young for marriage – and too young for Veronica. Perhaps he feared for my studies, my energies, my prospects.

'Wh'no'?' V tugged at his sleeve again.

Albert sighed. 'Because, dear Veronica . . . you are Michael's sister. Ach, you have always known this even if poor Michael does not understand.'

I said: 'Who gave you that absurd idea?'

'Your mother, Michael. After your father died. Please accept my sincere devotion to you both.' But he kept wiping his spectacles and I could see that he was quite shaken.

'Veronica and I have birth certificates – '

'Ja ja, but you don't speak from the heart, Michael. You are not surprised by what I tell you. Frankly, very frankly, this is shocking.'

'What can you prove?' I demanded.

He blinked apprehensively behind his boffin glasses. 'Just the word of a dear, honest woman.'

V laughed nastily. 'So honest that she deceived her own son? As for you, Albert, you and Mike's mother – oh, we all know about *that*.' (Not a vowel, not a syllable, was slurred.)

'I don't,' I said.

'Dear old Albert, I mean dear young Albert, he had his little time in our bed . . .'

Horrified, I searched her expression for frivolity but found only knowledge. Albert was silent and utterly miserable – proof enough! Then Leo's voice was heard:

'Albert had his time.'

I recognized Albert's present loneliness; not merely that of an exiled, on-sufferance foreigner quarrelling with two natives; but also the loneliness of the responsible, caring adult unable to curb children running wild with power and independence. When we got home Albert paid for the taxi, then hurried up to his room without a 'goodnight'. As for Leo, he faded away, murmuring.

V stretched herself across the big bed like a Hollywood siren, kicked off her shoes with a flourish, and raised both knees to display her limbs. It was the most wanton motion I'd witnessed.

'Drink,' she commanded.

I was tempted to refuse but poured her a small one.

'Cigarette,' she commanded.

I fetched her Lucky Strikes. She blew smoke in my face. 'Do Oxford men smoke?' She reached for my tie and tugged at it. I unfastened her stockings, carefully peeled them off, and stubbed out her cigarette. Could I have imagined, four years earlier, as I furtively entered the empty chamber of the absent goddess, and pilfered my way, slack-jawed, through the divine mysteries of her wardrobe with clumsy, awed fingers, that the mistress of my wretched dreams would, by a miraculous turn of fortune's wheel (not forgetting good management) – one day be mine?

She grabbed a wad of trouser. 'Such a big one,' she said, then pulled me down, forcing me on to my back and straddling me, wild-eyed, inviting a violence we'd never risked before. 'Show me what an Oxford man can do.' At last her locked-up energies broke over me; for the first and only time our two bodies merged like phials of molten glass.

Afterwards she threw her head back on the pillow like a lady pulled, too late, from the sea. A warm breeze fanned through the open window. The sky over London was silent. Poor Giovanni, I thought, too much helpless sentiment, too little administration. But V had a sixth sense for my thoughts.

'You never did send that telegram to Harold,' she murmured, 'did you?'

The war ended not a moment too soon. As the Allied armies

converged on the Elbe I was dangerously close to my eighteenth birthday and National Service. Lord Haw Haw delivered his farewell broadcast, snorting defiance: 'Es lebe Deutschland. Heil Hitler. Farewell.' Leo and I were for hanging him but Albert and V were against capital punishment. He on principle, she by instinct.

Public demonstrations of any kind were uncongenial to me but V insisted that we must join in the VE Day celebrations. I wouldn't have done it for anyone else. It rained during that May morning but the sun soon came out to salute the triumph of democracy. V, who carried a Union Jack in one hand, a Stars and Stripes in the other, and a small bottle of gin in her bag, pulled me into the crowds, linked arms with strangers, pitched into the songs as if her voice belonged to everybody, and even joined the thick mass gawping up at the balcony of Buckingham Palace as if it were one of those Central European clocks that produce gnomes on the chiming hour.

Down the Mall we drifted to Trafalgar Square, where the great British people, soon to vote Socialist, craned their necks and waved idiotically to a piece of stone crudely chiselled into the likeness of a long-dead admiral. Churchill's voice boomed over the loudspeakers, 'Advance Britannia. God save the King.' Flashy officers and their girls were pouring drink down from every available balcony.

As one of many conflicting tides carried us out of the Square towards Whitehall I felt a smart tap on my shoulder. A few minutes later, another. It was impossible to turn in the crowd (I had prudently left my wallet at home, though no doubt it would be a field-day for house burglars as well as prostitutes, pickpockets, bag snatchers) and hanging on to V was hard enough. The tapping continued, at intervals, down Whitehall towards Downing Street, something deliberate and personal like a morse code summoning me back into an unidentified corner of the past. The past was now behind me in more senses than one – and there was a mounting yattering, too, a chortling of cheeky cockney male voices. 'It's 'im I tell yer.'

Then V got tapped too. 'Miss!'

She turned into a pale, leering countenance which wore a film of stubble on its chin and projected an impudent knowingness. Its voice was three-quarters broken.

'Remember us, miss?'

V was radiant. 'Why yes, yes, it's Bert Frame . . . and Billy . . . and Eric . . .'

The urchin gang were all shouting and shoving now, competing for her attention. 'And *me*, miss . . .' She was marvellous, she remembered all their names, and they all got a victory kiss.

'Sorry yer left Greendale, miss,' said Bert Frame.

'I was sorry too, Bert. I missed you boys very much.'

'That Miss Lunt weren't a patch on yer. You's the tops, i'nt that so, lads?'

The glances shot in my direction were very different: guarded, hostile, contemptuous.

'Whyd'yer leave Greendale, miss?' Frame asked. 'You says you's comin' back, di'n't she, lads?'

'Didn't they tell you, Bert? I was conscripted.'

'Blimey! That beats it, lads, fuckin' conscripted, a piece of crumpet like 'er – no offence, miss, but why did 'ee go with yer?' He jerked a thumb in my direction.

I remembered that awful morning; the urchin bus disgorging its yelling cargo on to the gravel yard as we emerged from the Annexe, carrying our suitcases of shame. Now I lost my voice. V's voice was as posh as porcelain but she was the real thing to them, the genuine article, a sport, a friend, a real lady born to rule. She awakened their gallantry even if they'd never heard of it. But I was different and I knew it: sour, withdrawn, aloof – the kind of toff who didn't even qualify for their rasping wit. Plebeian hatred is reserved for those superior spirits whose intelligence lies quietly, forming concealed connections, not fast upon the tongue. They must detest what they cannot under-stand – it's natural – and the only breath they trust gushes continuously like an exhaust pipe.

'Why 'ee leave as well?'

(V's bare back had been turned to the window as that pale face scaled the scaffolding and thrust itself at the frosted glass between the curtains. The Sewer King had squealed – that illiterate scrawl dropped through Rowley's letterbox. Mister Roly that snob mikel Parson has it with . . . Ugh.)

V said: 'Mike came with me because we, he and I, are all that's left of our family.'

This occasioned a pause. But Bert Frame wasn't letting go; had he been literate, his reporter's notebook would have been out.

'Fam'ly? Yer bleedin' brudder yer mean.'

'Good lord, who told you that, Bert?'

'That Lunt,' he said defiantly. 'Call me a liar?' The gang leader confidently surveyed his minions. V didn't throw a single glance in my direction; she was keeping me out of it. But she didn't deny our relationship; I believe she was incapable of a direct lie.

The urchin mob of street arabs pursued us all the way to Westminster and there was no escape. I looked at Big Ben and noticed a wide fissure running the full length of it. Bert Frame grew ever bolder.

'Gimme a kiss, miss.' V offered her cheek. 'C'mawn, miss, a real 'un like 'ee gets.' (Whether V remembered the same dialogue during the grim Christmas dinner at the Rowleys' I doubt. Anyway she took Mac the Knife's rubbery slobber full on the lips without flinching; simultaneously his hand went up her dress and squeezed. Then they were gone into the crowd. V laughed at my engraved scowl.

'Bastards!' I hissed. 'Scum!'

'Don't look so glum, Mike. It wasn't only our sort that won the war.'

We drifted. Late in the evening darkness fell and there were fireworks. Wherever people were dancing the conga or engaging in other primitive rituals V forced me to join in. 'Be a good sport,' she whispered, squeezing my hand. Any sailor who wanted a kiss got one. She was quite reckless. Finally I tugged my gay (*yes*), flirtatious sister home through drunken crowds singing 'Roll out the Barrel' and 'It's a Long Way to Tipperary' – the last hurrah before the long, wintry years of reckoning.

That night she lay silent and motionless under my seething exertions.

GIOVANNI: What must we do now?
ANNABELLA: What you will.
GIOVANNI: Come then . . .

Afterwards she ran a hand through my hair and called me White Boy (I know, quoth I, I am her white-boy though humorous), then turned away straight into sleep.

My relationship with Albert was steadily deteriorating. The discovery of his clandestine affair with Mother was part of it; the general political climate did the rest.

In March the Conservative Party had spoken out in what seemed to me the required spirit, denouncing Socialist plans to nationalize the means of production as 'a system borrowed from foreign lands and alien minds'. I used to read the *Mirror* in the Brutus Hill sixth-form common room; it claimed that Labour's programme was a 'typically British solution for British problems': no more unemployment, poverty and misery. In France and Italy, meanwhile, the armed Communist partisans were making truculent noises; only Churchill's resolve put them down in Greece. The Russians were all over Eastern Europe. Leo wept – he would no longer speak to Albert, whose boffin glasses now glinted with a sinister new vision he called 'Peace'. Albert's 'Peace' meant 'the working people', the 'toiling masses' and puppet 'Popular Governments' planted like thorns by Moscow. Albert's 'Peace' smelled like a new order of things by which any refugee or squatter could take possession of your home supported by a new army of 'progressive' bureaucrats.

Work you that way, old mole? then I have the wind of you.

I told Albert more than once that we would not be offended if he felt he was out of place with us. He went off, cheerfully, to something hush-hush in New Mexico. I asked him what it was but he took obvious delight in an enigmatic silence. 'You might tell the Russians, Michael.'

In the first election broadcast of the campaign Churchill said: 'Socialism is in its essence an attack not only on British enterprise, but on the right of the ordinary man and woman to breathe freely without having a harsh, clammy, clumsy, tyrannical hand clapped across their mouth and nostrils.' He warned against 'the abject worship of the state ... this formidable machine, which, once it is in power, will prescribe for every one of them where they are to work; what they are to work at; where they may go and what they may say.'

Forty years later I wouldn't alter a word of it. Less tactically prudent, perhaps, was Winston's prediction that in a Socialist Britain 'all effective and healthy opposition and the natural change of parties in office from time to time would necessarily come to an end, and a political police would be required to enforce an absolute and permanent system upon the nation'. He used the word 'Gestapo' – with the benefit of hindsight, a mistake, although I was in two minds about it at the time. At Brutus Hill, where I was finishing the academic year in a luxury of idleness as a scholarship winner, sixth-form opinion generally relished the old man's bellicosity. Few feared that the language of war might rebound in the expectation of peace.

No two minds were required to react to the hateful Harold Laski's boast that a Labour Government would not be bound by the coming Big Three Conference at Potsdam. An outright Marxist and a past advocate of violent revolution (do they ever really change?), Laski was Chairman of the Socialist Party. As the *Express* pointed out, this was a clear warning that the Party would rule the Government, as in Russia or Germany. 'Who is the real boss of the party?' asked the *Express*. 'Who rules?' asked a *Telegraph* editorial. My spirits rose; we had tasted blood.

During the last week of June Winston made a fairly triumphal tour of the Midlands, the North and parts of Scotland (areas of the country foreign to me). When his campaign reached London during the first week of July, he met a good deal of orchestrated plebeian heckling. 'Another two minutes will be allowed for booing if you like.' At Camberwell Green his car was blocked by Socialists. This kind of loutish behaviour struck me as a good omen; the population at large wouldn't put up with it. It didn't surprise me when the *Daily Express* announced, 'Socialists Decide They Have Lost.'

I had, of course, no vote, but V was quite keen to exercise her rights. At breakfast on the morning of Thursday, July 5 she said: 'Mike, I'm not sure how to vote.'

I tossed her an indulgent smile. 'You state your name, they give you a ballot paper, you draw a cross against the Tory candidate, you put the paper in the box, you wink at the male tellers, they watch you walk out.'

'I mean I'm not sure who to vote for.'

I was flabbergasted. 'Not sure! This local Liberal of ours is a complete idiot. Anyway, why waste your vote?'

She said: 'Maybe it's time for a change, Mike. They say the servicemen are going to vote Labour.'

'The other ranks – what do you expect? I suppose Albert was brainwashing you?'

She said, 'There was a lot of poverty before the war. And still.'

'You imagine the Socialists, who believe in institutionalized idleness, can cure it? Do you really suppose things are better in Russia?'

She didn't seem the least bit abashed. 'Oh no. But I think Mr Attlee is quite a decent sort. He's rather dull, of course, and he wouldn't make a good war leader, but . . .'

'You want his Gestapo here.'

Her temper was rising. 'I think that's rather foul. The trouble with you, Mike, is that you're – '

'I'm what?'

'Never mind.'

'I want to know what I am. Perhaps I can engage in self-criticism, purge myself.'

'Don't you remember giving me *Sybil. Or The Two Nations* to read?'

'Great Heavens, you can't imagine Sybil would have voted Socialist!'

'Labour. That's different.' V looked quite stubborn despite my disparaging scowl. 'All right,' she added, 'I'm sure women don't understand these things. It was a mistake to give us the vote. I'll vote Tory if it makes you happy.'

The Socialists won 392 seats, the Conservatives and their allies 213. V pretended to share my anxiety about the result but I could tell that she was secretly pleased.

TWENTY-TWO

As my new boss, Nice Boy, put it, a scoop concerning the private life of a Cabinet minister could cost half a million in the High Court. A verdict of criminal libel could mean Nice Boy eating his muesli and cream in Wormwood Scrubs (the editor of the *Globe*, though a dedicated Sunday jogger in Richmond Park, did like his food).

It was the Home Secretary himself who obligingly untied my hands by publishing a White Paper amending the Sexual Offences Act of 1956. It was a crusading document, a pipes-and-drums parade up Backlash Avenue. The British public (explained the public relations firm hired for the job, yet another new departure) was sick of deviance, of unnatural displays, of Gay Pride streamers across the High Street at the ratepayers' expense, of propaganda designed to corrupt children under the guise of 'progressive' education.

The Rt Hon Michael Parsons, however, was an astute tactician. Various carrots and sweeties were tossed to the disarrayed platoons of progress: rapists, child abusers, paedophiles and porn kings were to be drowned in mid-Atlantic. Doubling the sentences on shameless dads and step-dads would be applauded from Limehouse to Hampstead.

The *Globe* responded in a no less Fearless and Forthright fashion than its rival left-of-centre tabloid, the *Mirror* (in whose service I'd laboured for twenty years before an offer of 25K and a boot in the Parliamentary Lobby carried me, kicking and screaming, to a champagne lunch on the eighteenth floor of

Globe House, where the Proprietor himself looked up from the various satellites, cables, channels and titles carved in onyx on his desk, waved me to an aluminium chair cast in the likeness of a satellite dish, and said, unforgettably, 'Mr Frame.')

Anyway, 'Too Little, too Late!' howled our headlines on direct instruction from the Proprietor's yacht. Nice Boy was instructed to 'grab the morality issue from the Tories, along with Law and Order'. Himself a liberal with a degree from the LSE, Nice Boy called a meeting of 'concerned' staff. It was a flop – most of us, though loosely pro-Labour, wanted, badly, to flog gays, burn lesbians and castrate child-abusers. Just how badly, few of us had known until little Michael produced his White Paper.

I mean, if only they'd kept quiet and got on with it, the traditional tactic of our public school queers and spies, but no, no, your post-modernist metropolitan queer has to queen his way through a strip-cartoon of designer postures at top squeal, private life is now 'political' just as washing up is 'political', it all has to hang out in a steady drizzle of *Time Out/City Limits* hysteria. Solid peasants living in East Anglian council houses and growing onions on Sunday mornings tell you they're turning their backs on Labour for the first time in their lives because loonies are handing London over to perverts and the IRA.

Little Michael couldn't lose. Parsons had surely earned his first five-minute standing ovation at the Party Conference. Or had he? Though no one noticed at first, tucked away as Chapter 7, paragraph 32, subsection M of his White Paper was a pair of free glasses for the blind.

Sibling incest between consenting adults was to be removed from the criminal statutes.

Not little Michael's idea, of course, oh no, he was merely implementing the proposals of the Criminal Law Revision Committee (including eight judges) which, in its infinite wisdom, had advised that incest between brother and sister over the age of twenty-one should be legal. Had the Rt Hon M. Parsons left it at that he might have got away with it. His White Paper, after all, drew attention to recent Scandinavian reforms and cited the Law Reform Commission of Canada, 1978, on the desirability of legalizing all sexual relations between consenting adults.

Yet little Michael pushed his luck beyond the frontier of public tolerance (as defined by the *Globe*). The Law Revision Committee had settled for twenty-one as the appropriate 'age of consent', but the White Paper noted that if marriage itself was legal at sixteen why not sibling incest as well? – perhaps twenty-one was as antiquated as a guinea.

My own hunch was that he'd had his own sister when he was fifteen or sixteen and he must have tossed himself off in the posh bathroom of his Albany flat night after night trying to screw up the courage to write 'sixteen' over the horrified protests of his civil servants and legal advisers. I dug under the Home Office sewers in search of a confirming leak and finally picked up an internal memo from a passing mole of Assistant Under-Secretary rank: 'Sixteen would be construed as provocative and medically insupportable.'

Little Michael had overruled him: sixteen it was to be.

But who among these civil servants, these Permanent, Deputy or Assistant Under-Secretaries, had a clue about the early years of the Rt Hon Michael Parsons, Her Majesty's Secretary of State for Home Affairs? Not a bean, sir.

The White Paper also committed a tactical blunder. It followed the Canadians in describing the evidence about genetical defects among the offspring of incest as merely 'controversial'.

The morning after the publication of the White Paper, the press scarcely noticed the legalization of sibling incest. Only the women's page of the *Guardian* commented that intercourse between sixteen-year-olds was likely to take place within the parental home, and possibly under constraint, with the girl normally the victim of superior force. The White Paper, said the *Guardian*, was therefore illogical in comparing it to marriage or normal sexual relations.

I had a word with that Nice Boy, my editor. He had a lovely house on Richmond Hill, the spot where Turner had done his picnic painting (Nice Boy told me), and a lovely Scandinavian wife and two lovely half-Swedish children, Tilly and Jimbo, who looked as if they'd come from Habitat – mass-produced handcrafted children in pine. The marriage smelled of mail-order catalogue: turn the page and either of them might have moved on. I was invited to Sunday breakfast (despite my hump and uncertain vowels) before Nice Boy did his jog in an Adidas tracksuit from Lillywhite's. He wore gorgeous trainers and there was a huge 'Viking' jug of cream on the table, huge Portmeirion coffee mugs, a huge loaf of 'farmhouse' bread and a huge seventeenth-century oak kitchen table plus benches – plus several huge Range Rovers in the car porch.

Nice Boy put the sibling incest question to his daughter, who had recently been debating AIDS, abortion, contraception, ozone layers, etc. at a famous girls' school in Hammersmith. 'Well, Tilly, at what age should you and Jimbo be allowed to climb into the sack together?' her father asked her, grabbing the muesli and cream which made him Fat as well as Nice.

Tilly pondered this for about the time it takes a Japanese cameraman to snap the attempted assassination of his Prime Minister.

'Oh me and Jimbo, we've been hard at it for years,' she said. 'We stopped because of the AIDS scare.' She shrugged slender, worldly shoulders inside a too-big T-shirt which said CIAO.

Nice Boy looked nervously at me, his smooth features testing several varieties of smile simultaneously. He then made a phone call to Miami (the Proprietor positively liked being woken at 4 a.m., it confirmed his presidential urgencies) and gave me the green light for a campaign against Parsons – 'as personal as possible this side of libel.'

'Got a title, Bert?'

'"Parsons' Pleasure".'

'You mean "Parsons's Pleasure". It's not a story about vicars.'

I could have choked. There was no way even Nice Boy could have detected a written anomaly on the basis of an aural or oral scan. (But is this my voice or little Michael's? – or that of a third party unknown to either of us? I have heard it said that the square of an author's ego is equal to the sum of the square of the egos of his two main characters.)

Nice Boy was heavy with suggestions for an alternative title. 'How about "Veronica – Or the Two Nations"?'

'Highbrow . . .' I muttered, but I didn't get the allusion. With three kids from my second marriage in private schools, I wasn't arguing.

We rushed the Scientific Facts on to page five, with a flag and trailer on the front page. Children of first cousins tended to show five per cent of 'recessive genes' compared to the normal four per cent. In the case of the child of a sibling union, one quarter of its genes would be present in both parents. Next we dug out a neglected report from the Institute of Child Health on thirteen children born from incestuous couplings (seven with sibling parents, six with father/daughter parents). It made 'disturbing' reading:

One child severely subnormal!

Four educationally subnormal!

Three had died in infancy!

Five were regarded as normal. Five out of thirteen!

Not for nothing had I grown a foot thick enough to wedge open the doors of queer schoolmasters, football stadium victims, Bereaved Persons in a State of Shock, child-abusers, pop stars on speed. We began sifting through the two or three hundred incest prosecutions which take place each year, discovering that very few of them related to siblings. The medical research teams showed us the door: the last thing their guinea pigs needed was publicity. Finally we tracked down a few suspect couples cohabiting in derelict lodging houses and rural pigsties. Even there, few of them had the good grace to look alike. If we could unearth a baby with two heads it would help but cross-eyes and funny smiles was the best we got. Most of them denied it anyway. They were sorry specimens and not worth the trouble.

Sections 10 and 11 of the existing Act forbade sibling incest with a maximum penalty of seven years and we on the *Globe* WANTED TO KNOW why so few prosecutions were brought and such lenient sentences handed down. No answer from the DPP's office; they, too, didn't work between meals.

TWENTY-THREE

I was browsing in Parker's Bookshop one idle afternoon, when I felt a faintly imperious tap on my shoulder. Turning, I was met by a rather diffident smile; the young man drew back a lock of hair from his eye.

'You are Michael Parsons, surely?'

'Yes, but I'm afraid I – '

'Christopher Charrington. We were at Greendale together.'

'Indeed we were.'

We didn't of course shake hands. At Charrington's suggestion we repaired to a pub in the Broad, where we exchanged conventional gossip about tutors, lectures, proctors' rules, the ghastly college food and the insufferable arrogance of the ex-servicemen who stormed around Oxford in their khaki greatcoats with the badges of rank ripped off, captains and privates on equal terms.

'We were awfully sorry when you left Greendale,' Charrington said.

'Oh – yes.'

'You just vanished. We rather wondered why.'

He looked quite innocent but I knew Charrington. I hadn't forgotten the three tarts in his father's bed or the bogus fund for orphans bequeathed by some 'Jew'. (I never forget.)

'My cousin Veronica was conscripted,' I said.

'*Was* she?'

'It also seemed a good idea for someone to take charge of our place in Hampstead. I mean it had fallen into terrible disrepair.'

'Bad show.'

'I found it full of refugees.'

'Lord. So where did you go to school?'

'Brutus Hill.'

'Don't know it.'

'Direct Grant school.'

'Ah. What's that?'

'You pay what you can afford.'

'Sounds a good idea. By the way, I hear you won a major schol. Congratulations.'

'Thanks.'

'Had to make do with an exhibition myself.'

'Congratulations.'

'Old Squeers was quite pleased. Must have broken his rotten heart to see *you* go.'

I shrugged. 'It's water under the bridge.'

'Look, Michael, I do realize we were awful bastards, Roger Brophy and I. Gave you a rotten time. I'd really be frightfully glad if you'd forgive if not forget.'

'Both,' I said. But he didn't seem very interested by my answer – almost disappointed. It reminded me of the invitations to stay with him during the Greendale holidays. I inquired after Rowley.

'Rumour is, he'll retire next year or soon after. They say he's got cancer of the something. Probably the spleen.'

'And Miss Murdoch?'

'Retired. About time.'

'Nancy Lunt?'

'Oh, that cow. She'll be there till the place falls down, which may be fairly soon. Confirmed spinster with rather suspect tastes, if you ask me. Great friend of your cousin's, wasn't she?'

I absorbed the word. 'A one-sided friendship,' I said.

'Oh quite. How is your cousin? Did she ever marry that American fellow?'

'No. He was killed in the Pacific.'

'Rotten luck. Is she still teaching games – she was quite a . . . quite something, I mean.'

I let this pass. A group of loud ex-soldiers entered the pub and bellowed their way to the bar.

'God,' Charrington muttered. 'Got deferment, did you?' he asked, somewhat *sotto voce*.

'Yes. And you?'

'Failed my medical. Bad leg.'

'You were the best cross-country runner of our year. Apart from Brophy.'

'Why don't you write and tell them?'

It was my round. I took the glasses to the bar, where the ex-soldiers contemptuously declined to make space. 'Past your bedtime, sonny,' one of them said. Very funny.

'Haven't seen you around the Union, have I?' Charrington asked when I returned with the beers.

'Is that the place to be?'

'Not if you want to be a don or a civil servant. What's your line?'

'I haven't decided. And you?'

'I shall eat my dinners.'

'Sorry?'

Charrington gave me a weary look I knew well. But the naked contempt of the boy had been wiped away by the assumed civility of the young man.

'Barrister, old chap. Follow in the old man's footsteps. Not very enterprising but there's a good living there once you take silk. If you want to try your voice out, or learn to argue a case you don't believe in, the Union's the place. Full of apprentice politicians, of course. You in the Conservative Association?'

'Yes, I did join but I –'

'Come along next Tuesday. Rab Butler's speaking.' Charrington drained his glass. 'Well, forgive me if I make tracks. Essay. Look me up in Trinity sometime, staircase four. I usually open a bottle around six.'

'I'll look in.'

'Yes, do.'

I drove my second-hand Ford 10 down to Greendale one

Friday in early summer. Coasting along the quiet country road from the town to the school, I noted the exact point where Harold had picked us up in his jeep after *Gone with the Wind*. Nothing had changed at the school (though the sandbags and fire buckets had gone) – why should it? More masters, less mistresses, probably. I had expected the school buildings to look smaller than they seemed during my childhood, but the 'Gulliver-effect' was denied to me. They looked the same. If the roof of the Staff Annexe had eventually been repaired you'd never know.

Having parked my car in the gravel yard, a satisfying gesture, I climbed the familiar stairs and knocked on V's door. No reply. I opened it. The furniture was the same only more dilapidated. A book of ration cards lay on the table. That divan bed . . . I thought of V and Harold and closed the door.

A short search revealed Nancy Lunt's new quarters – the late Miss Murdoch's chamber pot was now hers. A familiar voice or foghorn immediately boomed from within – whether commanding me to come in or stay out I couldn't tell.

She was marking exercise books and didn't look up – some squirt could wait.

'Hullo,' I said.

She stared at me – well she would, wouldn't she? Then she stood up, as if to mark an occasion.

'It's you,' she said.

'The other person is always "you", Nancy.'

'Hm. You haven't changed.' (Snort.)

'How's Winston?' This was considered unworthy of reply so I tried, 'How's things?'

'Could be worse. And you?'

'Still teaching games, Nancy?'

'Just the girls now. The blokes came back. Some of them.'

'Veronica never forgave you, I'm afraid.'

Lunt emitted a low moan, followed by a wail of distilled anguish, bottled up for three years, quite pitiful.

'I didn't do it! I'd never rat on Nicky!'

Evidently her vocabulary hadn't matured either – well, it doesn't, in a school. Close to tears (restrained only by her loathing of me), she couldn't resist asking, begging: 'Where's Nicky?'

I shrugged. 'She's back in South Africa with her mother.'

Lunt wary, sceptical, tongue-tied by passion. 'She didn't marry that American, then?'

'He got himself killed. I must go and see old Wackford Squeers. Still half-alive, I hear. I bet he's longing to see me.'

'He's showing prospective parents round the school. As a matter of fact the Head is extremely ill. Not that you'd care.'

'Come off it, Nancy.'

She was heaving and simmering. 'You really have got a cheek, Michael.' But the source of her distress lay elsewhere: three missing years in the life of her beloved Nicky, three years of loneliness, anguish and remorse, were securely locked away in my head.

'Have you got Nicky's address?' She couldn't help herself: Dutch peasant woman, artist unknown.

I winked. 'Show me your knickers.'

I found Rowley in the Library addressing a bemused knot of prospective parents – the usual flash Harrys and Jewboys with Lagondas, Jaguars, Italian-tenor hair and no fixed point of cultural reference. I slipped into a back seat unobserved; it was time I knew about this great school. Squeers was clearly in his element, parading his principles and pausing for laughter:

'As you know Greendale has a reputation as a "progressive" school. What does this mean in changing times? Does it mean our pupils can smoke behind the pavilion? No, because we don't have a pavilion. [Ha ha.] Do we beat them every morning after chapel? No, we have no chapel. [Groan.] What we encourage here is self-discovery.

'Liberty is not license. True freedom is not freedom to do anything they choose, but freedom *from* ignorance, bigotry, anxiety, fear, prejudice, dependence on others, and all the immobilizing forces [not bad, must use that] which encourage children to blame the world for every discomfort – teachers, parents, adults, everyone but Self. [The mums in the audience stir uneasily at the word 'discomfort' – does he mean bad food, lumpy beds, cold dorms?] We discourage the view that life isn't "fair" – of course it's not fair. Don't whinge.

'We encourage enlightenment. Now that's something you have to work at, like love. We believe this can be achieved only within a small community which is coeducational. Each of us here seeks the proper balance of male and female characteristics – the *animus* and the *anima* [ignorant sod]. We all confront choices; we must learn to take control of our own lives.'

He wobbles, clutches the lectern, hawks phlegm disgustingly with a paisley hanky which he then tucks back – ugh! – in the top pocket of the same old rotting tweed jacket. Will he survive another paragraph of his own erudition?

'Progressive schools are often criticized for being weak on intellect and strong on sentimentality. In the surrounding country and villages here they believe we never take a stand on anything. They believe our pupils are unkempt, grimy creatures who kick doors open, loll about smoking and invariably fail their exams. This, I am glad to tell you, is not true.

'The doctrine here is that as you grow older you must pay a higher price for your follies. Saturday detentions await the lax and laggardly, and I don't care whether it spoils parents' weekend plans. I call it my contribution to the era of petrol rationing. [Ha ha.] Get caught in any local pub and out they go. Lift a chocolate bar from a local shop and out they go. There is no room for delinquents here.'

(Parents now wear troubled faces; their children are without exception 'difficult' or 'disturbed' or in need of 'special understanding' – hence Greendale, the fashionable ratbag.)

'And what about sex? Nature is of course at work. We do not bring young males and females together to repress their natural instincts. Love and tender relationships – of course. But nothing blatant is allowed. ['Blatant'?] We encourage discretion, sensitivity to the feelings of others, maturity. Local opinion has it that the Headmaster of Greendale keeps a plentiful supply of contraceptives in his study, available on demand. [Nervous titters.] Let me disabuse you. Not one pregnancy have we had here in my time – our married staff excepted. [Huge joke.] Greendale's pupils leave the school as mature and responsible young adults for whom sex is not something furtive and shameful but a beautiful, life-enhancing

229

force with its proper time and place in the wider perspective of a creative life.'

(Will he ever stop? No.)

'Creativity is the motto of Greendale. Each pupil here is encouraged to discover his or her own special potential. Given the mixed-ability intake which we deliberately maintain, our academic results are, though I say it, remarkable. But passing or failing in life means more than a general certificate of education in this subject or that. It means discovering the whole person.'

(The sulking reader may skip.)

'Games? We build the body as well as the mind. But we avoid the spirit of competition on the hockey field as in the class-room. Occasionally we win a school match without cheating but it's not the end of the world if we lose. The friendships made after the match are more important.

'We seek to help our pupils, to understand them, to talk to them. If they lose a parent or their parents divorce, they can always come to me; they can always count on sympathy and understanding.

'Finally, there is, contrary to rumour, no adulation of adolescence here. I am not a great admirer of the young. They steal from one another – particularly games clothes – and their morals regarding property are appalling. Too much egocentri-city and self-indulgence; the sense of service, so prominent during the war, has rapidly been supplanted by the opportuni-stic spirit of the blackmarketeer. Having won one war, we must – alas – now face another. I shall not flinch from it.

'Now, I've talked for far too long, as usual. I'm sure you have questions to put to me.'

After the statutory awkward silence a woman inquired timidly about weekend exeats. Another wanted to know what provision was made for vegetarians. A man asked whether rugby was played [no] and a woman whether the sexes took part in sports together [sometimes, on Tuesdays]. These ter-mites disposed of, Rowley's pig eyes gleamed in anticipation of another bloodless victory. I raised my hand. Rowley nodded indulgently in my direction – the 'one more question' syn-drome – then executed the classic double-take: he recognized me.

'Excuse me, Headmaster, regarding your reference to *animus* and *anima*. Do these Latin words really refer to male and female characteristics? It certainly wasn't what we were taught during my time here.'

The flash Harrys and Jewboys sat up smartly, as if their entire lives had been devoted to the classics.

'Thank you, Michael. I stand corrected.'

'Another question, Headmaster –'

'Are you a prospective parent, Michael? Already?'

(This brought him a gush of protective adult laughter. Something not far removed from a child had been spotted: squash it.)

'A retrospective pupil, sir. I'm afraid my memory doesn't quite coincide with yours about pregnancies. At least three girls and four boys had to leave during my time on that account – we assumed that one of the babies had two fathers.'

This drew a somewhat mixed reaction. A pretty girl who looked like a potential sixth-form entrant (and delinquent) tossed me a delightful wink, but most of the papas and mamas looked downright distraught.

Rowley explained to his audience that I had been expelled from the school for 'persistent lying', adding that coffee and biscuits awaited the guests in Great Hall – 'an excellent opportunity for more informal discussions.'

There was an uncomfortable squeaking of chairs and a general shuffle towards the coffee and biscuits. A surprisingly large number of prospective parents immediately surrounded me and I held court for a few minutes, answering their anxious questions with great sobriety and moderation. 'The school is close to anarchy,' I told them, 'and won't improve until the old man can be persuaded to retire. As for the academic results, ask yourselves why you haven't been shown them.'

Rowley's house still smelt of boiled cabbage and linoleum polish. I waited at the foot of the stairs for more than an hour, flicking through the tatty copies of *Picture Post*, *Punch* and *Illustrated London News* which lay on the hall table. When Squeers finally shuffled through the front door he was much more obviously the dying man than when performing to an admiring audience.

I stared hard into his pig eyes.

'Get out,' he said.

He mounted the stairs so slowly it was a problem not lapping him. Uninvited I followed him into Yorkshire itself and waited to be sat in the electric chair. He wheezed badly, fiddled with the pipe he was no longer supposed to smoke, then pointed to the battered chair with a grunt.

'That's very decent of you, sir,' I said. 'I'm sorry to hear you're not well.'

'*Tempus fugit*. You look in the peak yourself. Now, Michael, since my energies are limited, let's get down to brass tacks. [Wheeze.] You didn't come here to commiserate on my state of decay. There's always a purpose in everything you do – oh yes [wheeze] I do remember that. So how's Oxford . . . pity we couldn't chalk that one up . . . helps with fund-raising. [Heavy coughing, spittle, drool, searches in rotting tweeds for indescribable hanky.]

'Oxford's fine,' I said through the bombardment.

'Hm. Career?'

'Haven't decided.'

'Go into politics. Or the law. But the law only brings money – you need power. And you're a gambler. [Wheeze.] No doubt you'll get to the top – string of corpses in your wake.'

'Really? None yet, surely?'

'I'll be plain with you. Quite a few nasty young characters have sat in that chair in my time – bully boys, delinquents, philistines – but none of 'em could hold a candle to you.'

I waited.

'Tell you why you're here? [New outbreak. Pause. Dog snoring.] Like all genuine villains, you couldn't rest until you were sure you'd disposed of the corpse.'

'Corpses again, sir?'

'Your sister Veronica was the nicest girl ever to set foot in Greendale. After your good mother died she was in a terrible dilemma, terrible. She came to me – at her wits end, poor girl – her own brother half-way up her skirt. [Wheeze.] I advised her to tell you the truth.'

232

I waited.

'Then that American came on the scene. She broke the rules on one occasion but she was a fine girl – hard to believe that you and she were cut from the same cloth.'

'Yet you expelled her. On the basis, if I recall, of an anonymous accusation.'

Rowley stared sadly at his stained cardigan bursting at the stomach.

'Anonymous? Balls. You were in a tight corner: Veronica about to be conscripted, Veronica anxious to hasten her marriage. So you engineered your own expulsion and hers. Brilliantly done. Two birds, one stone. You'll lead the Tory Party in the 1990s.'

'Machiavelli was content with Minister of Education.'

Squeers couldn't resist a chortle; the resultant coughing fit almost finished him. I was baffled by his logic: if he had believed that I wrote a letter containing a fabricated allegation against myself, why hadn't he just sat on it? Why expel us both?

Rowley sighed. 'Had to get rid of you. Didn't know what you'd do next. Doctor got nowhere with you. Too clever for your own good.'

'But Veronica? Was that justice?'

'Schoolmasters must sometimes consider claims other than justice. You were an orphan, wholly dependent on the love and loyalty of one relative. I couldn't in conscience destroy that love or that loyalty. Took my decision then made you both walk the plank – Captain Hook's justice. Out! Poor girl. I treated her like dirt. I'll never forget the shock and contempt in her face. But I gave you back what you should by rights have forfeited: her total devotion. Nancy lost a friend, of course, but that's life.'

Severe outbreak of coughing. Phlegm gushing up. Interlude. Bored, I ambled to the door. He raised a hand to stay me.

'Traditionally we confess on our own deathbeds. God may forgive you, Michael, if you confess on mine.'

'Call me when the time comes.'

'Hm. You haven't improved. And Veronica – how is she?'

'She's back in South Africa.'

'Ah. Didn't marry her American?'

'No.'

'You made sure of that? Now you must excuse me. Mrs Rowley insists I have my nap – though I tell her I'll have all the sleep I need soon enough.' He didn't attempt to move; indeed he was already snoring with his dog before I'd left the room.

TWENTY-FOUR

I was going to say the fucking Army taught me to read and write but what my two khaki years taught me was a bit more about them and us. After three years on building sites (I never wanted to follow my Dad into the docks) I was taken into the East Surreys at Kingston Barracks and put through hours of square-bashing by sergeants, CSMs and RSMs called Kelly, O'Brien or Mahoney. We would cheerfully have given all of them to the IRA but they'd opted for the King's shilling and a pleasant routine of ritual sadism sponsored by the languid public-school subalterns who rarely raised their voices and issued punishments in a casual drawl. These pipsqueak lieutenants were addressed as sir and styled themselves mister. Why not esquire? The noncoms did their dirty work for them, like factory foremen or colonized African chiefs. As for the specks of dirt that 'Mister' (Second Lieutenant) Rowcastle regularly found in our pulled-through rifle barrels, you can bet those specks had been implanted in his eyeball by some minor public school. The class code was as crystal clear in 1950 as when my Dad and my uncles were taken away in their time (though they never talked about it at home and that's interesting – when the head of the family comes home on leave there's no way he's confessing he's been treated with less dignity than his eight-year-old son in the elementary school). During my first fortnight at Kingston I was regularly locked up in the guardroom to teach me how to spell 'sir'. Within two weeks I was broken; within three I was physically fitter than I'd ever been in my life.

It wasn't the Army that taught me (I used to say 'learned me') to read and write but a frail, bespectacled phantom-individual called Corporal Braine of the Educational Corps. He was grammar school but not stuck-up. The point was, for the first time in my life the classroom was the best place to be – it couldn't be worse than RSM O'Brien, CSM Kelly and the exquisite Sergeant Mahoney.

Corporal Braine was a kind of genius. He'd say, 'Well, Frame, what did you do last night?' and I'd say, 'Well, Corporal, me and my mates was out on the town chasin' skirt an' lookin' for some geezer in need o' a bunch o' fives.' Corporal Braine would nod solemnly behind his thick, porthole glasses and copy what I'd just said on to the blackboard. 'Now write that out in standard English.' He made us memorize the first paragraph of the front-page story in the *Mirror* or the *Express* – then copy it out from memory. It's amazing how words and phrases stick when you do that. Or he'd turn on the radio for a news summary with the warning: 'You're going to hear fifteen seconds of it. After that write down every word you've heard.'

Your usual rotten teacher starts with something called 'life' or 'experience' and then kindly invites you to find words to describe it. ('My Father'; 'My Mother'; 'Where I Live'; 'Good and Bad Things About the Army'; 'The Best Holiday I Ever Had'; 'My Favourite Town/Tree/Food'.) But Braine knew he was dealing with adult illiterates – there were scores of us. He gazed at us through his portholes and told us that words come before 'life'. Slamming a few disconnected words on the blackboard (and breaking piece after piece of His Majesty's best white chalk) such as 'arrogant', 'victim', 'punish', 'discipline', 'obsession', 'severely', Braine then issued his challenge: 'Now write a sentence about someone you don't like.'

No problem: 'Sergeant Mahoney is an arrogant NCO with an obsession about discipline and a habit of punishing his victims severely.'

Braine understood that when you're given words (and grammar tucked inside them) you'll start finding bits of 'life' to attach to them. 'Play with words!' he said. 'Go on, show off, rob the *Mirror* headline wizard of his job!'

He was a quiet bloke, Corporal Braine, but he went straight for the passions: sex, murder, Communism, war. A favourite game was 'translating' from *Express* language into *Times* language (a paper I'd never seen before). 'Reds Murder Millions,' we'd write, then, 'According to unconfirmed reports, widespread disturbances have taken place in the People's Republic of China with heavy loss of life.'

OK, I didn't get to that level overnight and many of us never caught on at all, couldn't jump clear of years of under-nourishment. Some of the lads tried to take advantage of Braine and were sent straight back to O'Brien, Kelly and the gorgeous Mahoney. But the thing was, about that 'unconfirmed reports' sentence, most of us had previously felt that such language couldn't be for us, like stuck-up accents, so we'd never really listened to it, even on the BBC. What Braine said, essentially, was: 'It belongs to you if you want it. Drink it like tea and soon it'll taste like Watney's best bitter.'

Because – I'm sorry to go on – Braine also taught us to play with accents. He was teaching us to jump jail, to spring the handcuffs. 'Sound like the BBC,' he'd say. 'Sound like the Colonel. Sound like the vicar's wife. Sound like Jimmy Edwards. Sound like Frankie Howerd. Sound like Churchill – now Attlee.'

Brilliant Braine! He could do them all, without visible change of expression, rubber-tongued. He used words like paint. If you could half-sound like Clem Attlee announcing that rationing was over because there was no food at all, or Churchill saying never have so many owed so little to so few, you were half-way to the Press Gallery of the House of Commons.

Half-way from where? Looking back, I can see we was the dregs, football pool primitives taking life as it comes, which means stuffing coppers into the juke box or taking the local Kingston Teds apart – it was before the Rockers and no one could afford two milk shakes let alone a bleeding Norton 500cc. We sported American shoulders, vacant faces (like detectives), and our reading was just abaht confined to *Crime Unlimited* or

True Detective. (Corporal Braine always said *True Defective*.)
Build a husky body. Send for details. Create for yourself a
DOMINANT and ASSERTIVE personality! Send for details.
We was working-class scum and no mistake. Send for details.

After Braine, and a period in the glasshouse at Colchester
among the hard cases – I'd taken a swing at the angelic 'Sarge'
Mahoney in the Kingston guardroom while fairly pissed – I
found myself in the Korean slime on secondment to the Pioneer
Corps, mainly digging latrines, digging graves and lifting frozen
stiffs. Don't ask me where Korea is, I never knew.

Little Michael missed not only Korea but all the other
contemporary colonial wars: Malaysia, Kenya, Cyprus. It
doesn't surprise me. In Korea I was in my element and killed a
million Chinese with my bare hands. *Cockney Hero Slaughters
Red Fanatics* – How I Became Acting Lance-Corporal With My
Bare Hands. In point of fact our hatred was reserved for the
American fighter bombers whose pilots were too shit scared to
notice who they were crapping on. The Chinese? – they were
poorer than we were and merited our respect.

After I got out I began offering my services in Fleet Street as a
messenger boy. Actually our family knew several blokes from
Limehouse who were in 'the printing', which often meant
loading the bundles bound for King's Cross or Paddington. It
was all a racket, a kind of mafia, and I was in my element when
the going got heavy but I was dreaming of the upper floors
swarming with reporters in camelhair coats and snappy green
hats. I did legwork for some of them (lazy buggers), kept my
ears open for tips, sold a story about a conman masquerading as
a bookie, and enrolled with the Workers Education Association
programme for ex-servicemen.

I was told the WEA had ninety thousand students including
sixteen thousand manual workers. There was a kind of core
system of values in the WEA and a confused resistance to all the
bright lights now flashing cheap signals at working people. I
soon noticed what I've observed ever since: working people's
need for an anchor, a tradition, roots, call it what you like –
Levellers' Day, Peterloo Massacre Day, Tolpuddle Martyrs'
Day; whereas little Michael and the Tories no longer have any

real need for history or heroes because Moloch is now and tomorrow. At the WEA we were offered books that thousands of working people had read fifty years previously but even with the help of friendly tutors some of us had a real struggle to understand Henry George's *Progress and Poverty*, Blatchford's *Merrie England*, and even H.G. Wells. By now I was fighting to find out who I was.

Two years after I enrolled for WEA evening classes I received the best letter of my life. I was to be a student (magic word) at Ruskin College, Oxford.

My Mum said, 'If only yer Dad was alive today.' And maybe we both thought of that other letter which had come from the army in June 1940.

Of course we weren't Oxford students in the full sense, we didn't take degree courses or wear gowns, but I was walking the same streets recently trodden by M. Parsons, Esquire and his promising Tory farts. The great G.D.H. Cole was lecturing at Ruskin, an old tall thin balding man who held the key to the secret history of this and other nations – we revered him and when he advised us to read William Morris's utopian novel *News from Nowhere* we literally ran to the library. I often used to wonder about the great Corporal Braine and whether he was still casting his pearls before hooligan swine in Kingston Barracks.

Anyway, whenever I went home to Limehouse from Ruskin there were 'raised eyebrows' – we're quite a theatrical race, even if the music halls and vaudevilles have surrendered to bingo. (Name me a greater defeat than that.) I was told by uncles and aunties that I wasn't smiling at them with the whole of my face. 'Don't get above yerself, Bert boy.' Stone the bleeding crows! Isn't that just *it*. 'Thinks 'isself too good for the like o'us. Gives 'isself airs. Quite the Oxford gent.'

One particular incident sparked all this off. My Mum had learned to love Billy Butlin's holiday camps. They were huge and garish with cheerleaders linking everyone in pally groups. They dished out Light Programme Palm Court swing music night and day. My sister Elsie now had a young family of her own and I was the one chosen to take my Mum to Butlin's at

Clacton that particular year, it might have been '55 (rail strike, election) or '56 (Suez), I don't recall. Looking back I can see that, while my years with the WEA and Ruskin reinforced my notions of 'solidarity', they weakened my liking for group recreation: singing together, clapping together, all having a good time together, everyone together now, are we all together now. I didn't want to go to Butlin's and we had a blazing argument, me and my Mum.

'Is it the books' my Mum asked, 'that makes you stuck up?' Then she began to cry and said she wanted 'Abide with Me' played at her funeral so she could put her feet up at the end of a long life of work 'in a real friendly 'ome called 'Eaven'.

I remember relations were particularly strained with Billy and other members of our wartime gang. His big brother (always in the know, always not born yesterday, always knew a mug or a mug's game when he saw one, always said 'since when?' or 'who sez?' if in doubt) was now inside Wormwood Scrubs. Billy seemed to feel that my slowly rising fortunes were somehow responsible for his own family's decline – he himself had lost a job in the docks after a consignment of tobacco went missing.

I got a job writing copy for the TGWU, my old union when I used to work on building sites. But for some reason I knew my destiny to be the *Mirror*. It was not only the big-time tabloid, but it had always been our paper, the one we always had at home, plain speaking, on the side of the servicemen, the underdog, and full of bloody nerve. It was the paper of the Other Ranks and their 'Women', not of the Officers and their 'Ladies' (who once again ruled the country, as if they'd ever not).

Besides: the *Mirror* still had Jane in her scanties – how could we have won the war without Jane forever losing her clothes at the drop of a hat? She was indeed a strip cartoon and I couldn't count the number of times I'd jerked off in her honour in full view of my Limehouse gang in whatever bombed corner shop we were holed up. Jane reminded me of Miss Veronica King, who was real yet more remote, and on whose behalf we all beat our meat from Stalingrad to D-Day. (If little Michael likes to thank the big sister in *The Railway Children* for Veronica, me, I'd nod in the direction of Jane for my own contribution to Miss King.)

The *Mirror* at that time was 'Forthright and Fearless' – even about princesses. Come on Margaret! Please Make Up Your Mind! After a short period making the tea and phoning excuses to the Sports Editor's wife, I was given the job of choosing Baby Pictures (a regular feature). I always got the wrong one and was slagged off. The ideal *Mirror* baby was healthy but not fat, contented but not smug, impish but not cheeky. (Real babies are overfed, vain and bloody cheeky.)

After that I was writing captions for cheesecake ('Bikini Bombshell', 'Susie's a Smasher', 'Cheryl's a Cracker') and discovering that every little working-class girl with page-3 boobs 'adored' to sip bubbly in her bubble bath. Inventing their hobbies became a real headache: skiing, water skiing, horse riding, tennis and 'dining out' had real class, dancing was too much like every other girl, and photography was desperation.

I cut my investigative teeth hunting down queer schoolmasters in nasty, unregulated private establishments, notably choir schools which supplied choristers to fashionable churches. All those innocent faces and angelic treble voices masking wanking and buggery. And the middle-class parents of the terrified and corrupted little boys didn't want to know – anything could be rammed up little Nigel's arse so long as there was no public scandal. We ran headlines like 'Go! – Unfrock Yourself, Father O'Baloney'.

No one taught you the in-house vocabulary at the *Mirror* but you picked it up quicker than measles. Indecent. Urgent lesson. Dangerous. Wicked. Evil men. Silly, daft, pompous. Stunt. Smug. Upper crust. Clique. Humbug. Web of deceit. Guilty men. Sourpusses, grousers, wailers. Tin-pot (or pint-sized) dictators. Scandal. Shocked. Pervert. Conspiracy of silence. Traitors. See also Red Herring. Not a bad or vulgar vocabulary, either – as Corporal Braine had made clear.

As for style – no paragraph should ever be more than two

sentences long. If you forgot yourself and tried as many as three, the sub would snarl, 'What's this you're writing – literature?'

Of course the *Mirror* wasn't the only 'popular' you could work for but I was a political animal and wouldn't have walked further than its sister paper, the good old *Sunday Pictorial*. Not for me the *People* or the *News of the World* – though admittedly one of my heroes was Duncan Webb, of the *People*, who'd nailed the Messina brothers, a gang of Maltese running an empire of prostitution in Mayfair. Duncan knew where a piece of string ended. He'd been a dying man, too, though it was a well-kept secret. As for our despised rival, the *Daily Sketch*, when that struggling Tory rag raised its cover price by a halfpenny we congratulated it on being the only carbon copy in the world more expensive than the original.

Given the normal distinction between 'popular' and 'quality' papers, it was a matter of honour always to refer to the latter as the 'unpopular press'. What they did reg'lar, mate, was to reprint every horny, hoary detail of our latest 'disgraceful' story under the guise of nose-up disapproval.

The *Mirror* took a brave stand on Suez and on colonialism generally. 'No more Suez lunacy. No more Cyprus tragedies. No more Hola horrors – or perilous buckets of whitewash in Central Africa.' Right on. Hounded Eden out. And in Cassandra (William Connor) we had one of the truly great columnists with a real lively mind full of curiosity and respect for intellect – not your lowest common denominator stuff. But the Tories' third successive election victory in 1959 caused some panic. The famous masthead slogan, Forward With the People, first run up on May 11, 1945, was dropped without a word. The Richard [Dick] Crossman column, the best political analysis in the Street, also went. So did Jane. She was married off, an insult to all ex-servicemen. The paper now had a circulation of five million. Money was talking.

We were meant to be Socialists but our Chairman was a cynical, power-hungry tycoon who kept the lucrative *Horse and Hound* in the company stable while our tabloids ran nasty stories about the huntin' and shootin' set and editorialized against blood sports. Our bigwigs owned motor cruisers and yachts and dictated editorials from the English Channel on Pye coast-to-shore radio. I wanted nothing less for myself and had abandoned the quest of my years with the WEA and Ruskin College to find out who I was. I didn't want to know.

'Never mind, Bert, you can't afford a conscience and a mortgage.' This fearless and forthright piece of wisdom belonged to my new father-in-law, Harry Kilroy, Investments Editor and not strictly working class. I didn't intend to be strictly working class either, and by the time Harry retired me and Sharon had our semi-detached in Acton and Wayne on the way.

It had taken master diplomacy and a bottle of gin to get my Mum to the wedding in St Bride's, Fleet Street (Harry went the whole hog and Sharon's one hundred pound dress was cut to conceal the foundation stone of Wayne). Mum arrived in her war feathers surrounded by her family (Uncle Len, Aunt Elsa, my sister Elsie, and my baby sister Lizzie whose father was Uncle Len because my Dad had gone 'missing' on the beaches of Dunkirk four years earlier and it had taken until the Festival of Britain on the South Bank before Aunt Elsa and my Mum would speak to each other). Also on parade was my Mum's new husband, Jack Higgins. My Mum glowered at the Kilroys as if she expected a shoot-out. Despite Harry Kilroy's generosity to her she always insisted that they were stuck-up and smiled through half their faces.

My Mum had changed by the time Elvis was it. In the old days she used to love Gracie Fields, who could switch from a back-yard bawdy song to something 'classical' and 'religious' like 'Bless This House'. My Mum would sing at the top of her voice (which she fancied) while doing the washing:

> Bless this house, O Lord, we pray
> Make it safe by night and day.
> Bless the hearth ablazing there
> With smoke ascending like a prayer.

During the war she'd sing 'Ave Maria' and cry over 'Oh for the Wings of a Dove' sung by a male soprano or some kind of cultivated eunuch voice, but nowadays she was drooling over Frankie Vaughan and that Pearly King called Liberace. She was even on his side when he sued our paper on account of a few (expensive, as it turned out) sardonic comments by Cassandra. Since the Coronation my Mum had taken to antimacassars and flights of china ducks on the living room wall in Leyton (where she'd moved when she married Jack). In 1956 she put down a ten-pound deposit on a fifty-four pound Murphy V230 portable television; three years later it was an eighty-pound Murphy 410C Consolette. The one thing she'd talk about nonstop was the clannishness of the ex-East Enders in Leyton, and how they all thought themselves 'something special' and looked down on Jack because he was a former costermonger who'd done a stretch or two for receiving and straightening up fuzz after a job.

'At least I still know who I am,' my Mum used to say to Sharon when she came over to Acton to inspect Wayne.

TWENTY-FIVE

Following V's suicide attempt in North Wales (there are things that cannot be written about, though I shall try again) I'd chosen a nursing home situated in the Wiltshire village of Coombe Bissett – a two-hour drive from Oxford, feasible once a month for Jude the Obscure, but safely remote. On arrival I always asked the staff nurse whether there had been any other visitors; the answer was invariably negative.

'Such a pity, Mr Parsons. She does like company. It's terrible, isn't it, when people have practically no family.'

'How is my cousin?'

'Oh much better. We had quite a chat in mid-week. She's making a lot of sense.' She smiled. 'You know your way, Mr Parsons.'

I did indeed – the freshly painted corridor, the tea trolleys and starched aprons, the shuffling slippers, crutches, wheel-chairs. A single room had been beyond my means but at least this one, with its large windows overlooking a pleasant rose garden, was cosier, more intimate, than a public ward in a state hospital. And there were small comforts: better food, wireless headphones, and nurses who were never in too much of a hurry to attend a request.

There were four beds in V's room, three of them occupied by older women – inquisitive, incontinent and batty. Any visitor was a major event in their lives. When I arrived V was normally applying make-up with a compact mirror, intently dabbing powder on her nose, then angrily rubbing it off; she must have been absorbed in this for fully five minutes before she noticed me – or decided to. Today she was wearing her white ball gown but a large stain (possibly tea) now disfigured the skirt. Her hair was packed with curlers.

'How are you?' I took her hand.

As usual V didn't say a word until the nurse joined us.

'This is my other lover,' she then announced loudly.

'Yes, dear.'

'He's an Oxford man you see.'

'Yes, dear.'

The three old batty crones were goggling – I never quite immunized myself to this cackling audience. After the nurse had tactfully withdrawn I drew up a chair and presented my gifts – not only fruit, chocolate and flowers but also the cosmetics, nail varnish and false eyelashes she invariably demanded.

'Are these from Harold?' she inquired.

'Of course.'

'We'll be late for the dance. Tell him to hurry.'

The nurse came past again. 'Dr Yardley will be in later,' she said to me. 'You might like to talk to him.'

'Yardley?'

'He's the new one.'

V had drawn her skirt up her thigh. She was wearing suspenders and heavily laddered nylon stockings. She pointed to a bruise.

'Bruise,' she said.

'How did you get that, Veronica?'

'Kiss it better.'

I hesitated but she insisted and I kissed it. She screamed in pain: 'You hurt me!'

The old crones started yelling and the nurse hurried back.

'He hurt my bruise,' V complained.

'Did he?' (as to a child).

'Take him away.'

'We don't really want that, do we? Michael's only just arrived.'

'He raped me.' (Said with no expectation of belief in a flat, mechanical voice.)

246

'No, he didn't.'

V smiled. 'Daddy came.'

This, too, was part of the schedule. Dad (her invariable word) had become Daddy and Daddy had always come to see her just before I did. Three successive doctors had questioned me about it. By now I had become so bored with the myopia of the medical staff that I almost hoped for a doctor with a real spirit of investigation.

Nurse asked V whether Daddy had come by plane or car. But V had already forgotten about Daddy coming.

'Daddy's married Mummy again,' she announced. 'They're going to live in Hollywood . . . with Harold and me.'

After a while V ate a few grapes, pulled her gown off her beautiful shoulders to show me her breasts (how I longed to caress and suck them) – then told me to stop looking at her tits. 'You're looking.' This period of the performance was eagerly awaited by the three hags, who shrieked merrily. One of them, a deranged and hideous charlady, always urged me to 'have a go'. When the new doctor, Yardley by name, bounced in at about four in the afternoon I could tell at once that he was bumptious with healing zeal – the sort who is convinced that the history of real medicine began the night he was conceived. He'd whipped and creamed his hair up into something between a pyramid and a choirstall misericord – your real grammar school coxcomb. The 'case' (as he called it) 'intrigued' him. He meant to 'crack' it. The oaf talked about V in cramped, on-the-make Midlands English as if she wasn't listening and fully capable of understanding every word. Eventually I coaxed him out into the garden and across the lawn. I noticed that his cheap shoes soon began to stain in the wet grass.

'You're all we've got, Mr Parsons. Everyone else seems to be dead.'

'I'm afraid so.'

'Sex figures largely somewhere.'

I said: 'As you know, she took a massive dose of phenobarbitone the day she learned of her fiancé's death.'

'How long had she known her fiancé?'

'I'm not clear on that. We can ask her.'

'She never answers a direct question. The nurse asks, "Tea or coffee?" Veronica says, "Look at my bruise." Did you ever meet the American?'

'No. He was before my time.'

'You were staying in the same hotel when it happened. Sharing a room, according to the police report.'

'She was lonely.'

'If she loved this man, why should she take up with a cousin four years younger than herself?'

'She came to stay in my house during the war . . . We – she and I – were the only family each of us had.'

Yardley offered me one of his sceptical stares then lit a cheap little cigar.

'She must have been very attractive.'

'Yes.'

'Could have had anyone she wanted.' I let the insult pass. 'Did she make the running with you?' he asked. 'Sexually, I mean?'

'Does all this help the victim of an overdose?'

'She was traumatized before that happened.'

'I can't agree. I knew her. You didn't.'

'Tell me: what was the, er, understanding, if her fiancé came back? You'd move aside?'

'Oh certainly.'

'Why does she insistently refer to you as her brother?'

'It started soon after the overdose. The ambulance was an hour coming – remote village in North Wales. She must have been starved of oxygen.'

'She seems to be claiming that you and she had the same father.'

'She never knew her own father, he was killed in India soon after she was born. She liked and admired my father . . .'

'She constantly addresses you in sexual codes – but with a fierce resentment. Why?'

'I wish I knew. I wish you could do something for her.'

'What school did you attend' – he was consulting his notes – 'before Brutus Hill?'

'What's that got to do with it?'

'The relevance is that you baulk at the question. Why? There are elementary gaps in our biographical knowledge of the patient and of yourself. She is a displaced person. The real issue in my mind is whether you want to help or not.' Dr Yardley checked his stride and faced me. 'We might cure her, you see. Anything you tell me will be in the strictest confidence, Mr Parsons. Even if [he paused] we are discussing what may technically be a crime – attempted suicide.'

I asked him what he thought of the Socialist Government's new dispensation of free medicine.

We had walked full circle and were now almost back at the front entrance. No point in explaining to the self-made physiocrat physician Yardley that V's inconstant mother, Aunt Amanda, hadn't answered her letters for seven years; no point in explaining that, when the secret of Giovanni's love for Annabella was finally exposed, he had killed her, plucked out her heart, thrust it under the nose of her husband, then killed him too.

Finally Giovanni had been cut down like a mad beast. I would not be.

As for Call-Me-Kate Bracewell, I tracked her down without undue difficulty to one of the London teaching hospitals. Her nice bosom (artificially uplifted, I now suspected) had burst out of its twinset and her hair was all over the place in a vegetarian-bohemian sort of way. She had an office (partitioned with utility hardboard) and we sat in it.

'Are you surprised to see me?' I asked.

'Yes. How are you, Michael? What have you been doing since . . . when was it?'

'You've still got my confiscated books,' I said.

'Oh – I . . .' She fluttered her eyelashes (not her own, perhaps). 'To be honest, I'm not sure where . . .'

'I'd like them back.'

'Yes of course, I –'

'They're mine. Not that mine and thine mean much nowadays.'

'And your sister . . .'

'My cousin. As it turned out.'

249

I monitored Bracewell's thoughts through the skylight in her head. She was congratulating herself on not arguing.

'Did she marry her American?'

'They're Mr and Mrs Rascoe of Pacific Heaven Drive, Santa Monica.'

'Are you happy about that?'

'Why not?'

'It was hard to explain to you, but there's a certain type of predatory woman whose scalp-hunting is directly related to primal insecurity. She needs to have various males at her disposal, like a spider with its paralysed wasps, to take a bite whenever needed. I assume she did sleep with you, by the way?'

'I have little respect for people who qualify their most important question with a casual "by the way". It signals *mauvaise foi*, doctor.'

She grimaced. 'Now I remember you properly – an awkward customer.'

'Personally, since we're discussing sex, I've always felt that a pretty woman one has not yet enjoyed is more exciting – oh far more! – than the ones already possessed.'

'Yes?' Dr Bracewell waited for me to continue. 'Does that include sisters?'

'Your profession', I told her, 'is the most narrow-minded in the world. Every impulse which doesn't conform to "normality" is categorized as an inversion. And all because a Viennese charlatan called Freud –'

'Have you read him? No?' Seated democratically beside rather than behind her desk (as at Greendale General Hospital three years earlier) she re-crossed her legs and I couldn't help looking – thirty-love her smile said. 'She bewitched you, Michael – and deliberately. I could tell. In my opinion there are two solutions – otherwise this thing is going to tie you up for the rest of your life.' (I crouched before the woman doctor, helpless in my need.) 'Either it's got to be deep analysis, Michael, or it's got to be another woman.'

Was she offering herself? I couldn't be sure. I detest uncertainty; it diminishes.

On New Year's Day 1947 every coalmine carried a notice on the gate: 'This colliery is now managed by the National Coal Board on behalf of the People.' Governments don't make the weather but Socialism can turn a cold spell into a disaster. Power stations ran out of coal, and gasworks, and there was practically no transport; it was forbidden to use electric fires at home during factory hours. We worked by candlelight. Industry ground to a halt, unemployment shot up, exports fell to zero and hundreds of millions were lost in foreign currency. 'Starve with Strachey, shiver with Shinwell.' The Government lurched from one crisis to the next – as did Wilson after 1966 – and the official posters wailed 'We're Up Against It!'

Charrington had (rather flatteringly) invited me to share an elegant Park Town flat with him but my independent means were not such that I could afford the rent while maintaining the required and desired social life-style. I survived on spam, tongue, liver-sausage, salad cream, disgusting cream buns and cocoa. The local butchers generally hated undergraduates as intruders and I missed V's ability to get six ounces of mince more than the ration book said. On freezing winter mornings I lazily stirred my porridge with a wooden spoon, producing a congealed mess and, as often as not, a burnt saucepan. To sew up the seams of Utopia, there was also bread rationing for the first time.

I lived alone and did most things alone, I always have. I visited the Tate Gallery's Van Gogh exhibition and obtained a ticket (I always went alone) to Benjamin Britten's new opera at Glyndebourne. I saw *The Lady's Not For Burning* and – most poignant memory – Vivien Leigh in *A Streetcar Named Desire* at the Aldwych Theatre. My hand kept reaching out to take V's. There were times when her absence was an agony; her fate was the curse across my life.

I had grown fond of Charrington, who had a style of transporting his limbs as if they were only provisionally attached and could be rapidly dismantled in an awkward situation. My erstwhile tormentor had grown into one of those genuinely charming and handsome undergraduates who, meeting you in the Broad or the High, would simply turn and walk with you wherever you were going, his arm linked through yours, his eyes fresh as dew, his lips puffy with the kisses of last night's girls.

'The main thing in life, Michael, is not to be ignored.'

He carried a list of what he called 'notables' – undergraduates who had 'made a mark'. He was very keen on introducing them ('Mention my name') to each other and evenings on his staircase in Trinity were convivial affairs. I lacked the class and the money of most of Charrington's circle, but the demonstrative respect he showed for my opinions almost made up for it.

Though the 'main thing in life' (sometimes called 'the chief purpose') was constantly changing, Charrington issued each new edict with total conviction. Among the main things and chief purposes I best remember were: happiness, fame, wine, not being ignored or found out, art, shallowness, and setting fire to ex-servicemen (who constituted ninety per cent of freshmen in our year of matriculation). Charrington's charmed circle was of course regarded with contempt by these hairy brutes, not least because most of us had gained deferment from National Service by winning state scholarships.

In later years I read *The Last Enemy* by the romantic Battle of Britain pilot, Richard Hillary, an Oxford classicist and oarsman who had looked forward to war as an antidote to the 'false values and muddled thinking' of normal life and who regarded fighter planes as a revival of medieval hand-to-hand combat. My father had never talked like that but I suspect that in his cramped, inhibited mind lurked the same, dark Lawrentian (I mean T.E.) impulses of the romantic soul found in the literary pilots Malraux and Saint-Exupéry, whose 'dark sense of duty' was 'greater than that of love'. Ugh.

Hillary had been horribly burned in combat and came down in the same Channel over which I had flown after Father's last visit to Greendale, the day of the girls' hockey match when Father took V out to dinner without me and I was thrashed by Brophy and Charrington (will these nightmares never retreat?). Hillary had suffered agonies in hospital; he later pulled a woman clinging to a dead child from under the rubble of a bombed house. 'Thank you, sir,' she said, 'I see they got you too.' Possibly Hillary's niceness and very English tone of understatement, his aversion to flamboyant patriotism, has masked the fascist core of a man who could write, 'Life would have a purpose while it [the war] lasted.'

Gaining admission to the Oxford clubs was important – here again Charrington's patronage was crucial. As V had foreseen, money was needed, which was one reason for selling the house (it was the devil squeezing a higher allowance out of old Underwood even though I needed suits made to measure at Hall Brothers and dined whenever I could at Whites, which offered a sort of French menu on the blackmarket). Otherwise the food at that time was unspeakable and (if memory serves) considerably worse than during the war. The sport of the era was queueing to buy cakes made of dried egg – until the Socialist Minister of Food, the former Communist John Strachey, contrived the miraculous disappearance of the same – and greasy whale steaks . . . Ugh.

We made a point of cold-shouldering certain other categories of undergraduate, notably ex-servicemen (gangs of ex-Guards officers roaming in search of people to beat up), the effete dandies of the theatre set, plebeians, rugger buggers and rowdies, women in wool stockings and suspected of wearing serge knickers. This last embargo was rather forgotten when the great frost set in on the first Sunday of Hilary Term 1947 – snow storms, sub-zero temperatures and a ban on the use of electricity for five hours every day.

The main passion was politics, journalism and the Union debates. I was soon in print – at that time the only serious avenue of communication. Although without any previous experience of public speaking, I forced myself by effort of will to the despatch box. Too solemn in my first interventions, too eager to pile up facts in support of my case, I gradually learned to relax, to take my time, to spread my wit, to play with words. When the Socialist Chancellor, Stafford Cripps, delivered his austerity budget in April 1948, I led the attack. 'As this Government has taught us, if a job's worth doing, it's worth doing badly.' And: 'If at first you don't succeed, try, try and fail again.' Cripps, the first man to ration potatoes, rode out a sterling crisis in a Swiss clinic. When Socialist politicians like E. Shinwell and Dr E. Summerskill came to address the faithful, we derided them as humourless nannies. The most eloquent Oxford Socialist of the time was the Honourable Schoolboy, the Hon. Anthony Wedgwood Benn, who became President of the Union. He reminded me of a leaping salmon. Every time an industry was nationalized (mines, railways) we sent him a personal message of congratulation. The wording was always the same: 'You must be terribly happy today.'

But the Union was a broad church and certain debates were commandeered by wits and dandies of brighter plumage. Motions such as This House Deserves its Doubtful Reputation or This House Believes Sincerity to be the Refuge of Fools belonged to the satin-shirted aesthetes and their adoring female *claqueurs* (I do not find *claqueuses*) in the gallery. Women, of course, were not admitted as members of the Union. By 1948 they were wearing the New Look. I bought two dresses cut in the new style – both of them second-hand discards belonging to Charrington's bright young things – and took them to Wiltshire for my darling sister. I used to tell her at length about the Union debates and the points I'd scored but she never quite understood how one could argue a case one didn't believe in – her misted, uncertain eyes constantly searched my face for evidence of sincerity. And she knew virtually nothing about the world since the war. She could no longer read or write – I never received a letter from her in all my life, oh what I wouldn't give to be able to hold such a letter in my hand, to kiss the paper, to relive V through the words on the page, the large, rounded, naïve looping handwriting she had. She liked to gaze at pictures in magazines, *Picture Post* or *Woman's Home Companion*, clowns at the circus, models in underwear. The radio made her head ache except for the comedy half-hours. She loved Murdoch and Horne in *Much Binding in the Marsh*, which was set on a fictitious airfield, but the associations weren't good for her and by the end she was usually in tears.

Whenever I could I'd get down to Wiltshire on a Saturday to

take her to the shops. No use begging her not to cake her face in make-up and rouge before these humiliating outings. She fingered things like a child: 'I want it,' she'd say but a moment later she would lose interest. Sometimes she walked steadily, sometimes she needed to be supported, her sense of balance gone. When a Socialist Chancellor banned the use of petrol for private purposes I obtained an exemption on 'compassionate' grounds. My heart ached with love for her, but I could never again take her to a hotel, or sign the register 'Mr and Mrs Michael Parsons'.

This side of my life remained *terra incognita* to my friends, even Charrington. I trusted no one. My 'internal security' was flawless because effortless. Twenty years later I began to read the memoirs of bigamists with keen interest.

TWENTY-SIX

My Dad lifted me up with one arm on the platform at Victoria, my sister Elsie in the other, a lance corporal's stripe on his sleeve. First time he'd ever kissed me (and the last) and I was squirming. Before he went I remember my Dad laughing and teasing my Mum about French underwear and what he called ooh-la-la until my Mum said not in front of the children. My Dad said the French drank wine instead of tea, all the time. I wasn't sure what wine was.

Soon after my Dad went from Victoria we went from Waterloo. There was a WVS woman in green handing out sandwiches. We all wore name tags like parcels and carried gasmasks. We didn't know where we were going. The WVS woman said she hoped we'd all got three changes of underwear and my Mum nodded. Changes of what? Some of the other kids were crying. They wore grey caps and grey blazers and were stuck-up. We took their sandwiches. Some of them carried buckets and spades, so we peed in the buckets and they howled like mad until the teacher came from the next carriage.

When we got to this village we were lined up and the local women sort of handpicked us like us choosing West Ham v Arsenal in the street, only it was the opposite thing because the clean weedy ones got picked. When we got to wherever it was there was this big old house. The woman who took us home was quite shocked when she saw we didn't wear underpants. She scrubbed us in hot water and carbolic soap. 'Ungrateful'

256

was her favourite word. She'd wheel round to catch us with our tongues out. 'Ungrateful!' We was rubbish.

We slept on straw mattresses on the cold floor like kippers on a fishmonger's slab. I never wet my bed but most of them did. 'Filthy,' the woman said. Some kids were writing letters saying they wanted to go home but I couldn't write and didn't mind. I saw some cows with milk hanging underneath. Most of the time I was hungry. The local village shop was so stuck-up they'd bawl you out before they even saw if you had a penny. I was sick after eating some rotten pickled eggs. A boy got something I couldn't pronounce, then another; it must have been impetigo.

After some time, months I suppose, my Mum came down to see me all smiles and looking her best with the nine-carat wristlet watch which the bloke in Petticoat Lane had said was twenty-two. She described the barrage balloons and the shelters and said some of my mates like Billy had come home. My Mum took me home in time for the Blitz. The day after I came home a man came to the house to speak to my Mum. He said my Dad was 'missing' in France on a beach at Dunkirk. It sounded to me like maybe he'd got lost. I never wanted to hear that name again but you couldn't avoid it. They said we'd won a great victory, managing to escape.

I don't remember how the bombing started. My Mum wanted to send me back into the country where my sister Elsie was but I was staying. You could see the Dorniers, long and thin, we called them flying pencils, and our guns banging away, bits of shrapnel everywhere. Our planes were brown and green and the evil shapes of the Huns were black. We were sent down the underground at night until we got fed up. Billy was caught whizzing (picking pockets) by a plainclothes rozzer but I got away. Billy didn't squeal and I gave him one of my best pieces of shrapnel though not my prize bit off a Heinkel. (I always said it was off a Heinkel and no one argued. I had big fists like my Dad, who was still missing.)

Uncle Len said this war was nothing compared to the Last Lot. He'd been a soldier in the Last Lot. Uncle Len was a wardrobe dealer who used to travel out to Purley or Virginia

Water on a Saturday to pay five or ten bob for city suits worth a quid. Uncle Len got invited in by the ladies whose officer husbands were missing like my Dad. He said they always wanted to talk. My Mum used to sort of grunt when she heard that. 'Maybe,' she'd say. He used to take me with him to the Exchange Buildings, Houndsditch, where he sold some of the good clothes, and I'd keep watch on his stall in Brick Lane, Bethnal Green, Sundays. After my Dad went missing there was definitely something on between Uncle Len and my Mum though he was quite a bit older.

My Dad was a docker and a 'Bevin Boy' before they were invented. The man he hated most in the world after Hitler, Mussolini and Franco, was Ramsay MacDonald. My Dad's name was Joe Frame. Mum called him 'Dad' and he called Mum Ellen or Angel depending on his mood. Generally his mood was good. Once or twice he'd take us to see West Ham United. Arsenal was best but my Dad was a loyalist. There was more genuine wit on the terraces at Upton Park in those days and little of the violence you get nowadays from the likes of Bobby Dukes. When our centre forward missed an open goal, which he always did, there was almost affection in the 'Lor' what a load o'rubbish!'

He always read the sports page first then the politics. We never went to a match but the referee was biased towards the other team. ''Ow about that, ref!' my Dad would shout when he thought one of our boys was fouled, and 'Give 'im a chance, can't yer!' when one of our defenders got the whistle. It was partly partisanship but partly a code against authority in any shape or form. When the Blackshirts were beating up Jews in the East End my Dad and his mates in the TGWU turned out in their defence. I remember him going off carrying a heavy wooden stave. He said the police were definitely on the side of the fascists and the mounted police were the worst. My Dad was dead against the Blackshirts.

He never spoke a good word for our rulers. They were simply 'them' and you'd be a born fool to trust 'em. I was too little to remember the Coronation in thirty-six but he used to tell us that the only memorable thing about it was that the

docks were closed and they all had to lose a day's pay. Auntie Elsa (not my sister Elsie or my Mum, Ellen) said the Queen's family got rents from some of the worst slums in London.

I remember how ashamed I felt, for my Dad I suppose, when our dockers turned out in 1968 to support Enoch Powell against the coloured immigrants. They even abused Ian Mikardo, our local MP, and called him a Yid. That took me back to what my Dad used to say about the strong mob of Blackshirts in Hoxton chanting, 'The Yids, the Yids, we've got to get rid of the Yids.' I wrote to Mr Mikardo on *Mirror* notepaper and he wrote back. I've still got his letter. My Dad always said working people must stick together. 'Don't forget that,' he said, 'and you won't go far wrong.'

Mind you, I bet my Dad would have marched with his mates, I mean the cockneys were expected to absorb thousands of Pakistani immigrants by middle-class liberals who lived miles from the smell of their curries. Suddenly you had cinemas which only showed Indian and Pakistani films. Suddenly you had primary schools where a lot of kids spoke not much English and their mums none. Ain't it all a bloody shame, as the song went. I remember our dockers were denounced as racists and fascists by this wealthy, upper-class young Pakistani gent, President of the Oxford Union and a great showman, who was always flashing himself and his rent-a-mob student 'revolutionaries' in the streets when he wasn't on television. My Dad acted more on instinct and the spirit of the neighbourhood. His only trouble was the boozing and a weakness for skirt. Nothing serious but he was always chasing crumpet. He never let on but my Mum always knew. She cried a lot and said it was a sin. She once got into a fight with a barmaid. I offered my assistance but she made me wait outside the pub. She came out wearing a huge shiner on her left eye and supported by two women friends.

My Mum cried after my Dad went missing. It was about then that I began to turn wild and no one could control me but that side of me never really bothered her, a family needed men and lads who could defend the home; even among friendly neighbours who did fair by each other you had to look after your own.

I never carried my gasmask. You were soppy if you did. There was a rubber bit under your chin that flipped up and hit you every time you breathed. When you breathed out it sounded like farting. The bottom of the masks soon filled up with spit. The main use for gasmasks was fights – you could get your head cut open if you didn't dodge.

The barrage balloons were like silver elephants. The hawser would often break and you'd see it dragged across the rooftops, knocking off chimneys. Or breaking the trolley-bus cables. Billy said he reckoned he could shoot one down with his air rifle and I said he didn't have no air rifle. We had our big fight and after that I was leader of the gang until Hitler surrendered to me. We were still small but we knew how to fight dirty. What makes all the difference is growing up seeing bigger boys and even men fighting. I never feared for my Dad when he went to France because I'd never seen him lose a fight.

In Limehouse we had Limehouse oaths of allegiance different from Stepney and Hackney or Bethnal Green. You had to bring blood out of your finger. Quite a lot turned septic. Any lad under suspicion concerning his true allegiance or recent conduct had to say 'I swear' then 'I bloody swear' then 'I bloody bugger swear'. Fuck didn't come into it until we turned eleven.

The underground was worse than the bombs. Soldiers would force you on to trains to go further up the line. We never wanted to go further than Liverpool Street. If you didn't bag your patch right quick you might find yourself spending the night on the moving staircase which they switched off at night. That was no fun at all, you couldn't even filch things. People we knew were killed in the Bank shelter on January 11, 1941. Billy and his small brother Eric claimed they'd been on a tube train just out of Tower Hill station when a bomb had fallen down the lift shaft behind them killing everyone and electrocuting people on the line. I said it was a lie and Eric said, 'Ask my Mum!' But Billy just looked at me and said he hoped Hitler had one for me. That was a long fight. After the war Billy got the Borstal.

When the explosions shook the house my Mum raised her fist and cursed and cried for my Dad. Cannon Street station was flat. A lot of people used to spend the night in Epping Forest.

We never did that. My Mum said we weren't gypsies. The back of our house was blown in while we were in the underground. They boarded it up with plywood but we never went to Epping Forest.

When we stopped using the underground my Mum said at least we'll get killed together. It was too much aggravation.

When a house was hit we'd all come out to look, you could tell if they were dead because there'd be a blanket over the face, but you didn't always know which of the family it was and our Mums would grow hysterical. The wardens were always shouting, 'Get those kids indoors there's a bloody raid going on!' Pretty soon you'd make a gang den and light fires in the rubble, have a smoke, even if it was your neighbour's house. If I heard the words 'You kids ought to be ashamed' once I heard it a hundred times.

The big incendiary fires and the exploding gas mains were another matter. You could feel them sucking in the air and creating a wind which made it all burn harder. You could always smell what was burning down at the West India docks and even at the Royal Victoria if the wind was from the east. Sugar was worst, it made you hungry and sick at the same time. Rubber raised clouds of oily black smoke. The firemen were always in trouble when the Thames was at low tide and the pressure in the hydrants fell. We never felt on their side. I remember seeing some smart office girls coming out of the tube in the morning and giving their sandwiches to the firemen. You had to be stuck-up to give food away.

There was a dare on to try and cut the fire hoses with jagged bits of shrapnel. For a while we just talked about it but then it got serious and I had to do it. I was spotted but a fireman or Special couldn't keep pace with you through that rubble and I was wearing a rag round my face like the horseback robbers in the films. Finally all of us kids in the neighbourhood were made to stand in a line by a fire officer and told to own up but he was wasting his time. Then he said soldiers would be given orders to shoot us if we did it again. I suppose we half-believed him. Half-believing grown-ups was it. We knew that the Huns were only bombing poor people because they had a deal with the rich. Auntie Elsa said that. My Mum never said it but you could tell she was thinking it.

Terry Hare, whose Dad voted Tory and had the corner shop, said Jerry had bombed Buckingham Palace as well. I gave him a bunch of fives for contradicting. Mr Hare had always been dead mean about us paying off the grocery bills. If the debt rose above five shillings because my Mum was a bit short he'd refuse to serve her. After I spoiled young Terry's chances in life by removing his front teeth (just a couple) his Dad never again sold my Mum another packet of Capstans, just Turkish fags made out of camel dung.

My Mum used to smoke more than most and I took it up, on the cadge and scrounge, when I was about nine. She needed at least a dozen full-strength Capstans to get through the day. We knew men who'd call at the tobacconist on their way to work and go back to bed if there were no fags. My Mum always seemed to be in a crisis about her nicotine supply on Friday afternoons.

She and Auntie Elsa swore blind that that Mr Hare was in the forged clothing coupons racket operating up round Shaftesbury Avenue but selling all over the East End at 4d or 6d a coupon. Billy's big brother once offered my Mum a full book of clothing coupons for five quid saying it was a favour and he could get six. That was after a hundred thousand coupon books were lifted in a single job but the papers never said anything about it. Five quid was two weeks' wages for my Mum, who was by then working in a munitions factory. Another time Billy's brother's mob lifted thousands of stockings from a hosiery factory. There were always plenty of wide boys in crushed hats and flashy fish-tail ties who could get you things 'off the ship' for a consideration. In the docks you needed to be sure of your checker and your lorry driver. Our gang tried to work its own rackets but at eleven or twelve you don't get respect, just bovver and the boot.

You could say goodbye to two quid for a pair of real stockings. I bet Vera Lynn, the Forces' sweetheart, was never short of stockings. I liked Ginger Rogers and Fred Astaire, the tap dancing. Vera was an East End girl and when she sang 'We'll

Meet Again' or 'When they Sound the Last All-Clear' you couldn't resist a tear of pride. She didn't sing in American either and she had a catch in her voice that caught you. She was always one of us like Gracie Fields in Lancashire.

Sometimes we sneaked into the cinema by the fire exit at the back and saw stupid films showing stuck-up people singing in the shelters. There was two 'blitzes', the real one and the jolly-good tour of inspection by Winston or their Majesties. You never saw the looting on the films or in the papers. It was like those newsreels of Dunkirk: a great victory, thumbs up – and where's my Dad? My Uncle Tommy had come home a shattered wreck without his rifle saying Jerry will be here tomorrow.

I don't remember how much we went to school at that time. Sometimes there was a school and sometimes it had been turned into something else or flattened – raise a cheer – but I do remember this headmaster-character reading out the list of children who'd been killed and we had to pray for them. It was the only time we kept quiet, when he read out the list. The first thing to look for in a bombed house was tins of food. Then you had to make arrangements against the other gangs coming in there. I picked up quite a few things that way, including Terry Hare's electric train set, the only one in Limehouse, not a dent in it. It was the feel of the engine in my hand, the 'Flying Scotsman', that made me feel a bit sorry for him even though he was full of money and a Tory. He must have been killed just where I was squatting. Hare's corner shop was stripped bare within a day. They were all dead.

TWENTY-SEVEN

I had sold the house in Hampstead after Leo died. At that time I was quite naïve and had no thought of bricks-and-mortar as an investment; in any case I needed the money if I was to keep pace with my new circle of friends at Oxford (a more accurate word than 'friends' eludes me). I took some pleasure in being of no fixed abode – as they describe vagrants in the magistrates' courts. There was another reason for selling the house. Gangs of homeless people, some of them ex-servicemen, and all of them inpsired by the new Socialist dawn (known as *les lendemains qui chantent* in France), were roaming about and breaking into any large dwelling which looked empty. It was called squatting and the Communists were behind it.

When Albert returned from America a year later, to take up a post at the atomic research establishment at Harwell, he wrote a friendly letter asking after V and myself. I didn't reply. One afternoon he presented himself in College as an unwelcome visitor. We went for a walk (Albert was very keen on walking) along the river, passing the bathing place known as Parson's Pleasure. I inquired politely about his work. He sighed deeply:

'So much beauty given to us by nature, so easy to destroy it.'

'That's up to you boffins, isn't it?'

'Scientists make weapons not policies. Sadly, the Americans have now fallen victim to hysteria – so many loyalty oaths, so many FBI investigations, so many committees of Congress making hay out of spy mania.'

'The Soviet threat is real enough.'

'Listen: my friend Petersen returns to the Princeton University Physics Department after a period of work at the Brookhaven Laboratory. The rules forbid him to tell his students how many neutrons are given off in the fission of uranium.'

I brought my mouth close to Albert's ear in a whisper: 'How many neutrons?'

He smiled but thinly. In truth he'd been much more cheerful during the war. He told me that, if Max Planck's work on high temperature radiation had been classified, Einstein would never have postulated the equivalence of mass and energy through the concept of relativity. Or something like that.

'I assume you would have liked to sign the Stockholm Appeal, Albert?'

'Maybe, maybe.'

'No objections to the World Peace Movement?'

'They want peace. So do I. So should you. Even the Conservative Britain you desire to see restored will not be possible after a thermonuclear war.'

'But peace at any price? Appeasement all over again?'

'We start from different premises, you and I.'

He said he wanted to visit Veronica. 'She's very ill, ja?'

'Who told you that?'

'Why all this secrecy, Michael? My life is plagued by secrecy, most of it unnecessary, please believe me. Kindly tell me where I can visit your sister.'

'She's not my sister. I must insist, Albert, that you abandon this accusation –'

'It is not an accusation, my dear –'

' – which is deeply damaging to my parents as well as to Veronica and myself.'

Albert wrung his hands with 'guilt', explaining that Veronica and I had fallen into a 'tragic misalliance' (I laughed contemptuously), and that he, Albert, bitterly regretted that he had not intervened as soon as he recognized the nature of our relationship. But my mother had sworn him never to tell me; and the manner of my return home, expelling all his comrades, had further inhibited him from discussing something 'so delicate, so intimate, ja?'

I told him that his own, grotesque version of my relationship with Veronica could only impede her recovery. I therefore had no intention of divulging her whereabouts. I left him standing in the college quadrangle, his porthole glasses misty with grief. 'Goodbye, Albert.'

When I paid my next visit to the nursing home I noticed at once a marked difference of tone from the staff nurse on duty. It was not the usual chit-chat and 'you know your way, Mr Parsons'. It was 'Dr Yardley would like to speak to you before you see Veronica today'. I was thrown into the greatest alarm.

The Midlands coxcomb Yardley received me in the surgery.

'I won't beat about the bush. A Dr Albert Harting came to visit Veronica. He introduced himself as an old friend – she desperately needs friends. She not only recognized him at once but cheered up quite remarkably in his company. Interesting. He was pretty shaken by what he saw of her but didn't show it. She begged him to come again.'

'Well, good,' I said.

'Dr Harting told me that you had tried to prevent him finding her. Interesting.'

'That's nonsense.'

'He also told me a great deal about you and your family history. My first instincts were right, Mr Parsons; the sibling relationship may not be a fact in law because birth certificates can't lie, but I am convinced that Veronica is your half-sister and that you both knew this when you had sexual relations. OK, I'm not narrow-minded – special circumstances. But I've given you my professional opinion more than once: I believe we can help Veronica only with your honest co-operation.'

'I don't accept a word of what Harting told you.'

'Dr Harting occupies a highly responsible position.'

'Did he tell you he was my mother's lover?'

'Certainly. He was hiding nothing and in my view inventing nothing.'

'Did he tell you he's a Communist?'

266

'An interesting accusation. Communists don't occupy his kind of post.'

'They do until they're found out.'

'Oh, for God's sake! Look – what we need is for you to work through your entire relationship with Veronica, step by step, trauma by trauma: together. You and she.'

'And you.'

'Obviously. Tell me, please, in strict confidence: why did you conceal from me that you both attended the same boarding school?'

I made a familiar mental spot-check: Rowley now dead; Bracewell working in London and unknown to Yardley; Nancy Lunt the main threat if this forensic physician stopped posturing and actually got on his bike.

'Out of loyalty to Veronica,' I said.

'Please explain.'

'Veronica had been appointed games mistress at Greendale. The sad truth is . . . she was expelled after her fiancé was found to have spent the night in her room.'

'And why did *you* leave Greendale, Mr Parsons?'

'In protest. I was livid.'

'According to Dr Harting you and she shared a bedroom from the time you returned home. Now that's interesting – it's not an accusation, I'm merely trying to cotton on to the real source of Veronica's trauma.'

'A bottle of phenobarbitone is all you need.'

'I don't agree. Nor does Dr Harting.'

'That man was clearly after Veronica – no woman in our house could escape his attentions. As for this alleged sibling relationship, if I were to believe him, I'd have to accept that both my parents were liars. Harting did everything he could to make Veronica and myself unhappy and guilty – and I fear he may have planted poisoned seeds of doubt in Veronica whose bitter harvest we now see.'

'Hm,' said Yardley, 'interesting theory. It's an improvement on your phenobarbitone one.'

'With your permission, I'll now visit my cousin. I am, after all, paying the bill.'

He shrugged. 'But she's paying the price.'

I presented V with my usual sad and inadequate carrier bag of cosmetics, fruit, chocolate, cigarettes, gin and picture magazines. She immediately offered her fruit and chocolate to the old crones in the neighbouring beds – V always did this and it infuriated me, her relentless goodness.

Then she whispered in my ear: 'Mike.' Nothing more.

Sometimes she would ask me to read to her, sometimes her eyes would glaze over. The books she preferred were cheap novels, romances which bored me senseless but which I strove to inject with dramatic urgency and pathos. A useful trick is to lay heavy emphasis on one word in each sentence. I noticed that one can 'switch off' while reading (as while driving a car); the mind travels elsewhere, yet the reading faculty continues on automatic pilot. From time to time I tried her on the children's classics I'd never read – I remember ploughing right through a scene in *Alice* (a great favourite with V) describing how the heroine, having drunk from the unmarked bottle – not the Drink Me one – had grown so big that her leg was up the chimney and her hand out of the window, frightening the White Rabbit into the cucumber frame. But how, subsequently, had she grown tiny again and got herself out of the house to be confronted by a huge, frolicsome puppy which might just be hungry? I had no idea; I had read the passage without taking in a word. I glanced at V; her smile was relaxed and pleasant.

'Drink me,' she said and offered me a lock of hair. She always had one ready for me. 'Present,' she said.

On another occasion I tried her on *The Railway Children*, reading the passage where the two sisters tie Peter to the settle, then leave him as a punishment. As I read lines I had known almost by heart since Aunt Phyllis first introduced me to the book in Cornwall, I studied V's intent expression. Did she remember?

Abruptly her hand grabbed my trousers. 'Close your eyes and think of Hitler,' she said.

The old hags grinned. 'Have a go!' the charwoman cackled. 'Screw the bitch hee hee!' The walls of the room were stained with a crushed grey light.

TWENTY-EIGHT

There was a WVS woman in a green uniform who used to come down our way looking busy and concerned. You could tell she was the stuck-up sort that pride themselves on mixing with common people but you didn't slag her off because she might always have some clothes or food. My Mum called her Mrs Parsons from WVS. She was always telling my Mum that us kids ought to be evacuated. My Mum used to sigh in a kind of agreement. 'You know how it is, Mrs Parsons.' Then the green WVS woman came up with a scheme to have us all sent down to a school in the country during the school holidays. I didn't see the purpose but went along with it. It was called the London Boys' Programme and was mainly for kids who'd lost both parents but sometimes people who were skint like us had to go.

At Greendale they were stuck-up. You could go weeks at a time without an air-raid siren. We used to shit in the fire buckets. They were livid. The school didn't smell like London, where the air was always full of friendly dust and the smell of burnt things. The school was surrounded by 'fresh air'. The way the people spoke down there was also 'fresh air'. I soon got the hang of Mrs Parsons's big plan: they needed cheap labour to dig the allotments. We was it.

We'd snare rabbits or try to. The farmers were always complaining, not about the rabbits but about the fences we broke. We all knew they had as much to eat as they wanted. They could kill a pig and eat it for days until it went off. A local

269

farmer was offering a few shillings a week for digging trenches up to your knees in water and mud. Another wanted us banging the mud off sugar beet in the freezing cold. Rowley was all for it, keep us busy. By the evening you were always starving at Greendale, I was never that hungry at home.

I could make a deadly catapult out of just about anything and the 'ammunition' was easy. Spent cartridge cases littered the streets and you only had to fill them with wet sand. Two lads lost an eye in these exchanges. The main problem about Greendale was leaving the weapons behind. We had an arsenal in the rubble off Commercial Road. By the time you got back home from the sodding country the other buggers had lifted them. The worst thing was that some of the other gangs were getting sent to places where German planes fell like ninepins and then just rested in fields or haystacks waiting to be done over. All that lovely loot. The Narrow Street gang were boasting they'd lifted cannon and machine guns *with ammunition* from a bomber which had crashed near Clacton. The police and the RAF had given chase and the boys had been prosecuted before a judge. I knew this was true but pooh-poohed the story to keep my troops' morale up. Then Jack Jenkins, the Narrow Street leader, produced part of the jawbone of the German pilot complete with teeth. Jack held it under my nose because he was already big enough to lay the girls who worked in Woolworth's. That was clearly the worst moment of the war.

They said that round Piccadilly the tarts wore special heels that went click-clack like tap dancing. The slags who did the sailors down our way couldn't afford that. I never realized how much life there was on the streets until I was stuck among all those snobs, farmers and pigs at Greendale.

I didn't have so many words then, but in *Mirror* canteen language little Michael looked like a semi-quaver made of asparagus. He was the sort who'd save the stamp on a letter informing him of his Dad's death. I bet he'd lock the lavatory door even if he was alone in the house. Us, we didn't have a lavatory in the house. I didn't wipe my arse throughout the war. You have to smell bad to lead a gang. Stuck-up Michael walked around the school with that peevish look and his nose in the air, calling God by his first name. Shifty bugger, I always knew he was after that 'cousin' of his though I bet he only had one ball, like Adolf. When he got into the House of Commons he developed the habit of making his point by thumping his right fist into his cupped left hand. I used to sit in the Press Gallery and watch it coming. But you never heard the smack.

Every goose flying high above the world ends up a clump of feathers on some desolate shingle. So Auntie Elsa used to say.

They used to lock us in the dormitory at night. We broke several drain pipes getting out. Once Billy got his braces caught on the window latch and just hung there until a woman called Matron arrived. She went and got a man with a ladder who fetched Billy down then gave him a few lessons and half a hiding. But Miss King never slapped anybody. She might twist your ear, but friendly. She was a raver. I've never seen legs like that. You'd want to go on those bloody runs past the shitting cows just to see her legs. They were up to Betty Grable's, which we knew were insured for a million dollars though we had no idea what 'insured' meant. She had lovely boobs too. She used to tell us stories about South Africa, where she was a kid. She said the black people of South Africa were very friendly but very backward. She said the Zulus were the fiercest and told us about a king called Dingaan, who we nicknamed Dinner Gone. She'd seen Hottentots too. She was always trying to get us to read and do sums. You could stare at her for hours and never get bored, better than the barrage balloons. I used to imagine doing things with her though I knew she wouldn't. We boys used to fight over whether she would or not. The freezing cold day I went up the scaffolding and saw her in the bath with little Michael I got an anger that's never gone away. They weren't doing anything, in fact they were back to back – that got my wick. Maybe he never got his limp little dick into her. Billy said I shouldn't have written that note to Rowley. I'd have given my right arm to have Miss King. What a cracker and your real lady, too, I mean the genuine article. I'd probably have fainted on the job.

So there you are: Socialism is pure Envy. *The Times* was right all along though I never read it.

My Mum never really asked about Greendale. I think she felt it was a different kind of place she couldn't understand. She told us that the nice green lady Mrs Parsons WVS had been killed in her own kitchen by a bomb. I said, 'Jerry made a mistake then.' My Mum said she felt sorry for Mrs Parsons's son who was a boy at Greendale. I said he was a drip. Mum said he'd lost his Dad too. I didn't ever tell her about Miss King. Finally she began to unravel my Dad's old jumpers to knit us things and she cried.

Three years after my Dad went missing my Mum got a big tum. They used to say that you'd never get good meat unless the butcher fancied your Mum. The sausage we got was pink and no meat in it that's certain. But sometimes my Mum would come back with A.U.C. (Anything Under the Counter) 'butcher's sausage', the sort he made for his own family, and we'd all look at her until she'd say, 'What are you all staring at?' Billy said his Mum said my Mum had an A.U.C. bun in the oven from the butcher. I said it wasn't anybody and Billy's nose bled for an hour. My Mum never told me and I never asked though I knew it was Uncle Len because he started giving us things and Auntie Elsa cut my Mum dead.

My Mum called our new sister Lizzie to spite Auntie Elsa who'd been a Republican, home and abroad, ever since her Communist fancy man got himself killed in the Spanish Civil War.

I remember in 1945 there were rumours going about the streets that Churchill wasn't going to demob the soldiers and that he was keeping the German prisoners for the same reason, a war against Russia. We kids went up to Walthamstow to pelt the old villain with rotten eggs. The Communists (I can now reveal, world-exclusive) paid us to do it. But I did it for my Dad.

272

TWENTY-NINE

Albert's warm and expansive heart could not rest nor afford itself the normal human refuges: diversion, distraction, indifference. In Central Europe the burden of knowledge carries the burden of liberation. Doctors Harting and Yardley both saw themselves as scientists solvers healers; they believed passionately in information revelation therapy cure. I learned from Yardley that Albert continued to visit the nursing home (I had no legal authority to forbid Albert access to my 'cousin' and my threat to move V elsewhere cut no ice with Yardley while I remained a minor in law). According to the Midlands Physiocrat, Albert was gradually 'unwrapping' Veronica's tangled memory.

'In this case,' Yardley told me, 'repression is reinforced by physiologically induced amnesia – the destruction of brain cells. But Dr Harting has won her confidence. She talks to him. She makes sense. It was not only she who was expelled from Greendale, Mr Parsons, was it? And it had nothing to do with her fiancé, did it? She is beginning, now, to recall the last hour in that hotel in North Wales – but the blockage is immense.'

Fortunately history intervened in the shape of two plain-clothes policemen who presented themselves without warning at my modest but not entirely shabby lodgings in the Iffley Road. (I had purchased a reproduction of a Henry Moore – 'Man and Woman' – for two pounds, spent ten shillings on a plain frame, and hung the picture above the mantelpiece of what was now an electric bar fire framed in charred asbestos.)

'Inspector Rusk, Military Counter-Intelligence.' The senior of the two policemen presented his card while running an eye over my bookshelves. He was a real Home Counties ratcatcher. Suede shoes, sideburns, and probably spent his off-duty hours in the saloon bars of 1930s 'Tudor' pubs on the Great West Road.

'What have I done this time?' I asked, my feet planted wide, my hands in the pockets of my grey flannels, the briar pipe I'd latterly taken up between my teeth – the recently elected Chairman (proposed by C. Charrington) of the University's Conservatives at his ease.

Inspector Rusk, whose main feature was a conspicuous featurelessness – as if only dangerous foreigners had faces – explained that it was 'incumbent upon' him to 'manifest' a number of questions 'pertaining to a certain Dr Albert Harting presently employed in the Theoretical Physics Division at Harwell'. Would I tell them everything I knew about the said Harting?

I explained that Albert was a close and rather dear friend of my family.

'Go on,' said Rusk impatiently, examining his polished toe-caps for the speck of dust which might solve the case.

I reminded the Inspector that a friend is a friend. His sigh of impatience was cultural rather than temporal, of course: I've never met a policeman in genuine haste; their lives are studies in killing time while impatiently hoofing the carpet.

'I wouldn't want to prevail on you, Mr Parsons,' Rusk said.

Fascinating usage and abusage. I produced a notebook, at which his eyes narrowed somewhat. 'Just a record of what is said,' I smiled. Rusk seemed quite thrown by this – groping for some clause in the Official Secrets Act which forbids a man from writing down what he's just said.

'Albert Harting is my good friend,' I repeated. 'I have no obligation to tell you anything about him unless you ask me specific questions.'

'As Chairman of the Oxford University Conservative Association,' Rusk said, 'you wouldn't be particularly partial to Communism, I presume?'

'Quite the contrary. What has that got to do with Albert Harting?'

'How would you describe Dr Harting's political outlook?'

I told him that as a Conservative I was also hostile to Thought Police. 'We don't need to imitate the Russians here,' I added.

Rusk's rising irritation gratified me – another idiotic adult.

'You're a patriot, Mr Parsons?'

'I'd defend any man's freedom not to be.'

'You'd put your friends before your country, would you?'

'Of course. That's my understanding of Conservatism.'

Rusk look flabbergasted – was I taking the piss?

'We may be talking of treason,' he said.

'What – Albert! You must be joking.'

Comedy, he assured me, was not his line though he 'appreciated' a laugh as much as the next fellow. Had Dr Harting ever talked to me about German Communism or the Soviet Union?

'Well – yes, I mean he was very fond of me when I was a boy, a very dear friend of my mother's, and when both my parents died I suppose he felt himself duty-bound to look after my education.'

'He attempted to indoctrinate you?'

'Good heavens, no. Albert! No, no, he came from a certain refugee background and –'

'What background?'

'Don't you know? He must have been vetted for work like his.'

'The records of the Aliens Tribunals were destroyed after the war. An official decision but not a wise one.'

'It's really a most upsetting story,' I said. 'Albert was one of the many thousands summoned by the Aliens Tribunals early in the war. He was put in Class B (the "doubtfuls") and in May 1940) – if my memory serves, it may have been April – he was arrested along with three thousand others born in Germany, most of them Jews. Albert later told us that almost thirty thousand "enemy aliens" were interned by mid-summer 1940. I believe he was shipped to a camp on the Isle of Man where – I gather – there was an active cultural and musical life, including bad-smelling sculptures fashioned out of stale remnants of porridge by a Dadaist artist called Kurt Schwitters.'

Rusk raised a traffic policeman's hand, indicating that we must 'procrastinate' for his colleague, who took a slow note in a slow hand. Finally I got the nod.

'Then Albert had a stroke of luck – he missed being put on the *Andorea Star* and shipped to Canada only by a whisker. The same ship was torpedoed west of Ireland with the loss of half those aboard, including many German and Italian Socialists whom Albert had befriended.'

'Did Dr Harting describe himself as a Communist, a Marxist, or what?' asked the faceless saloon bar punter on whom our national security depended.

'Albert's father was a Socialist professor from Hamburg who used to take his children sailing on the Alster. Very much an idealist, I gather, and a strong supporter of the Weimar Republic. Then the world changed, the clock shattered, the Black and Brown Shirts moved in, and Albert . . . well, he joined the Reichsbänner.'

'The Communist para-military organization?'

I shrugged. 'You can call it that.'

'Thank you,' Rusk said sarcastically.

'Albert told us that some of the Communist students he met at the Humboldt University in Berlin struck him as very fine people – courageous and determined. His brother and brother-in-law were both murdered by the Nazis, you know.'

'So Dr Harting was already a Communist when he arrived in this country?'

No maiden guarding her virtue could have displayed more elaborate reticence than I in the face of Rusk's question. Indeed he repeated it with the implacable, metronomic beat of a firing squad drummer.

'He always *described* himself as a Social Democrat,' I said evasively.

'That was a cover, wasn't it?'

I sighed. 'Albert used to tell me that man becomes truly free when he understands and controls the forces of history. It's a respectable point of view, I suppose.'

'What about his friends?'

Again I looked acutely uncomfortable (I hoped). 'Won't you have some coffee, Inspector?'

Rusk declined. 'His friends, sir.' (A wolfish grin – gottya!)

'Well,' I mumbled, 'Albert did bring a number of people to the house. Some became lodgers. Mostly refugees. Very nice people, very friendly. I suppose you might describe them as a cell.'

'A cell? A Party cell, you mean?'

'Good heavens no! Well . . . hard to be sure. Albert wasn't very forthcoming about them. One gathered that they were united by common aims and activities. Friendship with the Soviet Union, anti-imperialism, international proletarian solidarity, that sort of thing. I'm not sure what they talked about among themselves. The conversation from Albert's room – more of a low murmur, really – was normally in German when it wasn't in Russian.'

'Russian, you say?' Rusk looked puzzled, as if there were a small herring-bone lodged unlocatably in the mucus of his throat. I asked him whether I should continue. He nodded, but with his low brow knitted in frowns by my sudden collaboration. 'Please go on, Mr Parsons: Russians came to your house?'

'There were these Soviet embassy types, they always arrived on foot, then hurried straight up the stairs to Albert's room.' I shrugged. 'They were our allies, after all. And – oh . . .'

'Yes?'

'It just came back to me. No – I really oughtn't to tell you this.'

'You have a legal obligation, Mr Parsons.'

I strove for the grimace of a man whose arm is being broken.

'My cousin Veronica used to darn our clothes, including Albert's. He'd torn an old suit, he was quite devoted to it . . . anyway, she found an old Party card lodged inside the lining. "Kommunistische Partei Deutschlands." We decided she should sew it back in the lining.'

The junior policeman was scribbling hectically.

'You'd swear to that?' Rusk asked. 'On oath?'

'Swear?' I simulated the greatest possible alarm. 'Oh no no, not against Albert, I'm sure he's absolutely above suspicion . . .'

Rusk gave me a look normally reserved for the discovery of rotten fruit on a costermonger's barrow. He then asked whether Albert had ever 'embarked' on 'conspicuous expenditure'.

'Well, he was never short of money, if that's what you mean. He was always bringing us gifts, little luxuries from the `ickmarket. He was tremendously generous, of course. When he took us to the theatre or a concert he always bought the most expensive seats. He once took us to a Soho club – I think it was when the Red Army captured Warsaw – we were treated to champagne, blackmarket steaks, a real feast, then he paid the bill from the thickest wad of notes I've ever seen.'

'More profligate than prodigal,' Rusk said. I was about to wrestle with this when I noticed that it wasn't a question, merely a note dictated to his assistant's slow-flying pencil.

'Can you remember the names of any of the people who came to your house at Dr Harting's invitation ?'

'I was never told them.'

'You mentioned your cousin – Miss . . .'

'Veronica King.'

'Can you advise us where we can find her?'

Reminded of the bubbles familiar to the dreary figures who sit on muddy river banks, waiting for perch, I handed Rusk the address of V's nursing home.

'She volunteered as a fire service auxiliary and almost lost her life. Multiple head wounds, shrapnel and glass. She . . . she no longer . . . I mean [my voice a whisper] she's been certified.'

Rusk pocketed the address. 'My condolences,' he said. 'You didn't have an easy war, Mr Parsons.'

'Frankly, you could only increase her distress if you taxed her failing and unreliable memory. It wouldn't be decent.'

Inspector Rusk almost stiffened to attention before he recollected my age.

Albert was never brought to trial, thank God, but not many months later, when his colleague, the nuclear physicist Klaus Fuchs, was sentenced to fourteen years for treason, Albert was quietly deported to East Germany. I took the opportunity to have Dr Yardley removed from V's case on the ground that he had shown atrocious judgment in paying attention to a Communist spy from whom I had wisely withheld V's address. Cold War hysteria was at its height (the Berlin airlift, then Korea) and no one wanted to argue.

By the end of 1947 V had forgotten I was at Oxford; a year later she'd forgotten who I was, though she still recognized me. 'G'way' was all she said. Lazily she would sweep my presents off the bed on to the floor, including the packets of Du Maurier and Balkan Sobranie cigarettes she liked to smoke from a long ivory holder. 'G'way.'

I wondered whether Olivia de Havilland's psychotic screams in Anatole Litvak's *The Snake Pit* might restore V's sense of proportion. Anne Baxter had turned alcoholic in *The Razor's Edge*, while Joan Crawford had gone mad in *Possessed* – would such films do V good or ill? But it was too late to take her to the cinema; she was now incontinent.

In desperation I told her that Harold wasn't dead after all; he'd been found on a Pacific Island; he was on his way back to England to marry her. I searched her veiled eyes (once a bright, catlike amber-green, sharp and provocative, but now the deadest tone of grey) for response or understanding but all she said was 'P'fic'. Oddly, it was when the mental collapse made itself most cruelly manifest that I experienced an insufferable, choking desire to recover her through her body. I could hear the flames.

As my final exams approached my tutors conceded that a first in History was mine if I didn't lose my head. But National Service also drew nearer. I detest uniforms. My cumulative horror of the armed forces – a steel arc of animosity – ran from Father through Harold to the arrogant ex-servicemen at Oxford. I had schooled myself to be my own master, to fashion my own destiny. I dreaded standing to attention – the return to the pathetic condition of obedience. No doubt I also dreaded a period of egalitarian contact with the Bert Frames, the fuck this fuck that fuck you rabble.

Yet I knew that military service put a Conservative in good standing. Constituency selection committees had a nose for any kind of evasion. A capable linguist with fluent French and German, I had the good fortune (and right connections) to be selected for the army's full-time Russian course – I would survive among kindred spirits after all.

The last piece I wrote for *Tory Challenge* before conscription was actually composed as I perched on the edge of V's bed while she flipped, glassy-eyed, through pages of magazine mannequins. By now she rarely enjoyed even ten minutes of such tranquil sanity and I suppose my relief was reflected through my article. Many years later I dug it out, subjected it to a thorough updating, ironed out its lingering liberal affectations, and published it in the same issue of the *Spectator* as a John Ford review of Sartre's play *Altona*. It was a risk I enjoyed. In my youth I had been almost blindly devoted to my own needs; thirty years later, as a politician approaching the pinnacle, the attachment had been transferred, eyes open, from ego to egoism.

Education [I wrote] is again in the news. The next Conservative administration must tackle this festering sore with vigour and determination. That means increasing the size of classes, reducing the number of ancillary staff, and discouraging any expenditure on school buildings other than bare necessities. We must also increase the range of choices genuinely available to parents. This can be done only if the stranglehold exercised by Socialist Education Authorities (notably ILEA) – and by the two main teachers' unions – is broken. They have never cared what parents want or think – observe Socialist teachers who've been 'working to rule' (i.e. drawing their pay without working), putting down some working-class Mum who complains that her kids are regularly sent home from school when there is no one in the house.

Socialists believe that if everyone cannot have it no one should have it. If every boy or girl cannot attend a private school then private schools must be abolished. If everyone cannot afford a quiet, smoke-free hospital room, then no one should.

In the long run the school system will thrive through competition and that means parents must (a) choose (b) pay for excellence. Those who won't will get what they deserve. As usual, the main obstacle to change is the semi-literate, 'progressive', polytechnic-trained Commissariat in control of the bureaucracy – teachers, social workers and librarians who insist that Biggles is bad for boys.

There is one problem that Conservatives must face: it isn't the parents who get what they deserve but the children who get what their parents deserve. Our party is too ready to assume that this is the natural and inevitable order of things. We sometimes forget that the health of a free society may be measured in terms of its opportunities for social advancement.

The prevailing sound-effects tell the story. Nowadays one can detect the approach of young working-class males at a considerable distance. They emit a kind of ritualized honking, like geese in the mating season. You hear it in the streets, the underground, the bleak courtyards of council estates. The blacks carry huge metal transistors everywhere, turned up full volume, like oxygen cylinders. These desperate tribal noises are abandoned as soon as a young man moves out and up.

I was in the army at the time (October 1949) and in any case far too insignificant to be invited, but we all enjoyed the printed menu for the dinner held at the Savoy to celebrate the Golden Jubilee of Winston's first election to the House. There was 'un sherry d'Oldham 1900', 'Les galettes de Dundee', 'Le Suprême de Sole de Douvres, Hastings, Sandwich, New Romney, Hythe et Manchester aux champignons de la forêt d'Epping.' A tribute to Clemmy in the form of 'Les Perdreaux Rotis sur Canapé Clementine', 'Pommes de terre toujours nouvelles de Woodford', 'Les petits pois d'un grand ami de la France', as well as 'mixed salad of political adversaries', and it all cost a guinea a head exclusive of wine. I would happily have paid five to be there and many more to have seen V relieved of her misery.

She simply could not give up the ghost. Visits became unspeakable. The nurses insisted she was fighting for life – 'Such courage' – and I didn't argue, but I knew that my love was fighting for death. She wanted to go. On a beautiful autumn evening in the year of the Coronation (she had watched it on television, unblinking) I held her hand, now a mass of swollen blue veins. 'Darling, you're almost there,' I whispered.

She died that night, while I slept in the chair beside her. I buried her in Coombe Bissett churchyard, the only person I have ever loved. It had been a passion sufficient to fill all the empty bottles. The gravestone gave her twenty-nine years but her effective life had ceased after twenty-one.

Not long afterwards a property company with which I was associated bought the nursing home and converted it into a private dwelling. After some legal conflicts regarding the incumbents had been resolved in my favour, the four-bed ward in which V had spent her last years became the master bedroom of my new home. It contains a single iron bed – hers once, mine now. I own a Sèvres porcelain collection but the iron bed has no price.

THIRTY

The Home Secretary, reported the chief political correspondent of *The Times*, was an increasingly isolated figure. An 'aura of malignancy' now kept even close colleagues and political friends at bay. 'This malignancy,' added the paper's leader-writer, 'is one with which we have grown all too familiar in recent years – a lack of personal frankness which takes refuge in the threadbare argument that those who have nothing to hide have nothing to reveal.' The *Daily Telegraph* urged Downing Street to intervene and withdraw the 'appalling' incest proposals in the White Paper. The Home Secretary's 'stubbornness' in their defence was adjudged 'inexplicable'.

Both newspapers had requested exclusive interviews. Both wanted me to hang myself in their parlour.

While transparently feasting off Bert Frame's personal allegations, both *The Times* and the *Telegraph* took care to deplore the 'blatantly political motivation' behind the *Globe*'s campaign. The *Guardian* also bit the vulgar hand that fed it with a joke designed to bolster the self-esteem of those who understood it. 'Bert Frame may yet win a Pulitzer Prize for investigative journalism, so dubious are his sources – if they exist at all.'

In the Commons, meanwhile, the Opposition fell into a fever of jabbing and stabbing, like matadors blinded by the midnight sun. I responded according to my best judgment, which was to repeat the humane arguments for legalizing sexual relations between consenting adults. The silence of colleagues seated beside me on the Treasury bench was only deepened by the restless stirrings on the back benches behind me. I reminded my Socialist Shadow that, 'The dogs of the Nile drink at the river running to avoid the crocodiles.' His caustic reply, taken from Belloc, surprised me: 'The press was squared, the middle class was quite prepared.'

According to Lobby gossip, I often lunched alone at my club; placemen glanced away when I entered, gazing at moulded cornices as if I were recently bereaved or had rescued myself rather than my wife and children following a boating accident. 'A milky way of starlets no longer girdles the Parsons planet,' announced Bert Frame. The 'infant prodigies' of my 'think-tank' had 'drained out through the widening holes in the colander.'

Mixed Metaphors: the Definitive Work, by B. Frame.

Charrington dined with me whenever his family and social commitments could spare him (I myself had none). More than once he offered to swallow 'pride and prejudice' by attempting to negotiate with the proprietor and editor of the *Globe*. I said no. He reached for a lock of hair which was no longer there. His hairline had receded very elegantly and no High Court judge could take against it. But I knew that the steady drip-drip of Bert Frame's 'revelations' was wearing down my friend's spirit. Frame's technique was to unpack his sack of mouldering bargains piece by piece, as if each new item had only just come into his possession. Call it the 'avalanche effect' – it works. Victim and spectators alike are engulfed by dust.

Bert Frame's proprietor, meanwhile, launched a new magazine called *Gaining the Edge*, whose promotional posters in the tube promised: 'Competitive working life in Britain. Excellent for people who mean business. Don't get eaten for breakfast. How to spot a bullshitter.' The way of life recommended was 'style and guile'. The first issue would – irresistibly – carry a feature article by Bert Frame, 'Fleet Street's No.1 muckraker'.

'I had a call from Frame.' Charrington delicately picked his words out of his disappearing avocado. 'He asked me, as Chairman of Greendale's Governors, for a copy of Rowley's report to the Governors in 1944 following ...'

'... my departure? Does such a report exist?'

'That's what we have to decide, Michael.'

'So it does exist?'

'Rowley referred to an "enforced emergency exit due to extremely difficult family circumstances". He invited the Board of Governors not to inquire further.'

'Did they?'

'Inquire further? No.'

As I absorbed this I noticed a slight tremor in the hand conducting a spoonful of the club's indifferent (today) fish soup to my mouth. Charrington was a friend but he knew (as they say) too much – I believe this is what the Red playwright Brecht meant by *Verfremdung*: secrets which separate us even from our own alter egos (not that anything as wet as Charrington could fill that bill).

'As you know,' I said, 'my cousin Veronica was about to be conscripted and sent God knows where. Having lost both my parents –'

Charrington touched my sleeve but quickly withdrew his hand.

'No need to explain, Michael. The question is do I send Rowley's report, along with the glowing reference he provided to Brutus Hill, to the proprietor of the *Globe*? It might scotch the whole thing . . .'

'Nothing ambiguous ever scotches anything. Don't forget they've lost three elections on the trot and they're desperate. They're now inhabiting Hobbes's state of nature. In the language of our friend Richard Hannay . . .' (I offered Charrington a small smile; Buchan's anti-Semitism had appealed to us both until we became friends of Israel) ' . . . they'll "stop at nothing".'

'I'm not sure, Michael. All newspaper proprietors are keen on a peerage. Besides . . . I have wind of further allegations.'

'Yes?'

Charrington didn't hurry. Years at the bar had taught him the rules of breathing.

'It concerns your time – rather long ago – as Chairman of Wiltshire County Council's planning committee. If you recall, I once discussed your career with Frame. He now points out that I didn't mention this episode. Hm. According to his information, you granted permission to build sixty-five upper-income houses across a rather attractive sweep of the Avon Valley – but failed to declare your interest as a principal shareholder in the property company involved.' Charrington wiped his mouth with a starched napkin that he'd been torturing in his lap. 'Shall I go on?'

'Please do.'

'Frame knows that you subsequently bought the nursing home in which your, er, cousin, died. He claims that you evicted the other patients.'

'We rehoused them.'

'Only after litigation. You may remember that I acted on your behalf. Tomorrow's *Globe* will accuse you of turning your . . . they call her your sister . . . of turning your sister's nursing home at Coombe Bissett into a private mausoleum. "A den of morbidity."'

'Ha! Complete with catafalque and embalmed mummy?'

Charrington had never been invited to my Wiltshire home. It is not a place for other people, whether friends or neighbours (though the villagers burn with curiosity about their distinguished resident whose normally reclusive presence has in recent years been signalled by policemen on duty). The local vicar had been much disturbed by the inscription I ordered for V's headstone; but the restoration of a perfect Norman column with richly decorated capitals, and the excavation of a medieval altar slab under the sanctuary floor (probably buried during the Reformation) – all cost money.

Charrington had finished his avocado and was picking peevishly at its exhausted skin. I shook myself like a dog clambering out of the warm, sluggish river of time.

'Cheer up, Christopher. Tomorrow's *Telegraph* is publishing my recent speech to the Young Conservatives, in full.'

Leaving the club, I handed him a copy of the text. He thanked me without enthusiasm and declined a lift in my official car. Doubtless he knew there would be photographers waiting on the pavement in St James's.

The British electorate [I wrote] crushingly rejected Socialism only when it was finally offered the experience of a

Government guided by, and faithful to, genuine Tory principles.

In every age one party or the other establishes a form of cultural hegemony. It imposes the dominant values; the other parties are mainly engaged in trying to steal its clothes while declaring it to be naked. From 1945 until 1975 it was the Socialist Party which dominated the national culture. Although the Tories won three successive elections and ruled for thirteen continuous years from 1951 to 1964, we did so mainly by arguing that private enterprise alone could produce the wealth to finance the welfare state, the education state, the health state, the benefits state, the equality state.

Indeed, if one aggregates the popular votes cast in the seven elections from 1945 to 1966, one finds that Labour comes out nine points ahead.

By 1970 it had become apparent to some of us that the solid 'Socialist nation' within the nation could be undermined only by a massive assault on the whole post-war 'settlement'. The excessive legal privileges of the unions, the right to strike at random and without balloting, to disrupt production by flying pickets and mob rule, to impose closed shops – all this had to be reversed by legislation. The great state monopolies had to be broken up, sold off; the welfare state itself had to be drastically slimmed down. Only then could we hand 'back' to the taxpayer his own money in the shape of vastly reduced direct taxation, reduced capital gains tax, reduced tax on investment income (which the Socialist bureaucracy typically called 'Unearned Income'), reduced inheritance and capital transfer tax, and attractive share options on preferential terms in the great privatized national industries: gas, electricity, aviation, telecommunications, oil.

We realized that to put Socialism down and out we had to destroy a whole infrastructure and create a new one. Our long-term aim is to introduce competition, choice, diversity all through the educational system. Similarly, there's no point in promising a Disraelian property-owning democracy unless you actually put council houses and company shares in the hands of the people. Give them possessions and a genuine 'enterprise culture' – and they'll never vote Socialist again. The Socialist

Commissars are naturally terrified of the spirit of ambition and self-help emerging in semi-detached homes, two-bedroom terrace houses and council flats.

In short, the British people will never again settle for equal shares of nothing.

THIRTY-ONE

I received a summons to his chambers in the Temple from Sir Christopher Charrington, QC. This noble pillar of integrity wished to assure me that no report by Rowley on the hasty exit of Parsons and King from Greendale could be found.

'I'm so sorry, Mr Frame. You obviously regard Michael as a symbol of social privilege. You couldn't be more wrong. His background is in fact quite humble and impecunious, the poor end of the officer class. Frankly it haunts me to this day that I so often suggested he should spend time with my family during the school holidays, yet never followed up with a firm proposal ... even though he'd lost both parents ... I suppose one felt he might not quite fit in. He didn't ride, you see, and he'd never held a sporting gun. Point to point and falconry both out of the question. Golf likewise. Tennis, pretty hopeless. As for the old-fashioned ballroom dancing which was *de rigueur* in those days, Michael didn't know a tango from a Highland reel. He would happily play chess or read all day. Solitary and faintly sullen – not at all the thing for a decent house party. I'm afraid he was the sort of fellow whom no girl wanted as a partner ...'

Charrington's voice tapered off, as if baffled by its own trajectory. I asked him why he was telling me all this – was I expected to identify with little Michael's shortcomings? Glimpsing the wound, Charrington hastened to apply antiseptic:

'Michael has made his own way in the world – as indeed have you yourself ...'

'Perhaps its the "decent house party" kind of Toryism which has lost the game?' I suggested. 'Power passed to the ones who never got invited?'

Charrington said: 'Michael is an honourable man of great ability. Why attempt to destroy him?'

I mentioned the *Spectator* columns of John Ford and the incest clauses in the White Paper. 'Unkind brother' were Annabella's last words to Giovanni, meaning not only cruel but unnatural (according to the opinion commissioned by the *Globe* from Dr Jorge Steinberg). I tossed that one at Charrington – had not Parsons virtually murdered his own sister?

Charrington mentioned libel and I mentioned that the Home Secretary had never accepted an invitation to speak at his old school – if such an invitation had ever been issued. Had it?

'It was kind of you to come, Mr Frame.'

It wasn't my first visit to Miss Nancy Lunt but it was my first summons. A 2.8 litre engine comes with the job and I was into the gravel yard at Greendale one hour fifteen minutes after crossing Chiswick Bridge. Not a drink on the way though I inhaled sufficient nicotine to face the smokeless zone in the Staff Annexe. Since I can't think without my eyes screwed up or write without a fag-end browning my fingertips, I approached that much-hated neck of the Hampshire woods with the class war loud in my ear. Only take away their fags and you bring the workers to their knees – quieter than Cossacks.

Three years had passed since Lunt had agreed to see me in connection with a book of wartime memoirs I happened to be editing for the popular end of the market, just lighthearted scrapbook stuff (I explained), lots of pics and, by the way, I'd been one of her charges under the London Boys' Programme so she couldn't decently say no. Almost an alumnus, give or take ninety social degrees.

I hadn't seen her in years and doubted my own childhood monsters, but there she was, fatter than ever, melancholic, shy, with a fine moustache and liable to lose her hanky and her temper just like old times. I walked nervously across the class gap, clinging to a fragile rope-bridge of Churchillian nostalgia and hoping my adversary wouldn't put both her feet down at the same time.

'You won't remember me,' I said and she didn't. 'When I was a kid I thought an Alp was a cheap glacier mint they sold from big jars, all stuck together. Now my kids go skiing.'

What possessed me to say that?

Miss King would have known me at once; I dropped her name into the conversation like a lump of sugar into a shallow teacup, watching Lunt intently on the crest of the splash. 'Oh yes,' I was saying, 'Miss King was a lot of fun, and a hard act for you to follow, Miss Lunt, and of course we were a handful I don't deny it. It was a great surprise to us lads when she left Greendale so sudden . . . ly.'

Miss Lunt's mouth was quivering at the corners.

'And her brother Michael,' I continued, 'of course he's a famous man now, some say our next Prime Minister.'

Lunt's shifting gaze was beset by uncertainties. 'You know more about that than I do, Mr . . .'

'Frame.'

'Mr Frame. I'm afraid I don't follow the political scene at all closely.'

'He *was* her brother?'

After a decent pause Miss Lunt managed to extract the fingers of one hand from those of the other and said yes.

'Of course it's all water under the bridge now,' I went on. 'History,' I chuckled, 'do we need it?' A guffaw: 'My bank manager needs it. Funny the way things nag at you over the years – mind if I smoke?'

'Yes.'

'Pardon? You do or don't mind . . .?'

'In the yard, please, not here. I have an allergy.'

'Did you know Miss King smoked? Secretly, of course.'

'It was Nicky you came about, wasn't it?'

I extended the palms of my hands in surrender, as if she'd cornered me at the climax of a long chase.

'Why she and he left this school in such a hurry. That's the question.'

'Oh – I believe Nicky . . . Veronica . . . was conscripted.'

'Yes? The version *I* heard must be wrong, then.

I could feel the heat of her curiosity scorching her code of loyalty.

'What version was that?'

'There was some scaffolding here, right on this building, during the war. Me and the lads – I don't want to be punished for this, mind, haha – used to scramble up and down, mainly to take a peep at Miss King.'

Miss Lunt's cheeks were alight.

'Well, you know boys,' I went on with a Limehouse wink (it lasts twice as long). 'Anyway, one day we were engaged in this outrage, me in the lead as always, and what did I see?'

Miss Lunt's haunted eyes stretched in search of her beloved's wanton secret trapped in the street arab's memory.

'Forgive my language, but what I witnessed on a very cold day in January 1944 . . . was . . . to be perfectly frank . . . no offence intended . . . Miss King and Michael Parsons together in the bath – hard at it.'

Not quite accurate, of course, but it served. Miss Lunt moaned. For a moment I thought she might pass out, but then a crazed grimace surfaced among those layers of flesh marinated in deprivation.

Now, three years later, I was back in the gravel yard, drawing on my last fag, climbing the scaffolding, peering into the frosted bathroom window, sick with memory, ambition, revenge. The assistant headmistress hadn't aged much, indeed she looked thinner and therefore more cultivated – the sort of tweed skirt and mortarboard that appears in the *Times Ed. Supp.* with its hand resting awkwardly on a sundial. 'New Principal Puts Clock Forward.'

For a moment she didn't recognize me. 'Frame, you say?'

'Yes. The one you telephoned two hours ago.'

I had only to go near a school to see bruised, blackened knees protruding beneath my filthy grey shorts. I reached for my fags, then remembered.

'I've seen his White Paper,' she said. 'Disgusting man. I wrote and told him.'

'You did?'

'I certainly did. And I warned him, too.'

'You warned him?'

'I warned him. He was down here like a shot. All alone. Not even a chauffeur.'

'No bodyguard?'

She chuckled grimly. It was now all of ten minutes since the nicotine from my last cigarette had entered my bloodstream as I hit the gravel yard like that American lover-boy of Miss King's who used to drive old Miss Murdoch barmy forty years ago. Miss King once confided in us, her London boys, tossing her golden-red hair and letting those breasts heave under her Aertex, making us promise to keep a secret, making us love her. She told us that old Rowley had roasted her because of her American fiancé.

We who were so streetwise gawped at this morsel of upper-crust cheese. I said to her once, just to get her attention for myself, I said, 'You let me win that last cross-country run, miss, you always let me win.' She tossed her hair kind of shyly because she couldn't ever tell a straight lie.

So Miss Lunt had 'warned' little Michael and I needed a smoke. I fought back the temptation to whip out my notebook. An inexperienced or nervous interviewee can panic and blow a fuse at the mere sight of pencil and paper. A Sony Micro-Cassette Corder M203 was turning in my open briefcase and I had to pray that she wouldn't notice the click at the end of the micro-reel.

'Threats?' I asked.

'Oh no, he pleaded.' Lunt laughed throatily, as if strangling little Michael with her garter. 'Michael said we shared too much in common to allow our enemies to . . . "exploit" was the word he used . . . to exploit our "misfortunes".'

'Did he refer to me?'

'Oh yes. He said he was surprised that a woman who'd been a schoolteacher all her life should be such a poor judge of character.'

'Whose – mine or his?'

'He called you a "guttersnipe" and a "cheap crook" rotted by envy.'

293

Her face was alight with almost half a century's distilled hatred and she needed to get it off her chest to someone who didn't count, someone who could sting, someone who wasn't one of her teaching colleagues, most of whom had not been born when little Michael got a sixpence in his Christmas pudding and I didn't. Ironically, many of them wouldn't blink at a passion such as Nancy's, but old Nancy was padlocked to the Forties Code of Conduct.

'Are you going to tell me what really happened in March 1944, Miss Lunt?'

'He was a worm then and he's a worm now,' said the assistant headmistress of Greendale. 'He deliberately engineered his own expulsion and his sister's disgrace.'

Gawd, she was mad.

'Oh yes he did!' she barked. 'He wanted to hang on to Nicky at all costs. He even stole my notepaper to make it look as if the poisen pen was mine.'

My heart was in my clichés – my prime witness had just turned out to be as cracked as an old vase – and I needed a smoke or two. Glancing at the tiny red light in the caves of my briefcase, I persuaded the old girl to map out the asylum. It came in rushes like water through an airlock, her big quarrel with 'Nicky' in the school gymnasium at the end of the spring term, the recriminations, the tears . . .

'He was so diabolically clever. He knew how to make it stick in her mind that I must have written that note to Rowley and –'

'Wait a minute. What note?'

She blinked. My hand was in my pocket stroking the mermaid lighter I'd bought in Copenhagen on my way home from the assassination of a Swedish prime minister. Desperate, I lit a cigarette and waited for the punishment. Frame! Stand in the corner with your face to the wall.

'Could I have one of your cigarettes, Mr Frame?' She giggled unhappily. 'Nicky used to smoke, you know. In secret.'

I pressed her hard. 'So you came back from the gym and entered Miss King's room?'

'The door wasn't even locked.' Miss Lunt would never forget what Nancy had seen. 'Never, Mr Frame.'

But what had Nancy seen?
'I saw what I saw.'
Heaving herself up, she opened a desk drawer, extracted an old envelope, and handed me a sheet of stiff, yellowing paper.
'Read it. He stole my notepaper.'
'This was sent to Rowley?'
'By Michael.'
'Then how do you possess it?'
'Rowley gave it to me shortly before he died.'

DEAR HEADMASTER, VERONICA KING AND MICHAEL PAR-
SONS REGULARLY COMMIT INCEST. I HAVE JUST WITNESSED
SUCH AN ACT IN HER ROOM, SHE DIDN'T EVEN BOTHER TO LOCK
THE DOOR. HE WAS WEARING A RUBBER SHEATH. YOU MUST
TAKE IMMEDIATE ACTION TO EXPEL THIS DISGUSTING PAIR OR
SHALL I REPORT THE OUTRAGE TO THE GOVERNORS? [SIGNED]
A FRIEND OF DECENCY AND OF GREENDALE SCHOOL.

She let me transcribe it, then slid it back into its envelope like some ancient lizard shy of the light of day.
'Miss Lunt, I respect a lady's feelings, but what exactly did you see?'
'It's all in that filthy little note, isn't it? Had to be exact, didn't he? – to convince poor Nicky that only I could have written it.'
'In that case, Miss Lunt, you saw the rubber sheath.'
'Yes.' Her eyes lowered. She was weeping now – genuine, too.
'On him?'
'Yes.'
'He wasn't inside her then?'
Nancy Lunt burst into tears: a storm. Then her heavy shoulders drew themselves back, like a soldier's, beneath her tweed jacket.
'What I saw, Mr Frame, was her infinite gentleness to him, and his limitless lust.'
Thankfully the cassette's final click in my briefcase was

295

smothered by the last word, so I had her on tape, unauthorized, unauthenticated – I could hear Charrington's swaggering scorn for this 'evidence' in the High Court – but it was enough to finish little Michael.

'Well, Miss Lunt, we can bring this enemy of the people down . . . with your help.'

Why, oh why, can't I keep my big mouth shut? Her small blackberry eyes focused on me, puzzled at first, then scornful.

'Do you know what he said to me when he was here yesterday? He said that Orestes had come to Greendale, then Electra, then the Furies – but Sophocles would never come.'

'Above my head, of course. Naturally you have your loyalties.'

'My loyalty, Mr Frame, belongs to the only person I've ever loved. She . . . I had a horse, you see, called Winston. He was fine with me . . . but when Nicky sat astride him Winston went wild.'

And so I left the old bag amid ancient spectres and phantom scaffolding, sirens warning of Sodom, or was it the All Clear? In the gravel outside, between the Annexe and my 2.8 litre saloon, I could see the hurried footprints of a small street arab who owed his shoes to the charity of Mrs Parsons WVS.

Later that evening Nancy Lunt would discover and read John Ford's final gesture of defiance in the *Spectator*. I'd left it in her toilet.

THIRTY-TWO

Yes Will, *BY JOHN FORD*

Regrettably this new production of *'Tis Pity She's a Whore* at the National Theatre reflects the banal modern tendency to stress Ford's debt to Romeo and Juliet, as if the young love of Giovanni and Annabella were as 'innocent' as that of Shakespeare's young lovers. Quite the contrary: Ford's passionate couple are well aware of the rules which they deliberately defy. It is surely significant that the play begins with Giovanni confessing, or 'shriving', his incestuous passion to his trusted confessor, the Friar – then openly disparaging the old man's stern remonstrances and prohibitions. Soon afterwards he casually, almost playfully, twists the truth when he tells his sister:

> I have ask'd counsel of the holy church,
> Who tells me I may love you; and 'tis just,
> That, since I may, I should; and will, yes will.

Annabella, of course, is not deceived; she merely shrugs off the religious dilemma.

What prevails, finally, between Giovanni and Annabella, is private honesty and honour. She for her part will not divulge to her maddened husband the identity of her child's father. Even when threatened with death, she scornfully puts her husband down as not a patch on the man she loves. Annabella does not back away from Giovanni until the relationship is discovered and her beloved brother's life is in danger. Giovanni's reaction is natural, simple and logical: he kills his sister, murders her husband, rubs his own father's nose in his children's incest, and generally takes as many of his own executioners with him as his tiring limbs allow.

> ANNABELLA: What means this?
> GIOVANNI: To save thy fame, and kill thee in a kiss.
> Thus die, and die by me, and by my hand.
> Revenge is mine; honour doth love command.

There will never be any lack of conventional souls to challenge the claim that incestuous lovers are propelled by 'honesty and honour'. Don't they resort to rank deception by concealing their bond from society? Does not Giovanni cuckold his sister's fiancé? Roundheads believe that truth and honesty are the same creature (or Siamese twins) but truth lies cheaply on a man's tongue whereas honesty resides in his dreams, and in the dark corridor between being and knowing. Honesty is a faculty, or gift, given to few; truth shouts from every hustings and every advertisement. Honesty comes in the filthy rags of Kim's Indian holy men; truth has always had a bath that morning. The honest man knows himself and remains faithful to his knowledge; the truthful man salutes the world and remains faithful to the world.

In murdering his beloved, and presenting her plucked-out heart to her husband, Giovanni does not merely fulfil the extravagant norms of Jacobean melodrama; the act is symbolic of the rebellion implicit in every serious sibling incest. Such affairs are nothing less than a suicide pact. Whether both die, or only one, or how, or when, is not the point; sooner or later both will perish. Only honesty survives.

Most editors of this play's text have been men of limited moral vision. As Lyly tells us (1582): 'So that whereas I had thought to show the cunning of a chyrurgian by mine anatomie with a knife, I must plaie the tailour on the shoppe-board with a pair of sheers.' Mr Henry Weber, whose 1811 edition of Ford's dramatic works has been one of my prize possessions for many years – though an edition I possessed as a boy was confiscated by 'progressive' bigots – regrets that Ford had squandered his talent on a plot which 'makes us shudder'. Mr Weber goes on: 'It is justly observed by Langbaine, that the loves of Giovanni and Annabella are painted in too beautiful colours.'

According to Mr Weber, Ford faithfully portrayed Giovanni's progression from 'utter detestation of his lust to a more moderate view of it, and from that to a complete exculpation of his guilt by "school points" and "nice philosophy" . . .' But this initial 'detestation' on Giovanni's part exists only in Weber's imagination. In the first scene of the play, Giovanni launches straight into the most profound of all justifications of incest:

> Are we not, therefore, each to other bound
> So much the more by nature; by the links
> Of blood, of reason; nay, if you will hav't,
> Even of religion, to be ever one,
> One soul, one flesh, one love, one heart, one all?

Mr Weber's stupidities naturally extend to Annabella also. When her enraged husband discovers that he's been cuckolded and deceived about her pregnancy, Annabella is defiant enough to sing a line or two in Italian and to shrug off Soranzo's threats. The ineffable Weber comments: 'The wicked assurance of Annabella is very properly introduced, though perhaps not with such a design, to erase the pity we had felt for her at first, when her perfections were painted in such strong colours.' Nonsense, of course: Annabella's 'wicked assurance' is merely an extension of her principled passion for her brother and should reinforce our admiration for her. Later still, comparing Ford's talents to those of the author of *Othello*, Mr Weber laments yet again that 'Ford has wasted his highest powers upon a play, the unfortunate plot of which will certainly make it unpalatable to many readers.'

And today? The spineless liberalism of our modern, ecumenical theatre not only discards the rather touching censoriousness of a Henry Weber (who was writing between the battles of Trafalgar and Waterloo) but pitches to the opposite extreme by depicting Giovanni as a naïve, wilful, hedonistic

boy who pursues his passion heedless of its probable consequences. Such an interpretation has one strength or perhaps
one-and-a-half: it allows the brooding brother to slouch,
furtive and disconsolate, among the shadows, balconies and
colonnades of his own home while pompous suitors pay court
to his sister. It also helps to account for Giovanni's helpless
panic when his sister becomes pregnant with his child. But one
must ask whether a naïve, slouching boy – hurt, wounded,
maddened though he is by his sister's marriage – would have
been capable of winding himself up to so savage and coldly
executed a holocaust of revenge. How to make the leap from
horseplay to knacker's yard? from refectory smells and pea
soup to an abattoir of blood?

In fact the sibling lover is likely to be more tenaciously
possessive (and ruthless towards a rival) than his conventional
counterpart. Though the romantic mythology must deny it,
Romeo can always find another Juliet, and vice-versa. But
sibling love is anchored to the unique and irreplaceable;
whatever their actual ages both partners are twins in spirit; they
are chips off the same block, Narcissus and Narcissa, Adam and
Eve, Jack and Jill. When they make love they find joy in flesh
which belongs both to the Other and the Self: the forbidden
motions of their loins join their bodies as sowers and reapers,
reapers and sowers.

As for the sister, every work of literature attests that once she
has given herself she can never thereafter break free of her
brother's hold. It is in celebration of that enduring bond that
the present writer has borrowed the honoured name of John
Ford since October 1956 when, inspired by our return to
Egypt, he first wrote about incest in the ancient world.

THIRTY-THREE

Dined with Charrington. He'd been to see the Moloch of the *Globe* in his penthouse – apparently the designers had come up with a suite which was post-Gothic, post-Regency, post-Bauhaus and post-Brutalist. The trade figures are going to be awful, I said. We may have to put half a point on base rate. The City won't be pleased, Charrington said. And the proprietor of the *Globe* would not bury Frame's story in consideration of a peerage.

'He thinks he'll get the peerage in any case.'

'The story is alive so long as Frame is alive,' I said. 'A Pinochet solution would be the only effective one.'

Was it a tremor of disgust in Charrington or merely a speck of dust on his sleeve?

'I suppose you've bugged Frame,' he murmured, 'on your own authority?'

'There would be nothing to discover.'

Why trust Charrington? This lean man had moved too swiftly to service my wound.

'This venison is rather tired,' he murmured, picking at his plate.

'Try more salt, it was the general medieval remedy. Talking of which, what version of Canossa do they want?'

'Canossa?' (He was always a slow starter, Charrington. Perhaps V taught him the habit. You couldn't study her lovely limbs unless you trailed behind her through Stokely Wood, past the Yew Tree Inn, then across the old ford and back by Smythe's Field. 'No slacking and any rotter I catch cutting the

course does an extra run before breakfast.' Darling V.)
'Canossa? Oh you mean the post-Frankenstein master of the *Globe*. He's clearly amazed that you haven't yet withdrawn those offending clauses from the White Paper.'

'Does the man still hope to buy St Paul's Cathedral? Will God sell?'

'Don't be frivolous, Michael.'

'Facetious.' No one else corrected Charrington.

'You – we – have been given the clearest possible warning.'

'How generous. Reminds me of the Texas prison doctor who swabbed the condemned man's arm in antiseptic before administering the lethal injection.'

'Michael, I wish you'd consulted me before paying a call on Nancy Lunt.'

Even Charrington did not realize what Nancy knew. And that bitch Bracewell, still in possession of my private library, the only person ever to have spoken ill of V (apart from Mother), would be called as an expert witness. Yardley I could understand, and old Albert Harting almost forgive, but Bracewell's vendetta was pure spite – forty years ago she'd been professionally humiliated by a mere boy.

'Have you heard who She's putting in charge of the Star Chamber?'

'Who?'

I told him. He raised his eyebrows. 'She's assuming the woman in the case won't surface again?'

'*That* scandal is dead. I'm next.'

'At least your skeleton can't jump out of the cupboard.'

Such a remark from Charrington was more than a reproach. How could he understand that the pair of buttocks he and Brophy had pursued through Stokely Wood was truly, with Wordsworth, a phantom of delight? Now he looks at me – what does he see? A face both etched by age and creased by cunnning? A parchment mask hiding its apartness of mind, its secret lair of being? The last of the seven ages of Tory man? Does he remember tipping a firebucket of sand over me during the stampede after a solitary Heinkel decided to put the school laundry out of action?

'Frame's problem is antiquated moralism,' Charrington said. 'Atavistic appeal to nineteenth-century values and –'

'Balls.'

Charrington's temper rising at last: 'Is it really the case, Michael, that you've booked yourself into the same room in the same Welsh hotel on the same day every year since 1945?'

'Yes.'

'May one inquire why? What did happen on that presumably awful day?'

'A bomb was dropped on Hiroshima.'

Would I have answered his question? We shall never know; my chauffeur had come in from the street and whispered to the porter, who now appeared in the dining room to whisper to the head waiter, whose duty it was to whisper to me. I had been summoned.

She invited me to sit down. Today it was a terracotta outfit in two parts with a busy pattern of what looked all too like snakes and ladders. The inevitable cravat, of course, a hailstorm of large beige polka dots. She brought Her big handbag from Her desk top to the foot of Her chair then folded Her hands in Her lap. She said She expected I knew why She had called me in but didn't pause for a reply – Her urgency to dominate every exchange can sometimes be mistaken for tact. Not sure which form of address the occasion would call for, I used neither – an old English tradition, like not shaking hands, which had not percolated down to the grocery classes. She uses one's name with almost American (or colonial) frequency. Of course She had been, rather briefly, the White Hope of White Africa, until clever Peter and the FO took advantage of Her novice status and the Pres. of Z, the weepy KK, he of the fluttering handkerchief, asked Her to dance. History or Herstory?

She invited me to share Her distress at what was happening to me. Normally She would extend additional commiseration to one's wife and children but I had none. She asked me whether it was all true. 'In essence, Michael, not the fine details.' (She is a chemist not a lawyer.) I said not true. She almost sighed; in Her experience my reply was clearly par for the course. She said She was of course extremely relieved and not at all surprised but would I share Her knowledge that even men of honour, in a 'position' parallel to my own (She almost hesitated over the word, as if associating it with the Edwardian butlers and maids of *Upstairs, Downstairs,* whose dramas She is rumoured to follow on television) had lied. She used that word – staring at me like a glacier mint, hard right through and lightly coated in sugar powder.

Her voice dropped half an octave: the disaster, She said, was always, *always, Michael,* the false denial.

A maid brought tea. Presently there would be lipstick marks on Her cup, like the Queen (whom She regards as a dangerous liberal – one confidently awaits the arrest of Her Majesty on a charge of *lèse majesté*). But V, too, had left the same signature on china; when unobserved I used to fasten my mouth across that delicious red smear. V, of course, would have been almost exactly Her age.

Then She turned to her chief janissary, H, who had been spreading out the morning's front pages with as much love and excitement as if he'd written them all himself.

'We have to make a move one way or the other,' he announced. 'The temperature is rising.' The words bounced off the imperious sweeps of Madam's lacquered hair. I had rehearsed this interview too many times. How could one explain to Her that honesty is precious whereas the word 'truth' is prized mainly by the running dogs of this stinking world? She sits there in a world all Her own believing that Ford was a man who made lots and lots and lots of cars. How could one explain to that corner-shop mind that our mission should be to carve out a plot of earth called England where truth is not the enemy of honesty? Heavens, one can either cleave to Whitman or embrace Wilde, but this woman has never read either.

Perhaps She expected me to resign. Yet She Herself had ridden out the Oman affair. The driest columnist in the *Spectator*, a person who published my pseudonymous literary pieces during the idyllic years in Opposition, had finally turned on me with a snarl: 'Mr Parsons is known to have brought

304

himself to the brink of resignation three times. On each occasion he drove to Downing Street in a taxi and returned home in a ministerial limousine.' The bastard. Never trust an intellectual who wears his hair short at Oxford then starts letting it grow when he passes forty.

H picked up the *Globe*, slapped the headline as if to punish it, then asked me whether I knew the reporter who was credited with the lead story, *Parsons's Pleasure*.

'Frame has had his knife into me for years,' I said.

H threw me his evil eye. 'Clearly this hack is insinuating a private kind of knowledge extending back over several decades.'

She nodded, Her glacier eyes already growing bored, the Chancellor's demand for a half-point off or on the interest rates infiltrating Her thoughts.

'Tell me about your "cousin" Veronica,' She said. The quotation marks were audible; the word 'cousin' was spoken so slowly it almost broke in two.

Does She wish it to be true or not? Scandals are bad for confidence. But a woman so frequently betrayed by male fragility merely gains in stature at each resignation. Had She already composed Her magnanimous letter of acceptance? One after another, each of us clinging to a capsized raft called Eros.

'You could always sue,' mused H, Her Commissioner for Words, knowing bloody well that I'd have to resign first.

She was gazing at the *Globe*'s headline.

'Parsons's Pleasure . . . I remember being told, when I was up, of a pond where men could bathe in the nude.' She was wearing Her little girl expression. 'Is that the point, Michael?'

When I was *up*! Does suburbia construe that because one eventually came down from Oxford one was previously, when crouched over one's bunsen burner in South Parks Road, working on the fluid properties of ice cream, 'up'? Yet no doubt they will eventually award Her, despite their unprecedented bitterness, the honorary degree She craves and which they refused Her on a previous occasion.

'Not exactly a pond,' I said. 'A placid and tree-shaded pool extending off the Cherwell. By legend the nude bathing was originally promoted by sporting clergymen of juvenile humour.'

'A place to get wet,' H suggested, very pleased with his wit.

'Well it doesn't surprise me,' She said.

Yes, She hates the clerics, dripping wet with tender concern for the inner cities, though I doubt whether She's moved one way or t'other by Durham's view that the divinity of Jesus is merely an option in the religious syllabus. Somewhere among the jagged iron railings of Her mind I am not only Parsons but parson too.

The mascara did not blink as She stood up to conclude the interview.

'Michael, we really cannot proceed with your bill in its present form. Frankly, I was never happy with the incest provisions. I've had a word with Sir Christopher Charrington. In his view the allegations in the *Globe* are substantially accurate. As a citizen you are innocent until proven guilty; as a member of this Cabinet we are all subject to a sterner law. Under the circumstances – and I *have* consulted widely, Michael – it is with the greatest regret that I must ask for your –'

One cannot be 'under' circumstances unless they constitute a halo. One can only be 'in' them.

My chauffeur opened the rear door of my official car as I came out. I shook his half-comprehending hand, then walked on to Whitehall, pursued by jostling photographers and journalists, passing like a deaf-mute through the wheeling flock of questions, no statement today, no, nothing to say. I flagged a taxi.

'So She gave you the boot?' the cabby said, plucking me from the mob. He was a cockney of roughly my own generation and determined to tell me his life story. Billy by name, he came from Limehouse and claimed to have known Bert Frame as a boy.

'Forgive the expression, sir, but that sister of yours was a smasher. She looked a real treat on VE Day.'

THIRTY-FOUR

They have pursued me to Coombe Bissett. The village is besieged by reporters' cars, radio vans, TV crews. The police have been helpful – I have twice raised their pay. The curtains are drawn, the shutters fastened, the servants under strict instructions. I have given myself forty-eight hours to force a passage down the last, forbidden corridor of my life – help me, dear, ugly Miss Levinson, to achieve what you called, clumping round Greendale, 'reinforcement'.

Here is my confession:

During the summer of 1945 my beloved V was still suffering from severe pains in the head and the numbing effects of phenobarbitone. Early in August I took her on holiday to North Wales. It was our first sight of Snowdonia and the broad sands of the Menai Straits, where glorious flights of birds wheeled and screeched in the salt air.

Our point of arrival was a modestly uncomfortable hotel called the Prince of Wales in the seaside village of Llanfairfechan. Here a sturdy little railway threaded bravely along the shore, the toy engine chugging between huge boulders and into tunnels hewn from coastal rock. We got off the train as happy as E. Nesbit's Bobbie and Peter.

As we walked up from the station V told me that I must enter 'Mr and Mrs Parsons' in the hotel register. We hadn't discussed this aspect of things though it had been in our normally convergent minds during the journey. I expressed my doubts but could offer no better formula.

'Mike, they won't put an unmarried couple in one room, not up here.' She smiled cheerfully and tossed her long auburn hair against the breeze. She looked a peach.

'Suppose they demand proof of your identity?' I objected.

She checked her stride, transferring her suitcase from one hand to the other. (I had offered to carry it, of course.) There was a trace of exasperation in her tone.

'Mike, you don't *have* to share a room with me.'

As my first term at Oxford approached, her fear of living alone had begun to surface, even though, as I reminded her, I would be away for only twenty-four weeks in the year.

I took her hand. 'It's you or Vivien Leigh.'

She smiled shyly, produced a gold wedding ring from her bag, and slipped it on her finger. Stunned, I stared at the familiar contours of Mother's ring.

'I took it from her hand, Mike. Not out of spite, I'd never do that, but to prove to myself that I was going to be a good mother to you.' She laughed. 'Some mother!' Then she fished out of her bag an old ration card bearing Mother's name. Dear, naïve V, how I adored her. In her company I was always happy.

In the event the hotel asked no questions, although the manager's peppery wife took every opportunity to refer to 'your young husband'. (Never mind Belsen or Auschwitz.) Some of the older guests gave us long stares; we in turn dubbed them Rowley, Murdoch, Bracewell – and I added Albert, though V remained fond of him. The day that Albert dropped his atomic bomb on Hiroshima – naturally we were unaware – we went into Bangor by train to see *The Way to the Stars*, all about heroic airmen and the women they fell in love with. But V, to my surprise, betrayed no emotion and afterwards led the way to a pub, drank several gins, and whispered in my ear, 'Fuck all airmen though I never did.'

This word always disturbed me. She was using it with increasing frequency. And it wasn't the only one. The country had just fallen under the control of people for whom such language was routine. I have never regarded obscenity as a friend of the erotic because Eros must remain a Secret God; foul language more resembles lower-class Puritanism kicking and screaming. But I never said anything when she chose this way of displaying the half-naked face of her despair – she who had never let me down. I loved her passionately.

How could I know, how could she know, that the journey back from Bangor by seaside train, hand in hand, humming our old cinema songs, was to be the end of our joint adventure in the buttercup meadows of a spring awakening?

Strolling into the entrance hall of the Prince of Wales Hotel, we found the manager's wife (who was more Liverpool than Llanfairfechan) stationed behind the reception desk and wearing her vinegar expression.

'Miss King?' she said to V.

'No, Mrs Parsons, as you well know.'

The woman produced a fat envelope addressed to Miss V. King.

'Then this won't be for you?' You could see the creature was simmering for a fight – one of those mean, nosey, semi-detached minds.

V simply lifted the envelope from her hand. 'My maiden name.'

We went up to our room. 'Bravely done,' I said.

'I think women are much better liars than men,' V said, putting the envelope down (I recognized Leo's handwriting) and stretching herself on the bed with the feline arching of her body that normally signalled an invitation.

'Gin,' she commanded me. She didn't get many letters.

As I reached into her travelling bag the gin bottle clinked against another bottle , presumably the phenobarbitone. (I have never, subsequently, heard the sound of glass against glass without shuddering.) I poured her a thin one and struck a match for her cigarette. As a matter of fact I didn't entirely care for the smell of stale tobacco in a small bedroom – and the tongues of smokers taste less than perfect. I mention these trivialities only to guard against my tendency to idealize my life with V.

V had ripped open the outer envelope with long, painted nails and produced an airmail letter from within. Abruptly her skin was ashen, her eyes luminous: XXI Bomber Command, 20th USAAF – Guam.

'Mike, give me another drink.'

My mind raced through a series of desperate expedients before collapsing into the same condition of paralysis which had gripped me in school while V lay in hospital and Harold's announced visit to Hampstead drew nearer.

'Would you like me to open it?' was the best I could do.

'No thank you!' (said with frightening intensity verging on fury – as close to a snarl as V could get).

I poured her another gin. She didn't touch it.

'Mike, how does one pray?'

She had difficulty in opening the letter. A sheet of flimsy airmail paper lay in her trembling hand. I caught sight of an official letterhead with a half-familiar crest. V's eyes followed the typewritten lines slowly, patiently, gradually glazing over until they resembled the irises of the blind. Then her head fell back on the pillow. A minor motion of her limp wrist indicated that I could read it.

July 10, 1945

Dear Miss King,

It is my sad duty to inform you that Captain Harold Rascoe, of Long Island, New York, was lost, now certified dead, during a raid over Tokyo on May 28 last. His private papers name you as his fiancée. Although it will be little consolation to you, perhaps I should add that 498 B29 bombers were despatched on Captain Rascoe's last mission, with the loss of 26 aircraft and 254 aircrew. I am also instructed to inform the relatives of the deceased that 17,021 officers and 20,040 other ranks of the USAAF lost their lives in the course of the war now terminated with the surrender of Japan.

Harold Rascoe, the son of Mr and Mrs Robert Rascoe, and brother of Mrs Daisy Jackson, was a brilliant officer with a *summa cum laude* graduation from Harvard and a degree from Harvard Law School. He will be remembered by all his colleagues and friends for his outstanding courage, skill and devotion to duty. He was an inspiration to us all. There was no more popular officer at this base.

For further information, please contact headquarters, USAAF, High Wycombe, Buckinghamshire, England.

Kindly accept my profound condolences.

Sincerely,

Bill Almond, Colonel, USAAF.

P.S. Found among Captain Rascoe's personal effects was a letter apparently written to yourself but never sent. It is always a difficult, often heart-rending, decision what to do in such cases, most particularly when the suffering of the bereaved may only be compounded. In times of stress, Miss King, brave men are not always themselves. It is our general policy to send on a man's effects to relatives or friends and I can only apologize if, in this instance, it would not have been your wish, or Captain Rascoe's.

V had been watching me with stony, hooded eyes as I read it, seated on the cheap utility bedspread beside her.

'I'm sorry, Veronica.' I hadn't used her full name, when alone with her, for five years.

'Mm.' She closed her eyes without touching the smaller airmail envelope which – void of either name or address – had emerged from the first with only the sinister inscription: 'To Be Opened Second'.

'You knew he was in the Pacific, didn't you?'

'No.'

'You knew. When did he go? While I was in hospital? Before or after you posted my letter and sent my telegram to him?'

I poured her another gin.

'Fuck off,' she said. But she drank. I could/should have snatched the unopened letter, flushed it down the lavatory, anything – but no, we all have our natures and my solutions are not physical ones. Besides, she might have begun to scream, rousing the hotel . . .

'Could you please leave me alone, Mike . . . just for a little while.' Her speech had slurred.

'You shouldn't be alone.'

'Oh for years and years – alone!' Abruptly she sat up on the bed, shivered, and folded her arms across her chest. 'I feel cold. When I look at you I feel cold all through me. You took away my honour. Yes you did, my honour as a woman.'

I reached for her hand but she shouted, 'Get out!'

I have always been horrified of scenes in public and I lost my composure. The lucidity in all circumstances which distinguishes a genuine leader instantly deserted me. Meekly I closed the bedroom door behind me and crept down to the homely little lounge to sit myself among the disgusting knick-knacks and figurines, the awful paintings of Snowdon and the Menai Bridge, of puffins and seagulls. Feeling the idle curiosity of the other guests settling on me, I hid behind a copy of the *Tatler*, staring blindly at debutantes and hunt balls, my entire being numb with pain and terror. It must have been thirty or forty minutes before two bottles suddenly clinked together in my mind, the gin and the phenobarbitone.

The bedroom door had been locked from the inside. For five minutes I dithered, knocking and scratching quietly and stupidly calling her name, fearful of shame and scandal; then a further fifteen minutes to persuade the manager and his sneering, I-told-you-so wife to break down the door (in fact she became quite human when she saw what she saw); then almost an hour before the ambulance came.

V was lying beside the basin. Her skin was grey and very cold. As soon as I saw her I felt almost no affinity, no connection, no kinship; what I experienced as I picked up the empty phenobarbitone bottle was a vast anger and repulsion: 'Tis Pity Shees a –

The police, when they arrived, were nice to the point of tediousness. Why was Mrs Parsons also Miss King? I confessed that we were cousins and unmarried. Why might she have done it? I studied their sleepy, rustic, sheepwool countenances and kept reminding myself that my entire future must hinge on this one hour of questioning.

'I suppose it was the shock,' I murmured and showed them the letter from Colonel Almond.

Their brows knitted and furrowed. 'The PS refers to a second letter, sir. Now where might that one be?'

I shrugged. No idea. The shape of that shrug secured my next forty years; it eliminated the one text that the verminous Frame needs to destroy me – this:

April 24, 1945

Dear Veronica,

Your chilling telegram finally found its way to the Pacific. OK, so what your revolting brother told me about you both was true. You knew I was coming to visit with you but you didn't have the decency or guts to tell me the truth to my face. Incest! I had to have it all from a cocky, sneering boy, your hollow-chested, perverted little lover. I don't believe you were out on fire duty that day. Women of your sort don't join the Fire Service, all they want is a good time and nice clothes from some sucker with an American accent. You certainly took me for a ride, Veronica. What a dupe I was. Of course you were both in it together. And I never did get my engagement ring back. Sell it? I loved you once and I love you still and I don't care if I die now, you whore.

Harold Rascoe.

THIRTY-FIVE

Police cars with blinking tits began to multiply outside the house. With the arrival of a howling ambulance Coombe Bissett finally fell to the Fourth Estate – never mind fences, flower beds, vegetable gardens, fruit trees, this was where you earned a living or lost one. There are no excuses on the eighteenth floor.

Jim Londis, a UPI photographer and former Olympic decathlete, was the first to penetrate the garage and snap the corpse.

Is it possible to commit suicide under the noses of three police officers and half a hundred hacks? It is. We had a clear view of the shuttered windows of the former nursing home but the garage was out of sight at the back.

We later discovered that he'd sent his domestic staff home for the night, despite the siege. What we didn't discover was why none of the policemen on duty heard the engine running in the garage or became aware of the build-up of carbon monoxide fumes which were being pumped through a rubber hose from the exhaust pipe into the car.

Her Majesty's former Secretary of State for Home Affairs had taken his leave in the rear seat, as befitted a backbencher.

A woman reporter from the BBC asked me whether I felt 'in any way responsible'.

When an enterprising publisher suggested splicing my reports into Parsons's autobiography, the same woman reporter asked me whether I felt no scruples (sorry, scruple). She also invited me to reveal the advance payment. I said that was my business wasn't it? As for copyright, little Michael's confessions virtually entered the public domain as evidence at his inquest; pirate editions appeared in Bombay and the Bahamas even before the coroner's verdict was announced.

His final will, evidently scribbled as a form of suicide note, was as oddball as the man:

I leave all my worldly goods and my intellectual property to Roberta (Bobbie), Peter and Phyllis, the Railway Children, whose virtues and passions embody the best of Britain. At the age of ten I longed to be Peter, and to have two sisters, the elder to love, the younger to be loved by. I remember, best of all, Daddy stepping off the train into the unsuspecting Roberta's arms . 'And now I see them,' wrote their creator, 'crossing the field. Bobbie goes into the house, trying to keep her eyes from speaking before her lips have found the right words to "tell Mother quite quietly" that the sorrow and the struggle and the parting are over and done, and that Father has come home.'

I used to gaze at Aunt Phyllis and beyond her at the fuzzy horizon off the Cornish coast, measuring the angle and distance to my own father and mother. Aunt Phyllis would point to any passing ship to distract me.

Now, half a century later, when I think of Bobbie I also remember the little boy sitting on the rocks near St Ives and not knowing that he had a sister of his own, a sister who would arrive, miraculously, to fill his heart with joy and longing.

Michael Parsons.

Comparing the two texts, mine and his, pedants noticed that Veronica King's hair was sometimes described as 'auburn', sometimes as 'golden red'. No photograph of her could be found – it seems that as a boy little Michael had never owned a camera. Not by bribery or prayer could we unearth a single snapshot; not even a smudged figure in the Greendale hockey team; not even a brave smile in Fire Service uniform. The 'hair' mystery was not resolved until the discovery, in a locked cupboard, of enough to stuff a small cushion. Unlike living hair on a living head, it had not darkened with age.

I almost forgot the headstone. When I first went down to

Wiltshire in my new camel-hair coat and snappy trilby, I'd assumed that Miss King had been cremated. But little Michael's papers revealed that he'd buried her in the grassy cemetery of St Michael and All Angels, Coombe Bissett. Nicely chosen, you have to grant it to him. Even nicer was the challenge he'd evidently thrown at us all thirty years ago, as a token of his contempt.

> In memory of
> VERONICA KING
> Born 1923, Died 1953
> soror et amor

They didn't teach much Latin in Limehouse before, during or after the Blitz. And they never will.

GLOSSARY

AFL-CIO: American Federation of Labor–Congress of Industrial Organizations

ATS: Women in the British Army

BBC: British Broadcasting Corporation

CGT: Confédération Générale du Travail (French trade union)

CSM: Company Sergeant Major (RSM: Regimental Sergeant Major)

CV: Curriculum vitae

DFC: Distinguished Flying Cross

DPP: Director of Public Prosecutions

EH: Edward Heath, Conservative Prime Minister, 1970–1974

FO: Foreign Office

GLC: Greater London Council

ILEA: Inner London Education Authority

IRA: Irish Republican Army

KK: Kenneth Kaunda, President of Zambia

LCJ: Lord Chief Justice

LSD: was never spelled out. It referred to the pounds, shillings, and pence of the pre–1971 British currency.

LSE: London School of Economics

NCO: Non-commissioned officer

NHS: National Health Service

OHMS: On His (or Her) Majesty's Service

PM: Prime Minister

QC: Queen's Counsel
RADA: Royal Academy of Dramatic Art
RAF: Royal Air Force
TGWU: Transport & General Workers' Union
TUC: Trades Union Congress
USAAF: United States Army Air Force
WAAFS: Women in the Royal Air Force
WEA: Workers' Education Association
WRENS: Women in the Royal Navy
WVS: Women's Voluntary Services